D0679826

RING OF TRUTH

RING OF TRUTH

Vernon Scannell

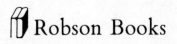

Robson Books

FIRST PUBLISHED IN GREAT BRITAIN IN 1983 BY
ROBSON BOOKS LTD., BOLSOVER HOUSE, 5-6
CLIPSTONE STREET, LONDON W1P 7EB. COPYRIGHT
© 1983 VERNON SCANNELL.

British Library Cataloguing in Publication Data

Scannell, Vernon
  Ring of truth.
  I. Title
823' .914 [F]   PR6037.C25

ISBN 0-86051-244-4

Printed in Great Britain by Biddles Ltd., Guildford.

Part One

Part One

CHAPTER ONE

H E GRINNED INTO the mouthpiece of the telephone and he looked excited, almost
mischievous and very young.

'Daft,' Aileen thought as she watched him over the pages of
Woman's Own, 'he always gets that daft look like a young lad
with his first girl-friend. And it's a lad he's ringing up. His
old mate. It's not right.' She was disconcerted by the
sharpness of her anger. It was like jealousy, but it couldn't be
jealousy. There was nothing like that about Dave. Or about
Tom Darwin, come to that. Tom was a funny one all right,
too clever by half, but not—well, not what you'd call nasty.
Not funny in that way.

Dave said, 'Hello... Dave here...' Then he laughed. She
never saw him laugh like that with anybody else. He said,
'That's right! I can't hardly believe it myself... I'll tell you
when I see you... Aye, I'll tell you about it... twenty
minutes. I'll be coming in the car... Right!... No, no
chauffeur, I drive it myself... Okay... yeah... see you
soon... Right!'

He put the telephone down and moved towards the door,
still grinning.

Aileen said, 'You going to be late?'

He paused and the private look of amusement and pleased
anticipation was still on his face. 'No. Most likely bring him
back here. He's never seen the house yet. That's all right,
love, i'n't it?'

She nodded. 'Mind and give us a ring if you do bring him
back. Where you going to see him?'

'The Oak.'

'Give us a ring then. I'll tidy up and have something for you.'

He looked round their sitting-room; it was as neat, dustless and polished as a shop-window display. His grin became very slightly broader and he came back from the door to her armchair and bent over to kiss her forehead.

'I'll ring you later on then, love.'

He went out into the hall, slipped into his sheepskin driving coat, switched on the porch light, opened the door and stepped out on to the gravel drive. The cold air slapped sharply at exposed skin of face and hands, nibbled at extremities of ears and nose. He opened the garage, climbed into his Ford Capri and, on the third attempt, started the engine. When he flicked on the headlamps the reflected light showed his hands on the steering wheel. They looked strong and competent, very sure of their function, the hands of a man who knew where he was going. He looked at them with a curiously pleasurable objectivity. 'Those are the hands,' he told himself, 'of the Middleweight Champion of the World,' and he gave a small grunt of laughter, but the warmth of delight and pride continued to glow inside him. He drove out of the garage and set off towards Headingley.

When he reached the Oak he parked the Capri and went into the lounge bar, preparing to be the target of the covert glances or frank stares, the cause of nudges and whispers or uninhibited exclamations of recognition. He was not sure about his own responses to these proofs of his celebrity. The professional fighter's contempt for the ignorance and fickleness of his public was quite strong in him; he had a fair idea of how superficial and how potentially treacherous the adulation of the crowd was; yet some part of him welcomed it, would have been disappointed by its being witheld.

The warmth of the bar seemed almost tangible, the bright noise cheerful yet excluding. He looked round and saw at once that Tom had not arrived. At one table three youngish men, all of them dressed in the kind of suits that shop managers or business reps favoured, had obviously recognised him. They all grinned in the same way, oddly tentative and suspicious as if they were afraid of being taken in. Dave could hear them muttering their recognition of him to each other, issuing their challenges. 'Goo on. Goo on. Ask him.'

'You go.'

'Goo on. He won't bite you.'

'No. But he might knock me fuckin' head off!' Loud, grinding laughter.

Dave ordered a ginger ale from the barmaid. She was not young, almost as old as his mother, he guessed, but quite heavily made-up, shiny blue stuff on her eye-lids, lashes like little black hearth-brushes, and silvery lipstick. She smiled at him automatically but there was no recognition in her eyes. She wasn't the kind to watch *Sportsnight* or read the back pages: though he'd take a bet that she'd spot anybody who'd been in *Coronation Street* or those poofy blokes who ran those daft games where they give away things like furniture or hi-fi stuff or even a car. When she had served his drink she began to dry glasses from the sink below the bar counter. He noticed that the veins on the backs of her hands were prominently corded, almost like a labouring man's. One of the three men who had recognised him came to his side.

'Am right aren't I?' he said, the grin ingratiating yet challenging. 'You're Dave Ruddock, aren't you?'

Dave nodded. 'That's right.'

'I knew you was. Will you come and join us? Do us the favour like. And let me fill that up. Have another. Anything you want.'

'I'd like to but I can't. I'm meeting somebody. Any minute now.' Dave looked at his watch. 'Some other time.'

'Eh, come on. You can spare us a couple of minutes. Just till your friend comes. What you drinking anyway?' The man glanced back at his companions who were evidently finding his encounter with Dave comical and somehow scandalous.

'I don't want a drink, thanks. And I told you. I'm waiting for somebody. Okay?'

Something in Dave's voice and look caused the man's grin to fade. He seemed about to retreat to his table when he paused, felt inside his jacket and brought out a used envelope and a ballpoint pen. He put the envelope, its back uppermost, on to the bar, and said, 'At least give us your autograph, Dave. It's for me nephew, the brother's lad.'

Dave took the pen and wrote on the envelope, *Best wishes, Dave Ruddock, Middleweight Champion of the World.*

'Could you just put "For Pete"?'

Dave added the required words. 'That your nephew's name is it?'

'Aye. That's right.'

By now the man's two friends had joined him, each with a piece of paper for the fighter's signature, and it was while Dave was autographing these that Tom arrived.

Dave said, with embarrassment, 'Just a minute, Tom. I'll get a drink in for you.'

He finished signing his name and he heard the last of the three men who had requested an autograph say to his original interlocutor, 'Come on then, Peter. Fill 'em up. It's your round!'

When Dave and Tom had taken off their coats and were settled at their own table Tom said, 'I expect you get a lot of that now.'

'What, the autographs? Aye. Enough.'

'I think you're going to get a bit more in a minute by the looks of things.'

Tom tilted his head slightly towards another table and Dave glanced across to see an older man leaving the woman with whom he had been drinking to advance towards them. He was heavily built and he wore his clothes as if they were an official uniform, drab necktie knotted tightly, all three buttons of his cocoa-coloured jacket fastened, large black toe-caps well polished. When he reached their table he said to Dave, 'You're the World Champion, aren't you?'

Dave nodded.

'Well, I just wanted to say thank you for what you've done for Britain and for Yorkshire.' It sounded like a carefully prepared speech. 'I'd be proud to shake you by the hand.'

Dave stood up, carefully avoiding Tom's sceptical and amused gaze. He took the man's outstretched hand, ready for the expected bone-crushing grip of sincerity and manliness.

'I won't take up any more of your time,' the man said, 'I just wanted to let you know from an old-timer—ex-Indian Army Champion—I just wanted to tell you we think you're the greatest.'

Dave said, 'Thanks... Thank you very much,' and sat down.

When the man seemed disposed to linger Tom asked quickly, 'How's Aileen, Dave? And your old man?'

'They're fine. I thought maybe you'd like come back and see my place...' The man moved slowly away. '... I'd like you to see it. We've had it all done up, new furniture, the lot. I told Aileen I'd ask you back. I'd as soon get out of here.'

Tom took a deep drink from his pint of bitter as if Dave was threatening to drag him out of the pub before he could finish it. Then he said, 'I've got to wait for a bit. Peggy's coming. You don't know her. She's the girl I'm living with. I told you on the phone I'd left the pad in Francis Street. I'm on my way up. We're living in her flat down the road from here. St Michael's Road.'

'How long you been living together?'

'Five, nearly six months. I've known her for ages. When we were students. She comes from the South, somewhere in Kent. She used to have another bloke in those days though. I always liked her, fancied her really, but never thought I stood a chance. Then we met up again last summer when she was in Chapeltown doing interviews after the riots—oh, I forgot to tell you. She works for local radio, BBC—well, we met up again and I did a bit of an interview about unemployment and racism, not that I had any qualifications for sounding off except I lived in an area—as you know—eighty per cent black and over half the kids leaving school without a chance in hell of getting a job, any kind of job. But that's all by the way. Thing is, I met Peggy again and we got together. She took one look at my pad in Francis Street and said it wouldn't do at all. So she threw me over her saddle and carried me away into the Headingley sunset.'

'Why didn't you tell me about her before?'

'I don't know. I only saw you for a few minutes at the

Vallejo fight. Haven't seen you since then. It must be over four months.'

'And what about the job. Looking after old people. You still doing that?'

'Still doing it.'

Dave shook his head. 'I don't know. I couldn't never understand you. I mean why you give up college—university—and that. You could be a teacher or something. By, I remember at school. You was clever then. Cleverer than what the teachers was. And here you are wasting your time wiping old folk's arses and not getting paid much more'n what you'd get on dole.'

Tom grinned. 'Aye. Seems daft, doesn't it? Still, somebody's got to do it and I don't suppose I'll stay there for—ah! Here's the lady from the BBC!'

Dave turned and saw coming towards them a small, rather plump girl with long, perfectly straight dark hair and the kind of bright, impudent snub-nosed face that he considered as unsuitable for a girl as the clothes she wore, the shabby anorak that she was unzipping to show the navy blue poloneck sweater beneath. Her maroon cords were tucked into ankle-boots and from one shoulder was slung an inelegant leather bag.

Tom and Dave stood up as she reached their table.

'Hello love,' Tom said. 'This is the great man you've heard so much about. David, this is Peggy Lawson. What are you going to have?'

Dave said, 'What about getting out of here and coming to my place? I told Aileen we most likely would. You can get a drink there if you want it. We've got beer and whisky and stuff. Aileen'll fix us a bit of grub too. Sandwiches or something. It wouldn't take us more'n a couple of minutes in car.'

Peggy and Tom exchanged subtly collusive glances. Then Tom said, 'Tell you what. We'll have one quick one here—Peggy's come straight from work. She needs a drink and a warm-up. Then we'll go and view your mansion. Okay?'

'Fine,' Dave said. 'What you having Peggy? I'll get them and then I'll go and phone Aileen, tell her we're coming.

What about you, Tom? The same again?'

They told him what they would like and watched him walk over to the bar with the part mincing, part strutting gait that fighters so often affect, the slightly exaggerated sway of the broad shoulders and dancer's gliding movement from the waist to the feet. Other customers in the lounge bar were watching him too and Tom knew that he was aware of this: the tension of self-consciousness could be seen in the set of the neat fair head.

'Well?' Tom said. 'What do you think?'

Peggy grinned. 'I think he's lovely.'

Aileen had sandwiches and coffee waiting for them when they arrived. Tom chose to drink beer.

Opening his third can he said, 'I'd have given a lot to see the Fournier fight. We watched it on telly but it's not the same.'

Dave chewed on a bite of beef sandwich and swallowed. 'You could have come with us. I told you. I got you a ticket.'

'Yeah, I know. But . . . well, you know, Paris, hotel, fares, time off work and half the staff away with 'flu—'

'Don't talk bloody daft! I said I'd look after the travel and hotel and that. It were your own bloody fault . . . what's that? What say, love?' He turned to Aileen.

'I said language. Watch your language.'

'Oh. Sorry . . . What was I saying?'

Tom smiled. 'You said it was my own fault. You're right. I should've gone. I know one thing though. Nothing, nothing in the world'll make me miss the Hayes fight.'

Peggy said, 'Hayes. That's the American isn't it? The black man.'

'Yeah. The black man.' Tom's dark eyes lost their customary gleam of sceptical amusement as they fixed themselves intently on his friend. 'What's it feel like, Dave? Can you tell me? They say this man's the greatest fighting-machine since Sugar Ray Robinson. He's fast, he can box and he punches like a heavyweight. Nobody's beaten him. Only one's gone the distance. Fournier didn't want to know. He was scared to be in the same country as Hayes, let alone the same ring. Okay, Dave. You were terrific in Paris. On that kind of showing I can't see anybody in the world staying with you. But, then, I've got to remind myself. What would Earl Hayes have done to Fournier? Maybe he'd have stopped him quicker than you did.'

Dave shrugged and smiled, relaxed. 'Maybe. We'll have to wait and see. Hayes is a good fighter. Nobody's beaten him. But nobody's beaten me neither. Right? And I've had more experience. He knocks 'em out. But don't forget. He's only had to travel the distance once. All his fights finish in three, four rounds. Except that one. Against what's-his-name—Tulloch. Tulloch took him ten rounds and remember: Fournier beat Tulloch inside the distance.'

'But that was a cut eye! Tulloch was cut. There's no knowing what would have happened. It was pretty close till that crack of heads in the seventh or eighth.'

Dave began: 'What you trying to say, Tom? You think I'm in for a hiding? You think Hayes is going to—'

But Aileen interrupted: 'Oh don't go on about it, Dave. Can't you ever talk about anything else? Peggy doesn't want to hear about nothing but boxing, do you Peggy?'

'Well...' Peggy said, smiling non-committally before Tom broke in:

'Sorry. It's my fault. I've not seen the lad for—what?— must be nearly three months. I never get the chance to talk boxing as a rule. But you're right Aileen. We'll talk about something else... The house is smashing by the way... It's great, isn't it Peggy?'

'Lovely.'

'Where do you live, Peggy?' Aileen said.

'Near Headingley. Just off the Otley Road. It's a flat. Not bad. Nothing special.'

'And you, Tom. I 'spect you're still in that horrible place in Francis Street.'

Tom and Peggy exchanged quick, amused glances. 'Well, no,' he said. 'I'm in the flat too.'

'Oh. You mean...'

'He means they live together,' Dave said.

Aileen's nod and over-bright smiled conveyed discomposure rather than disapproval. She began, 'Are you going to get—' then stopped as if she had suddenly realized that the question she was about to ask might be unwelcome.

'Get what?' Dave said. 'Are they going to get what?'

Aileen's cheeks had become pink. 'Nothing. It doesn't matter.'

Tom was smiling: 'Go on Aileen. What was it you wanted to ask? Are we going to what?'

The pinkness deepened into a dark flush. 'Well, I thought perhaps . . . I just wondered if you was going to get married.' Tom and Peggy looked at each other with mock conjecture and Aileen hastened on: 'You know. I thought like . . . well, some couples I've read about—heard about—sort of try it out—I mean it's what they call a trial marriage or something.'

Peggy said, 'You never know. But we haven't any firm plans at the moment. We'll just see how things go.'

Aileen nodded but she could not keep a suggestion of primness from the little smile. 'I expect I'm old-fashioned.'

Dave, heavily teasing, said, 'You wasn't so old-fashioned when you used to come up to London at weekends before we got married. Remember that little old creaky bed in my flat in Ealing?'

'Dave!' and the fading crimson flooded back. 'You shouldn't talk about—anyway, that were different. We knew we was going to get married . . . I mean . . . I don't mean it's wrong or anything . . .'

Peggy came to her rescue. 'It's up to the individual to choose. I agree. You're quite right. It's as silly for the would-be social rebels to say marriage should be abolished as it is for the establishment to say it should be illegal for couples to live together outside marriage.'

'That's what she said, was it?' Dave said grinning.

Tom, sensing that he could now turn the conversation back to boxing without displeasing Aileen, asked, 'Are you doing any training now, Dave? Or you just having a rest and a holiday?'

'Rest for another week. Then I'll start light training.'

15

'Is Harold King's gym at Roseville Road still going?'

'Aye. It's going all right. Harold's got one or two useful lads. There's Prince Cantrill—he's a black boy, light-heavy. Andy Flowers, welter, and Charlie Powell. Remember him? He's Central Area Middleweight Champion now. Very handy. The gym's been done up a lot since I first used it. Harold's got showers put in. It's okay.'

'No date or place or anything for the Hayes fight yet?'

'No. But Phil—' Dave turned to Peggy: '—that's Phil Richardson. He's my manager, my London manager—Phil says it's got to be in London. Hayes wants us to go to the States. Vegas. The purse'd be bigger—they reckon more than double what we'd get in England—but Phil says we've got the title and it's us that'll call the shots. We'll fight at home even if it means dropping a few thousand. Suits me.'

'You think the Hayes camp'll come to London?'

'They'll come. They'll argue but they'll come. They've got to. It's the undisputed title, see? If it was just the WBC I'd got maybe he'd collect the other one—the WBA—and say right, let's decide which of us is real champion. But I hold both versions. Everybody recognizes my title. So if he wants it he's got to come and get it.'

'And when do you think that'll be?'

'Not till the end of the summer. September or October. That's eight or nine months. Too long really without a warm-up fight. So Phil's already looking out for an opponent for a non-title fight. He wants a Yank, I think. Somebody to give me a good work-out but not dangerous enough to spoil things for the big one. He'll find somebody. He's a smart'un is Phil.'

'So you'll be in Leeds for a bit?'

'Couple of months at least. I won't be going down to London till Phil's got a firm date for the warm-up. He'll want me there for the last four or five weeks. I get intensive work there, a lot of sparring with different weights and styles, and the trainer at Phil's stable—Paddy Whelan—he's hot stuff. Puts you through it but he's a wizard at getting you in condition.'

Aileen, who had been talking to Peggy about the January

Sales, asked Tom if he would like more to eat or drink.

'I can easy make more sandwiches. What about you Peggy? I think there's some coffee left... yes, there is.'

Tom began to say that he wouldn't mind another beer but Peggy over-rode this suggestion and said, 'No. We'd better be getting back. I didn't tell them at the Studio I'd be going out. They think I'm at home and they might ring. I'm half expecting a call about a programme I'm doing tomorrow so we must get going. Can we ring for a taxi?'

'Course you won't,' Dave said. 'I'll run you back. No bother at all.'

Tom and Peggy exchanged with Aileen their goodnights and promises to meet again soon; then they and Dave put on their outdoor clothes and went out to the car which had been parked in the drive. The bodywork glittered with frost and the windscreen was thickly iced.

'Soon get rid of that,' Dave said. 'You two get in.'

He worked on the windscreen and rear window for a couple of minutes and then climbed into the car. 'The heater'll soon see the rest off.'

He carefully eased out of the drive and headed towards the Otley Road.

'How's Martin?' Tom asked.

'He's getting on champion. Likes it a lot. Coming home on leave next month. Me mam can't wait.'

'Martin's his younger brother, He's in the Paras.' Tom told Peggy, 'How old's he now, Dave?'

'Eeh... let's see now ... he must be coming up for ... No. I'm a liar. He's just past twenty. Birthday's in December. That's right, he's twenty.'

'He didn't take up boxing then?' Peggy said.

'Well, he did a bit when he was a lad at school. Joined the St Joseph's club. He wasn't bad. Good right hand. But not really cut out for it, not for the serious game. Didn't fancy the hard work, training and that. Bit too fond of his beer. Like Tom.'

'Yes,' Tom said, 'except for the beer I would have been a world-beater.'

Peggy made a derisive noise and Dave chuckled and said,

'You should have seen him with the gloves on, Peggy!'

Peggy said, 'Tom! You never told me you'd actually boxed.'

'I've done lots of things I don't boast about. But since you bring the matter up, yes, I did box. What's more I was only defeated once. That's true, isn't it, Dave.'

'And how many times did you fight?' Peggy said, and answered her own question with the same answer and in time with Tom's reply of 'once!'

'Which way do I go now?' Dave asked.

'Sorry,' Peggy said. 'Not far now. It's the . . . second . . . no, first. First on your left and it's about halfway down.'

When Dave let them out of the car Tom said, 'It's been great seeing you again. We'll have to have a good night out, the four of us. I'll give you a ring and we'll fix a date. Have a Chinese meal or something.'

Dave agreed that this was a good idea and when they had exchanged final farewells he drove away through the deserted streets, back to his home.

In their combined kitchen and dining-room Tom and Peggy sat at the table with mugs of coffee. It was nearly midnight but neither of them had to be up early the next morning and they were both wakeful and stimulated by the meeting with Dave and Aileen.

'She's so mousy,' Peggy said. 'Just about the last kind of girl I'd imagine a boxer to fancy. She looks—I don't know— like a sort of juvenile Baptist aunt. Does that make any sense? I mean she's sort of prudish, up-tight, in that sweet cachou-scented way. Don't get me wrong. She's not plain, not really. In fact she's quite pretty in a way. Or she could be. If she got rid of those granny specs and did something with her hair, used a bit of make-up, she'd look pretty good. And her clothes. They're not awful but they're negative. It's as if she wants to distract attention from her good points. I'd have thought Dave would have gone for something a bit livelier. A bit—you know—flashier. She's so dull.'

'She's got nice legs.'

'You would notice that. That's all that interests you about a woman. Legs, tits, bum and the rest of it.'

'I look only for what can be praised. It's a characteristic of the charitable.'

'Ha!'

Tom grinned. 'Well, you know what they say about the quiet ones. Still waters and all that stuff. Anyway, she's a Catholic not a Baptist.'

'She's not quiet. She's just dull. And don't be so literal. I didn't mean Baptist in that sense. Working class Catholics can be more puritanical than the puritans. How did he come to marry her?'

'I don't know. He was vaguely going around with her for two or three years before they got married in June—that's a year last June, nineteen-eighty. I've forgotten how they met. If I ever did know. I think what happened was he got very lonely when he went to London. The bloke he mentioned, Phil Richardson—he's a big time boxers' manager—fixed him up with a place to live, looked after his training and diet and all that. That was about three years ago. But I think Dave missed Leeds and his mates and family, got lonely and homesick. And Aileen'd go down once in while to see him—remember the stuff about the creaking bed? She was a bit of Leeds, a bit of the old Yorkshire to Dave. I think he probably married her out of gratitude. I don't know. It's never safe to think you know anything about these things. The heart has its reasons . . .'

'I wonder how she feels about him fighting. You couldn't even tell that, could you? I mean she was obviously bored when you two were talking about boxing —I can't blame her for that—but it didn't seem as if she hated it or was afraid of it, afraid of what it might do to him.'

'What? You mean the danger? Brain damage, cuts. That kind of thing?'

'Well, yes, those things I suppose. But other things too. I mean the whole thing's brutalizing, isn't it? It must be. You can't spend your whole time punishing your body and your mind so that you can turn yourself into a machine of

19

destruction. You can't do that and stay normal, human. Stands to reason.'

'Ah, wait a minute Peggy. Think what you're saying. You've just met Dave Ruddock. He's the Middleweight Champion of the World. And whatever some of them say about Fournier—that's the man he won it from—whatever they say about Fournier being a lucky champion and Dave being lucky to get the chance to take his title I can tell you this. Dave's a bloody good champion. He's up there with the very best. I've seen nearly every pro fight he's had. All the important ones anyway. I saw him win the British title when he went fifteen rounds with Redmond and saw the return when he knocked him out in the sixth. He's got better with every fight. He knocked out Ramirez the European Champion in four and he stopped Vallejo—and Vallejo was rated number three in the world—he stopped him in the eighth. Dave is one of the finest box-fighter's this country's ever produced . . . Wait a minute . . . hang on . . . let me make my point. He's been a pro for nearly five years and before that he was a top class amateur. He's been fighting since he was a kid of twelve. He's had about thirty pro fights and God knows how many amateur. And don't think amateurs play pat-a-cake. Now, according to your theory, this man should be well and truly brutalized, inhuman, just a—what did you call it?—a machine of destruction. Well, is he? Is that the way he seemed to you?'

Peggy made a shrugging gesture. 'I don't really know him. He's still very young—'

Oh come off it Peggy. He's twenty-four and he's been fighting for twelve years. If he's going to be brutalized it would've happened by now wouldn't it?'

'Well, he's not all that bright you must admit.'

Tom's fist banged on to the table and the coffee mugs jumped. 'Don't be so bloody stupid!'

She began to protest but he held up an admonitory palm.

'Listen,' he said jabbing at her with his forefinger, 'you know as well as I do you weren't talking about Dave's IQ. "Brutalizing" was the word you used. Of course he's not clever or educated and certainly he's no talker. But there's

20

nothing brutal about him. Surely you saw enough of him to tell that. Outside the ring he's one of the gentlest people I've ever known. Okay, call it sentimental. Anything you like. But I've known Dave since we were little kids and I've never seen him take the slightest advantage of being a fighter. Not without good reason.

'I'll tell you how we got to be friends, all those years ago when we were—what? Ten or eleven? No more. Two big lads—one was called Pollard and the other Ginger somebody-or-other—these two used to pick on me. I don't know, something about me made me good bully-bait. Maybe because I was a bit better off, compared to them, a bit posh. Cleverer too. Read books, cissy stuff like that. The bloody teachers liked me because I didn't give them a hard time. Of course Pollard and Ginger hated me. Who can blame them? But by Christ they made my life a misery. I'm not kidding. It really was hell. Fear, misery, shame, desperation, day after day, knowing you were in for a thumping if you hadn't got something to buy them off with—sweets, cash, fags, something they wanted. It was hell and there wasn't any end to it. Not that I could see. It wasn't just the thumpings. It was with you all the time. Fear. All the time. You spent the weekends waiting for Monday and school, and school meant Pollard and Ginger. You couldn't sleep. You couldn't enjoy anything. Your food tasted of fear. You couldn't read because your mind was full of it, full of fear. No room for anything else. Fear and shame because you knew you were too scared to do anything about it. Then, just like the *Bumper Boy's Annual* stories, the hero came along and caught the bullies at it and knocked seven kinds of shit out of the pair of them—it's true, absolutely true. They were a year older and both of them bigger than Dave but when he came into the bogs that day and found them working me over—one of them'd got my arms pinned behind me and the other was punching me in the guts—he just sailed into them. They didn't even try to fight back. They ran, Pollard bawling with a bloody nose. That was the first and only time I saw Dave use his fists outside the ring.'

'And what happened? I mean with the bullies. Did you

have any more aggro from them?'

'No. Because from then on Dave and I started to go around together. I used to live—you wouldn't know the area—not far from Dave. We used to walk back from school together down Harehills Road. We were mates. It was an amazing thing. I couldn't believe it at first. I couldn't understand it. There was something different about Dave, even then, even when he was a little kid. He looked different. He was very fair—I know he's still fair—but in those days his hair was almost silver or very pale gold. And he had that look of completion. You hardly ever see it in kids, not in white kids anyway. You get it more with blacks. D'you know what I mean? When they're ten or eleven their faces, their features, haven't got that soft, blurred look that most white kids have. The features are completely formed. They're there, just the way they'll be in ten, twenty years time. Well, Dave was like that. He was very quiet, very good natured. Smiled quite a lot but hardly ever laughed out loud. Nobody ever tried to take the piss out of Dave. Not even the teachers. As you said, he's not very bright, not in any sense that teachers would understand. Most kids as slow as Dave would've copped a lot of hassle from teachers. But I never saw any one of them try and give him the treatment. There was something that everybody recognized that put him apart. He was different. And for some reason—I've never understood why—still can't—for some reason he wanted me for his mate. He chose me. I still find it amazing.'

Peggy said, 'Aren't you romanticizing a bit? Wasn't he just a tough little boy who could use his fists? Not very clever but his fists could do his arguing for him? Nice enough. I quite see that. Very likeable and very simple.'

Tom shook his head. 'No. There's more to it than that though I don't think I can explain. It's maybe something only men know about. And that's not a sexist remark. The opposite in a way. Maybe women are too rational, less primitive or something. Because there is something primitive about the thing I'm trying to get at. It's the mythic thing. The idea of the hero. That's what Dave was. We all knew it in our bones, in our blood, on our pulses. He was the hero.'

Peggy laughed. 'Oh darling, you're talking about a prize-fighter. A pug. I think he's a very nice chap but he's not Parsifal. He rescued you from the little thugs and you got to be friends. You were very grateful. You still are. But it's overdoing it a bit—isn't it?—to pretend he's a great and extraordinary man. He's not. Don't think I'm knocking him because I'm not. He's a very nice, fanciable bloke. But ordinary. Very ordinary.'

'You wouldn't say that if you'd seen him fight.'

'I wouldn't—? Tom, what's that got to do with it? He can hit people hard enough to put them to sleep? His whole life's devoted to smashing people in the face as hard as he can? You can't really think that if I saw him doing it—hitting someone and being hit back—you can't really think that a sudden mystical illumination'd descend and the scales fall from my eyes and I'd be granted a vision of human nobility and heroism that'd change my life forever! We're talking about a game, a sport—though there're lots of people who'd question that description of it.'

Tom said, 'Okay, okay Peggy. Let's drop it. There's no point in going on. Either you see it or you don't. Maybe you'd see nothing more than two men wearing shiny pants and big gloves trying to knock each other's head off.'

'But there isn't any more to see, Tom. Deep down you must know that's true. You must know that your—whatever it is—obsession isn't really too strong a word—you must know that it's all to do with your childhood. You felt inadequate physically. I don't mean there's anything wrong with you physically. Of course there isn't. In fact I think you're lovely. But you weren't a muscle-bound fighting-man and you were brought up in an environment where that was the thing to be. You felt you'd failed. But you're grown up now, Tom. You ought to get rid of those infantile fantasies, see them for what they really are, Cock-fighting, bull-fighting, boxing, wrestling, hunting big game—all the Hemingway macho stuff—it's all pathetic really. Feel my muscle, baby, I'm a big strong man! You know as well as I do that the important human qualities are nothing to do with killing and hurting. They're to do with compassion,

23

imagination, love, intelligence, creativity. Your passion for boxing should've disappeared with all the other little-boy excitements—war games, cowboys and indians, Batman, all those.'

He finished his coffee. Then he said, 'Let's not go on about it any more. I don't really mind what you think or say, I know it's something different from anything you've ever known. The fact that you talk about wrestling and cock-fighting and—whatever it was— in the same breath shows invincible ignorance. Saying there's any connection between boxing and that ludicrous obscenity, professional wrestling, is the same as mixing up the worst kind of showbiz revivalist meeting with high mass. You can call them both religious events but they're not the same. But let's drop the subject. It's something you can't understand unless—oh, I don't know—maybe it's something that no woman can see.'

Peggy said, 'It's something this woman certainly can't see!' Then she laughed and added, 'But what was that about you boxing? I really can't imagine that!'

Tom tried to look stern and offended but could not sustain the expression which crumbled into a grin and then a chuckle. 'You might well laugh.'

'Did you really have a fight? I mean a proper boxing match, in the ring?'

'Well, yes, I suppose I did. If you could call it a fight.'

'When was that? How old were you?'

'Thirteen, I told you Dave and I did most things together. Well, I used to go along with him to the St Joseph's Club on training nights. That's when I first got interested. My God I'd have given anything to be a boxer. Not even a specially good one. Just to be able to go in there and move around properly, jab and slip and duck, maybe land a good right-cross or left hook. I wouldn't want a title. Wouldn't even mind whether I won or not. Just to do it without looking like a mug, a no-hoper.'

'And what happened?'

'One day, at school, I told Dave I'd like to have a go. I'd like to join the club. Anybody else'd've told me I was barmy. But not Dave. He said okay but maybe it'd be a good idea to put the gloves on and learn a few moves before I actually joined. So I went round to his house—he'd got a set of very old gloves that his dad'd used when he was boxing—and we went out into the back yard and he showed me how to stand, how to lead with a straight left and keep your guard up, the very basic stuff. We sparred a bit and Dave kept saying I was doing all right but he never once hit me except on the gloves or arms or very lightly on the chest. So a couple of weeks later I went along to St Joseph's and got into the ring to spar with another novice. But he wasn't a bit like me. I stood up there the way Dave had taught me, correct orthodox stance. The other lad just put his head down and came at me like a little tornado. He knocked the stuffing out of me. The instructor stopped him a couple of times to tell him that he wasn't there to try and murder me but to learn how to box but the lad just nodded and carried on swinging his haymakers and belting me round the ring.'

'So that was your one and only fight.'

'Oh no. That wasn't a fight. That was what they euphemistically called sparring. Dave had another shot at teaching me to defend myself and even do a bit of attacking before the next club-night but I never got much better. Funny thing was I kept at it, week after week. Every training night I got a bloody nose or a black eye, sometimes both. But I kept going, even though I knew I was in for a hiding. Somehow I hung on to the dream that one day it'd all come right, I'd suddenly start moving the way Dave did, jabbing, hooking, weaving, ducking, slamming in the combinations. I put my name in for the Schoolboy Championships. I knew they were all trying to put me off—the trainer, the other lads, all of them—but I was going to give them all a surprise. I didn't though. The only one who got a surprise was my opponent. He couldn't believe his luck! He hit me with every punch he'd ever learnt. I was on the canvas three times before the referee stopped it in the second round. And that was my first and last fight. After that I never had the gloves on again. But here's the odd part about it. I've always been glad I had that one farcical contest. Ridiculous as it was, hopeless as I was as a boxer, at least I have some idea of what it's like to be in there. I've been under fire. I know it was a silly little skirmish, it wasn't a real battle. But we used live ammunition and I'm glad I did it. Daft, isn't it?'

Peggy smiled and paused before answering. 'I don't know. Perhaps you're right. Maybe it is something women can't understand. I've tried to see it. I've read Norman Mailer—'

'Oh Christ! He's the last person to explain it. In a funny sort of way he's got a feminine attitude to the game. All that hectic over-writing, the sexual metaphors and so on, the way he licks his chops over the pain and violence, I bet he wears drag when he's writing that stuff. You might not believe this but boxing's got very little to do with physical pain. That's why nearly all the writers and movies get it wrong. Films like *Raging Bull*. All that ketchup, all those punches landing like bombs. Comic-strip stuff. Wrong, wrong, wrong.'

'And you're going to get it right.'

Tom looked at her with a small, guarded smile; then he looked quickly away.

'That's it,' Peggy said, 'isn't it? That's what you'd like to do? Get it right. In a book. That's your dream now, isn't it Tom? You want to write a book about it.'

He pushed his chair back and stood up. 'Not tonight,' he said. 'One day perhaps.'

She said, 'Listen. Sit down a minute. I've just thought of something.'

'I'm going to bed. I'm tired.'

'No, just a second. Please Tom.' He sat down again. 'You and Dave were talking about this fight he's going to have with what's-his-name, the black man.'

'Earl Hayes'

'That's right, Earl Hayes. Well, do you think you could persuade Dave to come on the programme? Just ten minutes or so. Talk about his early days in Leeds. How he feels about being World Champion, marriage, human interest stuff. D'you think he'd agree?'

'I don't know. He's not a great talker. You might have noticed.'

'He'd be all right. I'd keep the questions nice and simple. Please Tom. Would you ask him? Please.'

'I don't know. I'll think about it.'

'Give him a ring tomorrow.'

'I'll see.'

'It'd help me a lot, Tom. You know that, don't you?'

'I told you. I'll think about it. Now let's go to bed.'

'All right. I'm coming... He wouldn't be shy with me. I'd get him to talk. It'd be marvellous. For me I mean.'

'Bed.'

They switched out the lights and went out of the kitchen. In the bedroom Peggy was first in bed. A few moments later Tom joined her, drawing her close to him and kissing her quickly, without passion.

'Goodnight,' he said.

'You will ask him, won't you?'

'Yes. I'll ask him... Goodnight.'

'Goodnight, darling,' Peggy said, and soon they were both asleep.

CHAPTER TWO

THE SALOON BAR of the Pack Horse was busy but the two middle-aged men, the shorter one wearing a flat tweed cap and his companion in an unfashionably wide-brimmed felt hat, were able to find seats on two low stools at a table where a young couple was already sitting. Neither of the men removed his headgear as they both raised their pints of bitter in brief salute before taking a long draught, exhaling appreciatively and replacing their glasses on the table. The man wearing the felt hat was Dave's father, Jimmy Ruddock, and he and his friend, Micky Rice, had been attending a meeting of the Leeds Ex-Boxers' Association. The faces of both men were slightly disfigured by the marks of their former profession, the thin trickle of scar tissue gleaming white through the bristle of eyebrows, the flattened noses and eyes set back more deeply in the skull than is common among non-fighting men. The left ear of Micky, the smaller man, was misshapen and swollen, like a large dried apricot.

He took a second less deep drink of his beer and said, 'It was right good of Dave to come to meeting tonight. He's a good lad is that one. There's not many youngsters'd want to waste their time with the old'uns. And him World Champion at that.'

Jimmy Ruddock nodded. 'Aye, he's a good-hearted lad is Dave.'

'Pity he had to get away early. Would a been nice to see a bit more of him. He still don't take a drink then?'

'No. Never touched it. Not as far as I know. Never had a

smoke or a drink. Not even at Christmas. Now Martin, he's different. Not like any of us really . . .' The young couple rose to leave so Jimmy and Micky moved from their stools to the more comfortable wall seat. 'Aye, Martin's a different lad all together. Likes his pint, he does. Maybe a bit too much. He's only twenty. I never drunk much till I was older'n that, not till I'd hung up gloves. Can't afford it now.'

'Finish that and I'll get you one. I can take a hint, you poor old bugger.'

They both chuckled hoarsely and drained their glasses. Micky went to the bar and returned with fresh pints. 'How's Martin getting on then?—Still likes it does he, the Paras?'

'Seems to, far as you can tell. He's not a great one for writing letters. Dot's happy now 'cause he's coming home on leave in a couple of weeks. We had a card on Tuesday. February the twelfth. We're going to have a bit of a knees-up that night. Just family. Jean and Jeff and Dave and Aileen. Bring Freda. Nothing posh. You know us Micky. But we'll have a laugh and a joke and few jars. Okay?'

'Sounds champion. I'd like to see young Martin again. Pity he packed in game. Had the makings, didn't he? He could've gone a long way if he'd took it serious.'

Jimmy took a drink of his beer. 'Ah well. One champion in family's enough. We have to give t'others a look in.'

'Dave tells me he's going to start light training a week on Monday. It'll be nice working with him again. I've never known a lad work like he does. He's a trainer's dream. Good as gold. Pity some of Harold's other lads don't train like him?'

'That's why he's World Champion. Well, part the reason. Hard graft, it's half the battle. You know that, Micky. You can have all the talent in the world but it won't take you to top if you can't graft.'

Micky nodded and drank some beer. Then he said, 'Listen Jimmy, You and me's been friends a long time. I reckon if we can't talk to each other straight now we never will. Right?'

Jimmy nodded.

'Well, what do you think? What's your honest opinion? I mean like compared with best. Compared with the really big 'uns. Sugar Ray Robinson, Joe Louis, Jake La Motta, this young Ray Leonard. How do you rate Earl Hayes?'

Jimmy's shoulders heaved and sank and his head tilted from right to left. 'I don't know. You can't tell for sure. I mean I've never seen him. Only on telly. 'Course he's a good 'un. No doubt about that. He can dig with both hands. Got all the punches. He's fast too. But who's he fought? Jerry Foster was past it. The others we don't know about except Tulloch and Vallejo. True, he knocked Vallejo out quicker than what Dave did but you can't tell a lot by that. It took Dave eight rounds. Okay. But Dave's a different kind of fighter. He doesn't take any chances. He were never in trouble with Vallejo, not once, not for a second. The Mexican never laid a glove on him. Not solid. You saw Dave after fight. Not a mark on him. Didn't look as if he'd been in a fight.'

'Aye. But Vallejo never gave Hayes no trouble neither. And that left hook that finished it was a beauty. Nearly took Vallejo's head off.'

Jimmy Ruddock nodded. 'Oh, I'm not denying it. He's a good 'un and no mistake. He's fast and can dig with both hands. But I think Dave can do it. He's punching harder than ever. You could see when he hit Fournier, even the jabs sickened him. And that right hand. That's the one that blows the fuses. When Dave gets it on target the other fella's got to go. I don't care who he is. There isn't nobody that can take that kind of punch and stay on his feet. And another thing. Dave can take a good punch himself. We've seen him. Terry Vincent caught him with that left hook—you remember? In the eliminator?—and there wasn't many that could take Terry's Sunday punch and stay on their feet. And what happened? Dave came right back at him with a combination' like the bloody Alamein barrage.'

'True enough. Dave's never looked like being knocked out. So far. It's just—I don't know. This Earl Hayes looks like something special, something different. But you're right, Jimmy. He's not been tested. We've never seen him against a really big puncher. And if Dave catches him he's got to go.'

'Aye, We'll just have to wait and see.'

30

'Any more news about date?'

'Nothing definite. Phil Richardson rang Dave a couple of days ago. Seems the Hayes camp still want it in America or San Remo. They reckon Dave could get a couple of million dollars or more in Vegas. But Richardson says it's only a matter of time till they agree to London. We've got the title, he says. If they want a crack at it they've got to come and get it. He says it'll be Wembley in the autumn some time. September, October, somewhere around then.'

'Will he get Dave a warm-up fight? It's a pretty long time to wait. He could get rusty.'

'Aye. Richardson's looking out for somebody to put him in with. It's got to be someone that can give him a good hard fight without being too bloody dangerous. I don't mean they're likely to beat him. But we can't have him getting cut or busting his hands or anything. Here, sup that drop up and we'll have one for road.'

Jimmy Ruddock took their glasses to be refilled at the bar. The landlord who was talking to some customers and their wives in the snug saw Jimmy through the hatch and called to him, 'Hello there! How's the Champ? They tell me he's back in Leeds.'

Jimmy just grinned and nodded before carrying the drinks back to the table. Micky drank some of his beer then said, 'Henry Walker was telling me at the meeting we've got more licensed boxers today than we've had since about nineteen-fifty. He reckons it's unemployment.'

'Bound to make a difference. These young amateurs. A few years back they had good jobs. They could get time off if they was fighting abroad like the Commonwealth Games or Olympics. A lot of good lads never even thought of turning pro. Why should they? Maybe got a trade earning good money. Not much going on in fight game. A few dinner shows at these bloody sporting clubs. Half-a-dozen big promotions a year in London. That was about it. But it's all changed now. It's more like the old days when I was a kid. Remember the thirties? There wasn't a town in Britain that didn't run regular shows. It'll soon be like that again... Well, maybe, not quite. Telly'll stop that. But it's going to be more like the old days.'

'Let's hope you're right.'

Jimmy took a drink and returned his glass to the table. 'I'm not so sure, Micky. It's a big price to pay, unemployment. They talk about the good old days but I can remember my old man being out of work. It wasn't so bloody funny. You know what we had to us teas on bad days? Bread and lard with a bit of salt on it. Bread and bloody lard.'

'Aye, it was hard times all right. There was fights to be had but you didn't get much wages. Remember old Fred Casey that used to train boys at St Clement's Club? He's dead now, God rest his soul. I remember Fred telling us about when he was fighting. You had to fight two, three times a week to make a living. Fred said one time he had a ten-rounder at Belle-Vue Manchester on Monday, a twelve-rounder at Blackfriars on Wednesday and another ten rounds in Glasgow on Friday and when his expenses and manager's cut was taken off he ended up with sixteen quid. And he thought he was well off!'

They both chuckled. Then Jimmy said, 'I remember one time telling him I was boxing eight rounds in Birmingham. First time I'd gone more than six. It'd be—when?—about 1949 or 50. Anyway I were getting sixty quid and expenses. Old Fred couldn't believe it. He thought I was kidding him. Sixty quid for eight rounds, bottom of the bill! The most he ever got paid—and that were for a twelve-rounder, top of the bill at the Holborn Stadium Club—the most he got paid were twenty pound. God knows what he'd say about things nowadays. Bloody half-baked heavyweights getting paid thousands and they can't punch their way out of a paper bag. By! If Dave was a couple of stone heavier he'd be a millionaire by now.' Jimmy looked at his watch. 'Eh look at the time. Twenty past ten. Dot'll have my guts for garters. Sup up lad. We'd best be on us ways.'

They finished their pints and went out into the malicious cold night.

'By, it's parky.' Micky said. 'There's a number ten. You're lucky. Go and catch it. See you a week next Tuesday if not before.'

Jimmy trotted the few yards to the bus-stop and climbed aboard the bus seconds before it moved away. Micky saw him through the misted windows as he took a seat and peered out into the night failing to find his friend, his hat tipped forward at a slight angle, cocky, pugnacious, a good mate, a good man.

When Jimmy let himself into the living room he knew that his wife was not in a good mood from the tight, slightly downward curve of her pressed lips, the rigid set of head as she rose from her chair to switch off the television set.

'All right then?' he said with unhopeful cheeriness.

She allowed a slight but significant silence to intervene before she spoke: 'Do you want a drink? I'm going to make some cocoa.'

'Aye. A hot drink. That'd be smashing.' He took off his hat and coat and was about to throw them on the sofa when he thought better of it and went out into the tiny entrance hall and hung them on the combined clothes and umbrella stand that occupied most of the space at the foot of the stairs. Back in the living room he could hear from the kitchen the clink and chime of the cocoa being prepared.

He called, 'Dot! Have you got any of that parkin left? I just fancy a bit of that with me cocoa.'

She did not answer but when, a few moments later, she came into the room he saw that there was a plate bearing a slice of the dark ginger cake on the tray with the two mugs of cocoa.

'I'm going to take mine up to bed,' she said. 'I'm tired.'

'Aye you do that love. I won't be long after you.'

She picked up her mug of cocoa but did not at once go out of the room. 'You didn't bring Dave back then.'

Jimmy was about to take a bite of his parkin and he paused, mouth open, as if astonished. 'Dave? No. He wanted to get back home. I expect he thought Aileen'd be a bit lonely like.'

'So was his mother a bit lonely like. But she's used to that.' She spoke with more resignation than bitterness and went out closing the door carefully behind her. He heard the faint

33

creak of the stairs and then the sound of their bedroom door being closed. He chewed his parkin and drank some cocoa, but not with great relish.

Women had a rough deal, he thought. No doubt about that. Getting old was bad enough for anybody, but men were better off than women. Like tonight. He could see his old mates at the Association, have a couple of pints and a crack with Micky. He'd still got his interests. But what about Dot? There wasn't much for her to look forward to. Her kids all grown up and flown the nest. Hardly ever saw them. Jean had got her own family now so you couldn't blame her for not coming round very often. Martin away in the Paras and Dave a celebrity, up there in the big time. Not that he was a snob. Not Dave. He still came for Sunday dinner most weeks. When he was back in Leeds. But he'd got his own home now, a wife and most likely he'd have nippers before very long. Dot wasn't interested in the fight game. In fact she hated it. It was just another worry for her. She got no pleasure out of Dave's success. She'd sooner any day see him manager of Lewis's or something. There really wasn't a lot left for her when you came to think of it. Her looks were going. No doubt about that. Not that she was an old bag or anything but she wasn't a young smasher any more. Like she'd once been. Still, she wasn't at all bad for her age. She was pushing— what? Fifty-one? fifty-two?—and when she was dolled up she could still look pretty good.

Funny this getting old. Again men seemed to be the lucky ones. Going thin on top, wearing specs, getting a bit of a gut didn't worry a man so much. Specially when you'd never been an oil-painting anyway, even at your youngest and best. As long as you didn't *feel* old it was all right. You got a bit short-winded, not so nifty on your pins, your chest might slip down to your belt but inside you didn't feel all that much different. It was still a good life. You could get the old thrill second-hand, watching Dave do the things you might've done yourself. It wasn't a bad life at all.

Jimmy drank more cocoa and ate the last of his parkin. 'I'll make it up to her,' he told himself. 'I'll think of something. When Martin comes home. She'll enjoy that. She can get a new rig-out or something. Go to the hairdressers. Something like that. I'll make it up to her.'

He drained his mug, turned off the gas fire and the lights and left the room to climb the stairs to the bedroom.

CHAPTER THREE

D AVE DROVE QUITE slowly along Woodhouse Lane as the pale wintry sunshine sparkled and gleamed from the chrome and windscreens of other cars and danced on the still frosty surface of the road. He was driving slowly because he was reluctant to reach his destination, the studios of Radio Leeds where he had agreed to be interviewed by Peggy Lawson. Tom Darwin had telephoned two days ago and asked him if he would agree to making the short broadcast. Tom had been apologetic. He had said that he knew well enough how much Dave hated any kind of public performance other than those held in a boxing-ring but Peggy would make it as easy as possible for him. It wasn't going to be a sports programme with those so-called experts talking in what they believed to be the language of the game. Just Peggy herself asking a few simple questions, like what he ate for breakfast, the kind of music he enjoyed, where he liked to go for his holidays, that kind of thing. Then Tom had said, 'If you can't bring yourself to do it, Dave, don't worry. Just say nothing doing. But if you can—and it only means going in there on Wednesday morning about eleven-fifteen for twenty minutes or so—well, Peggy'd be thrilled. She's got this idea there's some kind of plot to get her kicked out. Anti-feminist prejudice. So she thinks getting you to give an interview'd kill the opposition once and for all.'

It had sounded easy enough the way Tom had laid it out, but now the mild apprehension which had troubled Dave since he had awakened that morning had become something sharp and abrasive; now it was moving in his bloodstream

36

like an infection. His mouth was dry and his bowels and bladder were potentially treacherous. It was crazy. He felt more scared than when he was waiting in the dressing-room before the fight with Fournier. It didn't make sense. All he had to do was go and answer a few silly questions from Peggy. There was nothing to be scared about. He was the Middle-weight Champion of the World. People wouldn't believe he was afraid of anything. Yet here he was, shaking like a jelly. It was crazy.

He turned into the car park and found a space to leave the Capri. He got out of the car, made sure it was locked, and walked with what he hoped seemed nonchalance towards the entrance of the old Broadcasting House. A girl at the reception desk looked up at him from beneath eyelids so darkened by makeup that she might have been on the loser's end of a few accurate left jabs. She said in a curiously mechanical, sing-song voice, 'Can I help you?'

'I've to, er—got an appointment with, er, Peggy Lawson. It's, er, I'm—'

'Name please?'

'Ruddock. Dave Ruddock.'

She lifted a telephone and spoke into it. 'Mr Ruddock's here ... yes, I'll tell him.' She said to Dave: 'Would you go through to the left there and just take a seat in the waiting area. Peggy'll be with you in just a couple of minutes. Okay?'

He went through the swing doors that she had indicated and found himself in a corridor which led to a recess with a couple of seats and small tables bearing an assortment of BBC periodicals and publicity material. He sat down facing a studio door which had a red-light burning above its lintel and picked up a copy of *The Listener* and began to flick over the pages without really absorbing anything of either text or illustration. Then he looked at the gold watch on its glittering bracelet which Aileen had given him for Christmas. Almost quarter-past. He would wait another couple of minutes and then, if Peggy hadn't shown up, he'd clear off. They'd said a quarter-past and he was there on time. Who the hell did they think they were to keep him waiting? Champion of the World and they kept him sitting around like somebody applying for a job or social security or something. Another minute, just one more minute and he'd get out of there. But he knew that his anger was not an authentic passion: it was an expression in other terms of his fear of the coming ordeal and he knew, also, that he would not leave the building without fulfilling the promise he had made to Tom.

Then the studio door opened and Peggy came out, advancing on him as he rose to his feet, releasing an effusion of greetings and apologies: 'Dave! Lovely to see you. I'm so sorry we're a bit behind time. Hope you haven't been waiting long. Tom sends love and—oh, by the way, this is Judy Styles... you know each other?'

Until Peggy had spoken the girl's name Dave had been only vaguely aware of someone female accompanying her as she emerged from the studio. Now he recognised who it was and recognition struck like a shocking and perfectly timed blow to the heart. He felt the blood scorching beneath his facial skin and for a moment vision blurred before it cleared again to confirm his first impression of her beauty.

'He won't remember me,' Judy was saying. 'You don't do you, Dave?'

His first attempt to answer was choked by a constriction in the throat. He coughed it away, aware of the warm stinging of his blush, and said hoarsely, 'Yes. I do. 'Course I do. I remember you.'

Peggy sounded delighted: 'So you do know each other! How marvellous. How long? When did you meet? I wish I'd known.'

Judy was smiling at Dave, half conspiratorial, half mocking. Her eyes were exactly as he remembered them, that strange dark green colour, slightly slanted, foreign-looking, and her hair too was just the same, very pale, gleaming like some fine-spun precious metal. She said, 'We've known each other for ages. Ages and ages. Though it's a while since we last met, isn't it? But I've heard about you, Dave. And seen you on the box. I'd have thought you'd have forgotten me by now though.'

Peggy saved Dave from having to reply. 'Look,' she said,

'We've got to get into the studio. Judy, we won't be long. Twenty minutes at most. Why don't you sit in the fish tank and listen in and then we can all go across the road for a drink? How about it? Yes?'

Judy hesitated only for a moment. Her smile widened. 'Why not. If you don't mind, Dave.'

Dave muttered his indifference and before he could correct the ungraciousness of his reply Peggy said, 'Great. Come on then.' She opened the studio door. 'You go through there Judy—see you soon—over here Dave at the table.'

He sat down before the microphone and Peggy took the chair opposite. An old Carpenters' hit was spilling into the studio from a speaker on the wall. Peggy said, 'The music'll be over in a minute. It's okay, we can talk while it's on. That little green light there'll tell us when we're on the air. Don't worry, Dave. I'll just be asking you a few questions and you can answer any way you like. I won't ask you anything technical about boxing, only very general stuff. You'll be able to tell when we're finished. I'll wind things up and there'll be more music. Just relax and let's have a chat like we would over a cuppa... okay?'

Dave nodded, swallowed with difficulty and wondered if he would be able to speak at all. Through the glass which separated the studio from the control cubicle he caught a glimpse of Judy smiling at him and nervous apprehension stretched taut and quivered inside him like steel wire strained to. the point of snapping.

The music had finished and Peggy was saying, 'Later in the programme you'll be hearing more golden oldies. But now we have in the studio a special guest, a local boy who's reached the very pinnacle of his profession, a young man whose name's a household word literally all over the globe. He's Dave Ruddock the Middleweight Boxing Champion of the World. And here's a coincidence. Unless you've only just switched on you'll know I've just been talking to Judy Styles, the popular Leeds soprano who's well-known from *The Good Old Days* and other television shows as well as for solo performances all over the north and elsewhere. Well, it seems Judy and Dave are old friends. How did you come to meet each other, Dave, and how long ago was it?'

Dave stared across the table and for a moment Peggy's face blurred. Then he cleared his throat and said, 'We're not really what you'd call friends. I think Judy were kidding when she said that. It's just that we met a couple of times when we was youngsters. Me mam—my mother—used to work for Mrs Styles. Did a bit of charring or something. I don't know. I didn't really know Judy. We was a different class.'

'Well, Judy's still on the premises. Perhaps you'll be able to talk over old times after the broadcast. But let's get on to the subject nearest your heart. Not old friends or sweethearts but the rough and tumble of what must be the most violent professional sport there is. When did you start boxing, Dave?'

'When I were a lad. About eleven.'

'And what started you off? What was it at such an early age made you decide that you'd be a pugilist?'

Dave frowned. 'Well... my dad were a pro. Jimmy Ruddock. He were Central Area Welterweight Champion in—I can't be sure exactly—but it were around the early fifties. About 1952, I think. Before that he were Army and Combined Services Champion. He must have been pretty useful.'

'And he started you off boxing?'

'Aye. That's right. When I were a little'un, no more than five or six, he used to get down on his knees and I used to belt away at him. He'd show me how to stand and all that. How to jab with the left, block and deflect. Simple things like that. So when I joined St Joseph's—that's my old boxing club—I knew the first moves. It all came natural. It were like I were born for it.' He grinned, a small flicker of private amusement or self-mockery. 'Still is.'

'So your father started it all by making you fight when you were little. If it hadn't been—'

Dave interrupted. 'Here! Wait a minute. You said my dad *made* me fight. That sounds like he were forcing me to do something I didn't want to do. It weren't like that. I liked it. I *loved* it. Right from start. And another thing. You said he made me *fight*. He didn't. My dad were dead against scrapping, like in the street. What he did were different. He taught me how to *box*. It's different, see? He taught me tricks of trade. Well, the simple ones. And he showed me how it were daft to lose your temper. You've got to keep cool. If you lose your cool and try to start throwing your bombs like a madman you walk right into trouble. Every time. Self-defence. That's what my dad taught me. The art of self-defence.'

Peggy smiled. 'But Dave, be honest. I mean I'm the first to admit boxing's a closed book to most women but even I can see that the object is to bash your opponent until he's senseless. No! Wait a second! Let me put it this way. When you go into the ring it's your intention to knock out the other man if you possibly can. You might not succeed. You might just win on points. But that wouldn't be as satisfying. The knock-out's the thing. That's what you're after, isn't it?'

Dave frowned and pondered the question.

'Come on, Dave. Be honest.' Peggy said. 'You go in there to knock the other man unconscious. That's what it's all about.'

He nodded slowly. 'Aye. I suppose you're right. In a way. I go for the knock-out. Most fighters do except maybe those that haven't got a punch. But you said that's what it's all about. Well, it isn't. Boxing's about a lot more than landing the big punch. It's about skill and defence and fitness and heart.'

'What was that last word? Art?'

Dave was by now sufficiently at ease to be able to find this quite funny. He gave a little grunt of laughter. 'No, not art like in noble art... *Heart* ...' He over-emphasised the aspirate: '... That means guts, bottle, brave.'

'Yes, of course. I see. But tell us, Dave. Don't you ever worry about hurting your opponent really badly? There've been cases, haven't there—I believe there was one not so long ago—of a young boxer actually being killed? How can you justify a sport where one of the participants might kill the other? And not accidentally but as a result of a blow that's intended to knock the man unconscious. In other words a blow that's deliberately meant to cause more or less serious injury.'

'No,' Dave said, 'that's not right. It's not like that.'

'But it *is* like that, Dave. You've said so yourself. You said you go for the knock-out. That means you're trying to hit him as hard as you possibly can. And from what I'm told, you hit harder than most. That's why you're the Champion. You know quite well that the kind of blow you've been trained to deliver could kill a man. I'm not saying it's likely to but it could. It's actually happened and it could happen again. That's true isn't it?'

He knew that there was an answer to this, that Peggy was distorting the reality of the game, but he was confused. He needed time to think things out. He wasn't a quick thinker or talker like her. She was not sticking to her promise. She'd said it would be easy like having a chat over a cuppa and here she was, outspeeding him, tying him up inside.

He said, 'It's not like that. You don't understand. Women don't understand boxing, not many. One or two maybe. It's something they can't usually see. I mean like you talking about causing injury. A boxer's not trying to hurt anybody, not really, not *hurt* them. Boxers are like—I don't know— well anybody who does something different, something special. Say actors or doctors or coppers. They've all got their different ways of talking. They might use the same words but they mean something different. You'll hear a fighter maybe say something like "I knew I'd hurt him so I went in for kill." Now, he doesn't *mean* it, not like you mean "hurt" or "kill". You never feel vicious. It's not like that. Sure, fighters get hurt, may even be killed. It's that kind of game. You've got to have a bit of danger, a bit of pain, or there wouldn't be no point would there?'

Peggy was smiling slightly, sympathetic but entirely un-persuaded. He knew that he had failed to express what he believed.

She said, 'You're married, aren't you Dave? What does your wife think of your boxing? Does she watch your fights?'

His frustration and mild anger with himself for not being able to present the case for boxing more convincingly faded before the relief at being faced with a simple, easily answered question. 'No, she's never seen me fight, not even on telly. She's not interested. Like you, she thinks it's just a couple of lads trying to hammer each other's brains out.'

'Doesn't she get very anxious—afraid you might be badly hurt?'

'You'd better ask her.'

'Oh come on. Surely you talk about it with her.'

'No. It's my work. Just like a bloke going off to pit or something. It's a hard job. A little bit of danger maybe. But she gets on with her work—looking after the house an' all that—and I get on with mine.'

'And what about children? I know you and your wife haven't any as yet, but if you were to have a boy. Would you like him to follow in your footsteps, be a boxer?'

'I don't know. I haven't really thought a lot about it. Well, yes. I mean if he wanted to. Not if he didn't though. I wouldn't make any lad take up game if he didn't want to. It'd be all right by me whatever he wanted to do. If it was legal.'

Unsmilingly Peggy said, 'What are your interests outside boxing? How do you like to spend your spare time? Music for instance. What kind of music do you like?'

'I don't know. The usual. I mean most kinds of ordinary music. I'm not that bothered. It's not my line, is it? I mean it's like you asking Judy Styles what she thinks about southpaws. Tell you the truth boxing's the only thing I'm really interested in.'

'Oh surely there must be other things in your life, Dave. All right, music you can take or leave. I don't suppose you read much—' He shook his head '—or go to the movies or theatre. But what about people? What above love?'

Dave stared at her without expression. It was obvious to her that he had no intention of speaking.

She went on quickly: 'You've been married—what?—just under a couple of years. Well, that was pretty well in mid-career wasn't it? I mean you must have found time for thoughts about something different from boxing, musn't you? For romance? Love? Dare I say it, sex?'

Dave continued to look at her steadily.

Peggy's eyes were suddenly bright and slippery with panic. She began, and her voice sounded a little breathless: 'All right you don't want to talk—' when he cut in:

'That's private,' he said. 'Love, marriage, sex—all that—it's personal. It's my business. Nobody wants to hear what I think about them things. Or if they do, they need their brains testing. I told you. Boxing's what I'm interested in. It's the thing I know about. And I'll tell you something else. You've got to be—what's the word—you've got to give it everything. You can't mess about.'

'Dedicated,' Peggy said.

'That's it. Dedicated. You've got to be dedicated. Every inch, every ounce, every breath. You've got to think and dream and sleep and eat boxing. Anything less and you'll never make it. You'll just be one of the others, one of the also-rans. I'm lucky. I was born dedicated. I love the game. I always did and I always will.'

'I think you've made your point, Dave. So, just before we have a bit more music, a final question. Your next fight is to be with Duke Hayes. Right?'

'Earl Hayes.'

Peggy gave a little yelp of embarassed laughter. '*Earl* Hayes. Sorry. I knew it was something aristocratic. Now he's supposed to be one of the greatest Middleweight boxers ever—or that's what my expert advisers tell me. He's never been beaten and apparently nearly all his fights end almost before they begin. Right?'

'Something like that. Except I'll probably have one fight before the defence against Hayes. What they call a warm-up. That'll most likely be in May against a good foreigner, most likely a Yank. Then I'll have a bit of a rest before I start training for the big one.'

'The one against Hayes. And that will be... when?'

'September's the most likely. They're still fixing details. But it's fairly sure to be September in London.'

'Now my last question. Does it worry you this man's got a fearsome reputation? And—to put it bluntly—are you absolutely confident you can win?'

'He's got a good record has Hayes. Nobody can't deny

that. I'd be a fool if I took no notice. I've watched him on film and I'll be watching a lot more. He's a very good fighter. It won't be easy. But I've got a fair record myself. Couldn't be a lot better really. Nobody's beaten me yet and I've fought more than Hayes. And I'll tell you this. I'm stronger than ever and I'm punching harder. I don't believe Earl Hayes can keep his chin out of the way for fifteen rounds. Sooner or later I'll find it. And he'll go. I can promise you that.'

'Well, thank you Dave Ruddock and the very best of luck to Yorkshire's own World Boxing Champion.' For a few seconds Peggy held her index finger to her lips in a warning to keep silent; then she said, 'Okay. Let's get out of here.'

Judy joined them from the control cubicle and they went out of the studio into the corridor.

Peggy said, 'Now, I've got half-an-hour free. Lets go over to the Fenton and I'll buy you both a drink.'

Judy was smiling with an expression of wondering delight. 'You were marvellous, Dave,' she said. 'Wasn't he, Peggy? Wasn't he terrific?'

'Terrific,' Peggy confirmed. 'And he made a monkey out of me.'

Dave was again confused and embarrassed by the burning that he felt on his face and neck.

He muttered, 'I'd better be on my way.'

'Oh no!' Judy said. 'You can't walk out on us. You promised! It was all fixed. We're going for a drink across the road. No argument.' She took his arm and they all began to move towards the reception hall and exit.

The light pressure of her fingers, the faint scent that seemed to be part of the aura that she carried with her, a sweet starriness, a silent tune, worked strangely and potently on Dave's consciousness. Her closeness brought with it a sense of unreality, a deep and vibrant awareness of her which seemed to involve taste, sight, scent and hearing and which reduced all the commonplace furnishings of the moment to a dreamlike remoteness. His strength had been drained away. He could do nothing but submit to that ever so gentle insistence of her small hand on his sleeve. There was a steady humming through his blood, a small bee in his heart or skull.

45

Then they were out into the street and crossing the road to the pub.

He said, 'I don't drink.'

Her laugh was scarcely more than a smile made briefly and softly audible. 'Not anything?'

They were entering the pub.

Peggy said, 'You two go and sit over there. I'll get the drinks. What are you having, Judy?'

'Just something soft. Orange juice.'

'I'll get them,' Dave said. 'What you drinking, Peggy?'

'No. This is on the Beeb. Do as you're told and sit down.'

'Come on,' Judy said and led him to a table in the corner farthest from the bar, calling over her shoulder to Peggy, 'We're both on Britvic Orange.'

'I haven't been pushed around so much since I was at school,' he said as he seated himself on a stool at the table.

'Not there,' Judy objected, taking his hand and moving him to the long seat against the wall behind the table where she joined him, sitting so close that he could feel her shoulder touching his upper arm and, more disturbingly, her thigh against his own and the fragrance of her pale golden hair haunting his nostrils.

Peggy came from the bar with the drinks and took the stool from which Dave had been removed. She looked from one to the other, smiling mischievously. 'Cheers!' she said, taking a drink from her half-pint of bitter. 'It's nice and empty here now. You get quite a few in later on. Can I get either of you anything to eat? Sandwich or a pie or something?'

Both Judy and Dave decline the offer of food.

'No. Well, I always bring a something from home myself. And a flask of coffee. It's a lot cheaper and nicer. In fact I'll be going back across the road in a minute for a quick scoff before the next programme. I expect you two've got plenty to talk about . . . Oh Dave, I almost forgot! Tom says can you and Aileen come out with us for a Chinese a week on Saturday. That's the thirteenth. He's on nights next week till Friday or we'd have made it sooner. Saturday the thirteenth. Hope that's not an omen. Tom's bound to give you a ring before then but he asked me to mention it.'

Dave felt in his inside jacket pocket and brought out his diary. 'I'll make a note now,' he said. 'Tell Tom I'll look forw—we both will—look forward to it.'

When Peggy had finished her beer she said, 'Good to see you both. I must rush. 'Bye now.' She left the pub, waving and calling a farewell to the barman as she went. Judy said, 'You handled that interview very well, Dave.'

He glanced sideways at her then quickly away.

'You're kidding. You're taking the Micky. I were petrified.'

'I'm absolutely serious. You were good. You didn't let her get away with anything. I mean most people, when they're interviewed on the air, they're too anxious to please. Do you see what I mean? They'll say what's expected. They're not honest. They go along with it. Not you. When Peggy started on the personal stuff you just told her to shut up. None of her business. That was marvellous.'

'I didn't mean to be big-headed, bad manners like.'

'You weren't Dave. You just showed a bit of independence. A bit of dignity. And that's a pretty rare thing in that world. Don't get me wrong. Peggy's a nice girl. I don't know her well but I've met her a couple of times before and I like her. But I must admit I enjoyed seeing you slap her down.'

'Slap her down!' Dave sounded horrified. 'I hope I didn't do that.'

'Don't worry. She won't mind. It was good radio.'

He said, 'Would you like another Orange?'

She smiled. 'No thanks. All right, I'll change the subject. Did you really remember me?'

'Course I did.' He did not return her smile or even look at her. Then he said, 'How's your mam and dad—your parents?'

'They're all right. Retired now. Got a nice little bungalow at Robin Hood's Bay. I don't see them as often as I ought to.'

'You're not married then? Or are you?' Then he added quickly before she could answer, 'Sorry, it's none of my business.'

'Don't be silly. Nothing to be sorry for. No, I'm not

married. And I can't really say I'm wedded to my career, like you. Except you found time for marriage as well. What's she like, your wife? Is she a Leeds girl?'

He nodded, 'Aye. She comes from Harehills. Went to the same school.'

'How lovely! A boy and girl romance, first and only love. It's nice to know it happens in real life.'

Dave grinned slightly, 'Not really. It weren't like that.'
'Oh?'

He said, 'I'd best be off now. Aileen's expecting me. She'll have my dinner ready.'

'My turn now,' Judy said.

'Eh? what was that? What do you mean your turn?'

'My turn to be slapped down.'

Again the heat of confusion on forehead, cheeks and neck. 'No! I didn't mean to—that's not what I meant to do. I didn't mean to be rude like. I just thought it were boring. You talking about romance and love and that. I didn't want to disappoint you. Aileen and me, we wasn't like that at all. To tell you truth I sometimes wondered how the bloody hell we ever got wed.'

'Oh dear.'

He shook his head like a man who is taking a count and trying to clear the fog in his skull. 'No,' he said. 'It's not like that either. She's all right, is Aileen. It's me shouldn't have got married. It's like Peggy was saying. Dedicated. You've got to be if you're in fight game. Maybe after, when you've hung gloves up. Maybe there's time then. But—I don't know. I'm not much good for anything except fighting. And that's a fact.'

Judy touched his hand gently and only for a moment. 'I'm sorry. I shouldn't have poked my nose in. I'm sure things'll work out for you both.'

He nodded gloomily. 'Aye!' Then he said, 'What was you doing over there, on radio with Peggy?'

'Same as you. Small stuff, of course, in comparison. I'm singing at a concert in Harrogate on Friday. I was just doing a little interview. My life and hard times. How I rose to stardom kind of thing.' She studied his serious face. 'I'm

48

joking, Dave. About the stardom. I'm a little fish in a little pond.'

'But you've sung on telly. Peggy said so.'

'A couple of times or so. I do all right in a small way but I've no illusions. I'm not a bad soprano and I look all right. I get by.'

'I heard somewhere you was a singer. I'll have to look out on box.'

'Why not come to the concert?' You and your wife—what's she called? Eileen?'

'Aileen.'

'Why don't you bring her along? It's a charity do at the Harrogate Theatre. Not heavy stuff. Light music, quite painless. Musical comedy, Gilbert and Sullivan. That kind of thing. She might enjoy it.'

Dave nodded and made a sound that conveyed both agreement and doubt.

'Look. I'll leave two tickets for you at the box-office. If you can't make it, don't worry. But if you can, you must come backstage and see me. We'll go out for a meal or a drink or something. That's Friday, day after tomorrow, at eight o'clock. You will try, won't you?'

'I'll try, yes. Aileen's not all that keen on going out.'

'She only needs persuading. I'm sure she'd like to dress up and have a night out. You tell her she's got to come.'

'I'll see if I can. I'd like to hear you sing.'

'Well, don't expect too much.'

He looked her full in the face for the first time since they had sat down, and as they smiled at each other he felt a momentary breathlessness and the sense of drifting out of the ordinary, daily world on to another level of existence. Abruptly he said, 'We'd best be going.'

She nodded and they left the Fenton, which was beginning to fill up with lunch-time customers, and re-crossed the road to the BBC car park.

'Can I give you a lift?' Dave said when they had reached his car.

'No. I've got my Mini.'

49

'Oh ... Where d'you live, anyway? I mean, if it's not being nosey ...'

'A turning off the Wetherby Road, near Lady Wood, opposite the Park.'

'Eh! Not so far from us. We're just off Lidgett Park Avenue.'

'You will try and come on Friday, won't you? Tell your wife you'll go on your own if she won't come. That'll change her mind.'

'We'll see.'

'I'll leave the tickets at the box-office anyway. I'll be very disappointed if you're not there.'

'So will I,' he said, and as she smiled and walked away he wondered if somehow he had made a declaration of more significance than those words would normally contain. He watched her fair head, bright in the cold sunlight, as she moved between parked cars; then he saw her pause at a red Mini and bend to unlock the door.

He got into his Capri and quickly switched on the engine, engaged first gear and drove out into the lunch-time traffic. When he looked in his rear mirror as he waited at the red traffic light he saw no sign of the Mini. The lights changed and he moved forward, driving as fast as was prudent, for he was already quite late for his mid-day meal.

The table in the dining-room was set for their meal when Dave came in, rubbing his hands together and puffing out his cheeks.

'By' he said, 'it's a lovely day but it's still nippy.'

Aileen who was in the kitchen, called from the serving-hatch, 'Come and get these and put them on table.'

'These' were a casserole and dish of mashed potatoes. He did as she asked and then took a chair at the table as Aileen came into the dining-room and joined him.

He said, 'That smells good.'

She did not answer or even look at him as she began to serve the meal. When his plate was filled he did not at once begin to eat. He watched her as she served herself, replaced the casserole lid and picked up her knife and fork.

Then he said, 'Hey up. What's the matter, love? You're very quiet.'

She did not reply but started to eat.

'Aileen. I asked what's wrong. Are you feeling poorly?'

She looked at him and he saw that the blue eyes behind her glasses had lost their usual brightness and become misted and withdrawn and her lips were joined and pushed slightly forward into a pout.

She said, 'Why are you late?'

'Late?' He looked at his watch. 'It's only twenty past now. I wasn't more than ten, fifteen minutes after I said. Traffic were heavy. What's up with you?'

'Nothing,' she said and forked a very little food into her mouth and began to chew.

'Oh, come on. Something's wrong.'

When she next spoke it was with lowered head. 'You never told me you knew Judy Styles.'

'What?... Oh that! You heard about that on radio. Hey, listen Aileen. Don't be daft. You heard what I said. It was that Peggy Lawson. She got it all wrong. I never knew Judy, not really. Like I said, my mam worked for hers. I haven't laid eyes on her for years, not since we was kids. So don't be bloody silly.'

'And don't you swear at me! I'm not so daft as you think. She were there, weren't she? They said so. She were waiting while you was talking. That girl Peggy said you'd be meeting afterwards to talk about old times. Old sweethearts, that's what she said. So don't tell me you didn't know her. And where've you been till now? You finished on radio at twenty-five to one. It doesn't take you three quarters of an hour to drive from Woodhouse Lane. You could walk it in that time. So what you been doing?'

Dave threw his knife and fork down. 'What do you think I've been doing? You think me and Judy Styles—oh for Christ's sake Aileen grow up! I told you. I told Peggy Lawson. I never knew her. It's just she remembered my mother working for hers. And once—just once—mam brought Judy round home for tea. Her Mam and Dad was out somewhere and we was looking after her. She couldn't have been more than ten or eleven. I never said a word to her after that. Not even then, I shouldn't think. So belt up and don't be so daft.'

Aileen was quiet for a few moments; then she said. 'You still haven't told me what you were doing for all that time.'

Dave had picked up his knife and fork and begun to eat again. He chewed quickly and swallowed. 'We went to a pub across the road and had a drink. Very wicked. I had a Britvic Orange. So did Judy. Peggy had a half of bitter. That's all. We wasn't there more'n fifteen, twenty minutes, so I don't know what you're going on about.'

'What did you talk about?'

'Talk about? I don't know. Nothing much. The weather— oh, yes. Tom and Peggy's asked us out for a Chinese meal a week on Saturday. That all right?'

Aileen looked at him, her expression still sullen and brooding.

'You mean you and Judy Styles never talked about nothing except the weather? Try and pull the other one! She wouldn't let go a chance to get her claws into somebody that's famous like you are. She'd be after you quick enough.. And I bet she were, weren't she?'

Dave shook his head in exasperation. 'I don't know what you're on about. What you got against her, anyway? Do you know her? What's she done to upset you? You seem to know a lot about her. How did you come to meet her?'

'I don't need to know her. I know about her. Everybody does.'

'What d'you mean? Know about her? Everybody does? What d'you mean? What is it everybody knows? Cause I'm buggered if I know.'

'Everybody knows what kind of woman she is! And watch your language!'

Dave dropped his knife and fork again. 'Oh, do they? Well here's somebody that doesn't. So tell me. What kind of woman is she?'

'You know.'

'For Christ's sake—'

52

'She's a whore!' Aileen released the words with a kind of bitter, strangled shout in a voice which Dave had never heard before, just as her face wore an expression that was unfamiliar to him, a look of hatred and revulsion. For a second he was shocked, almost frightened by this transformation in someone he thought he knew so well; then this first response gave way to a feeling of anger and disgust.

He said, 'Where do you get your information from? You don't know the woman but you know she's a whore. *How* do you know? Does she advertise? She got a plate up like a bloody dentist or something? *How* do you know?'

'Everybody knows.'

'For Christ's sake stop saying that! You sound like a bloody half-wit. Everybody knows! Who the fuck's everybody?'

'Dave! You've never used that word before! That's terrible. In front of me.' She sniffed and he saw a tear creep from the corner of one eye and begin to trickle down her cheek.

'You'd make a bloody saint swear,' he said. 'You sit there calling somebody a whore and God-knows-what and when I ask you where you get your information from you keep saying, "Everybody knows", like a bloody parrot. Well *I* don't know, so everybody don't know do they? So just you tell me where you get your information from or shut up and admit you're talking bloody rubbish.'

She said, 'When I worked in Lewis's. All the girls talked about her. It were common knowledge. I saw her myself with different men, all the same type they was. Flashy. Where d'you think she gets her smart clothes from? Fur coats, jewellery, car. She's not top of the charts. Not even on them and never will be. She doesn't make all that much, singing at charity things and clubs. They used to laugh about it. I've heard them. "Judy was in with another this morning. Bought her a nice gold bracelet." Then there was Sharon Harper, she worked in Lingerie. Sharon told us. Judy Styles and one of her men. That Colin Hunter it were. In Lingerie! Choosing underwear! With a man! She'd no shame.'

Dave pushed back his chair and stood up.

'Where you going?' Aileen said. 'You haven't finished your dinner.'

'I'm not hungry. Keep it in oven. I'll eat it later. I'm going for a walk.'

'What's wrong, Dave? Why you so upset about it, me calling Judy Styles what everybody knows she is? It's upset you, hasn't it? Why?'

He said, 'The only thing upsets me is you. Talking like a bloody fishwife. Scandal. Gossip. It's jealousy, that's what it is. I don't know if Judy's what you say she is or not. And I don't care. It's not my business. But one thing I do know. You've got no right to talk about anybody that way unless you know for a fact that it's all true. She's a whore, you say. And how do you know? Because Sharon somebody-or-other sold her a pair of knickers in front of a man. Bloody marvellous!'

'You *are* upset. She must have got under your skin without much trouble. Your old sweetheart.'

He turned quickly and walked out of the dining room and into the hall.

Aileen called, 'Dave! Where you going?'

'A walk! I told you!'

He grabbed his sheepskin coat from the stand and shrugged it on as he moved towards the door.

'Dave!' she called again, but the door slammed like a gunshot, silencing her.

CHAPTER FOUR

P EGGY WORKED LATE that evening because one of her colleagues, Mike Taylor, who was suffering from the onset of 'flu, suddenly decided that he must go home to bed, leaving her to handle the two studio interviews he had arranged with an instrumentalist and a singer on a Country and Western programme. By the time she had finished work and returned to the flat she was tired, cold and hungry and her already prickly temper was not soothed by Tom's absence and the inhospitable darkness of the place. She set about preparing herself a meal of bacon, eggs and toast and a large mug of instant coffee and she had begun to eat at the kitchen table when Tom came in.

He stood, leaning with his back against the door, looking at her with a slightly crooked, not very friendly smile. His face was pale and the dark swarthiness about the jaws and upper lip showed blue in the brightness of the unshaded light. His black hair was untidy and it needed cutting; a heavy lock fell across his forehead, down to his right eyebrow. She knew that he had been drinking though she had to wait until he spoke before she could tell whether or not he was drunk.

'Make yourself some coffee,' Peggy said, 'and come and sit down.'

He stayed where he was for a few seconds and then heaved himself from the door and crossed to the cooker and began to prepare a mug of coffee.

She said, 'You've had something to eat, have you?'

'Yeah. Enough.'

He took off his duffle coat and hung it on the back of the

door. Then he sat at the table with his coffee.

'You had a good day?' he said.

She chewed her bacon and egg and swallowed. 'All right. Too much of it. Mike Taylor was feeling rotten—'flu or something—and he buggered off home. That meant I had to do his stupid interviews. I don't have to go in till eleven tomorrow. Thank God.'

'I heard you and Dave this morning. At work. Old Arthur Fox and I listened on his tranny.'

'Oh.' She looked up at him cautiously as she ate. 'What did you think?'

He appeared to consider; then he shrugged but said nothing.

'Oh come on,' Peggy said. 'I can tell you didn't like it. What did I do wrong?'

'It was all right.'

'No it wasn't. At least you don't think it was. I can tell. Come on, Tom. Out with it. What was wrong?'

'No. It was okay. It came across pretty well really. But it mightn't have done. It could have been a balls-up. Dave surprised me. He handled you a lot better than I thought he'd be able to.'

She lowered the fork, that was about to carry the last fragment of her meal into her mouth, and stared at him. 'What the hell do you think you're talking about? I can see you're a bit pissed but, really, you can't have had that much. Handled me! What's that supposed to mean?'

Tom sipped some coffee. 'I mean your stupid bloody questions—questions you promised me you wouldn't ask him—I mean he wasn't flattened by them. He might have been. I was surprised.'

'Stupid questions, were they? I'd promised not to ask them? What questions are we talking about? I asked him how he felt about the dangers. What he felt about hurting people badly or being hurt himself. I was talking to a prize-fighter. How can you avoid questions like that? I asked him what his wife felt, whether she watched him fight. Whether he'd let his kids—if he had any—take up boxing. What's so stupid about that?'

Tom grinned slightly. 'Okay, Peggy, simmer down. Okay. They're the questions you asked. But there are ways of putting questions, aren't there? . . . No, just let me finish . . . Listen. When you were talking about the dangers—hurt and getting hurt—you also talked about death, didn't you? You talked about killing. You even got him to the point where he had to admit that he always went for the knock-out if he could and there was a chance that he could literally kill his man. Now, I said I'd ask Dave to give you the interview on condition you stuck to simple questions. Well, that's hardly a simple question! In fact he answered it pretty well. But I don't want to see him worried by things like that. Christ, if he started worrying about the possibility of killing someone it could finish him. Can you imagine him going in against Hayes with that kind of weight on his mind?'

'It was a fair question, Tom. If you weren't so biased you'd be the first to want an answer to it. It's a moral question and I owed it to my listeners to ask it.'

'Owed it to your listeners! What the hell do they care? Anybody who listens to that programme isn't going to be looking for answers to moral questions. But it wasn't only that. It was the way you tried to belittle him, all that stuff about what music he liked—books, theatre. You know damn well he's never been to the theatre in his life unless it was the City Varieties or panto. And what was that business you started with about some woman, some singer. You said Dave and she were old friends. He didn't sound too pleased by that.'

'That was Judy Styles.'

'Who's she? Why bring her into it?'

'Well, it was rather interesting. She's a kind of local downmarket Moira Anderson—I don't suppose you've heard of *her* either—a sort of Victorian ballad, musical comedy soprano. Tell you the truth I've never heard Judy sing but she must be at least passable because she's been on telly and radio a few times and she seems to get quite a lot of bookings. She's certainly a stunning looker, if you like that kind of thing— and I guess most men do—and I don't suppose that spoils her chances.'

'Go on. What about her?'

'Well, I was doing an interview with her about some charity concert she's appearing in on Friday and when we came out of the studio Dave was waiting. Judy greeted him as if she knew him very well. The way they went on—well, the way *she* did, I suppose—well, I just assumed they were old friends.'

'And you were wrong.'

'I don't know. Dave played it down. But you know what he's like. Anyway, we all went over to the Fenton for a drink afterwards and I left them there. Maybe you're right. I shouldn't have said anything on the air. It just seemed a natural thing to do. I'd just been talking to Judy, a few minutes before, and I really thought they were old friends.'

'Did you ask him about the meal, him and Aileen coming out with us next weekend?'

'A week on Saturday. Yes, I did. He said that'd be okay. I told him you'd probably give him a ring before then.'

They sat in silence for a few seconds then Peggy said, 'Would you like more coffee?'

He looked into his empty mug. 'There isn't anything else, is there? Any of that vodka left?'

'You finished it on Sunday.'

'Oh yes. So I did.'

She stood up. 'Well. Do you want any more coffee or not?'

He reached out and took her hand. 'Yes please ... we'll have one more coffee and go to bed. How's that sound?'

'It sounds great. I'm knackered.'

He rested his right elbow on the table, his chin cradled in the palm of his hand, watching her as she made the coffee. He said 'Sorry I was shitty about the programme. It was all right really. I'm over-defensive about Dave. I shouldn't be. He can look after himself.'

She brought the refilled mugs back to the table and sat down again. 'He was a lot more articulate than I expected. That stuff about words meaning different things to different professions was very smart. He's right in a way. I mean there's enough truth in what he was saying to fool a lot of people that he was telling the whole truth.'

'I think he was telling the whole truth. As he sees it.'

Peggy smiled. 'You do? Really? Well, I doubt it. I think our simple, honest Dave was doing something quite clever. He said different people—actors, coppers and so on—use the same words to mean different things. Boxers the same. When they talk about hurting or killing they mean something different from what a policeman means by the same words. That's probably true, but only when the boxer's using the words as metaphors or half-metaphors. See what I mean? When a copper talks about killing, someone killing another person, the word 'killing' is unambiguous. It's got one final, unarguable meaning. It means taking away someone's life. Making them dead. When Dave says he goes in for the kill he claims he's talking about something else, not death, just knocking a man unconscious for ten seconds. The word "kill" is a metaphor. But you see what he's up to? He's implying that the whole thing's a metaphor. There's no real pain, no real death, in boxing. And he's lying, and I think he knows he's lying. He *must* know, because the facts are there. People *are* hurt, they *are* killed, literally, physically. They're made dead.'

Tom breathed out, a long audible expulsion of air as if he had been holding his breath throughout Peggy's speech. Then he said, 'I think you're doing Dave a bit of an injustice. I mean that "honest, simple Dave" stuff was a bit of a sneer wasn't it?'

Peggy shook her head, 'I wasn't trying to—'

'All right. It doesn't matter. You ended up by saying he was lying and he knew he was lying. But what you didn't mention was what he said at some point: sure, boxers get hurt and they even get killed, he said. He even said that pain and danger—and we know what he means by danger: he means the possibility of death—he said those things are necessary. I can't remember his exact words but something like there wouldn't be any point if the dangers weren't there. Now what he was really trying to make clear with the language business was that those words "kill', "hurt", "murder" and so on, when the boxer uses them, are in fact metaphors. The reality is violent all right. But it's purpose isn't either sadistic or lethal. When a fighter says he's going in for the kill or he's going to murder his opponent, obviously he doesn't mean that literally. He means exactly what Dave said and no more—he's aims to knock him out. If a boxer suffers serious injury or gets killed in the ring it's an accident. Certainly it's an accident that's made more likely by the nature of the game, but it's still an accident.'

'But Tom! Is it worth it? There's Dave, your dearest friend, from all accounts a nice gentle sort of chap. How can you bear to see him risk awful injury or death? Or for that matter how can you bear to see him inflict these things on other people? I just can't understand it.'

Tom sat brooding, in silence, and when it seemed that he was not going to reply Peggy said, 'It's not worth the risk, is it?'

'Yes,' he said, 'it is.'

'Oh Tom. How can you say that? What about that Welsh boy? The one who was killed in America? Surely you can't justify any sport—if you can call it a sport—that involves that kind of sacrifice. It's intolerable in a civilized society and you know it.'

'In a civilized society? You mean Britain? Europe? The Western world? Civilized? Just look around you, Peggy. Never mind about South Africa, El Salvador, Afghanistan, Ulster and so on. Just take a look outside your front door. Football yobs smashing each other—and anyone who happens to get in the way—bicycle chains, knives, knuckledusters and God-knows-what. Go down the road and see what's on at the movies. *The Chainsaw Massacre* and *Confessions of a Window Cleaner*. Your local pub gives you four full strips with lunchtime ploughmans and a pint. Or music. Christ, listen to *Top of the Pops* if you want to be labotomized by shitty, ugly, utterly uninventive noise. Your own local radio pumps out either syrup or piss. Just take a look at the Best Sellers lists in the Sunday heavies. What do you find? *The Wit and Wisdom of Mark Phillips* or the *Guinness Book of Bollocks*. And what about high culture? Sam Beckett's last crap or Andrew Lloyd Webber's musical version of Loyola's Spiritual Exercises. And government? Thatcher and her little coven of toadies? Stupid, selfish, cruel. Swollen up with crazy pride and greed. And the Opposition? Much the same, except for the few who haven't any voice, any real power. It's a dark world we're living in, Peggy, and it's getting darker. You know it's there, even in the sunlight. You can smell it, the darkness. You can taste it. And it's thickening, spreading all the time.'

'And what's that got to do with boxing?'

'What?' Tom, who was staring down at the table looked up at Peggy. 'Oh. Yes, boxing. Yes, well... you'll probably laugh at this, but I think it's important. In this darkening, stinking world there isn't much left that's not been dirtied, corrupted in some way. I'm not saying boxing hasn't been. God knows the money boys, the promoters, managers, the entrepreneurs have tried hard enough. But somehow there's something there, among the fighters themselves, that can't be touched. And I'll tell you what it is. It's a sense of the heroic. I know that sounds ridiculous but let me try and explain.

'Everything's being debased, smeared, filthied. Okay, maybe not absolutely everything, but damn near it. Art, literature, religion, theatre. There might be some real stuff around but if there is you can't see it because it's buried under the shit. Now, boxing's different. It resists vulgarization. You might say it's intrinsically vulgar so it can't be vulgarized any more. But I don't see it that way. It's primitive, I suppose, but my God, it's pure. There's nothing sham about it, when they're in that ring they're on their own. All the razzamatazz and commercial crap is left outside. It's a moment of truth. It really is. The kind of courage and skill and strength and beauty you see in the ring can't be seen anywhere else. Nowhere else at all. It's heroic because it's pure. You'll find courage and sheer resolution in other places I'll agree. But they're different. You'll find people behaving bravely and unselfishly in, say, a rail crash or fire or earthquake. Certainly in war. But it's expedient. Contingent. Is that the word? Do you see what I mean? It's manipulated. The soldier's being *used* by politicians. The hero of flood or fire's manipulated by special circumstances. With the fighter it's an end in itself. He's not forced to do it by circumstance or from some notion of patriotism or honour. And not for profit. That's where so many people make a mistake. Because there's big money in the fight game they think boxers are in it for the cash or they're being exploited by the managers. Maybe. But when two fighters are up there in that ring nothing matters—not money, fame, country, nearest and dearest—nothing matters except the fight itself. And they'll fight, if necessary, to the death. It's heroic. It's a little gleam of pure light in a dark bloody world. It's beautiful. And it's got to be to the death. The possibility—however remote, and it's always remote—it's got to be there.' He looked at her, smiling and reached again for her hand. 'But if you can't see it you can't. It's no good trying to explain. It's like talking about the thrills of cricket to an Eskimo. That right?'

Peggy nodded. 'That's right.'

'And in any case, as you said, I'm a bit pissed.'

'Finish your coffee.' She stood up and took her plate and cutlery to the sink.

He followed her with his empty mug and stood behind her. 'Let's leave the washing up,' he said.

She looked upwards, over her shoulder, at him and smiled, 'All right, you old boozer.'

'Randy old boozer.'

She turned, took the mug from his and put it into the sink with the other dishes. Then she raised her face for his kiss.

When he withdrew his mouth from hers she said, 'Come on, Darwin. Let's to bed. The talking's got to stop some time. So come on. Let's go.'

CHAPTER FIVE

THE BRIGHTNESS, WARMTH and noise inside the foyer of the Harrogate Theatre seemed welcoming yet confusing after Dave's walk through the cold dark streets from the car park. The scent of cigar-smoke seasoned the air which was loud with the chatter and laughter of the smartly dressed men and women who stood about in groups, smoking and gossiping. One man, in a dinner jacket, wore round his neck a chain of office and his little party was conspicuously the noisiest.

Dave felt a sudden impulse to turn and get out of the place. These people were not of his kind; they were old and rich and very sure of themselves. Those great honking laughs were not expressions of merriment; they were loud advertisements of confidence, wealth and power. He was the lad from the back streets, the boy who delivered their newspapers; his mother scrubbed their floors. He did not belong there. They were the same kind who sat at the ringside at the exclusive sporting club shows, the kind who might throw into the ring the casually screwed-up fivers if a couple of boys had given them a bit of excitement by cutting each other to ribbons. They were the brandy-drinkers, the cigar-smokers, the big-bellied, the bosses. Then he saw that one of the men in the group which included the civic dignitary was glancing in his direction with that now familiar look of furtive excitement and recognition, and was muttering to one of his companions who flicked a quick glance towards where Dave was standing. Then, quite abruptly Dave's feeling changed: he felt something of that remote sense of assurance and superiority which he experienced before the start of a fight when he was standing in his corner and the anonymous, featureless crowd was down there, below him, making excited, wordless, almost animal noise. He knew what the noise meant; just as he knew what those quick furtive glances meant. They feared him. They held him in awe.

He walked over to the box-office and said to the girl at the cash desk, 'Miss Styles—Judy Styles—said she'd leave tickets for me. I'm Dave Ruddock.'

The girl smiled. 'Oh yes, Mr Ruddock. Here you are.' She pushed an envelope towards him.

He tore open the envelope and found inside it two stalls tickets and a single sheet of pale-blue notepaper on which was written:

> 'Please come and see me in my dressing-room in the interval. Mr Pringle the manager will show you the way. I have told him you may be coming. I hope you enjoy the concert.
>
> J.'

Her handwriting was large and it swooped and curled across the page with a generosity of gesture, an expansiveness, almost a recklessness that seemed to convey something of her character. Dave looked quickly around before bending his head and briefly sniffing the paper. He has hoped for something of her fragrance but he could detect no scent at all. He returned the note and one of the tickets to the envelope which he slipped into his inside pocket and, holding the other ticket in his hand, he approached an attendant at one of the entrances to the auditorium from whom he was able to buy a programme before she halved his ticket and directed him to his seat.

The place was rapidly filling with the audience and the hum and rattle of their conversation grew louder. It was a quite different noise from that made by a fight crowd. However much the volume rose the sound contained nothing raucous, gruff or menacing; it remained genteel, prepared at any moment to submit to an appeal for silence. Dave looked at his programme and saw that Judy was to sing a group of solos from Gilbert and Sullivan, Lehar and Kern in the first half and, at the beginning of the second, she was to conclude her performance with an aria from *Madame Butterfly* and a duet from *The Maid of the Mountains*, in company with Richard Palmer, tenor. This information meant little to Dave. He looked around him and grinned secretly as he wondered what his mates at the gym in Leeds or London, his fellow pros, would say if they could see him sitting among these stuffed shirts and their blue-rinsed old bags waiting to hear high-class music.

When the concert began, with an overture by Edward German, Dave found the music quite pleasant and for the first few minutes he was beguiled by the glitter of brass and silver, the dark chestnut gleam of wood, the way in which the conductor seemed to wield the baton like a long needle which stitched together the tapestry of sound, but by the time the piece had come to an end, and a stout baritone had begun his interpretation of *The Road to Mandaly*, Dave was aware of little of his surroundings. He was now preoccupied with feelings of guilt and excitement, anticipation and an uneasy sense of his betrayal of his wife's trust and, perhaps most strongly, of profound misgivings about his own intentions and hopes and about the way in which Judy would receive him, if indeed he found courage enough to visit her in the interval. Since the afternoon two days ago when he and Aileen had quarrelled after his broadcast on Radio Leeds neither had made any reference to the argument or to its cause, but he had been conscious of a slightly uncomfortable constraint, a guarded and not quite natural politeness between them. He had tried to forget his meeting with Judy but his efforts to do so seemed perversely to intensify his memories of her and regenerate the sad yearnings of adolescence which had not troubled him for almost ten years.

Dave had been eleven years old when his mother had agreed to work part-time for Mrs Styles whom she had known slightly when they were both young girls. Judy's mother had, in Mrs Ruddock's words, done well for herself. She had married a responsible white-collar worker, Frank Styles, who had been employed in the investments section of a big insurance company and had risen to the position of Departmental Head. They lived in a nice house on the Harrogate Road and their only child, Judy, was not only very pretty but, or so they claimed, remarkably gifted. When Judy was about twelve her mother took a job as a dentist's receptionist not, as she emphasised, because they needed the money but because she found, now that her little girl was growing up, that the days were long, lonely and boring and she needed some interest to fill those hours when her child was at school. Dave's mother was not asked to do any heavy work; a cleaning lady came in three times a week to do the more taxing chores. All that was demanded of Mrs Ruddock was that she should do a little tidying up, perhaps some shopping and be at the Styles's home ready to provide tea when Judy returned from school.

There were a few occasions, for Dave strangely compounded of joy, fear and embarrassment, when Mr and Mrs Styles would meet each other in town after their day's work to attend some exclusively adult social function and Mrs Ruddock would bring Judy back to the Ruddock's terrace house in unbeautiful, uncompromisingly plebian Harehills to wait until the child's parents arrived to take her home. At these times Mrs Ruddock would bring out the best table-cloth and china, and rare delicacies such as tinned pears and ice-cream would be served after the fish-paste sandwiches and sausage-rolls, but Dave would show a most unusual lack of appetite because Judy's effulgent, shimmering beauty, her delicacy and sheer poshness were powerfully disconcerting presences before which the enjoyment of food seemed too coarse, too irreverent an activity, to indulge. She became for him the graceful embodiment of all that was mysterious, delicate, and lovely, an ideal of the feminine which had never been entirely dissipated. He could not remember now anything she said to him or whether in fact they ever spoke to each other. It certainly did not occur to him that there could ever exist between them a friendship of any kind, far less a romantic one.

Later, when Judy was old enough to come back from school to an empty house, or perhaps her mother had given up her job with the dentist, the visits to Dave's home ceased but the beautiful girl continued to haunt his waking dreams and, now, as he sat in the theatre, he could remember summer evenings when he would spend hours patrolling the area in which she lived, hoping for a glimpse of her, sometimes, but not often, being rewarded by seeing her, almost always with friends, returning from the tennis court, those slim, smooth brown limbs, that glittering opulence of hair, piercingly, intoxicatingly ensnaring him. Winter nights, too, outside her house, seeing the lights behind the curtains, imagining her there, warm, flushed by the firelight, hearing sometimes the faint sound of music and troubled by a profound hopeless longing, a sick vacancy that ached to be filled with sustaining sweetness and comfort but which he knew must remain unsatisfied, a pain that was strangely precious, one for which he did not seek, but feared, relief.

The people about him were clapping and the baritone who had reached the end of his group of songs was bowing and retreating to the wings. Then the orchestra played a selection of Strauss waltzes after which Judy came on to the stage to be introduced by the compère. For Dave it was a moment of such mystery, such erotic and aesthetic intensity, that his physical response was almost frightening. He literally gasped, as if he had taken an accurate and powerful body punch and was gulping suddenly for air, and for a moment his vision blurred so that it seemed that Judy was cocooned in a shimmering radiance, an unearthly nimbus, which gradually faded until he saw that she was wearing a long dress of dark maroon velvet from which her shoulders, arms, and the partially exposed bosom with the shadowy division of breasts gleamed with milky smoothness, and he realized that her pale golden hair had been taken up and secured by glittering clasps, emphasizing the slender and delicate column of neck, the fragility of that small head in which those slanting, brilliant, now strangely darkened eyes gazed out at the audience with a kind of mocking defiance, a withholding which was sealed by her small secret smile.

The applause faded, the clapping palms in the darkness petered out with a few last, weakly assertive flutterings; the opening bars from the orchestra sounded and then she began to sing. Her voice was very pure, sweet, crystalline, like spring water at dawn, and it startled Dave for he saw no relation between this beautiful and artfully controlled sound and Judy's ordinary speaking voice. At the end of each song he clapped so energetically that his palms tingled; the violent slapping together of his hands, the fleshy explosion, like fireworks, attracted the amused attention of some of the audience sitting around him and, though he was aware of this, his knowledge did nothing to moderate the vigour with which he expressed his approval and admiration. His clapping was more than formal appreciation of an artistic performance; it was an effort to convey to her his astounded praise and it was an exultant advertisement of his at least momentary enslavement.

At the interval he returned to the foyer and after enquiring from an attendant the whereabouts of Mr Pringle he was directed to a man in a dinner jacket to whom he showed Judy's note.

The manager waved it away and said, 'Ah yes! Judy told me you might be coming. Very pleased to see you Mr Ruddock. Where's your good lady? I understood, er, ah . . . ?'

'Good . . . ? Oh. Yes. No. She couldn't make it. My wife couldn't come.'

'I see. Oh yes. What a pity. Well, perhaps you'd like to follow me. We'll go backstage. This way . . . '

Dave followed Mr Pringle through a couple of doors and along a corridor to Judy's dressing-room on the door of which the manager tapped and waited, with his head slightly bowed and tilted, until they heard her voice call, 'Come in!' Mr Pringle opened the door and stepped back, allowing Dave to enter.

Judy was sitting on a stool at her mirror but was turned away from her reflection and facing the door. She said, 'Dave! How lovely you could come.' The manager had waved to her from outside the room with a coy fluttering of the fingers and then disappeared. 'Come in and close the door.'

She was wearing the maroon dress and her shoulders and bosom were almost dazzling in their whiteness. But it was her face that disturbed him most for, although it was clearly the face of the Judy he knew, it was, at the same time, changed almost shockingly by the heavy stage make-up which transformed her features into a mask-like, ornamental, hieratic imitation of themselves. There was a coarseness, too, that was thrilling in its extravagance, its blatancy and exaggeration.

He said, 'Aileen couldn't come. She wasn't feeling too good.'

'Oh. I'm sorry.' The mysteriously different yet still familiar face smiled: 'But I'm glad you could make it. Sit down.'

'I won't stay a minute. You was great. Terrific.' He remained standing.

'Thank you. I know I'm not, but it's nice to be told all the same.'

'You were!' he protested. 'Never heard nothing so—oh, I can't put it in words. Just smashing. And you looked like a—I don't know—better'n anything, anybody. Magic. Like a princess, a fairy story. I don't know. I can't put it in words. Not what you was like.'

'You're doing pretty well,' she said. 'You're going to stay for the second half, aren't you? . . . Good. Well, look. Are we going to have a bite, or a drink after the show? When I've finished? Or have you got to get back? Aileen not being well, I mean.'

'No. I mean yes, we'll have a drink or whatever you like. I haven't got to get back. No hurry anyway. Aileen's all right. She only had a bit of headache. I told you. She doesn't like going out much.'

There was a knock on the door and Judy called. 'Yes?'

The door opened, a man looked into the room, glanced from Judy to Dave and back again to Judy. 'Sorry darling,' he said, 'didn't know you had company.' He wore evening dress, his dark hair was lustrous with pomade and his face looked almost as heavily made up as Judy's.

She said, 'What did you want?'

'Nothing important.' He glanced back at Dave and away again.

'I'll see you later darling. On stage.' But he stayed in the doorway, smiling and looking from one to the other of the dressing-room's occupants.

Judy said, 'This is Dave Ruddock, an old friend . . . Richard Palmer. He's my other half in the duet, Dave.'

The singer darted forward into the room and took Dave's right hand in both of his, gave it more of a squeeze than a shake and relinquished it. 'How exciting,' he said. 'The great boxer. Wonderful, wonderful. I'd no idea, Judy. Fancy you never letting on. But I won't intrude. I'll see you later darling. And it's been a great thrill to meet you, sir.'

When he had gone, Judy said, 'Now, where were we? Oh yes. After I've finished my bit. That shouldn't be long, Dave. I'm on in a few minutes and I've only a couple of numbers. You came in your car I suppose?'

He nodded.

'Good. I got a lift you see. One of the orchestra, Tony Blythe, gave me a lift. I'm not all that keen on driving at night, specially when the roads could be slippery. I'll tell Tony I won't be going back with him. Then perhaps you could take me home when we've had a bite or whatever we're going to do. All right?'

Dave tried to shake off a deepening sense of unreality. Judy's beautiful but mask-like face, the surroundings of the dressing-room with the huge mirror framed with electric light bulbs, the litter of cosmetics on the table, the frothy scraps of feminine clothing, at which he carefully avoided looking after the first glance, the splendour of her white flesh against the dramatic dark red velvet, all of these increased the theatricality, the incredibility of his situation.

He said, 'Won't he mind?'

'Won't who mind what?'

'This bloke, Tony. I mean won't he mind you not going back with him?'

She smiled. 'No, of course not. He's just an old friend. We were at college. He plays the clarinet. He won't mind. Be pleased in fact. It'll mean he can get home to his wife quicker.'

'Oh.' Dave hesitated before he began: 'What about the—' But then he stopped.

'What about what?'

'I dunno. I was just wondering. About the other one. The singer. Not my business really. I just wondered.'

'Just wondered what?'

'Is he . . . ? I mean you and him seemed very friendly. Like the way he came in here. The way he talked. He called you "darling". Things like that.'

Judy laughed. 'Dave! Do you mean are we—are we . . . *courting*?'

He knew that he had made a blunder, though he was not sure quite how. 'Summat like that,' he muttered, his accent becoming broader in his embarrassment.

Traces of laughter were still in her voice; 'Oh dear, no! Didn't you notice, Dave? Richard's a little bit— well, not very what you might call manly. He was a lot more interested in you than me.'

'Aye . . . Ah, well, yes. I thought so. It was just him calling you "darling". I just wondered.'

She stood up. 'Everybody calls everbody else "darling" in this business. It doesn't mean a thing. It's just a silly habit.'

'They don't in mine.'

'What?' She had been moving past him towards the door as he spoke and it seemed that she had not heard or not understood.

'They don't in my business,' he said. 'Call each other "darling".'

Judy's eyes widened fractionally and briefly and she laughed: 'I can imagine!' She placed one hand on the door-knob. 'I'll be on again in a minute. Listen, Dave. As soon as I've finished the duet with Richard. Could you go and get your car? Bring it round to the stage-door. You'll be able to find your way, won't you? Okay? I'll change as quick as I can, so I shouldn't keep you waiting more than a few minutes. Is that all right? You don't want to stay for the rest of the show, do you?'

He told her that the arrangement was fine and that he would be waiting for her.

She touched his hand, not holding it, a soft, brief stroking motion, and then she opened the door and said, 'See you soon,' and he found himself out in the corridor, still partly dazed with the sense of unreality yet filled, too, with an excitement that was unequivocally physical, a conturbation of blood, nerve and flesh that was not very dissimilar from the sensations he experienced before going into the ring for an important and possibly dangerous contest.

Dave parked outside the stage-door but kept the engine running so that the car-heater would have warmed the atmosphere by the time Judy came out. He switched off the headlights but kept his sidelights on and he sat remembering her on the stage in her dramatic long dress, the frosty glittering of pearls at her white neck and in her hair, the fragile, menacing sweetness of her, the danger, opiate and surely irresistible. But those images, though present, were never properly articulated or focused. What Dave was touched by was a memory, not only personal but generalised, of his childhood and its environment, of his own mother, and, he was sure, of all mothers of her kind: the recollection was of confectionery, of those lovely, brightly coloured cakes composed of sugar icing, perhaps sprinkled with tiny silver sweets like miniature ball-bearings, oozing with cream and rubious jam, the pastry flaked and feathery, the 'shop-cakes' that his mother spoke of with such contempt and which she so sternly forbade him to touch, commending the sustaining virtues, the honest goodness of her home-made, unglamorous, unexciting rock-buns and scones. Judy was a shop-cake, thrilling, colourful, sweet, tempting and bad for you. And Aileen, he thought, at first with a fleeting, sour grin and then with sudden guilt and melancholy, was a rock-bun.

He tried to think of her but it was impossible to prevent the image of her face appearing before him, the eyes hurt and suspicious behind the gold-rimmed glasses, her mouth set in a look of sullen injury which erased completely the knowledge that, in cheerful mood, she could look quite pretty with a dimple in her right cheek and a smile which showed regular little teeth as bright and white as miniature bleached almonds. She would be reading one of the many women's magazines that she ordered each week from the newsagents in Oakwood, or watching television, and in about an hour's time she would go up to bed and continue reading until either he returned or she was overwhelmed by sleep. Women didn't have much of a life, he thought; at least not women like Aileen.

The darkness outside was brilliantly split for a moment by the opening of the stage door and he saw Judy silhouetted against the light before she moved quickly towards the car. His instant reaction was one of disappointment. The image of her that he had been cherishing, beautiful, almost ethereal, yet also, as seen at close quarters in the dressing-room, slightly coarsened by the extravagance of make-up yet no less mysterious, was obliterated by the complete change in her appearance, by her ordinariness. She wore a scarf tied over her head, a three-quarter length fur coat and trousers and in one hand she held a grip, not unlike the bag in which he carried his training gear. He leaned across to the passenger side and opened the door for her and he saw, in the interior light, that her face had been cleaned of the cosmetic mask and she looked pale, quite pretty, but no longer magical. He took her bag and heaved it over on to the back seat. Then, as she settled beside him and her faint scent reached his nostrils, the unexplained sense of disappointment faded and was replaced by a glow of pleasure, excitement and the stirrings of an astonished gratitude that the marvellous creature he had seen and listened to on the stage was now humanized; she had been translated, a warm breathing, terrestrial woman. And she was with him.

She said, 'What's the time?'

He looked at his watch. 'Five to ten.' Then when she did not immediately speak, he added, 'Where shall we go?'

She made a small murmuring sound of reflection or hesitation, but nothing more, and Dave was troubled by a feeling of uncertainty.

He said, 'What's up? You want to go straight home? That's all right. Just say the word.'

She sounded relieved. 'Yes, I think so. I'm not hungry. Never am after a show. And I don't particularly want a drink. Anyway we can—'

'Okay,' he broke in, 'I'm easy. Best be on our way.' He flipped on the headlamps, engaged first gear and they moved away from the pavement. 'I shouldn't have come,' he said.

'Not without Aileen. I nearly didn't. But then I changed my mind at the last minute.'

He thought he heard a small, quick intake of breath as if she had been startled or even slightly hurt. Then she said, 'I'm glad you did come. I don't mean I'm glad your wife's ill. But—well, I'm glad it didn't stop you from coming.'

Mollified, Dave tried to explain: 'I didn't mean I didn't want to hear you. You was terrific. It was great. I just meant—well, I thought you maybe wanted to get home—not go for a meal or anything—'cause you didn't want to go out with a married man. On his own. Without his wife.'

Judy had begun, very softly, to laugh before Dave had finished speaking and, when he had finished, her amusement was quite audible, though only very gently mocking. Then she said, still with traces of laughter in her voice, 'No, Dave. You've got it wrong. I'm not in the least worried because your wife couldn't come. Tell you the truth I'm glad. It was you I wanted to see, not your wife.'

'Oh.'

'Is that very—what's the word? Is that very *forward*. Does it shock you?'

'No,' Dave said and, evidently sensing that his voice had not carried complete conviction, he repeated, 'No, 'course it doesn't.'

'Good. Well, what I was going to suggest was we could have a snack or drink or something at my place. And it isn't because I don't want to be seen with a married man. It's just I think it'd be nicer, more comfortable. If you've got time, of course. What time's your wife expecting you back?'

'I don't know. I mean I didn't say any special time.'

His mind seemed like a run-away merry-go-round, spinning at ever increasing speed, and through the channels of blood and nerve moved a faintly buzzing fever that contained fear and the promise of unimaginable delight.

As they drove back to Leeds he was content to listen to Judy's talk of the concert and of her singing career. She was not a great singer, she said, but she had been well-trained and she had a voice that everybody told her was unusually pure. What she lacked was power—in a hall of any size she needed a microphone—power and, just as important, real dedication. That was one of the things she so admired in Dave. Of course he was lucky to be blessed with lots of other gifts, physique, courage, natural talent, but it was his single-minded, ruthless driving of himself that had taken him to the top. Now she was different. Even if she had been given a voice of great power and range she was sure she would not have been able to apply herself with the kind of self-denial needed if you were to climb or soar above the run-of-the-mill, the competently mediocre.

Dave had little more to do than nod and, occasionally, make little noises of assent or, if Judy seemed to be too self-deprecatory, of vague protest until they reached the Wetherby Road when he had to ask which turning to take.

Judy said, 'Daft of me. I'd forgotten you didn't know. It's just along here, past the park gates—there! Park in the road just there by the lamp post. My car's in the drive.'

He took her grip from the back seat and they got out and went through the wide gates of a detached medium sized house that looked as if it had been built at the turn of the century. There were lights in the upper rooms.

He said, 'It's big. Who do you live with?'

'No one. I've got the flat on the ground floor. There's a couple upstairs but I hardly see anything of them. I've got my own entrance at the back. Here . . . take my hand. It's a bit dark round here.'

He held her small, delicate fingers and followed her to the back of the house where she unlocked the door, went forward into a little hall and switched on lights. She took the grip from him.

'Here we are,' she said. 'Bathroom and loo on the right. This door—' she indicated one facing them as they entered '—is into the bedroom. And here's the kitchen.'

She opened a door on the left of the entrance and they went through it into a kitchen which was large enough for a small table and four chairs. 'And through here—' she opened a door on their right—'We've got the living room, sitting room, lounge, call it what you like.'

He said, 'It looks very nice.'

'It's okay. Now you sit down there while I make us some

75

coffee. And what about food? I could do you ham or cheese sandwiches. Or eggs. Scrambled, omelette, any way you like. And that's about all.'

He shook his head. 'Nothing thank you. I'm not hungry.'

'You quite sure?'

He was.

'All right. I won't be a couple of minutes.'

She went into the kitchen, leaving the connecting door open, and he moved round the room, looking at its furnishing with respectful curiosity. Two armchairs and a small two-seater sofa occupied most of the centre and against one of the window-less walls was an upright piano and opposite this a music-centre with a large collection of records and tapes stored beneath. The whole floor was covered with a thick-pile carpet and heavy, expensive looking, green patterned curtains hung from the top of the tall front windows to the floor. On the left, as you came into the room from the kitchen, stood a shelf-unit taking up most of the wall and displaying a couple of plants, a few books and glossy magazines and some vases and trinkets. Among the four pictures on the walls was a studio photograph of Judy, a head and shoulders portrait taken, Dave guessed, two or three years earlier. She looked beautiful, but not, he thought, as disturbingly so as she was in reality.

She called from the kitchen. 'Take sugar?'

'Just one.'

'I'll bring it in. You can help yourself.'

He thought of her hand resting softly in his as she had led him along the dark path to the back of the house and he remembered her saying that she wasn't worried that Aileen couldn't come, that she wanted to see him, not his wife. Could it be that she was giving him the come-on, the green light? Was there something, after all, in all that gossip that Aileen had heard? And yet she was so classy, such a lady. She'd been to the High School and then the music college. She belonged to the tennis-club. She sang those high-class songs. She was beautiful. Could she possibly fancy him?

'Here we are.' She came into the living-room and placed a loaded tray on to a small wheeled table which she pushed across to the two armchairs. She had removed her coat and head-scarf and her hair had been taken down and combed out. He saw the rounded definition of her breasts beneath the pale blue sweater she was wearing and for a moment he was dazzled again by the remembered whiteness of her arms and shoulders, the shadow between that creamy smoothness where the breasts divided.

'Sit down,' she said. 'You make me feel uneasy, prowling about.' She began to pour coffee as he sat next to her. 'Would you like some music?'

'I'm not fussy.'

'No. Perhaps we'll just talk. About time I gave you a chance to say something. God I was awful in the car, wasn't I?'

Dave was genuinely puzzled. 'Awful? I didn't—what d'you mean?'

'Well, going on and on. I never stopped talking. And all about myself. You should have told me to shut up.'

'It were very interesting.'

'That's sweet of you, Dave. But I'm sure you were bored out of your mind. It was nerves. I always gabble on when I'm nervous.'

'Nervous? You? You can't mean it.'

'Of course I was. Who wouldn't be? I might be pretty thick-skinned but even so. After all, look at it. I saw you at the Beeb. Hadn't seen you for—what?—donkey's years. Since we were little kids. Almost forced you to come to the concert. You were too nice to hurt my feelings and stay away. And there I was. Alone with just about the best-known, most popular man in Yorkshire—probably in England—and trying to entice him into my little web. Of course I was nervous.'

Still sceptical Dave said—'Well, that made two of us.'

'Oh come on! You must've been wondering what you'd let yourself in for. You probably still are.'

Dave sugared and stirred his coffee. Then he said, looking down at the tray. 'All right,' he said. 'I'll tell you what I've been wondering. I've been wondering why you asked me to go to your show. Okay. You asked us both. Me and Aileen. I s'pose you might. I mean just kind-hearted, maybe wanting to show somebody you're a pretty good singer. But then—when I never brought Aileen. Well, no. I don't really understand. I

77

don't really understand why you asked me to come here. Not really.' He risked a glance at her face and saw she was smiling very gently, almost compassionately.

She said, 'Very well. I'll tell you. Or I'll tell you as far as I'm able to. Do you understand that? I mean there're things we do that we don't really know the reason for ourselves. Things we do on impulse. It's afterwards you ask yourself why. As soon as I saw you on Wednesday I knew I wanted to know you better. And it's funny, I remembered you straight away. Mrs Ruddock's son. You were a funny little lad then, Dave. Very, very serious. I remember the way you used to stare at me. You were very fair. You still are, I know. But when you were small your hair was nearly white. Very short, cut in a fringe, absolutely straight fringe. And you just used to stare at me. You wouldn't speak or smile, just stare with those serious, big blue eyes. I used to pretend not to notice. I'd ignore you. Pretend you weren't there, stuck-up little bitch that I was. But all the time I was wondering what you thought of me. Did you like me? Did you hate me? What were you thinking . . . ? What *were* you thinking, Dave?'

He took a sip of coffee and replaced the cup and saucer on the tray. He said, 'I don't know. I don't know as you could call it thinking anything. I just used to think you was the prettiest girl I'd ever seen. No. Pretty's not the word. More than that. I thought you was like magic, something out of fairy stories. Sounds daft, doesn't it?'

She shook her head slowly, her smile quizzical and faintly sad. 'And what about now? What do you think now? Did you recognize me on Wednesday? At the studio?'

'Yes.'

'And?'

Dave looked into her eyes and, for a fraction of a second, he was aware of a sense of physical vertigo as if he had awakened from sleep to find himself on the very edge of a precipice. He knew that he had arrived at a moment of decision where whatever choice he made would be irrevocable.

He said, and his voice was scarcely louder than a hoarse whisper, 'The same.'

Her smile had now gone. She, too, looked almost afraid.

'You mean . . . ?'

'I mean the same. I felt the same. Just like I did when I was a lad.'

'You . . . Dave . . . ' She pushed the table away with one foot, stood up and held out both hands to him. He took them in his and, feeling her slight tug, he too rose from his chair and they stood, facing each other, hands still lightly clasped, looking into each other's eyes.

He said, 'I'd best be going.'

'Yes.'

But neither of them made the least move to separate.

Then she raised her face and her lips parted; her eyelids flickered, then partly hooded the slanting green eyes and his own lips were drawn down to hers until they met, quite lightly at first but, as the pressure increased, both of their mouths opened wider and their hands released themselves and started to touch and stroke each other's heads, faces, bodies. He felt the stabbing and flickering of her tongue against his own and he pulled her closer, harder against himself, feeling the taut plumpness of her buttocks, squeezing with both hands, kneading, pressing her more tightly to him until he was aware of her thighs parting as he pushed his knee between them so that she was partially straddling his left thigh, moving rhythmically under his coaxing hands and releasing little cries and whimpers close to and into his mouth.

Suddenly she pulled her face away from his and held his head between her hands, staring up at him, now wide-eyed. Slowly her eyes began to close and her mouth was loose and swollen with the force of his kissing. Her body was shaken by a shudder and she moaned something unintelligible. The shudder passed and she whispered, 'Come on Dave. Come to bed,' and she took one of his hands in hers and led him through the kitchen to the hall, then into her bedroom. She switched on the bedside lamp and began, without looking at Dave, to take off her clothes, first the sweater, then the brassière, sandals, trousers, tights and lastly the tiny briefs. Then she stood by the side of the bed, facing him, her hands at her sides, looking submissive, beseeching, almost afraid.

She waited while he removed his clothes, leaving each

garment where it fell on the floor, and when he, too was naked she again held out both hands to him and, as he came towards her, she said, 'My God, you're beautiful.'

When they embraced once more he knew he could wait no longer to be inside her. He held her, cupping one hand under each buttock and lifted her clear of the floor, feeling her arms entwined about his neck and her legs about his waist. And so he drove his swollen penis deep into her, and after a very few thrusts which brought him perilously close to orgasm, he fell with her upon the bed where, with contrapuntal cries of need, amazement and exultation, sweating and bucking and rearing they rode towards the dark.

At ten minutes to two she woke him by switching on the bedside light and leaning over him to kiss and nibble his ear.

She said, 'Nearly two. You'd better be going.'

He groaned, screwed up his face and knuckled both eyes as he sat up. 'What's up . . . Two? What?' Then he saw the time on his watch. 'Jesus! You're right.'

He moved to slip out of bed but she held him by one arm. 'Kiss,' she said.

He turned to her and found that her lips and mouth were still fresh and sweet. Punctuating each word with a quick kiss Judy said, 'You . . . are . . . incredible!'

'Not me,' he said swinging his feet to the floor and moving over to his pile of clothes. 'You're the incredible one, love.' He began quickly to dress.

Judy got out of bed, went to her wardrobe and slipped on a dressing-gown.

He said, as he put on his jacket and stuffed his tie into one of his pockets. 'I've got to use your toilet. Okay?'

'Through the door, first left.'

After he had eased his bladder he washed his hands and splashed water over his face. Carelessly he patted and stroked his hair into comparative tidiness and was about to leave the bathroom when he noticed, on the shelf above the washbasin, among various toilet requisites, which were undoubtedly feminine or could be used by either sex, a razor and a tin of shaving foam. He was surprised by the sharpness of the pain that struck at him, leaving behind a faint nausea. Of course she slept with other people. Maybe all those rumours that Aileen had gone on about were true. What the hell difference did it make anyway? She was a beautiful woman and a marvellous fuck. He was lucky to be with her. Even if he never saw her again he had a lot to thank her for. She wasn't his wife. He'd no claim on her. They'd had a great time together. She'd enjoyed it too. She'd said so, said he was incredible. Three times in a couple of hours or so. Incredible. But something of the pain and a shadow of the sickness still lingered. One thing he assured himself, he would not ask who owned the razor. That would be to show himself up as gormless. Judy had been around. She was a classy girl and he mustn't make a fool of himself.

'Whose is the razor?' he said when he returned to the bedroom.

'Razor? Oh that! It's mine. Why?

'Yours? You mean you shave?'

Judy laughed. 'Yes. Under here.' She indicated one armpit. 'I couldn't wear dresses like that one tonight if I didn't. Why, what did you think? I kept a razor handy for gentlemen friends?'

He hoped that his blush would not be taken as a confession that this was exactly what he had been thinking.

'I just wondered,' he muttered. 'None of my business really.'

She came close and rested one hand on his upper arm. 'Dave. Tonight—this morning—it's been lovely. And I hope you feel the same. But listen. We mustn't, either of us, start getting possessive or asking too much. D'you understand? You've got a wife whether you like it or not. Whether I like it or not. I've got my own life, too. If you want to see me again—and I hope you do, because I certainly want to see you—you'll have to accept things as they are. You, a married man. Me, a—I don't know—what? A career girl? Anyway, we'll have to be careful.'

'Sorry,' he said. 'I didn't mean to be nosy. It was just—oh. I don't know. I'm sorry.'

'Forget it. By the way where does your wife think you are now? Tonight? Last night, I mean.'

'I told her I was going to Manchester. Watch some boxing. She won't be worried.'

'Still, it's after two. You'd better go. Ring me tomorrow. I'm in the book.'

'Yes.'

They looked into each other's faces, not quite suspiciously, but with the uncertainty of the half-committed, both asking with their eyes what neither would, or perhaps could, put into words. Then they kissed, quite briefly, almost asexually, and she walked with him into the hall and let him out of the back door.

She said, 'Can you see all right?'

'Yes.'

He touched her face lightly with the tips of his fingers as if making sure that she was a thing of substance. Then he said, 'Goodnight. I'll give you a ring,' and he made his way to the front of the house, past her Mini which stood in the drive, and out into the road where he climbed into his car, started the engine after a couple of abortive attempts, and drove home.

Aileen was asleep when he cautiously entered the bedroom but she awoke as he was undressing and mumbled, 'What's time? Where been?...You're late.' But when he did not answer she mumbled something incomprehensible and instantly went back to sleep.

In bed by her side he thought of Judy with an excitement that kept him awake for a while, but gradually he became drowsy and he turned, as was his habit, towards Aileen, who lay with her back towards him, and placed his right arm across her body in a loose embrace. Then, to his half amused, half horrified incredulity he felt desire stiffening against her insenate buttocks and turned away on to his other side.

'Incredible,' he said to himself. 'I'm a sex maniac. I'm a monster.'

But when he fell asleep, a few moments later, the smile on his face was contented and without trace of self-censure.

CHAPTER SIX

JIMMY RUDDOCK WAS pleased with the way the little 'do' was going. There was more than enough booze, thanks to Dave who had turned up in the morning with half-a-dozen of those big 'Party' cans of bitter as well as bottles of sherry, gin and vodka so, with what he and Dot had already got in, they had enough drink to open a pub. Martin looked great in his uniform. He'd filled out quite a bit, got the build of a natural light-heavyweight, and now he'd grown that moustache he seemed a lot older. He wasn't twenty-one till next May but you'd take him for five or six years more than that. Funny how your kids turned out. There was Jean—she'd been a right little mischief—and there she was, a proper lady with her own nipper now, driving a car, living up in West Park. Not that she was a snob. She still came round for tea with Dot nearly every other week and brought little Lucy with her. And Dave. Well, it was like a dream. Champion of the bloody world! A national title, a Lonsdale Belt. These were more than you could really ask for, but they weren't enough for Dave. Nothing less than the first prize, the jackpot, the place at the top, nothing but that was good enough for him. The undisputed world title.

'How's it going then, lad?' Micky Rice came into the kitchen holding an empty glass. 'They've run out of ale in there. Plenty of t'other stuff but the beer's finished. Dave says you've got some in here.'

'Aye. Lots of it. Help yourself. Here y'are. This can's got plenty left in it. Or open one of them over there if you like.' Jimmy filled his friend's glass and topped up his own. 'Freda enjoying herself?'

'Aye. Her and Dot's getting all weepy-like over your Jean's little 'un. They've made up a bit of a bed on sofa in front room and Lucy's sleeping like a kitten. They're enjoying themselves all right.' Micky took a long drink. Then he said, 'Who's the bit of stuff with Martin then? Tracey they call her. Is she what they call punk or something?'

'I couldn't tell you. He only got home tea-time yesterday so he must've picked her up somewhere last night. Here y'are. Let's have a fill-up and we'll go and see what everybody's up to. You take glasses and I'll bring in a new can.'

In the front room Tracey, a small girl with short spikey green hair and clownish make-up, dressed in skin-tight trousers of black leather, pantomime silver boots and a shapeless short smock decorated with many badges, was talking—more relentlessly than animatedly—to Dave who was holding a glass of Coca-cola and looking down at her with a tentative and rather puzzled smile. Martin Ruddock, wearing Army uniform with the insignia of the Parachute Regiment, was half-listening to Jeff Holroyd, husband of his sister, Jean, and father of the sleeping Lucy while his mother and Freda Rice were sitting on the sofa, at the other end of which the child was curled. The two older women were holding glasses of gin and orange and nodding solemnly over what one or the other had recently pronounced.

Tracey was saying to Dave, '... see what I mean? Women don't have the same chances like fellers do. I mean look at you. You get paid a lot of money for it. We couldn't do that could we? And like music and that. I know there's some women make it but it's mostly men, isn't it? And DJs. Simon Bates and them. And the groups like Police and Adam and Ants. It's all bloody men i'n't it? They talk about Women's Lib and all that but it's a con. It's always been the same. Always will be.'

Aileen and Jean came in from the living room but Dave's momentary hope of rescue was disappointed when they joined Martin and Jeff.

'Come on,' Jean said to her husband, 'it's nearly half-past eight. We'd better get Lucy back. You've had enough to drink anyway. It's been great seeing you, Martin.' She kissed her younger brother on the cheek and, as she began preparations for departure, he moved away to where Dave and Tracey were standing.

He said, 'Come on Tracey. Come and have a natter with my dad, he's very interested in Women's Lib and he's a big fan of Sting... Hang on Dave I want to talk to you in a minute.'

He took Tracey by the elbow and led her towards Micky Rice and his father who were sitting in the two armchairs drinking their beer. He said, 'Don't get up—as if you would—but here's Tracey to have a chat ... Give us your glass, love, and I'll fill it up. Vodka and lime i'n't it.'

He went to the sideboard and came back with her fresh drink. 'Dad'll tell you about the time he fought Ginger Sadd in the eliminator and got robbed. You sit there on the arm, or sit on Micky's knee if you like—No, don't get up, either of you. She's all right, aren't you love?'

Martin returned to Dave who had moved across to the sofa where Jean was now holding her still sleeping little girl, and making her final farewells. All of the women went to the front door to see Jean and Jeff get away, and Dave would have followed except that Martin held him by the arm and said, 'Come on our Dave. I want to have a talk with you. Come on upstairs.'

They went into the hall and up to the landing where Martin led the way into one of the three bedrooms. It was the one which they had shared until Jean had married and Dave had moved into her room leaving Martin in sole occupancy. On one wall was a huge coloured action picture of the first Ali-Frazier fight and a smaller photograph of Dave having his hand held aloft in victory after his British title win over Harry Redmond at Wembley. The small bookcase at the side of the bed was filled with paperbacks and on another wall a selection of photographs of naked girls had been displayed but these were not of the hirsute pubic kind to startle or disgust their mother but smoothly mamillary or gluteal, curvacious but sanitized, as if moulded from sweet smelling soap.

'Brings back memories, this room,' Martin said.

'Aye, it does that.'

'I remember Christmas times trying to keep awake so's

we'd see them bring us presents in.' Martin sat on the bed and lit a cigarette. 'Come and sit down.'

Dave did as he was asked. 'What was it you wanted to talk about?'

'Oh nothing special. Just get away from that lot for a bit. Old Jeff there was boring the backside off me. He's not a bad lad, means well and all that, but I can't think how she puts up with him, our Jean. Just wanted to get you on me own for a bit. Haven't seen you for—what?—nigh on five month i'n't it? Since the Vallejo fight in September. Haven't seen you since you won bloody World Title either, man! By, that was the night! We got it on news in morning. Just after reveille. Eleventh round knockout! You should've heard the lads. We shifted a few pints that night, I can tell you.'

Dave said, 'I couldn't believe it myself. Still can't.'

'And you'll do the same to Hayes. One thing you can be sure of. Everybody in Two Para's going to be right behind you, you'll beat the bastard all right.'

Dave felt uneasy, a superstitious fear of witnessing such a challenge to providence. He said, 'Hayes is a good fighter. Never been beaten. You can't be sure. Nobody's unbeatable. There's always somebody's got your measure. Maybe I've got his measure. Maybe he's got mine. We'll just have to wait and see.'

Martin inhaled cigarette smoke and blew it out. 'We'll see all right. You'll flatten bugger. But listen. What I really wanted, Dave, was for you and me to have a night out. Tomorrow. What about it? We'll have a trip round a few of the boozers and end up having a good feed somewhere. Just the two of us. What about it?'

'Martin, you know it's no good. You know I don't drink. What's the use of going on a pub-crawl with a teetotaller? We'd both be bloody fed up. And anyway. I've got something fixed up for tomorrow. You remember my mate, Tom Darwin? Me and Aileen's seeing him and his girlfriend for a Chinese meal.'

'Tom? 'Course I remember him. Brainy bugger, weren't he? He were all right though. He'd always have a bit of a laugh and a joke with you. But listen, Dave. Why don't I come as well? Me and old Tracey down there. That'd make a nice little party. Tom wouldn't mind, would he?'

Dave hesitated. 'I don't know. I mean perhaps I'd better—

'Course he wouldn't mind! I'd pay my whack. Don't worry about that. I'll pay the lot if you like.'

'It's not like that, Martin. It's . . . well, he's just expecting the two of us. And you've not met Peggy—that's his girl—and—well—he's probably fixed up, you know, reserved a table just for the four on us.'

'Don't be daft! All you've got to do is give him a buzz tonight. Tell him me and Tracey's coming. They'll change the booking quick enough. Specially if they know Dave Ruddock's in party. I tell you. They'd probably pay us to eat there.'

'I don't know . . .'

'Come on Dave. I don't often get chance to see you. You'll be going up to London soon, won't you? I'm your brother. Tom Darwin's all right but he doesn't come first, in front of family, does he? You fix it. Give Tom a ring. Yes?'

Dave nodded. 'All right. I'll try. You ring me at home. Tomorrow dinner time, about one. I'll let you know then if it's all right.'

' 'Course it'll be all right. We'll have a good night. I'll tell Tracey to dress a bit more sensible. She's all right. Stupid but all right. Come on then. Let's get back to merry throng. See if mam and old Freda Rice's pissed yet. We'll have a great night tomorrow, Dave. You see if we don't.'

Dot closed the front door and went back into the room which, a few moments before, had been noisy with leave-takings. She could hear Jimmy laughing as they walked down to the bus-stop. He had said he would see Micky and Freda on to the bus. That meant he wouldn't be back for at least another hour and a half. After closing time in fact. As soon as they'd caught their bus he'd be off to The Carpenter's Arms or the Institute, one or other. As for Martin, God alone knew when he'd be back. Not that she wanted either of them under her feet while she had to clear this bloody lot away. Aileen had offered to stay behind and help but you could tell she didn't want to be taken up on it.

Dot began to move about the room collecting glasses, and when she had taken these into the kitchen she returned with a waste-paper bin in which to empty the plates of half-eaten sandwiches and cakes and the ashtrays of cigarette-ends left by Martin and Tracey. There were sticky marks on the sideboard and someone—almost certainly Jimmy—had spilt beer on the carpet. She felt tired and rather dizzy. The gin she had drunk had not had the effect of lifting her spirits. On the contrary she felt depressed, a little sick, and her sense of balance had been slightly impaired so that in her journeys from the kitchen to the other rooms she occasionally felt herself sway and even stagger. To hell with it, she told herself, I'll just wash up these things and leave the rest till tomorrow.

As she worked at the sink she thought that Aileen hadn't looked right somehow, not so much poorly as miserable. Yet what had the girl got to be miserable about? She'd got a lovely house in one of the best parts of Leeds. She and Dave had been married less than two years, still on honeymoon really, no kids to look after, very little housework with all those gadgets, washing-machine, latest thing in carpet-sweepers, electric mixer, God knows what. Maybe that was the trouble. Not enough to do. Bored. And yet she shouldn't be, unless. She shouldn't be. Dave was a good lad. He'd be a good husband to her. He was like Jimmy in some ways. Gentle. Funny that. The pair of them professional fighters but no harm in either of them. Jimmy had always been soft. Anyone could take advantage. Dave was a bit different though. He was gentle all right, even when he was a toddler. Needed a lot of pushing before he stood up for himself. But he had an obstinate streak that was all his own. Jimmy hadn't got it. Once Dave set his mind to something you couldn't budge him. He was determined, a sticker. Jimmy was never like that. And what about Martin? Different from either of them, harder, more selfish. But a nice enough lad underneath. They'd been lucky, her and Jimmy, with their kids. No trouble really that wasn't easy enough to handle. Except of course you still worried about them, Martin jumping out of aeroplanes, likely to be sent to Northern Ireland among the bombs and snipers. Dave, a boxer, could be cut, injured, brain-damaged. No. That was terrible. That couldn't happen to him, not like that poor little starved-looking lad from South Wales they sent to America and he was. No. Dave was too strong. He wasn't like that poor boy who looked as if he needed a good feed, something round his ribs. Dave had always been a good eater, always been sturdy. A lovely lad, right from the very start.

But they were grown up now, on their own. They grew up, they went their ways, made lives for themselves that you knew nothing about. And you were left with nothing to look forward to except old age, your hair, going grey and dried up like wire-wool, your body slack and wrinkled and disgusting, nobody to give you a second look. Of course not and why should they? You weren't worth looking at. But you had been once and that was the sad part, the part that hurt the most. You'd been worth looking at once but you'd never really known it, you never really knew that it was all there for you to take—life, excitement, beauty, adventure—you didn't have the confidence. You thought things like that were for the others, the lucky ones. And you settled for Jimmy Ruddock.

Poor Jimmy, he wasn't to blame. It was wicked of her to feel bitter towards him. It wasn't his fault. He was a good man. A bit soft, not much sense, but kind. He'd always been kind. He was selfish in little ways, but then, who wasn't? He was like a rough old dog, grinning, anxious for everybody to be happy, everybody to like each other. Yes, he was like a dog and he didn't know what was happening any more than a mongrel would know. He didn't know that the brightness, the gleam, the glitter had gone. First it had been dulled and darkened and then it wasn't there any more. He didn't know that he was dying. If you told him that he was going to die he'd say yes, of course, he knew that. Everybody's got to go some time. If your number's on it and all that. But why worry? Worry doesn't get you anywhere. But he didn't know. He didn't really believe it. Like a dog. He didn't see it in the mirror or feel it in the dried and wrinkled skin, the aching muscle and bone. And if she tried to explain, it would be hopeless. He'd say age, that's right love, we're not getting any younger. And off he'd go to the pub, grinning, wagging his tail.

She had finished drying the glasses and she began to put them away, giving each one a final polish on the dry cloth before she placed it in its proper place in the cupboard. That's what she was there for: to clean, to cook, to make things comfortable so that everyone thought life was like that, clean, nice and comfortable. And it wasn't. That's what she now knew. And it looked as if young Aileen was. beginning to suspect the same thing. But Aileen was too young. She ought to be happy. She was healthy and if she took a bit more trouble with herself she'd look quite pretty. She ought to be making the most of it because it didn't last long, that little time when things sparkled and glowed and it seemed that the darkness would never come.

'I'll have a word with her,' Dot thought. 'See what's wrong I don't suppose I'll be able to help but you never know. I'll see what I can do. She's not the one I'd've picked for Dave—specially her being Roman Catholic—but she's there now. She's my daughter-in-law, like it or not.'

She hung up the cloth, went into the living-room and switched on the television. Then she sat before it, unrelaxed and unbeguiled by the antics of a short, fat comedian and his tall thin partner. When the ten o'clock news replaced the comics' show she continued to watch with the same expression of guarded neutrality, a slightly oblique, suspicious gaze, withholding repudiation or consent, waiting for her husband to return so that she could go to bed and, with luck, escape for a few hours from the anxieties and fears of wakefulness.

Dave and Aileen, causes of some part of Dot's unease, were at that time sitting in their lounge drinking coffee.

Dave said, 'What's up, love? Feeling tired?'

She did not look at him. 'I'm all right.'

He stood up, put his cup and saucer down on the trolley and, perching on the arm of her chair, lightly placed an arm about her shoulders.

'If you're all right,' he said, 'I'd hate to see you when you wasn't. Come on, love. What's wrong?'

Still she kept her lowered head turned from him. 'Nothing wrong with *me*.'

He hesitated between abandoning his mollifying role and risking investigation of that significantly emphasized 'me'. Then he decided that evasion would merely delay confrontation and that it would be better to attempt to clear the air now.

'What's that mean?' he said. 'Nothing wrong with *you*. You trying to say there's something wrong with *me*?'

For a moment she did not answer. Then she raised and turned her head to look up at him and he was surprised, even a little alarmed, by the unhappiness and resentful anger in her eyes.

'Well, isn't there? You think I'm daft or blind or something? You're hardly ever in the house and when you are you're no more company than that sideboard. Last week you stayed out three times past midnight. All I'm here for is to cook your food and do washing and cleaning. It's not a wife you want, it's a servant. And you ask me what's wrong!'

Dave withdrew his arm, rose and returned to his own chair. It was difficult to face the pain and accusation of her gaze.

He said, 'It's not that bad, is it? There's lots of women would envy you, Aileen. You've got a lovely house. You don't want for nowt. I can't see you've got that much to complain about.'

Very slowly she shook her head three times, as if in wondering disbelief at either his obtuseness or duplicity.

'You really think anybody'd envy me? You really believe that? A husband that can't stand to be with me more 'n half an hour at a time except when he's asleep. One that goes out three or four times a week till after midnight. I'm just part of furniture to you, Dave. You don't want me, not really, and I often wonder if you ever did.'

He felt pity for her and guilt, aching somewhere inside his chest, thickening in his throat as he tried to combat them with false indignation, but all he could say was, 'It's not that bad.'

'Isn't it?'

'You make it sound worse that what it is. You say I'm

always going out. What about tonight? What about tomorrow? We're going out with Tom and Peggy, aren't we? You don't do so bad.'

Aileen smiled, faintly and sadly. 'Lucky me. Oh Dave, you know I'm not talking about things like that. You know what I'm talking about all right. I wouldn't care if I never went out. You know that. If I had a husband that stayed at home and *wanted* to, a husband that liked being with me, instead of disappearing as soon as he's had his tea and not coming back till next morning.'

Dave knew that he had been led on to treacherous ground. He said, 'I can't help it if I've got to go to club shows and that. I'm World Champion. It's natural. I get asked to do things. Present the prizes at amateur shows. Go to the ex-Boxer's nights, be introduced from ring. All that. It's part of job. Phil says I've got to do it. Be a popular Champion he says. It pays off at the box-office.'

'And what was you doing on Wednesday night? I've forgotten. Was it ex-boxers or amateurs or what?'

'Wednesday?' Dave hesitated. 'I told you didn't I? I had to go to Sheffield. A dinner show. They wanted me to take a bow, that's all.'

'And who sprayed you with perfume?'

'What?'

'Where did the perfume come from? Smelled like expensive stuff. You reeked of it Dave. I had to wash sheets and pillowcases yesterday to get rid of it. How did you get like that at a boxing game?'

He felt the sudden upsurge of confusion and shame burning on his face, blurring for a moment his vision. He knew that his guilt must be plain, yet he could not admit to it.

He said, 'I don't know. Don't know what you're on about?' Then becoming bolder. 'Where d'you think I was? A knocking-shop or something?'

She shook her head, and the small, sad smile returned. 'No. I don't think you'd have to pay for it. There's plenty'd do it for nothing, only too willing. Dave Ruddock, the World Champion, the great hero. Like that one at your mam and dad's this evening, Tracey or whatever they call her. She was making eyes and waggling her backside at you. Not that you objected.'

Dave was genuinely affronted by the suggestion that he had been anything other than tolerantly polite to Tracey but he also recognised that an exaggeration of this indignation might serve to distract Aileen's attention from the matter of Wednesday night and the origin of the perfume she had detected on him. He said, 'If she was—you know—doing what you said, I never noticed. She were yapping away like an old washerwoman. And if you think I were interested, fancied her like, you must be going soft in head. She was horrible. I don't know what Martin see in slags like that. So if you believe I were after that one it just shows you'd believe anything.' Then, before she could protest at this imputation of gullibility he hurried on: 'And it looks as if we're going to be stuck with her tomorrow.'

This proved an effective diversion. Aileen stared. 'What do you mean? How we going to be stuck with her? We're going out with Tom and Peggy.'

'Aye. And she's coming too—our Martin asked if he could come and then he said he'd bring Tracey. Keep the numbers even or something.'

'And you said yes?'

'Well, why not? Tom and Peggy won't mind. Martin asked me. I couldn't say no, could I? And she won't make any difference. I'll tell Martin to keep her quiet. He won't stand no nonsense won't Martin.'

'And what's Tom and Peggy going to say? They just asked us didn't they? Not the rest of your family and friends.'

'Ah, come off it love, I'll give Tom a ring in morning. He won't mind. I wasn't going to let him pay anyway. Martin and his bird coming with us gives me a good excuse. I'll tell him it's my treat for Martin being on leave. Don't worry. That Tracey won't spoil it. We'll have a good time. You wait and see.'

Dave left his seat again and resumed his perching on the arm of her chair. This time he took hold of her left hand in his right and, bending over, he kissed the top of her head.

'Just don't worry about anything, love. Things'll work out. Try and remember. I've got this big one coming up, this fight with Hayes. I know you don't understand it but take my word for it. It's going to be a world-shaker, one of the greatest fights ever. And I've got to win it. I've got to. It's a responsibility see? It doesn't give much time for anything else. I can't think about nothing except Hayes. I don't expect you to understand. But you'll just have to take it. After, when the fight's over, we'll see about—well, everything. We'll work things out. All right?'

She looked up at him and her eyes were both melancholy and mistrustful. 'I don't have a lot of choice, do I?'

He gave her hand a little shake. 'Come on, cheer up. Tell you what. You can get yourself a new dress or shoes or something tomorrow. We'll have a nice evening and things'll look better.'

But, although her lips formed the shape of a smile, her eyes remained miserable and he felt relief when she said that she was tired and would just tidy away the coffee things and go to bed.

When she had gone upstairs he stayed in the lounge and opened a copy of the current *Boxing News* but he could not fix his attention on the print. He was uneasily aware of Aileen's unhappiness like a sickness in the house; he could sense it, restlessly breathing upstairs, and he knew that he was its progenitor. Yet he was unable to prevent himself thinking of Judy, of her lightness, brilliance and softness, the way she had looked on Wednesday night. At first so exquiste, so sparklingly cool and graceful, then later, when they were both naked, her calm loveliness had changed to a passionate, clamorous hunger, when she was both imperious yet supplicatory, vulnerable yet voracious, outrageously candid in her greed. Desire swelled and hardened. He groaned, just audibly. This was agony, but it was a pain he would not be without, a pain whose absence would be the worst of conditions, a precious affliction.

The magazine on his lap was open at a page of which half the space was occupied by an action photograph of two lightweights swapping body-punches in a bout of in-fighting. It was the kind of picture that would normally send a little frisson of excitement through him, the white blaze of light from the arc-lamps, the geometrical taut ropes, the straining muscle and sinew of the two fighters, their faces masks of aggressive concentration, but in contrast with the warm, seductive images in his head it now seemed, static, frozen and ugly.

He threw the magazine on to the carpet, stood up and went into the kitchen. All was clean and orderly, the table laid for breakfast. Aileen was a good girl. Not glamorous maybe but she was all right. She kept things nice and tidy. She wasn't the kind to get in the way of his training. She wouldn't make him lose concentration. If he had any sense he'd stick with her and get down to work and forget the other one who sent him mad and dizzy with longing and sucked the strength out of him like a vampire. But instantly the images of Judy, which had become mistily imprecise, were sharply refocussed; he felt a melting warmth at his heart and he knew that he was enslaved.

So what was to be done? One thing was clear. He couldn't let his training slide; he had to get back that piston-drive of complete resolution. And no reason why not. The old-timers like his dad and Micky Rice still believed the stories their dads had been brought up on: sex was bad for you, it weakened you. You couldn't fuck and fight. When you were in training you had to live like a priest. The trainers now knew better. Like Phil Richardson had said: better to fuck than fret, but get it over quick and back to work.

But Dave was still very uneasy. He could not think of Judy in that way. She possessed a magic that was more powerful than anything he had encountered since starting to box, so potent that it could now make him almost completely forget boxing. A couple of weeks ago that would not have seemed possible. Somehow he had to sort things out, get everything into order so that he could get on with his work in the old way. Aileen, Judy, the Title defence, he had to do what was right for everybody, but what ever happened he mustn't lose his edge. He was Middleweight Champion of the World, unbeaten and unbeatable. That was the most important thing and anything that threatened it had to be swept out of the way. Anything. Anyone.

He went to the sink and poured himself a glass of water and drank half of it.

'Anyone' chimed faintly in his head like an echo and, as he put the glass on the draining board and switched off the kitchen lights, he nodded assent and went back to the lounge, picked up *Boxing News* and sat down to read. He would give Aileen another twenty minutes or so. She ought to be asleep by then. And tomorrow, all being well, she would be feeling better.

CHAPTER SEVEN

THE MEAL AT the Chinese restaurant began amiably. Tracey was dressed just as garishly as she had been on the previous evening at Martin's homecoming celebration but she was less voluble and evidently impressed by Peggy's being a regular broadcaster on local radio. Martin, who wore civilian clothes, a blue blazer, polo-neck sweater and grey hopsack trousers, had obviously enjoyed quite a few drinks before joining the party at the restaurant but he seemed coherent, though inclined to raise his voice rather more than was necessary for normal conversation. Aileen was wearing a dark suit and a white blouse with a lace collar as if to emphasise by this austerity her rejection of Dave's offer to buy her a new dress, but her hair, which she had washed that morning, gleamed softly in the subdued lamplight and she seemed to be enjoying her Peking Crunched Duck and mushroom sauce.

Although it was a Saturday night the restaurant was not crowded for they had come early, and the other occupied tables were taken by couples who evinced no interest in the party of six, even when Martin's voice, either in laughter or expostulation, became obtrusively loud. A round table had been provided at which Tom sat between Tracey and Aileen on whose left were Martin, Peggy and Dave. Tom and Martin were drinking claret. Peggy had chosen a Sauternes for her and Tracey while Aileen and Dave both refused wine, and it was this refusal, uncommented on at first, which later occasioned the slight change of atmosphere from conviviality to something which hinted at possible conflict.

Peggy and Tracey had drunk only a glass each when Martin was calling for another bottle of claret and Tom showed no reluctance in helping to consume the contents of this one with at least equal speed; so it was with the serving of a third bottle that the first faint danger signals might have been detected. Martin filled Tom's and his own glass and then, brandishing the bottle, he said, 'Come on our Dave. A drop of this stuff won't hurt you.'

Dave smiled and shook his head. 'You know I never drink. You're wasting your time.'

'Come on,' Martin said again and gave the bottle of claret a flourish. His elbow struck the top of the Sauternes bottle, which still contained three inches of wine, sending it clattering among the dishes, soaking a part of the tablecloth from which wine began to drip on to Peggy's lap.

'Fuck!' said Martin very loudly.

A waiter quickly appeared with a napkin and began to dab and wipe at the tablecloth.

'Bring us another bottle of that stuff,' Martin said to him.

Peggy at once intervened. 'No. We don't want any more, do we Tracey? We've still got some in our glasses. We don't want any more.'

Martin looked at her belligerently for a moment. Then he shrugged. 'Please yourself.' He drank some claret, half emptying his glass. Then nodded to his right in the direction of where Tom sat: 'Your boyfriend's not so slow at supping the old free booze, is he?'

Dave was still smiling but a slight frown had appeared on his forehead. He said, 'Take it easy, Martin. Everything's all right. No harm done.' He noticed that Aileen, on Martin's immediate right, had her mouth set in what he had come to think of as her Sunday School teacher's look. He pointed towards the hot-plate in the centre of the table: 'There's lots left. Spare ribs, rice, sweet-and-sour prawn. Dig in everybody.'

Tracey and Peggy helped themselves to more food, Aileen said that she had eaten enough and would have some coffee when everybody was ready for it while Tom and Martin drank more wine. Briefly it seemed that harmony had been restored;

then Martin lit a cigarette and Peggy, who had probably not forgiven the crude jibe at Tom, elaborately waved away real or imaginary smoke and put down her fork with an abruptness which spoke of exasperated finality. Martin dragged more deeply on his cigarette and exhaled more smoke. Then he reopened the packet and extended it towards her. 'Have a fag, love,' he said.

'I don't smoke,' she answered, 'and I don't eat either, not when some oaf's blowing that filthy stuff all over the place.'

Aileen, on his other side, said, 'You should've asked, Martin. It's manners.'

He looked from Peggy to Aileen, then back again. He was grinning and the cigarette was held in his mouth. He drew on it again, removed it and blew out more smoke.

'I should've asked, should I? And s'posing I'd asked, Peggy. S'posing I'd said, "Do you object to me having a fag?" What'd happen then? I'll tell you. Either you'd've said, "Yes I do" or you'd say, "Carry on. It's a free country." But whichever you said I'd light up anyway. So there's no point in asking, is there?' He turned again to Aileen. 'Manners is for them that's scared to do what they want, love. I don't give a monkey's what other people think. You've got to be hard to get by in this world. That right, Dave?' Martin's face was red and his slightly bloodshot eyes looked as if they might not be perfectly focused.

Dave shrugged, still smiling faintly but the frown was deeper and his eyes were both wary and puzzled.

Tom said, 'Perhaps we should all have some coffee.'

There were sounds of assent from all except Martin who exclaimed, 'What's up, Tom? You scared of the women? Come on lad, there's some vino left. Let's have your glass.'

Tom, who was himself quite flushed, did not need further persuasion. 'Okay,' he said. 'We'll finish the bottle. But order the coffee, Dave.'

Martin smoked and drank in a moody silence until the coffee was served. Then he said to Tom, 'You still red then?'

On his left Peggy gave a little snort of unamused laughter. 'You both are by the looks of you.'

Tom had not heard, or had not understood the question. He

said, 'What's that? What did you say, Martin?'

'I said are you still red? Commie? Bolshie? Call it what you like. You know what I mean.'

'I wonder what gave you that idea,' Tom said quite amiably.

Martin was frowning and there was a thrust of aggression about the lips and jaw. 'You always was. Say what you like but you was always a Lefty.'

Peggy remarked to no one in particular, 'Expect Martin thinks anyone who doesn't worship Tebbit and Thatcher's got to be a wild revolutionary.'

'I'm not a Tory,' Tom said, 'but that doesn't mean you've got to be a Communist. Not that I'd be ashamed to say so if I was. You can be a good man and a Communist. Misguided, maybe, but morally straight. But anybody who supports the Conservatives—well, Thatcher's kind of Conservatism—'s got to be either stupid or vicious.'

'I'm a Conservative,' Martin said, staring hard at Tom, jaw and brow resembling even more the warrior's visor.

Tracey squeaked, 'Give us a fag, Martin,' but he took no notice of her.

Peggy picked up the packet of cigarettes which were on the table in front of Martin and passed them to Tracey.

Aileen said, 'It's about time we were going home, Dave.'

Tom was smiling benignly as if unconscious of the tension in the air. He said, 'I suppose you're bound to be if you're in the Army.'

Peggy said, 'That's enough, Tom.'

'Bound to be what?' Martin demanded.

'Conservative, of course. At least I'd have thought so. I know the Army's the tool of whatever government's in power. That's the theory but in practice it's unchangeably Conservative. It's got to be. It's a kind of model of the class system, isn't it?'

'You said Conservatives've got to be stupid or—what was it?'

'Vicious,' Tom said cheerfully. 'In other words you don't understand how evil the system is, or you do understand but don't care because you're gaining from it personally. At the expense of others. Look at unemployment since—'

'So you're calling me vicious, are you?'

Dave said, 'Shut up Martin! We've had enough of this. You're spoiling the evening.'

'What about him! He just called me vicious. What about that smart-arsed little bastard! He's been creeping round you ever since I can remember. You know why? 'Cause you're somebody and he's nobody. You're the World Champion. He wants to get in on the act. I'm your brother. Who the fuck's he? Look at him! He's a poofter, that's what he is. A Commie poofter.'

'Wrong,' observed Peggy. 'Wrong on both counts.'

Tom said, 'I'm sorry Martin. I apologise. I didn't mean to get at you. We've both had a drop too much. I have anyway. I was just arguing for arguing's sake. Okay?'

Martin still glowering, muttered indistinctly what might or might not have been something conciliatory. Dave called for the bill and shortly afterwards the party left the restaurant. Out in the brightly lit street the cold air seemed to exacerbate Martin's drunkenness and Dave had to take him by one arm to prevent him from staggering about the pavement.

Tom said, 'Peggy and I'll get a bus up there. Sorry I upset Martin. Hope it didn't spoil things for everybody.'

'My fault. I shouldn't have brought him.' Dave was propping up his brother who, with sunken head, now seemed oblivious of anything that was taking place.

'I'll fix up with you about the bill some other time. I wanted to take you and Aileen out for a change. Now you've been landed with the lot as usual.'

'Don't be daft Tom. Makes no odds to me. We'll get this fella back home and sober him up. We're parked over in Harrison Street.'

They exchanged final goodnights and Dave guided his brother across the road, followed by Aileen and Tracey. The two girls sat in the back of the car and Martin was slumped in the front passenger seat. He was not completely unconscious for he occasionally muttered a few words of which most of the comprehensible ones were oaths.

Dave said, 'Where d'you live, Tracey? Better get you home I s'pose. Not been much of a night out for you, has it?'

'It was okay. I live off Chapeltown Road. Mexborough Avenue.'

'That's fine. It's on our way.' They moved off. Dave spoke over his shoulder to Aileen: 'When we've dropped Tracey off we'll take our Martin home and see if he sobers up. If he feels up to it I'll take him back to mam and dad's later on. Or he can kip down at our place.'

Aileen said nothing and all four then remained silent except for Martin's sporadic and profane mutterings.

Dave experienced a good deal of difficulty in extracting his brother from the car and he was forced to half-carry him into the house where Martin slumped into an armchair and relapsed into a deep sleep.

'He must've supped a lot more than we thought,' Dave said. 'He was likely at it all afternoon. There's a club he knows that stays open. I've never seen him this bad. He can take a lot of booze as a rule, can Martin.'

Aileen looked at the crumpled figure of her brother-in-law with an expression of distaste which Dave found irritating. 'What are we going to do with him?' she asked.

Dave considered. 'Can't take him home like that. Doubt if I could shift him anyway. Best thing is let him sleep it off in chair and when he wakes up he can go to bed in one o' spare rooms.'

'What about your mam? Isn't she expecting him home?'

'Aye. I'd best go and tell her he's staying with us.'

'You're not going out again!'

'I'll have to. They're not on phone and I can't have 'em worrying all night what's happened t'lad.'

'He might be well enough to go back when he wakes up.'

'Aye. And he might not. No, I'd better go and see her. I'll just say he's made up his mind to stay with us tonight.'

'What if he wakes up when you've gone?'

Dave looked puzzled. 'What d'you mean?'

'What d'you expect me to do with him? You know what he's like. He's horrible. He might do anything.'

The mild irritation thickened to real anger. 'The worst thing he's likely to do is piss himself. There's nothing you can

102

do to stop that so you might as well go to bed or watch telly or do what you like. It's only ten past ten. I'll be back by half past or near enough. All right?'

He put on his coat and went out to where the car was still parked outside the garage. It was a cold, frosty night and stars glittered like small scattered crystals in the high vault of the sky. As he drove down towards Harehills he could see the lights of the city, the high-rise blocks, the illuminated squares of countless windows stamped symmetrically on the darkness, the glow from street lighting, the electric jewellery, vulgar and brilliant and exciting. Leeds was a good town, he thought, as he turned off the Roundhay Road into the street in which his parents lived.

When he knocked on the door there was a pause before it opened fractionally and he heard his mother's voice: 'Who is it? Who's there?'

'It's me. Dave. It's all right, nothing to worry about.'

The door was opened wide and she said, 'Come in. You'll catch your death. Where's others? What's happened?'

'Nothing.' He followed her into the living room. 'It's just that Martin's staying up at our house tonight. I thought I'd tell you case you waited up for him.'

'Is he all right?'

'Aye, he's fine. He had a few drinks, maybe a couple too many. But he's all right. Just sleepy. He'll be round in morning.'

'What happened to that girl? That Tracey? She were with him, weren't she?'

'Earlier on, yes. But we took her home. Dropped her off on way back to our place.'

'Sit down love. Take your coat off. I'll make you some tea. Or would you sooner have something else? Your dad'll be back soon. He just went out to Carpenter's for an hour.'

'No. I can't stay, mam. I told Aileen I'd be back by half past. I only came to let you know about our Martin.'

'Did you enjoy your meal? And how was Tom? Haven't seen him for a long time.'

'Fine. The meal was okay and Tom's all right. I'll bring him round to see you. He always asks after you.'

'Aye, he's a nice lad is Tom. Is he still looking after old folk?'

'Yes. But I must go mam. Tell dad I'll see him if he looks in at Harold's gym on Monday. I'll be doing a workout in evening. And we'll be round here—me and Aileen—for Sunday Dinner next week or week after. We'll fix it definite tomorrow when I bring Martin back. Be seeing you, mam.'

She followed him to the door and, despite his exhortations to go inside out of the cold, she stood on the step, silhouetted against the light in the hall, a figure of pathos and reproach, small and vulnerable, yet exasperatingly obstinate, watching as he climbed into the car and started its engine. He touched the hooter in farewell as he drove away, back towards home, and he caught a glimpse of her waving on the pavement in the light that spilled from the open door.

It was a few minutes after half past ten. He drove as far as Oakwood Parade and stopped the car. He got out and went into a telephone box and dialled. The double rasping of the bell at the other end of the line sounded as he placed the coin over its slot in readiness to press it into the box once contact was established. He was aware of excitement moving in his gut, drying saliva, and the sound of his own nervous cough was loud in the kiosk. Then he heard the faint click as the ringing stopped, the stuttering bleeps and then her voice, low and a little breathless, cautiously interrogative, said. 'Hello . . . ?'

He said, 'It's me, Dave.'

Judy's pleasure was unmistakeable. 'How lovely! I didn't expect you to ring. I wondered who it could be. I thought you said you were on the town tonight.'

'I was. We got back early. My brother, Martin, had a bit too much to drink. He weren't all that bad but we had to get him home.'

'Where are you now?'

'Oakwood. A phone box.'

'Are you coming round?'

'I can't love. I left Aileen with Martin. He's passed out. I've got to get back. I just thought I'd phone. Wanted to hear your voice.'

'I wish you could come round. Just for a little while?'

'So do I!' He felt his need for her rise, hard and unequivocal, sweetly painful. 'Don't I just! But I ought to've been back ten minutes ago.'

She said, 'All right. I'll see you on Tuesday then?'

'Aye. Have a good concert on Monday—Halifax, i'n't it?—An' I'll see you about six on Tuesday.'

'Will you be able to stay?'

'Not all night, worse luck. I'm supposed to be in Liverpool for a show at the stadium. Genuine. I got invited to a VIP dinner and all that. I rang them today and said I couldn't make it. But Aileen thinks I'm going. Trouble is, though, she knows I never stay the night anywhere if I can get back. Still, we'll have plenty of time. I mean there won't be no hurry about getting away.'

'All right. I mustn't be greedy. See you on Tuesday then.'

'Yes.'

'It seems a long way off.'

'Aye it does to me.'

'Goodnight then, love. Sweet dreams. Till Tuesday.'

He said goodnight, replaced the instrument and went back to his car. He did not at once switch on the engine but sat remembering the soft, warm texture of her voice, thinking of her face, the emeraldine eyes, the pale golden hair, the fresh welcoming lusciousness of her mouth. But the pleasure generated by these images was tainted by feelings of guilt that he could not dismiss. It was bad enough having to tell lies to Aileen and to watch her unhappy, suspicious expression when he said he was off to Sheffield or Manchester, or wherever it might be, as guest to some boxing promoter. It would be better perhaps to tell her the truth. But he was not sure what the truth was. People talked about being in love, but he wasn't too sure what they meant. He and Aileen hadn't, as far as he could remember, used that sort of talk, even when they were courting. It would have embarrassed both of them. He'd never been much of a one for the pictures or reading. Aileen read a lot of those women's books that seemed to be about nothing else but people falling in love, but she never talked about them. They were her means of getting away from the boredom and misery of daily life. He suspected that you wouldn't learn much, however many of them you read, because they weren't about real people like him and Aileen. And Judy.

Was he in love with Judy? If thinking about her nearly every minute of the day, breaking into a sweat and getting collywobbles in your guts when you heard her voice, getting a hard-on just by picturing her body, if these things were signs of being in love, then he was in love with her. And another thing. She had taken his mind off the fight game. That was powerful magic. For ten years and more he'd lived and breathed boxing, given it every bit of himself. It had always come first, ahead of anything or anybody. But could he truthfully say that now? Could he honestly say he would give Judy up for the sake of boxing? Could he say, 'If she's going to spoil my chances in the Hayes fight—bring in a risk that wasn't there before—if she's going to get in the way of my defence of the title I'll give her up. I'll never see her again.' Could he say that?

Dave shook his head slowly and said, aloud, 'I couldn't give her up. I love her.' And then, as if those three words had magically exorcised the demons of anxiety and doubt, he felt an unprecedented sense of release, a buoyancy and drench of joy that tingled, fizzed and sang through him so that he wanted to leap and shout for pure gratitude and delight. He thumped the steering-wheel with his right hand and said more loudly, almost a shout, 'I do, I love her! And I'll still beat that bugger Hayes!'

CHAPTER EIGHT

THEY LAY TOGETHER in the almost darkness and the ghosts of their voices which had, a few minutes earlier, been raised in wild supplication and exultation seemed to linger, gossamer presences in the now becalmed bedroom. The intermittent sounds of traffic could be faintly heard, distant, scattered, mingling with the sigh of the night wind. Dave felt her hand moving slowly, thoughtfully over his chest, gently pressing and stroking down to the abdomen, then prowling in the pubic hair before going on to touch lightly his languid penis and delicately cradle and caress his balls.

She whispered, 'You're beautiful.'

Strangely, the compliment no longer embarrassed him; instead he felt almost as if it was his own and not Judy's hand that was investigating and approving the velvety smoothness of skin over the relaxed muscle, the luxuriant soft bush of pubic hair, the well-filled purse of his scrotum.

She said, 'Are you sleepy?'

'No. Just sort of comfy.'

'Hungry?'

'No. Are you?'

'No.'

They lay side by side, each with a hand on the other's groin. Then she said, 'Are you worried?'

There was a hesitation of perhaps two seconds before he answered, 'Worried? Why should I be?'

'You are, aren't you?'

Another, slightly longer pause and then he said, 'Well, I s'pose I am a bit.'

'About Aileen?'

Again, a momentary hesitation: 'Yes. Mainly her.'

'Does she know anything?'

'No. Well, not really, not for sure. But I think she's got a good idea something's up. She reckoned she could smell scent on me after the last time.'

'What did you say?'

'I can't remember for sure. Told her not to be daft or something.'

Judy removed her hand to a more decorous place on his thigh as if the mention of Aileen had magically rendered them vulnerable to her suspicious vigilance.

Then she said, 'I don't want to be nosy, Dave, and you don't need to tell me anything if you don't want to, but I can't help wondering how you and Aileen got together. I mean you don't seem exactly crazy about each other and you've only been married—what?—a couple of years?'

Dave, too, removed his hand and took hold of Judy's.

'I don't really understand it myself,' he said.

'How did you meet in the first place?'

'I can remember that all right. It were in seventy-eight, September or October. I know 'cause it were about a week before I fought Johnny Bain in Manchester. Anglo-American Sporting Club. I knocked him out in three rounds. Aye . . .'

'Never mind about Johnny Bain. How did you meet Aileen?'

'Oh yes. Well, it were on a Saturday evening, or late in the afternoon. It must have been about six o'clock. It were light anyway. I've told you about my mate, Tom Darwin. Well, he was away, down in London an' I was on me own. Bit fed up, nothing much to do. So I went for a walk up Roundhay Park and I met a lad I was at school with. Brian May they call him. We was never mates or anything but he were all right. We got talking and we was walking up towards the Mansion and we caught up with these two girls. One was called Carole Sugden and the other were Aileen. Aileen Watkins as she was then. I didn't know her then but she reckoned she knew me. Said she remembered me at school. We was in different forms. She were nearly two years younger than me. I didn't remember her. Anyway Brian wanted us to take them for a drink at Mansion but it worked out Aileen and me didn't drink so we split up and I took her to pictures.'

'And that was it. Love at first sight.'

Dave grunted. 'I dunno. It just started like a habit. When I took her home that night I said something like see her again sometime and she said, "When?". So we fixed a date. And that's the way it went on.

'But she's all right, is Aileen. She's good-hearted and she's good at looking after the house an' all that. But . . . eeh, it's hard to say. She's not very—I was going to say womanly but that's not the word. She's not—well she's nothing like you.' What he meant was that Aileen possessed nothing of Judy's mysterious, provocative feminity, those deeply thrilling contradictions of feral, dark, pungent magnetism and fragrant, elusive, daintiness. 'She's not glamorous and she doesn't like—well, she's not very passionate.'

Judy chuckled softly. 'Poor Dave, poor love.' Then she said, 'But why marry her?'

'Aye, I sometimes ask myself the same question. But there didn't seem any choice somehow. When Phil Richardson took me over—that were in seventy-nine—I went to live in London, Ealing they call the place. It weren't too bad. I mean they fixed me up with a flat, and Rose—that's Phil's wife—give me most of my meals at their house. Phil's gym and the sparring and training and all that was good. I wouldn't never've got the title without Phil. I know that for sure. But I never liked London. Still don't. That's why I came back and got a house here, in Leeds. London's all right if you've always lived there I expect, but I thought it were bloody terrible.'

'Dave! You're supposed to be telling me why you married Aileen!'

'Oh . . . yes. Well. I was getting around to that. I was homesick. I know it sounds daft but I was. And in a funny way Aileen were like a bit of Leeds. She'd come up and see me at weekends. Phil wouldn't let me go home—not even for a weekend—not while I was training—so Aileen'd get on train after work on Friday and go back on Sunday. She'd stay at the flat and that's how we got into bed together. Not at first. It was about the third or fourth time she come to stay. At first she slept on couch in sitting room. Any road, once it'd happened she just took it for granted we was going to get married. There weren't no talking about whether or not. It were suddenly a fact. "When we're married," she'd say, "We'll do so and so." And that's what happened soon after her mam died—that were early in nineteen—what? seventy-nine. No, nineteen-eighty, the year we got married. About March, it were. And we got hitched three months after, in June.'

'Is her father still alive?'

'No, he died way back, ten years or more. Mrs Watkins—that's her mam—she were a right old bible-thumper. Catholic. Didn't fancy me at all for a son-in-law. A professional boxer! Oh dear no! Maybe if she'd stayed alive Aileen wouldn't've had nerve to take the jump. Specially being a Roman Catholic an' all that.'

'What about other girls? You must have had others.'

'No. Not what you'd call girlfriends. I never had time. It were a fluke, meeting Aileen. As a rule I was training. I never had time for discos or anything like that. Places where you meet girls. I had a couple of—you know—what you might call pick-ups before I went to London. You sometimes get them at boxing shows. Not often. Once in a while you get them hanging around after show's over. There were one in Nottingham the night I fought Stan Cooper. I were usually with Harold King—that's my Leeds manager—but he couldn't make it that night. Ill or something. So I went by train. I didn't have a car in them days. Anyway, this woman—girl—whatever you call her, was waiting outside the hall. I come out with my gear, hoping I hadn't missed last train to Leeds and she pops up from nowhere and says she's seen me fight a couple of times and thinks I'm the greatest and all that and what about a bite of supper. Tell you the truth I thought she meant in a café or something, but not her. In a couple of minutes we was in a taxi and off to her house.'

'Really? And she wasn't a—I mean you didn't have to—she didn't expect you to pay?'

'No. She weren't a prostitute. I couldn't make it out myself. She were quite good-looking too, not an old bag or anything.

110

And she talked sort of posh. Her house was all right as well. Good furniture and everything. She were a good bit older than me—about thirty-five, something like that—but she was really nice.'

'Oh, I'm beginning to feel jealous.'

Dave was at once alarmed and anxious to assure Judy that she had no grounds for jealousy. 'Christ, no!' he exclaimed. 'It was nothing. I mean she weren't—well, nobody ever has been, ever could be, anything like you. Like this. Honest. You're the—well, you're terrific. The most beautiful woman ever. Perhaps I shouldn't've said nothing about them others. They was nothing.'

She squeezed his hand. 'All right. I forgive you. But what about Aileen? Does she know anything about your boxing groupies, or whatever you'd call them?'

'Never! We don't talk about things like that. We don't talk about nothing much, really.'

'It sounds peaceful, if nothing else.'

'Aye.' They were silent for a few seconds then he said, 'I'll have to be going back to London fairly soon, in a couple of months. This warm-up fight's been fixed. May twenty-fifth at Wembley. Phil wants me there about five weeks before night. I've got to leave around the last week of April.'

Judy said, 'I don't quite understand about Phil and—who was it you said? Harold? Managers and the rest of it. How does it work?'

'Aye. Well, it's a bit complicated. You're quite right, I've got two managers. It's like this. When I turned pro—that's about five years ago now—it was a bloke called Harold King that managed me. He's got a stable—that's what they call a bunch of fighters—in Leeds. A nice gym in Roseville Road. I worked with him and his trainer, Micky Rice—he's an old mate of my dad's—and we did all right. Harold got me plenty of fights but the trouble was that they was all outside London. Liverpool, West Hartlepool, Belfast, Glasgow, Birmingham, all over the place except London. It was all good experience but you've to to get to Wembley or the Albert Hall if you're going to make the big time. And there's a couple o' blokes there that've got the whole game tied up. If you're not in with them you can't get a look in. Bernie Slater and Des Pickett, they're the two lads. Slater's the promoter and Pickett's what they call match-maker.

'Anyway, Harold got me a fight, an eight-rounder, at York Hall, Bethnal Green, and I struck lucky. It were only a small local show but it were London and one of Phil Richardson's boys was on the same bill. Phil come along to watch his lad and he saw me fighting this bloke Joe Simmonds. Joe was rated number eight in country and I knocked him out in five rounds. Well, to cut a long story, Phil got in touch with Harold and put it to him. If I joined Phil's stable in London I'd get to top. He guaranteed fights at Wembley and overseas and the way I'd shaped that night he reckoned I'd have the British title inside twelve month. Harold weren't all that keen at first but they come to some arrangement and, sure enough, Phil did everything and more than he promised.'

'So that was very nice of Harold. He must have had a contract. He wasn't obliged to let you go, was he?'

'Oh he's a nice old fella, is Harold. He didn't want to stand in my way. But he didn't do badly either. I think he's still got ten percent of me. He's got ten and Phil's got fifteen. I think that's the way it works.'

'Twenty-five percent! But that's criminal. My agent gets ten, and I hate parting with that. You mean they take a quarter of everything you earn?'

'Aye. That's right. It's the usual in boxing. I s'pose it does seem a lot but the way things are you can't do without a manager. Lads've tried managing themselves but they always come unstuck. I'm not complaining. Phil's a good manager. He cares about his lads and he knows the game. He's taught me a lot. And his trainer, Paddy Whelan, he's a good'un too. We work well together. They got me to the top, didn't they?'

'And they have contacts with those two you mentioned—what were their names?'

'Pickett and Slater. Aye. Phil's well in with them. He's got the best stable of fighters in London, has Phil. They want him as much as he wants them. And he's got contacts all over the world. He got me fights in Hamburg, Adelaide and Madrid *and* the big one—the world title—that was in Paris.'

112

Judy said, 'It's fascinating. It's a new world. But tell me something . Maybe I've got this all wrong. Of course I don't know anything about boxing but I heard or read somewhere you were supposed to be lucky to get the championship. I don't know. Something about the man you beat—the French-man—not being the proper champion. Something like that.'

Dave sounded weary rather than angry. 'Aye well, yes, I know what you heard. That's what a lot of 'em said. Fournier—that's the Frenchman you're talking about, Marcel Fournier—he were maybe a bit lucky to get title. Don't get me wrong. He's a good fighter, is Fournier. His record proves it. He only lost three in forty-odd fights, and he were the recognized contender when he fought Bonetti. Bonetti was a good champion. He was undisputed. That means the WBA and the WBC both recognised him—they're the two main governing bodies as they call them, World Boxing Association and Council. He beat Bonetti over fifteen rounds, unanimous verdict. He defended once before I took the title off him. That was against a black fighter called Dwight Tulloch. Well, he beat Tulloch on a cut eye, eighth round. Could have been anyone's fight when the referee stopped it. But Tulloch's a good 'un. He's the only one to take Hayes the distance. Now, what a lot of the papers said was that I should've fought Tulloch or Hayes before getting a crack at Fournier's title. They reckoned the Froggie took me on 'cause he thought I was an easier touch than them two. Well, if he thought that, he got a shock didn't he? 'Cause I gave him a right pasting before I put him away in the eleventh. And whatever the papers say I were legitimate number one contender. *Boxing News*—and that's the only paper that knows anything about the game—backed me all the way. Legitimate number one contender, that's what they said. I was outright winner of a Lonsdale Belt—three successful defences of the British title—European Champion and I'd beaten Vallejo and Corrigan, number one and two. I've had more fights than Hayes. Better opposition. He's a good fighter. I'd be a fool if I said he weren't. But he's going to be fighting away from home for the first time and he's going to be fighting the hardest middleweight in the business.'

'My God,' Judy said. 'It's exciting.'

'I'll get you a seat. Ringside. Would you like that?'

'I—well—I don't know. I mean yes, part of me says yes, terrific, thrilling, wouldn't miss it for the world. But then I wonder. I don't think I could stand seeing you hurt. I don't know, but I don't think I could.'

'I tell you what. You come and see my warm-up in May. It's going to be against a Yank called Wayne Harvey. Don't know much about him. Phil told me last night on phone, he's seen him fight and he's useful but not brilliant. A good workout, that's what Phil said.'

'We'll see.'

'I'll miss you when I'm in London.'

'Perhaps I'll be able to come down and see you. Like Aileen. Or will she be with you?'

'No. She's stopping in Leeds. But, I don't know. It might not be . . . I don't know. I'll have to concentrate. I'll be living with Phil and Rose, in their house. They've got somebody in the flat I used to have and, anyway, they've got to watch what I'm eating, see I get to bed early and all that. I can't take any chances with this one. If Harvey licked me I don't know what would happen.'

'He'd be the champion then I suppose?'

'No. It's a non-title bout. Ten rounds. No he wouldn't be champion but it'd take the icing off the big 'un wouldn't it? Here's me and Hayes, both of us unbeaten. Both of us big punchers. It's a sell-out. World TV Rights, closed circuit in every big city. They reckon we'll be splitting three-quarters of a million between us. At least. But Jesus, if I dropped this one to Harvey it'd be a right balls-up—sorry. Language.'

'Balls-up is right,' Judy said. 'But did you say three-quarters of a *million*? *Pounds*?'

'That's right. Maybe a bit more, Phil says.'

'My God. I'd no idea.' She sounded dazed, even awed.

'Aye. It's big money these days if you're lucky and make the top. I'm lucky. I've worked hard but I've had the luck too. So you see. I can't take it easy with the warm-up. I've got to take it just as serious as the Hayes fight.'

'You mean you wouldn't want me getting in the way,

taking your mind off your work, is that it?'

'I'd want you right enough. Trouble is I don't think strict training and seeing you'd be a good mixture somehow. Even now it's hard enough.'

'What do you mean?'

'Training and coming here and seeing you. Like this. Making love. And I'm only in light training.'

'I'd have thought it'd make a nice change.'

'Aye, it does that. But it's thinking about it, thinking about you, that's the trouble. Even in light training you didn't ought to be thinking on owt else, just on fight in front of you, getting into shape.'

'What do you do in light training? How is it different? Is it just doing less of the same thing or what?'

'Well yes, you're doing the same things. Some of 'em anyway. I mean you do roadwork—that's running—and you work in gym. Groundwork—that's for your stomach muscles—skipping, punching the heavy bag. I'm doing a little bit of sparring, but only a couple of evenings a week. Eight, ten rounds, something like that. But once I go down to London with Phil and Paddy it's all a lot tougher. Everything's timed to the second. And you work your way up to a peak. The first week you're running maybe five miles a day, skipping six threes—that's three minute rounds—punching the bag for six, and sparring three or four then doing half an hour's exercises. But it gets stepped up till you're doing it all twice as long and twice as hard. It's murder. And old Paddy's watching like a hawk. He's got to, 'case you reach your peak too quick and then go stale for the fight. I've seen that happen more'n once. But old Paddy's good. He gets you so's you're like whippet on a leash, rarin' to go.'

'And you'll be able to forget me, put me out of your mind?'

She felt the movement of his head in denial. 'No. I won't be able to forget you. I'll just have to try. That's all. Put you away somewhere in the back of my mind. Like a photo in a drawer. You know. Take it out and have a look at it once a day. It'll not be easy.'

'What about another girl? I mean a casual one like in Nottingham. Is that allowed?'

'But I wouldn't!' He sounded shocked. 'I wouldn't want to. I don't want anyone but you.'

She said. 'You're sweet . . .' but there was a teasing note in her voice. 'All the same. You'd've thought with all that exercise, building up your strength, early to bed and all that . . . well, I don't know, but I'd guess most men'd get to feeling a bit . . .' She released her hand from his and touched his penis once with a delicate forefinger '. . . perhaps a bit frisky?'

He did not answer and she took his hand again. 'What's the matter, love? I haven't shocked you, have I?'

He cleared his throat. 'No. No. I was just wondering . . . No, 'course you haven't.'

'You were just wondering what?'

'Nothing. It doesn't matter.'

'Come on Dave. Out with it. What's worrying you? Don't be shy. You can tell me anything. Honest. I won't be shocked.'

'It's not *telling* you anything really. It's more asking.'

'Oh.' A tiny pause and then a slightly cooler, perhaps cautious tone tempered her voice: 'What did you want to ask?'

'Well . . .' he was plainly uncomfortable: 'You wanted to know about me and Aileen getting married and all that. And then about any other women . . . you know . . . well, I just wondered about you. I mean a girl like you must have lots of lads fancying her. And you're not exactly—well, I mean it wasn't your first—'

Judy broke in crisply: 'Just a minute Dave! Get this quite clear. The first time you came here I told you. You're a married man and I'm not your wife. I've got every right to ask about her, about your marriage, because she's part of the situation that I'm in, that we're in. Do you see what I mean? If I thought that you and Aileen were happy. If I thought I might be busting up a good marriage, maybe I'd've had second thoughts about—well, about us, being here, like this. I'm not married. 'Course I've had friends, men friends, but I'm not tied to anybody. That's the difference. But Dave . . .' Her hand remained in his as he felt her move, rising and turning so that he could sense rather than see her face as it hovered above him. '. . . don't think I'm like one of your pick-ups—' He began to protest but the index finger of her free hand pressed on his lips. 'Shush! I don't usually jump into bed after knowing somebody for five minutes. You're different Dave. You're special. And it's not because you're a champion boxer. It's because you're you, Dave Ruddock that little blond lad with the blue eyes. Serious, nearly a scowl. Like an angry cherub. And, if it helps you to know this, there's nobody and there never has been anybody, that's made me feel the way I feel about you.'

He felt the whisper of her hair on his forehead, then the warmth of her breath before her mouth settled upon his in a kiss that was at first gently, reflective, reassuring, then gradually becoming demanding, seeking, hungry. He released her hand and caressed, with both of his the suave contours of her flesh. She began to mutter endearments and fragments of entreaty and delight: 'Oh love, darling, oh please, yes darling, yes, I want you to . . . ooh, you're marvellous . . . oh love, so big, so . . . oh . . . please do, yes do . . . oh my love . . .' and then she was astride him, and he reared up, thrusting into her and she cried out in a voice that seemed to mingle ecstasy and despair. 'Oh my love, oh yes! Oh love, oh yes! Yes! Yes!'

CHAPTER NINE

THE SMELL OF Sunday and of childhood was unchanged; in the kitchen the roast was in the oven, the greens were simmering in the pan and elsewhere all wooden furnishings had been aromatically polished. Dave and Aileen sat in armchairs in front of the gas fire while his mother finished laying the table.

She said, 'Your dad ought to be back any minute now. He says he can't eat his dinner without he's had a couple of pints. Half-past one I said and not a minute after.'

She wore a cotton apron over her good Sunday dress and her dark greying hair had recently been released from its curlers. There was even, Aileen noticed, a faint touch of rouge on her cheeks and lips, but it did little to soften the severity of her expression.

Dave was glancing without great interest at the pages of a Sunday tabloid.

'Unemployed well over three million,' he said.

'Aye. An' here comes one of 'em,' Dot observed as they heard the front door opening and closing and the sounds of her husband removing his hat and overcoat in the hall.

Jimmy Ruddock came into the living room rubbing his hands and grinning cheerfully. 'It's a fine bright day but a bit parky out there. How are you, Aileen love? An' how's the champ?'

Dot said, 'You can all sit up at table now his lordship's back.'

They took their places and the meal was served and eaten. Conversation was sparse and desultory. When Jimmy tried to engage Dave in talk of boxing he was instantly rebuked by his wife.

'Can't you think on owt else?' Dot said. 'Boxing and beer's the only thing you ever talk about. Aileen doesn't want to hear about it, do you love? I shouldn't think you get much else out of our Dave, either.'

Aileen said, 'I think myself lucky when he talks to me at all.'

If the remark was aimed at that note of flippant banter which accompanies mild marital dissent it misfired. Her smile was vestigial and melancholy and her voice petulant. Dave was aware of his mother's quick glance from him to Aileen, the shrewd, undeceivable eyes questioning, concerned.

Jimmy spoke of the rail strike and of the folly and greed of the trade union leaders and, when no one seemed inclined to pursue this topic, he embarked on a vigorous if sketchily informed attack on the Labour party as a whole and Tony Benn in particular who, he said, wanted to get rid of the Royal Family and turn everybody into communists.

Dot said, 'Eat your dinner. It's getting cold. And if we want to hear about politics we'll put wireless on . . . Aileen, you're not doing very well. Is it all right?'

'It's lovely. I'm just not hungry.'

'Aye. Well, don't eat it if you don't want it, love.'

Dave said, 'It's great, mam, like always. Aileen never has much of an appetite, do you love?'

Aileen who had placed her knife and fork together on the plate, nodded her agreement but did not look at her husband.

'You're not at this slimming game are you?' Jimmy said. 'Can be dangerous can that. You need good grub to keep healthy. You look as if you could do with a bit more beef round your ribs, Aileen.'

'Ha!' Dot sounded derisive. 'He's the diet expert now! Doctor Ruddock. Leave the lass alone, Jimmy. If she doesn't want to eat her dinner she doesn't have to. So be quiet and finish that up.'

When the meal was over Dave said, 'You have a sit down, mam. Put your feet up. Me an' Aileen'll wash up pots.'

For the first time that day Dot smiled at him with all of the old affectionate, slightly mocking warmth. She said, 'That's kind of you, son, but no. You an' your dad go out and get a bit of fresh air. Go on. Go for a walk in park. You can chat about boxing or whatever you want to talk about to your heart's content. Aileen and me'll clear up have a cup of tea. Go on, the pair of you. Off you go.'

In the hall Dave slipped into his sheepskin coat while Jimmy carefully put on scarf, overcoat and hat, tilting the brim at a cocky angle. Then they went out into the street and walked briskly towards Potternewton Park.

In the living room Dot said, 'Well, we might as well get this lot put away,' and she and Aileen began to clear the table and pile the dishes in the kitchen in preparation for washing them up. A few minutes later they were working in the steam that rose from the bowl, Dot washing and Aileen drying, both silent until the older woman said, 'How's things with you and Dave then, Aileen? You happy up there?'

Aileen dextrously wiped two dinner plates at once. 'At Lidgett Park? Aye. It's lovely. You've seen it. Don't you think it's lovely?'

'I'm not on about the house, love. 'Course the house is all right. Ought to be at that price. I'm on about you and Dave. You don't look very happy to me.'

'Dave's all right.'

'And what about you?'

Aileen picked up two more plates and began to dry them. 'I'm not complaining,' she said.

'Happen you should be.'

There was a silence of a few seconds. Then Aileen said, 'Complaining doesn't help anybody.'

Dot added more boiling water to the bowl and continued to clean the dishes and other utensils. 'Sometimes it does,' she said, 'If it's only yourself. Gets it off your chest like. Walking around with a face as long as a fiddle and never saying more'n a couple of words to anyone doesn't help much either.' When Aileen did not reply she went on: 'What d'you do with yourself all day? I'm not criticizing, love. Don't think that. But I just wondered. Dave's out a lot, isn't he? Training and boxing and all that. You must get lonely.'

'I've got friends.'

120

'Oh? You see a lot of them do you?'

'Quite a lot. There's Madge Phillips. I used to work with her at Lewis's. She's married and lives near Gledhow Woods. And I sometimes go to Carole Sugden's coffee mornings. She's a girl I went to school with. She's married a policeman.'

'Doesn't sound all that lively,' Dot said, 'but as long as you're not lonely.' Then she added. 'What about church? R.C. wasn't it, you used to go to when your mother was alive? Your mam brought you up very religious, didn't she. You still go, do you?'

Aileen started on the cutlery. 'No. . . . Sometimes I wish I . . .' the sentence was not completed.

'Oh? No. Well, none of us has been great ones for church. Nothing against it, mind, but you find more real Christian feeling outside than inside I reckon.'

There was no more conversation until their work was finished and they were back in the living-room sitting by the fire with cups of tea.

Then Dot said, 'Listen, love. Earlier on you said complaining doesn't help anyone, didn't you? But that's not the same as saying you've nowt to complain about, is it? In fact it's saying the opposite. You're saying you've got your troubles but complaining about them isn't going to make them go away. That's right, isn't it?'

'Everybody's got troubles,' Aileen said, looking into the gas fire.

'Aye, that's very likely true. But some more'n others. Talking to somebody doesn't do no harm. Might even help if it's somebody who cares about you and wants to see you enjoying your life. You should be, you know, at your age. You've got everything to look forward to.'

'Have I?' Aileen's usually soft and placid features surprised Dot by their look of bitterness. 'I don't see as I've got anything to look forward to.'

'Aileen!' Dot's voice was genuinely shocked as if the girl had uttered an obscene blasphemy. 'You can't say that, love. You're nobbut a young lass. You can't say you've nothing to look forward to. It's not right.'

She put down her cup and saucer on the small table at the

side of her chair and leaned forward as if she was going to touch her daughter-in-law. But the hand that had moved impulsively towards the girl was withdrawn as though some instinct had warned her that the physical contact would be unwelcome. 'Listen. I want to help you. I know you think nobody can help, but give it a try, love. You know the old saying. Trouble shared is trouble halved. You've nothing to lose. If it's Dave not treating you right, you don't have to think I'll take his side and put blame on you. I know what men are like. Come on love. Tell us what trouble is. You're not happy. I know you're not. Tell us all about it, there's a good lass.'

Dot's voice had taken on a soothing, motherly note, almost a crooning sound and she saw Aileen's face soften and her mouth tremble and droop at the corners. 'Go on love. Have a good cry. It'll do you good. Let it come out. Tell me all about it then.'

But Aileen surprised her. The girl shook her head and tightened her lips. 'I'm not going to cry. I'm not a baby.'

' 'Course you're not,' Dot said in the slow placatory voice she would use if indeed she was speaking to a baby. ' 'Course you're not a baby. You're a married woman. But all of us have a cry sometime, it's human nature. Many's the little cry I've had all on me own. It helps. A bit. Not much, but a bit.'

Aileen looked straight at Dot for the first time since they had sat down. She said, 'I think Dave's got another woman.'

The older woman nodded. 'Aye, well, so that's the trouble.'

'No. It's more than that. I wouldn't mind that—well, I'd mind, but I could put up with it. But it's everything else. He's hardly ever there and when he is he's got nothing to say. He might as well be a hundred miles away. Maybe he's thinking about her, whoever she is. I don't know. One thing's certain. He's not thinking about me.'

'You're quite sure? About this other woman? 'Cause it's not like Dave. He were never much of a one for lasses. He were always so shy.'

'I'm sure all right. Unless he's started using Chanel

Number Five, and that's a bit unlikely. He's always reckoned it's cissy to use after-shave.'

'You don't know for a fact then?'

'I know all right. Three times last week he's come in well after midnight. Last time it was past two in morning. He were supposed to be at some boxing thing—guest at a dinner show or something—in Preston.' Aileen nodded, her lips compressed.

'How d'you know he weren't there?' Dot asked.

'I looked at his mileage in car when he was out running Thursday morning. That's the night he were off to Preston, or so he reckoned. I checked it on Friday. Guess how far he'd been.'

Dot waited.

'Three mile,' Aileen said with a kind of bitter satisfaction. Then she went on: 'He were never in Preston. He were with his woman whoever she is.'

'And you can't think who it can be?'

'No . . . well, aye, I've got an idea but I'm not sure. I'm not saying till I find out for certain. But if it's who I think it is she's a right bad 'un.'

Dot made a little gesture of incomprehension with head and hands. 'Ee, it's hard to believe. I'm not saying you're wrong, Aileen. But it doesn't sound like our Dave. I mean not just him being so shy but the boxing. He never had time. If it was our Martin I'd understand it. They was as different as chalk and cheese. When Martin were nobbut a little lad he were after lasses. Kept pin-ups in bedroom. Dave never seemed bothered.'

'Well, he's changed then.'

'You sure you're right about car and mileage? I don't know how these things work but couldn't it've gone wrong? Got stuck or something?'

Aileen shook her head. 'He'd never been to Preston. Never been out of Leeds. But I'd know anyway. The car mileage was just proof. I could tell a month ago he'd got a fancy woman.'

'The scent? Well, happen there's some explanation—'

'No! Not just the scent. Him. Dave. The way he acted. He

didn't come near me unless he had to. He hasn't—you know—bothered me for four or five weeks.'

'*Bothered* you.'

'You know what I mean. At night. In bed.'

Dot looked at her with eyes which showed pity and an appalled comprehension. '*Bothered* you? Aileen, love, is that the way you see it? Making love. Is that what it is to you? Being bothered? Eh, there's something badly wrong somewhere. I thought the young 'uns today never had them sort of worries. The pill before they're out of school. Permissive society and Women's Lib an' all that. By, you sound like a Victorian lass, Aileen. Is that really true? I mean do you really feel that's what it is? Being bothered. I mean—look, you can talk to me straight, love—d'you mean you don't like it? You don't get any pleasure? You really mean that?'

Aileen's face had flushed a deep red. She looked into the fire. 'Well . . . no, not really. Not . . . not the part they like. Men I mean. I don't mind—I mean I like a cuddle and a kiss, but it's when they get—you know—nasty. Crude. You know.'

Dot released a long sigh. 'Oh dear,' she said. Then: 'Here, let's have your cup love. I'll pour us another.'

As she was pouring the tea Aileen said, 'I never refused him. Not unless I were poorly.'

Dot handed Aileen her tea and sat down again. She took a sip before saying, 'What are you going to do then?'

The girl did not answer.

Her mother-in-law went on: 'It isn't easy to talk about these things but you've got to try and see both sides, love. I know you haven't been married more'n eighteen month but to tell truth I'm surprised Dave's not gone off rails sooner.'

This seemed to startle Aileen. She looked up sharply. 'I thought you said you wasn't going to take Dave's side. Blame me. That's what you're doing though, isn't it?'

Dot shook her head slowly. 'No, I'm not blaming you. But I can see why Dave might get himself another woman. I'm not saying that he's right but I'm not saying he hasn't got some cause either.'

124

'Why? What cause? What d'you mean?'

'Oh, Aileen, What d'you think I mean? I'm talking about your marriage, your—well, the way you talk about it—about sex. You talk about him *bothering* you, about being *nasty*. Honest to God I never thought anybody talked like that for the last fifty years or more. Making love isn't nasty and it shouldn't be a bother. It ought to be something lovely and there's something wrong somewhere if a young wife feels like you do. And I'm not saying it's your fault, Aileen, But it's not natural.

'Natural thing's to enjoy it. If you don't there's something wrong and you want to find out what it is. You ought to go and see a doctor. See a lady doctor. Talk to her. Tell her how you feel. Or one of these marriage guidance places you hear about. The two of you could go. I'm not saying Dave's right if he's gone to another woman but I can see how he might be driven.'

Aileen's face had become set in a heavy, sulky look of reproach, that held, too, an obstinate defensiveness which told Dot that there was little hope of fruitful discussion on this topic and that it would probably be wise to alter her tactics.

'Has Dave and you thought about babies? No rush about it, I know, but it's nice to have 'em when you're young. When our Jean left school I wasn't forty yet. Her and me were like—well, not sisters exactly, but I don't think many would've thought we was mother and daughter.'

'I don't want babies,' Aileen said. 'Not yet anyway.'

'And what about Dave?'

'Dave doesn't want anything to do with me.'

Dot made a final attempt at sympathetic communication: 'Aileen, love, I'm not criticizing you. I'm doing my best to help. 'Course you can't be thinking on babies while you're not happy with your husband. But I want you to believe me when I tell you this. If you're not both happy in bed you're not going to be happy out of it. That goes for all marriages. I'm not saying sex is everything in a marriage. 'Course it's not. There's a lot more to being wed than that. But it's got to be right. You go and talk to somebody. A doctor like I said.

125

Tell 'em what you told me love, how you don't really enjoy it. They might be able to do something for you. For both of you.'

Aileen nodded miserably.

'And cheer up. Things are never as bad as they might be. Look on bright side. You're young. You're a good-looking girl and if you made a bit more of yourself you'd be a smasher. Why don't you go to beauty parlour. See what they've got to suggest. A change of style happen. Make-up. Facial. A bit of glamour. You can afford it now. No good sitting round moping. you'd feel like a different person. Give Dave a surprise. That's what I'd do.'

Aileen managed a pale smile which encouraged Dot to continue:

'And have it out with Dave. No messing. Be blunt. Tell him you know what he's up to. Get things out in open. Then there's a chance of sorting things out. If you keep quiet it'll all fester and get so bad there's no cure. All right, love?'

Aileen said, 'What about him? What about Dave? Why don't you talk to him?'

Dot smiled. 'That's what his dad's doing. I hope. That's why I sent them out for a walk.'

Dave and his father walked quickly because of the cold. The sun was still shining but already a mist had formed to dim its radiance. They went through the gates of the park and set off along the rising path; the swings and slides on their right stood unused and disconsolate and the hard tennis courts were deserted. A few people were exercising their dogs, trying to keep them away from the two or three disreputable strays who were engaged in mock combat or investigating each other's private parts.

Jimmy Ruddock said, 'It's a while since we been in Potternewton. Remember you used to come here when you was a kid? Do your roadwork. Three times round the park. You didn't like coming in daylight. Felt daft didn't you? Remember? Nowadays nobody wouldn't notice. Joggers all over bloody place. It's the ones walking that look funny.'

Dave remembered setting his alarm to wake him early, often before daylight, and forcing himself to leave his warm bed and put on a sweater, old trousers and heavy-boots before letting himself quietly out of the house into the deserted streets where the lamps still slopped their pale yellow pools of light on darkly gleaming pavement and road. Then he would run down to the park and, breathing out smoky blossoms of breath, pound three times round it.

'Seems a long time ago,' he said.

'Aye. You've come a long way since then, son. I never thought you'd be what you are. I knew you was good. A natural. Anybody could see that. But world title! That's dream stuff, i'n't it? I can't hardly believe it now.'

'No more can't I,' Dave said, though this was not true. He knew that he had been lucky to be given a shot at the crown but there had seemed to be something inevitable about his success. He had not lost a fight since he was thirteen, and that, had been a disputed verdict which he had convincingly reversed in the return bout. Eleven years—Schoolboy Champion of Great Britain, Junior ABA and Senior ABA Champion, a Lonsdale Belt, the European title and then the pot of gold, the Championship of the World—eleven years without dropping a decision. He was a winner. He'd never got the habit of losing. He knew only how to win.

His father was saying '. . . I told her there were nothing to worry about, but I just thought I'd ask you. Well, I promised your mam I would. See?'

Dave said, 'Sorry dad. I didn't catch what—I was miles away. What was you on about? You promised mam what?'

'By! You're a dozy bugger sometimes, Dave. You never heard a word, did you? You wasn't listening was you?'

'Sorry.'

'Ah well . . . I was just saying. Me and your mam was talking t'other day and she were a bit worried about you and Aileen. She said I ought to ask you how things is going—you know, if everything's all right.'

'Me and Aileen? Aye, we're okay.'

'Aye . . . well, that's good. It's just that your mam thought Aileen wasn't looking too bright, not very happy like. And tell you the truth I thought the same. Everything's all right with the pair of you then? No complaints, like they used to say in Army . . . Carry on sarn't . . .'

Dave said, 'She doesn't have a lot to do. I think she gets a bit fed up sometimes.'

'Aye. Well then, you know the way to keep lass busy, don't you?'

Dave wondered for an uneasy moment if his father, astonishingly was about to make an improper joke. 'How?'

'Nippers. Have a kiddy. That'll keep her busy. Changing nappies, pushing pram. She wouldn't have no time to be down in mouth.'

Dave made a noise which might have been taken for agreement.

'Have a little lad,' Jimmy went on. 'Another champion in family. I bet what you like Aileen'd cheer up if she had a nipper to look after.'

For the briefest fraction of a second Dave felt the temptation to tell his father about Judy, but common sense snuffed out the impulse before it was fully alive. He knew that his father would not understand. He doubted if Jimmy Ruddock had ever considered the possibility of adultery in his own marriage. To Jimmy it was the kind of thing you read about in the papers or heard people making jokes about. Dave thought of his father at the dinner table, talking of things the old boxer knew little or nothing about, and he remembered with sudden clarity Jimmy's hands, gripping knife and fork, slightly swollen and freckled with brown spots like those first, heavy drops of rain on a dusty pavement in summer, presaging a storm. His father most certainly would not understand about Judy. He was getting old and his life now was drained of hope and expectation. Whatever excitements came his way were second-hand, Dave's success in the ring, the possibility of becoming grandfather to a young fighter, of Martin gaining promotion in the army. Yet he seemed happy enough, Dave thought, and felt a small stab of oddly protective love.

'We'll go once more round,' Jimmy said, 'and that'll do. Then we'll be ready for us tea.' Then he added, 'Did you see

128

Martin before he went back?'

'Aye. He come up on Friday night. He said he didn't mind going back. Misses his mates when he's on leave. Reckons the first couple of days is great but after that you just want to get back to the lads.'

'I never felt like that,' Jimmy said. 'I'd've stayed home forever if they'd let me. But it weren't bad really. I might've told you, I were a PTI. Boxing got me that. I won the Army and Combined Services Championship in 1949 and they sent me on a PT course. PT—Physical Torture.

Dave had heard the joke often before but he was able to offer a token grunt of amusement.

'Rest of the time I were PTI Corporal. Real cushy job. No guards, no bullshit. That's what they called the square-bashing. Aye, the army weren't too bad. And they let me turn pro while I were still in it. Not like it is now, mind. Our Martin gets paid more'n a bloody officer did in my day. Aye, an' grub! They get a choice like a posh hotel or something. All we ever got was meat and veg and duff. I was telling Martin. He ought to take up game again. He's young enough. I don't mean serious like you. Not turn pro. Stay in the amateurs. He'd do well in army.'

Jimmy went on talking about his days in National Service just after the Second World War and then, predictably enough, he switched to his own professional ring career. The familiar stories, which Dave had loved to hear as a child, touched lightly at the edges of awareness and, in the way that well-known tunes played as background music to conversation do not interfere with communication, so Jimmy's anecdotes provided an unobtrusive accompaniment to Dave's thoughts of Judy. Father and son, in their own different ways, were, at least for the time being, quite content.

129

CHAPTER TEN

THE MARCH SUN was bright and the young daffodils were out in Sue Davitt's garden as Judy turned her Mini into the drive and parked in front of the house. Sue must have heard the car, for the front door opened before Judy had reached it and the two friends embraced briefly before going indoors. In the sitting-room a coffee table had been laid with cups, saucers and a plate of biscuits.

Sue said, 'Sit down. The coffee's all ready. I've only got to bring it in.'

She went out of the room to return a few seconds later with a silver coffee-pot and, when she had poured from it, she took her seat opposite Judy and leaned forward with a smile of brilliant, almost hungry anticipation and said, 'It's such ages, Judy love! Now tell me what's been happening. All the news. All the gossip. I never hear anything. How's the singing? How's Colin? And what's this great mystery you were on about on the phone? You've been spotted by a talent scout, you're off to Hollywood. West End musical. Colin's getting a divorce. Let me guess. No, don't let me guess. Tell me.'

Judy sipped some coffee and looked at her friend with a small, uncertain smile which seemed to interrogate and doubt and even contain traces of apprehension. 'I don't think you're going to approve,' she said.

'Come on. What is it? What you been up to?'

'I had to tell somebody. You were the only person I thought might—well, the only person I *could* tell really.'

'Tell *what* for Heaven's sake? What you talking about? Get it out, lass. Let's have it.'

'I've started an—well, I'm in—God it's hard to explain. No it's not! I'm in love. I've fallen in love. I think. No, I know. I have. I must have. I'm daft about him. He's lovely. I'm in love. Yes. I am.'

Sue leaned back and looked steadily at Judy. Then she said, 'Who is it?'

'I don't think I can tell you. He's quite well known. Well *very* well known. But it's not that so much. I don't think I ought to talk about it unless he knows. I mean I feel a bit—you know—not deceitful exactly but, well, like going behind his back.'

'And what about him? Is he in love with you?'

'I think so.'

'Hasn't he said so?'

'Yes—well, not exactly in so many words. But neither have I. We don't talk in that sort of way. I mean he's made it pretty clear.'

'He's married, I suppose?'

Sue began to nod affirmation to her own question before Judy answered. 'Yes. If you can call it a marriage.'

Sue nodded twice more then said, 'What's he do? Or can't you tell me that either?'

'No. I'm sorry, but I can't. Not without giving away who he is.'

They both drank some coffee. Then Sue said, 'Okay. It looks as if we'll have to play guessing games. He's very well known. You can't say what he does without letting on who he is. So there can't be very many of him, if you see what I mean . . . Mmm . . . How old is he?'

'Young. About my age. Our age. About a year younger than me actually.'

'Into music? Showbiz? Not a pop singer, I hope.'

Judy smiled, 'No.'

'Oh come on, Judy. You can tell *me*. It's a bit unkind love, isn't it? I mean what you're saying is you can't trust me. You ought to know by now I wouldn't give away anything you tell me in confidence. I wouldn't. Honest. You know that, don't you?'

'What about your husband?'

'Andy? He wouldn't be interested. I wouldn't tell him

131

anyway but he's never interested in that kind of thing.'

'What kind of thing *is* he interested in?'

'What? Andy? Oh the usual man's things. His work's his main interest—Company law. Reads journals and books about it. And cars and sport. That's about it, I suppose. Sounds dull, I know, but he's a good husband and a good father. I wouldn't swap him for anyone.'

'He'd be interested in Da— in my man.'

'Oh? Is he a lawyer?'

This time Judy laughed aloud as she shook her head.

'I don't see what's so funny about lawyers,' Sue said with a note of asperity. 'Andy's a damn sight more interesting and attractive than most of the men you meet in the music set-up. And he earns a damn sight more money.'

'I wasn't laughing at lawyers. Certainly not at Andy. Of course he's a lovely man. I've always said so. It was just the idea. Well, my chap's what you might call distinctly physical. I can't see him in an office or a black suit or anything like that. He's—well, he's an athlete.'

'You mean—?'

'Can I have a drop more coffee?'

As Sue was pouring she said, 'You mean he's a professional? Professional what, I wonder . . . ? I know! He's a footballer!' She looked up from her own cup which she was now refilling. 'Am I right?'

Judy shook her head. Then she said, 'Look, will you promise on your word of honour you'll never tell anyone, not even Andy, no one at all, if I tell you?'

'Of course I promise. I told you. Andy won't be interested!'

'But supposing he *is* interested. And I'm pretty sure he will be. Do you swear you won't tell him, however much you're tempted?'

'Yes. I swear. Guide's honour.'

'All right. I'll tell you then. You'd better get ready for a shock. It's Dave Ruddock.'

'Dave . . . ? Who? Dave . . . ?

'Dave Ruddock. The boxer. World Champion. Don't tell me you haven't heard of him.'

'Oh him! The boxer! Well . . .' Sue's frown of perplexity

had been replaced by a look of pure astonishment. Her dark eyes were very wide and it seemed that her breath had quite literally been taken away, for she had to inhale deeply before she could speak again: 'But how did it happen? I mean how did you meet him? He's not the sort of person—well, you know, the sort of person I'd have thought you'd come across in the ordinary way. Of course I don't know anything about him. I don't suppose I'd've ever heard of him if Andy didn't go on a bit about things like that. Boxing and football and all that stuff on the box on Saturdays. And him being a local boy, the boxer I mean. How did it start?'

'I knew him when we were children.'

'Judy! Why didn't you ever tell me? All that time at school and college. All the heart-to-hearts we've had! You never mentioned him. I'm sure you didn't. I'd remember if you had.'

'No. I'm sure I didn't. I'd forgotten I ever knew him. Well, that's not quite true either. I didn't really *know* him. I mean we weren't ever friends or anything. It was just that his mother used to do a bit of housework for my mum and, for some reason I can't remember, Mrs Ruddock took me round to her house a few times. I remember the house quite well. Slummy but kind of nice and cosy. And there were three Ruddock kids—an elder sister, two or three years older than me, a little lad about five years younger—and Dave.'

'But you must have been—what?—I mean you weren't old enough. To start anything. I mean how old were you?'

'When I first saw Dave? I don't know. About ten or eleven, I suppose. Of course we didn't start anything. Nothing like that. We hardly even spoke. But he fascinated me in a funny sort of way, even then. Something about him. Innocent, very quiet, gentle, but —well, sexy, animal, even a bit dangerous.'

'You never felt like that about a little lad when you were ten!'

'No, of course not. Not consciously. But I can see it now. I mean I recognise the funny feeling he gave me then for what it really was.'

'But how did you meet up again? How long's it been going on?

'About a month or so. Just over. Not long. We met at the

local radio place on Woodhouse Lane. Both doing interviews.'

'And then what?'

'And then—pow! Right away. My God, Sue, it was amazing. The kind of thing I never believed in. It was electric. Nothing like—well, nothing like anything that's ever happened before. It wasn't just the way he looked. Not just that, though he looked terrific. I mean we've all seen blokes we've fancied, nice looking, good figures, sexy movers, that kind of thing. But this was different. I could have melted on the spot. And the thing is, he's so damned *nice*. He's like a—God, I don't know—like a beautiful panther or something, sleek and powerful and dangerous. So bloody strong. But he's gentle, too. He's—'

'All right, love! I get the general picture. You're stuck on him. But what we want to know is where you go from there. What about Colin Hunter? Where does he fit in? How much does your—what's-he-called, Dave—how much does he know? About you and Colin and everything. Where's Colin now? Wasn't he going away? South America or somewhere didn't you say?'

'Florida. He's still there. They went the beginning of November, the kids as well. He's doing some business deal about holiday property or something but he wanted to get away for the winter 'cause of his chest.'

'When's he coming back?'

'I don't know for sure. I've only heard from him a couple of times. No, three. A couple of cards and one phone call on New Year's day. He said something about they'd rented a place for six months so I reckon he'll be back in May some time.'

'And then what?'

'I don't know.'

Sue looked at her friend with an expression which contrived to show concern, a touch of amusement, some exasperation and, behind all this, a conspiratorial excitement. 'There's a drop more coffee left.' She refilled their cups. 'You said your chap Dave's married. Has he got kids?'

'No.'

'All right. And what about Colin? Does Dave know

anything about you and Colin?'

'No. I've been meaning to tell him but it's not easy. It looks bad. I mean it looks worse than it is, Colin owning the flat and that.'

'What d'you mean, worse than it is?'

Judy looked up sharply, 'Well . . . it looks . . . you know . . . You know exactly what I mean. It looks as if I'm Colin's bit of stuff that he keeps for a nibble on the side. Rich man's tart. Old fashioned little kept woman. That kind of thing.'

Sue said nothing.

Judy's face was suddenly and noticeably pinker and her eyes showed anger. 'Oh! I see! You think that's exactly what I am!'

'No. Of course not,' Sue said quickly, 'but I'm not sure . . .'

'You're not sure of what?'

'Well, I'm not sure that most people wouldn't see it that way—Wait! Just a second, love!—I'm not saying the same thing. I know different. I know you got trapped, in a way. When Colin found you that flat you didn't even know he owned the place. And even when you did find out you could take it as a friendly bit of help. Same with the low rent. But once he started coming on with the presents and the invitations and finding you little engagements in those clubs of his you must've known he wanted something in exchange. But how could you get out of it? He'd got you in a kind of honey trap. That's the way I always thought of it.'

Judy still looked angry. 'But you still think I'm his little bit on the side. You think I'm cashing in. Isn't that right? And that makes me a whore, doesn't it?'

Sue returned her friend's indignant gaze steadily and very seriously. Then she said, 'Look Judy. We've known each other a long time. What is it? Must be ten years or more. We've always got on well because we haven't tried to fool each other. We've always been very different. Maybe that's why we've got on. We always respected each other's difference. All right? No, wait . . . let me finish. It's important to get this straight. You always thought I was a bit square, a bit cautious and maybe a bit on the soppy side. Believing in love and marriage and all that. Not fooling around—well, not going

135

the whole way unless it was likely to be serious, likely to lead somewhere. A real relationship. You took it more lightly. Always. Right from the early days. I never blamed you. Tell you the truth I admired you for it. But I knew it wasn't for me. I still do admire you. Even this crazy thing with the boxer. But don't let's start fibbing to each other, Judy. You and Colin Hunter. You knew he was a married man with three kids. You knew what his reputation was with women. Once you realized he owned that flat of yours you must've known you either had to get out of it or play along. Right?'

Judy's expression of indignation had slowly changed into a heavier, sulky look. She said, 'I liked him. It wasn't just because of the flat and the—well, work and things he put my way. It wasn't that. I thought he was kind of glamorous. I know that sounds daft. He's thin on top and pushing fifty but he had something.' She grinned suddenly. 'And I don't mean a Rolls and a couple of million in the bank. He'd got style and he'd been everywhere and done everything. It was a kind of—what's the word? You could depend on him. He only had to flick his fingers. Authority. That's the word. He had authority. And, you know, it wasn't a bit the way it must seem to you. I mean he'd go days, sometimes weeks, and I'd never see him. I was never his property, Sue. He never came round without ringing up first. My life was my own. That was understood. And the other thing. Bed. Sex. That wasn't really very important. After the first few times—and they weren't anything to get excited about—he didn't seem bothered. He liked taking me around. Showing me off to his business pals. Last couple of times he spent the night at my place—just before he went to the States—nothing happened. His chest was bothering him and he was tired. All he wanted was a bit of sympathy. And I shouldn't think he gets much of that when he's home, not from what I've heard of Mrs Hunter.'

'What's going to happen then? Is there any chance of Dave leaving his wife? You said—or you sort of hinted—their marriage wasn't up to much. Though you've only got his word for that of course. All right! Don't get all defensive. I'll take your word for it, though you must admit it does seem a bit odd. I mean you tell me he's only—what?—twenty-four or five? So he can't have been married all that long and already he—'

'It was a mistake! They should never've got married. I know, I know. You'd expect me to say that. But honest. It's true. Dave doesn't run her down. Well, he doesn't mean to. But even when he thinks he's talking about her good points she sounds like bad news all round.'

'So there's some hope of . . . ? I mean you're looking for something—well, something more than just an affair? Something more permanent?'

Judy made a helpless, shrugging gesture. 'I don't know. Yes. Maybe. I don't know. It all seemed to happen too fast. I made the running, not him. And once I'd started I couldn't stop. It's only a few weeks ago but it seems he's always been there. In a way. It's funny. In one way it's like a dream that could finish any moment. All over. The end. Nothing left. All a dream. But in another way it's more real than anything that's ever happened. It's like I've been waiting for it all my life. I know that all sounds as corny as . . . I don't know. If anybody talked to me like that I'd tell them to cut the crap. But it's true. It's the way I feel. And I can't think of anything except being with him. Not marriage. Not forever. Just the next time. I know I've got to work things out. I know I've got to sort out the thing with Colin. I wanted to do that anyway, even if Dave hadn't come along. It was laziness stopping me. You're quite right. I knew the set up was wrong. I *was* his kept tart. I knew I ought to break with him. And I will. As soon as he gets back from America. I'll tell him it's all over.'

Sue looked at her wrist-watch. 'God! Look at the time! I've got to pick up Emma from nursery school. You'll stay for lunch, won't you? Just soup and bread and cheese.'

'Okay. I'd love to. I'll come with you to pick Emma up.'

The two young women left the sitting-room, put on their out-door clothes and went out of the house into the bright noon sunlight and the cold clean breeze of early spring.

At that moment Dave was completing a sequence of exercises designed to strengthen his abdominal muscles. He lay on the gymnasium floor looking up at the ceiling while Micky Rice crouched at his feet holding the heels firmly down while Dave, with fingers interlocked behind his head and elbows pressed back, sat quickly upright, pushed his face down towards his knees twice before resuming the supine position. He executed this manoeuvre fifty times before Micky released the boxer's feet, straightened up and said, 'Okay Dave. That'll do you.'

The gym consisted of a single cavernous room with dressing accommodation, two showers and a lavatory partitioned off from the main space which was occupied by a floor-level ring, three heavy bags suspended from beams, a speed punch-ball and a couple of exercise machines. Even on such a bright day artificial lighting had to be used. Dave jumped to his feet and joined Harold King and Tom Darwin who, with the trainer, had been watching his work-out.

Micky said, 'Don't hang around, son. Have your shower and get changed.'

Dave, who was wearing a one-piece woollen sweat-suit under an old pair of trunks, nodded. 'Come and talk to us, Tom, while I'm getting dressed,' he said, and made for the dressing space, followed by his friend.

There, he stripped and stood under the shower for a minute or so and then emerged to towel himself vigorously. Tom sat on a bench watching him.

Dave said, 'Good to see you Tom. You on nights again?'

'Until tomorrow. I finish in the morning and then I'm free till Monday. Start early shift then.'

'You doing anything special tomorrow night?'

'No. Don't think so. Why?'

'Thought you might like to look at some videos of Earl Hayes's fights. Phil Richardson's coming up to Leeds tomorrow. He's got some business he wants to talk about with old Harold. So he's bringing these films. Me and dad and Harold and Mickey's going to have some grub with him at Queen's. That's where Phil's staying. Then we're going to watch films after meal. Why don't you come?'

'What? Join up with you after you've eaten— Wouldn't the other's mind?'

Dave began to get dressed. 'No, 'course they wouldn't. One more wouldn't make no difference. Come and eat with us.

They all know you. They know you're my old mate. Another few bob wouldn't worry old Phil. He's got plenty.'

'No. I won't do that. Thanks all the same. But I'd like to see the videos. Do you know what time you're eating?'

'Aye. We're meeting at Queen's about seven. You can come about half past, see how we're getting on. Have a drink or something if we haven't finished. Then we'll all go up to Phil's room and watch fights, he's got half-a-dozen tapes I think. Got them sent from America.'

'Well, if you're sure it's all right.'

' 'Course it's all right. I'll tell Harold and Micky now if you like. You're part of the old firm, Tom. They know that. Anyway, there's something I want to talk to you about, after like, when I run you back home in car. Okay?'

'All right. I'll look into the restaurant about half seven or a bit later.'

Dave bent to tie up his shoes. 'Good lad. How's Peggy?'

'She's fine. And Aileen?'

Dave stood upright. 'Aileen . . . Aye. She's all right. Well, that's one o' things I'd like to have a talk about, after we've looked at films tomorrow night.'

Tom looked at him with curiosity but decided not to ask any more about his friend's wife. He said, 'None of the other lads training this morning then?'

'No. They work-out at night mostly. Prince sometimes does a work-out in morning but Charlie's with Securicor I think. I'm not sure what Andy does. Driving job of some sort. I, come in odd nights for a bit of sparring but Phil's not keen on that. I'll be going down to London next month. That's when I start training proper.'

'That's for the Harvey fight in May.'

'Aye. Phil's getting a bit jittery like. He knows I can lick Harvey but he's scared something could go wrong. Thinks I might get cocky and walk into a sucker-punch. Get a cut eye or something. He don't trust anybody with my training except him and Paddy Whelan. He gets on all right with Harold and Micky but he's a right Londoner is Phil. Thinks he knows it all. Reckons we're fifty years behind times up here.'

'He seemed very bright, the couple of times I met him.'

'Oh aye. He's bright enough. Best manager in country. No question. It's just that he thinks everybody else is a bit daft or something. Treats me like a bloody ten-year-old sometimes. Still, I didn't ought to complain. I'm dead lucky really. I'd never've got where I am without Phil, that's a fact.'

Dave picked up his bag containing his gear and he and Tom rejoined Harold King and Micky in the main gymnasium.

'Tom's coming to the movie-show tomorrow night,' Dave said. 'Not for the meal, just to see Hayes. That's all right i'n't it?'

Harold, tall, heavily built with thick-rimmed glasses, looked like a retired senior officer of a provincial police force or perhaps the head of a decent, small town firm of solicitors, solid, dependable and shrewd, accustomed to authority but not to quick decision-making. He said, 'No reason why not. Don't see why Phil should object. I'm sure he won't.'

'That's all right then,' Dave said. 'I won't be coming into gym tomorrow. I'll just do a run in morning. See you both at seven.'

He and Tom left the gymnasium and walked to where Dave's car was parked on a patch of waste ground.

'Can I give you a lift anywhere?' Dave said.

'No thanks. I'll walk into town. I've got one or two things to do. So I'll see you tomorrow night at the Queen's.'

They exchanged farewells and Dave opened his car door, threw his training-bag on to the back seat and settled at the wheel. As he started the engine Tom turned and waved and Dave touched the horn before moving away towards home.

CHAPTER ELEVEN

THE HOTEL BEDROOM was warm and, although only Harold King was smoking, the air was hazy and pungent with cigar-smoke. Tom, Dave and his father, Jimmy, sat on the bed while the other three men occupied chairs. Except for Dave everyone was holding a glass, and on a small table at Phil Richardson's elbow stood a much depleted bottle of Scotch, a jug of water and a soda-syphon. Phil put down his glass, rose from his seat and switched off the video. He was a man of medium height and build with closely cut grey hair, gold-rimmed spectacles behind which very pale blue eyes moved from one face to another of his guests with a detached curiosity which might have held a touch of amusement. He remained standing in front of the blank television screen, evidently resolved that he would not be the first to break the silence in the room.

Mickey Rice spoke. 'By, he's a good 'un all right is that lad! He's got the lot. Speed, digs with both hands, clever, all the punches. I couldn't see no weaknesses.'

Harold, who was sitting next to him said, 'Reminds me of Sugar Ray Robinson. Same style. Maybe not quite so flashy. What d'you think Phil?'

Richardson allowed a pause of two or three seconds before answering. 'Hayes is a very good fighter,' he said. 'No one in his right mind is going to say any different.' Another slight pause. 'He can box and he can punch. He doesn't take chances. Never gets careless. You saw him yourselves. He's always positioned right. Near perfection as any fighter can get. Right?

141

Tom could not prevent himself from grinning: the self-important, commanding-officer manner was both slightly comic and slightly irritating. But the others waited respectfully for the lecture to continue.

'Right,' Phil went on. 'We saw Hayes knocking 'em over like nine-pins. Don't let's kid ourselves. They weren't push-overs. There was some very useful fighters among that lot. None of 'em gave Hayes any trouble at all. He out-classed them. I've watched these tapes dozens of times. Taking notes. Looking out for any weakness, any technical flaws. And I'll be honest with you. I haven't seen one. Not one. Earl Hayes is as close to the perfect fighting-machine as you'll ever get. But he's not a machine. He's a human being. Flesh and blood. Right? He's human and he's got his weaknesses. Not technical. He don't seem to do anything wrong that way. When he's on top he looks unbeatable. And we've only seen him when he's on top. See what I'm getting at? We've never seen him under pressure. We've never seen him worried. And it makes you wonder. Has he ever been under pressure? Look at his record. Amateur: National Golden Gloves, World Champion, Olympic Gold. Same as a pro. Only one fight went the distance and he was never in trouble, never under pressure. And there's the big question-mark. How would he be if he was pressured? If he was bulled out of his rhythm? And how would he be if he was hurt? Never once on these tapes did he have to take a punch. Not a real punch. The few that got there he was moving with them, riding 'em. And here's the thing. He's never met a puncher like Dave. Tulloch's got a fair dig but he tried to outbox Hayes. And I can't see anybody doing that. He fought the wrong fight. And we're not going to do that. Dave's going to get close to him and worry him and break his rhythm. And he's going to hurt him. Hayes carries a wallop. Both hands. But he doesn't hit as hard as Dave. And we're going to make that the crunch.'

Jimmy Ruddock said, 'Dave's a boxer. He's a box-fighter. You don't want him going in there throwing punches and forgetting all about the clever stuff. He's got to make his openings like he always does. He's not a slugger, isn't Dave. Never was.'

'That's right,' Micky confirmed. 'If Dave goes in there to mix it he'll likely walk into trouble. Hayes is a smart counter-puncher. I reckon we'd be playing right up his street if we was to go in there and try and take him out of his stride. That's not Dave's style.'

Phil picked up his glass from the table and took a drink, but he remained standing. 'Listen,' he said. 'I think you've missed the point a bit. You've just seen what Hayes is like. I don't reckon there's any way you could win if you was to go in there and play him at his own game. He's too fast, he's too clever and he carries to much artillery. You talk about box-fighters Jimmy. Well, Hayes is the greatest. Now, don't get me wrong. I'm not belittling Dave. Dave's the best middleweight we've had in England. I'd put him above Turpin. Dave's faster than Turpin was. He's got more variety and he punches a bit harder. But this Hayes is something special. Christ, you've just seen him! He's like lightning. Never puts a foot wrong. Not as long as he's dictating the way the fight's going. What we've got to do is take the initiative away from him. And I'm telling you. There's only one way to do that. And that's give him the shock of his life. He's coming over here to fight a Britisher. You know what he'll expect? He'll expect someone that stands up straight and comes in behind a left jab and maybe crosses with a right and tries the odd left hook. I was over there a few weeks back and I heard them talking. They think Dave's a push-over. They think the title's in their pockets. They think British fighters are all easy touches. Well, we're going to show them different.'

Harold King said, 'Aye. That's all very well Phil, but like Micky and Jimmy says, Dave's not a slugger. You can't expect him to change overnight. You can't make a Rocky Marciano out of a lad who's always been a smart mover.'

Phil listened, nodding patiently. Then he said, 'Here. Let's finish this stuff. Who wants topping up?' He went round with the bottle, replenishing glasses and then sat down. He leaned forward and pointed at Harold. 'Okay, Harold. You've all had your say. I understand your worry. But I think you're wrong. It's as simple as this. If Dave goes in there to fight his usual fight he'll most likely lose—Now! Just a minute! Let me explain—Hayes just isn't going to be beaten at his own game. My guess is that Dave would take him a long way. Maybe the whole distance. But I think he'd be outscored. I can't see him matching Hayes for speed. And don't forget, Hayes is a wicked puncher. You saw the way he flattened that Mexican—what's-his-name—Garza. Nearly took off his head with that left hook. And Garza's no mug. No, Dave's got to go in there and stay close, rough him up, work away at the body, get the guard down and then slam over the big bombs to the head. The Hayes camp'll be taking a good look at Dave's fights on film. They'll be expecting the upright style. The way he fought Fournier. And we've got to give 'em a big surprise.'

Harold said. 'What about Dave? How d'you feel about it, son? Changing your style like Phil says?'

Dave shrugged. 'Phil's the boss. Everything he's taught me so far's worked. And I reckon he's right about Hayes. Looks like he's never taken a real punch. He's a good boxer all right. About the best I've ever seen. It'd be wrong to try and out-smart him like. But I bet I've got the edge regarding punching power. So that's what we'd have to work on I reckon.'

'And that's just what we're going to do,' Phil said. 'I've been doing a bit of planning. When Dave comes down to London next month to work for the Harvey fight we're going to have two training programmes. I'm talking about tactics now. He'll do his sparring for the Harvey fight with the usual lads. Johnny and Paul and Harry. Nothing different. Usual style and tactics. The press boys can come in and watch him. Okay. But then we'll bring in two new kids I've got. Tommy McGuire. I expect you've seen him. A light-middle from Belfast and a good 'un. He can punch a bit and he's very fast. And Jake Nemko, Commonwealth Welterweight Champion. Now, he's a strong boy and he's a speed merchant. He'll be perfect for Dave to try his new tactics on. He won't let Dave get away with a thing. If Dave gets careless he'll be punished. So we're going to be preparing for the warm-up, just the way we always do, Okay? But, at the same time, we're getting ready for Hayes. Behind closed doors. The Hayes camp'll be watching like hawks. They'll see Dave going about his usual routine. They'll see the Harvey fight. Touch wood, Dave'll box rings round him and stop him around the ninth or tenth. That's what I'd like to see, anyhow. A good work-out. Harvey's going to see the usual stand up, jab-and-move, orthodox Dave. And when we get down to training for the big one we'll follow the same plan. Dave'll have his ordinary sparring sessions for the media. But then we'll get down to the new tactics when the doors are shut. I'll bring in at least one extra sparring-partner. I've got him signed up. A kid called Leroy Coombes. Black Canadian light-middle. He's good. He's going to be perfect for Dave to work with. We're going to give Hayes the shock of his life.'

Phil leaned back and smiled. He looked at once excited and complacent.

Jimmy said, 'I dunno.'

'What?' Phil asked. 'What don't you know, Jimmy?'

'I don't know as you can change a fighter, not once he's found his style like. It's all right with youngsters. Novices. You can do anything. You can turn 'em round. Southpaws into orthodox. Anything. But once a lad's got it together it's different. And all this about closed doors. Secret work-outs. That's the kind of thing you get in comics.'

Phil shook his head. 'No Jimmy. You're wrong. This is for real. We're in the nineteen-eighties. You've got to be scientific. Psychology. The old days it was all simple. The boy did his roadwork, skipping, sparring and all that. Got himself ready physically. But nowadays you've got to get mentally ready too. Fights can be won and lost inside the boxer's nut. Look at Ali and Foreman. Ali, or his handlers, had worked that one out to the last full-stop. On the form book Foreman had to win. He'd smashed Frazier who'd beaten Ali. He'd half-killed Ken Norton in a couple of rounds and Norton had broken Ali's jaw and licked him on points. No way Ali could win that one. And what happened? Ali went into the ring and everybody, including Foreman, knew what to expect. Ali would use his speed and skill. He'd jab and move. Float like a butterfly, sting like a bee. The only hope he had was to outbox the killer. All right. And what did he do? He shocked everyone in that stadium. They couldn't believe their eyes. Everybody was bewildered. Especially Foreman. Ali, the dancing-master, the stick-and-move man. What did he do? He leaned back on the ropes and invited Foreman to hit him. He stood still, flat feet, back to the ropes and said, "Come on George. Come and hit me!". And Foreman was the hardest hitter in the world! Terrifying! And we all know what happened. The impossible. Ali foxed him, fooled him, psyched him, bewildered him for eight rounds. Did everything he wasn't supposed to do. And then he did the last thing that he shouldn't have done. He knocked Foreman cold.'

Phil's audience was quiet for a few moments. They seemed impressed.

Then Jimmy said, 'Aye. You're right, Phil. I s'pose I'm old-fashioned. I don't even know what they're on about sometimes. The way they talk. I heard that chap on telly the other week the one with the big moustache. On about Tommy Hearns or somebody. "He can take you out with one punch," he said. Take you out! That's what we used to do with girls, take 'em out.'

Micky chuckled. 'I know the one you mean. Fat-faced chap. None of 'em knows nothing about game. There's that other one. Barry Parsons. Funny little fella with a silly grin. I heard him doing the commentary on one of Pat Cowdell's fights. Can't remember Cowdell's opponent—Italian or Spaniard I think. Anyway Pat moved inside a left hook and catches this chap with a beautiful short right to the solar plexus. Lovely punch, smack on target. Down goes the Italian. And what does Barry say? "He's slipped!" he says. "So-and-so's slipped. It doesn't look as if he's getting up. I can't understand it." Everybody else could understand it all right. Poor bugger was paralyzed.'

Jimmy snorted. 'Experts! They don't know nothing.'

Phil said, 'It's just after ten. If you'd like another drink we could go down to the lounge. More comfortable. What about you, Dave? I expect you'd like to be on your way. Harold can take your dad home if he wants to stay for a nightcap?'

Dave stood up and the others also rose to their feet. 'Okay. Tom and me'll leave you to it then. That all right dad? You want to stay?

'Aye. Just have one for road. Harold'll run me back. I'll see

146

you early next week at gym. Give Aileen my love.'

Tom thanked Phil for the whisky and video show and he and Dave put on their coats, went out of the room into the corridor and descended in a lift to the ground floor. They did not speak until they were outside the front entrance of the hotel.

'It's bloody cold still,' Dave said. 'Let's get to car.'

City Square was fairly quiet. In the distance Tom heard the whiplash whirring of a police siren sting the night air. He hunched his shoulders and hurried at his friend's side to the car park where Dave unlocked the Capri and they both climbed in. The engine started on the second attempt and they moved off towards Headingley.

'Well?' Dave said, 'What did you think?'

'Of Hayes?'

'Aye.'

Tom paused. Then he said, 'I'd say he was unbeatable. But then, that's exactly what I felt about you when I saw you beat Vallejo. I think you're both unbeatable.'

Dave gave a little grunt of amusement. 'Nobody's unbeatable,' he said.

'No. That's what commonsense says. But some fighters are damn near it, aren't they? And what about Marciano? Nobody ever beat him?'

'Aye, he was a good 'un. A lion. Heart like a lion.' Dave slowed the car as it approached red traffic lights. The bright lozenges changed to orange, then lime, and the car moved forward. He spoke quietly almost as if to himself: 'So you think Hayes is going to lick me.'

'No! I didn't say that!'

'All right, mate. Don't get excited. And don't try and soft-soap me. I listen to you, Tom. I've got respect. You know that. So don't pull your punches.'

'I'm not, Dave. I'm trying as hard as I can to tell the truth. About the way I feel. I wasn't being funny when I said you both seem unbeatable. You do. Hayes tonight. I just couldn't see anyone staying with him. But it was just the same with you and Vallejo and what I saw of the Fournier fight on the box. They're both bloody good fighters but they looked like a different class, a different breed. I mean there was nothing they could do. Even when Fournier caught you—I think it was the fourth or fifth round—with that right hand over the top. It was a big punch. But I wasn't worried. You just came back at him and punished him. Poor sod. He must have known it was no good. Nothing could save him. You were in charge. Unbeatable.'

After a brief pause Dave said, 'You're as good as t'other fella let's you be. That's an old saying. And it's a true one.' Then he went on: 'I know what you mean. I feel same. It's funny—I mean it sounds like I'm bloody big-headed—but I can't see anybody licking me. I know it's daft. I ought to be shitting myself watching Hayes there tonight. All the punches. Even that bloody bolo punch that he winds up like a mangle or something. Talk about telegraphing a punch! You ought to see that one coming a mile away. But he caught 'em every time. And they wasn't mugs neither. He's a helluva fighter—brilliant. No doubt about it. But...' Tom sensed, rather than saw his slow grin. '...it's a funny thing. I'm not bothered. There isn't nobody at middleweight stronger than me. Nobody punches harder. When I catch 'em solid they've got to go. No question. And sooner or later I'll catch Hayes. I'll get to his chin and bugger'll have to go.'

Tom said, 'What do you feel about Phil's tactics for the fight?'

'That's Phil's job. He tells me what to do. He works it out. Then I go in there and do it... Ah, this is turn i'n't it?'

'What?... Oh yes. Round here. There you are, near that lamp-post, just behind that Datsun or whatever it is... Fine.' The car came to a stop. 'You going to come in for a coffee? It looks as it Peggy's there. I can see a light.'

'No I won't come in. Thanks all the same.'

'Okay. I'll give you a ring some time next week.'

'Aye.'

Tom moved to get out of the car when Dave said. 'You think Phil's wrong, do you? About pressuring Hayes. Roughing him up. Getting close.' He switched off the car lights.

'Wrong?' He settled back in the passenger seat. 'No. I don't know. I suppose I feel a bit the same as your dad. I can't imagine you changing your style like that. I mean I never thought of you as a smash-and-grab fighter. Maybe it'll work. I can see the reasoning. Why try and beat him at the game he's best at if you can force him to fight a way he's not used to. Surprise him. Break his composure. Rhythm. The theory's all right. But can you do it? Can you fight that sort of battle?'

'I don't know. Aye. I can if Phil says I can.'

'You've got a lot of faith in him. In Phil Richardson.'

'I have that.'

'Well, I hope it's justified.'

'Oh aye. It's justified all right. Think on 't, Tom. I'm World Champion. I wouldn't never've been without Phil. That's a fact. And another thing. Not many knows this. It were Phil taught me how to punch.'

'What? But you could—'

'Aye. I know what you're going to say. I could punch before Phil had me. True enough. I could punch all right. I punched like an amateur. A good amateur but not a pro. Not a real pro. Not a world class pro. There's a difference, Tom. And it was Phil taught me the difference. You've seen it yourself. I used to stop 'em, wear 'em down, put 'em on floor a couple of times before they stayed there or the ref come in and stopped it. Right? But after Phil took over you saw the difference. Mark Price, knocked out in three rounds. Clean knock-out. No messing. Joe Simonds, five rounds. Werner Bauer, three. Ramirez, four. I know the referee rescued Vallejo but he was out on his feet. Fournier, clean knock-out in the eleventh. And these was all world-class fighters. See what I mean?'

'But how? I mean how did Phil do it? What was the trick?'

'Well, it's not that easy to explain like. Not for me. Phil could tell you. He's bloody brilliant is Phil. They call him professor, the lads in London. I know it sounds a bit like dad said, comic book stuff. But it works, Tom. See, when Phil got me in gym after I'd signed with him he watched me work out and then he said, "Very nice Dave. But we've got to teach you to punch." I felt like putting one on his chin! Bloody nerve, I thought. But I didn't know him then. I soon learnt though. It's psychology, see? It's in the mind, partly. I know it sounds daft, but listen. You get one boxer. He's a nice mover. Punches correct. Clean. Knuckle part of glove. Shoulder, body-weight behind the punch. But the other fella stays on his feet. Why? That's the question Phil says you've got to ask yourself. Another fighter seems to punch just the same way and his opponent's flattened. What's the difference? The mental state, Phil reckons. It's like this, he says. You get a few fighters, not many, and they've got it natural. It's what they used to call a bit of tiger. They're killers. Every time they throw a punch, even a jab, it's meant to destroy you. Marciano was like that. This fella, Duran. Old timers like Dempsey. Not just heavy punchers. They're out to smash you. Kill you. I know. Sounds terrible don't it? But that's the game. Most of us haven't got it natural. Too civilized, Phil reckons. See what I mean? And if you haven't got it natural you've got to learn it. You've got to tell yourself every time you throw a punch—even a jab—it's going to break your man. Smash him. All the time. In the gym. Punching the bag. Sparring. Every punch you throw's got to be a bomb. Your fist's got to be a rock. It's got to be iron. You've got to get the habit. And that's what I learnt. I never throw a punch now that's not meant to kill.'

Dave broke the following silence with a sudden chuckle.

'You're a bit shocked, Tom, eh? It's a long way from the old St Joseph's Club. It's a different world.' Then he added, 'Anyway, don't worry. I wanted to talk to you about something else. We've had enough boxing for tonight, I reckon.'

'Something else? Okay. Fine. Look, why not come inside? Peggy'll fix us some coffee. Something to eat if you fancy it.'

'No. No, what I want to talk about isn't—well, I don't want anyone else to know. Nothing against Peggy, mind. It's very personal like.'

'Oh? All right.'

Dave was silent.

'What is it then?' Tom felt mild alarm. 'What's worrying you?'

'It's not worry exactly. Well, it is in a way. Aye, yes. I am a bit worried like. But it's all right. I just wanted to tell somebody. Ever since it happened I've wanted to talk about it.

You're the only one, Tom. I mean I can talk to you. Always could.'

Tom waited.

'It's hard to say it. Without I sound like a soft bugger.'

'Go on.'

'It's about me and Aileen and—well—somebody else.'

'Oh. Somebody else?'

'Aye. A girl.'

'Yes. Well. I thought it might be a girl.'

Dave, it seemed, detected no irony. 'Aye. I'm serious. She's terrific, Tom. Beautiful. I can't get her out of my mind. All the time. I can't think of nothing else. She's bloody marvellous.'

'You say you can't get her out of your mind. But do you see her? I mean it's not somebody you fancy from a distance? What I mean is you're—well, having an affair, sleeping together, fucking, call it what you like. Yes?'

'Yes.'

'I see. And what about Aileen? Does she know what's going on?'

'I don't know. Yes. I think she does. She's got a good idea anyway.'

'But you haven't talked about it?'

'No.'

'She doesn't know who the girl is?'

'No. She's just got suspicious. Me being out late and that. She smelt scent on me too.'

'And you denied everything. Yes?'

'Aye. That were a while back. She hasn't said nothing since. But I think she knows.'

'She must be very unhappy.'

'Yes . . . well . . . I'm not sure. I mean she seemed fed up at first. Miserable like. But the past two or three weeks she's changed. She's gone all sort of quiet. But not unhappy. Doesn't seem unhappy. Sort of dreamy, like she's thinking about something else all the time. It's hard to explain. I mean she doesn't seem to care when I go out now. I give her like excuses and that, but she don't take much notice. She just listens with a funny sort of smile. It bothers me a bit. I don't understand it.'

'Maybe she's got somebody herself. A lover.'

151

'Aileen? Never!' A pause. Then Dave said, 'You don't think so really, do you?'

Tom said, 'No, I don't. But how would you feel if she had?'

'How would I feel? Great. Terrific. It'd solve everything. I'd be able to have Judy—that's her name, the one I've been on about—and Aileen'd be happy as well.'

'And then what? Would you want to marry this girl, Judy?'

'I don't know. Aye. I think so. I haven't thought about it. It's hard to imagine it. Judy's not the kind you think of like that. She's not—ordinary like. She's more like—I don't know how to put it. Sort of glamorous. You know. You can't think of her like ordinary, with curlers in an' all that.'

Tom thought, 'Yeah, you think of her on her back with her legs in the air.' Aloud he said, 'What does she do for a living?'

'Judy? She's a singer. Classy stuff. She's been on telly. Sings at concerts and that. She's singing tonight. Some place in Bradford. A club, or something.'

'Oh.' Tom remembered the radio interview with Peggy. 'Oh yes. What's her second name?'

'Styles. Judy Styles.'

'Yeah. I remember. She's the one you met at the BBC with Peggy. That right?'

'That's right.'

The vague anxiety that had troubled Tom since Dave had first spoken of the girl deepened and sharpened. 'She's the one Peggy talked about on that radio thing you did. That's the girl isn't it?'

'Aye.'

'But didn't you know her before? You said you met her a few weeks ago. Wasn't there something about you and her being old friends?'

'Aye, but that wasn't right. Not really. I didn't really know her. I'd seen her a few times.'

'Christ!' Tom said, 'we could do without all this!'

There was an uncomfortable silence before Dave said, 'What d'you mean?' He sounded defensive, perhaps ready to be angry.

Tom spoke more cautiously: 'Well, it's not the best possible time to find yourself in this kind of mess, is it? I mean you've got the fight with Harvey in May and the whole build-up to the big one. Hayes. You know as well as anyone that you've got to be a hundred percent involved. If you're worried about Aileen and thinking about this girl, Judy. Christ, Dave, you don't need me to tell you. Between now and September you shouldn't have a thought in your head except licking Hayes. You *know* that, mate, don't you? I've heard you say the same thing about other fighters. You've got to be single-minded. You've got to be obsessed. I know you can't help falling for the girl. Don't think I'm blaming you. But you've got to admit it's not happened at the best of times.'

'I don't see as it's got to make any difference.'

'No Dave. Don't let's kid ourselves. Don't start lying to yourself. That's not going to help anybody. You're an honest man, Dave. I don't think I've ever known you to lie to anyone. And you've never lied to yourself. So don't start now. You *know* it makes a difference. How can you be thinking of nothing but destroying Hayes when every instinct says you want to be in bed with Judy. Love, infatuation, passion—call it what you like—it's an obsession, just about the most powerful magic there is. It bloody well scares me, Dave. And on top of everything you've got guilt. Worrying about Aileen. What she's feeling.'

Dave sat without speaking, his head lowered. Then he said, 'Aye. You're right, Tom. It's true. Like I said. I can't get her out of my mind. And Aileen. She don't seem so unhappy now but I'm still worried. I don't want to hurt her like. I mean she hasn't done nothing wrong. If I could get that sorted out. Me and Aileen. We never was what you might call in love. We shouldn't've married really. It just seemed what everybody expected. It were bloody daft, looking back. But if I got that sorted out and it were just Judy and me, I'd be all right. If things was tidied up like. See what I mean?'

'Not exactly. What d'you mean by getting you and Aileen sorted out? Are you talking about splitting up, divorce, or what?'

'I don't know. Aye. That's what I'd like. But I don't want to hurt her.'

'If she knows already. Or she's a good idea you're having it away with someone else, she's going to be hurt anyway. Telling her the truth won't make it worse. It can only help. That's what I'd do Dave. Tell her you've fallen in love with someone else. See what she says. If she's reasonable you can talk things over properly. You'll have to decide what you're going to do. I mean what sort of set-up has Judy got? Could you move in with her? What would you do about the house? You've got a solicitor, haven't you? At least Harold's bloke represents you, doesn't he? Oh, Jesus, it's a mess. I don't know. All I know is you've got to get yourself right quickly or you're going to blow the Hayes fight. Even the bloody warm-up. You've got to get yourself sorted out.'

'I won't blow it. I'll be all right.'

'Yeah. I hope so. I hope so.'

Neither spoke for a few seconds. Then Dave said, 'Listen Tom. Could you talk to her? To Aileen. I mean you're good at explaining. You know I'm no good at—'

'No. No I couldn't Dave. She'd hate that. She'd hate you and she'd hate me. She'd be furious if she knew you'd told me all this. You'll have to tell her yourself. Just tell her the truth. Don't commit yourself with the other one. With Judy. Box clever, Dave. Keep your sights on the next two fights. If you beat Hayes the whole bloody world's yours. You'll be set for life. Get your problems out of the way. Shelve them if you can. Listen you're going to London next month, aren't you? To get ready for Harvey. You want to get the whole thing tidied up by then or you'll be fucked. Have a talk with Aileen. See what happens. Be as nice as you can. Tell her you're fond of her but. This other thing's bigger than both of you. That kind of crap. See what happens. But for Christ's sake get your priorities straight. You've spent your whole life so far to get where you've got to. The world title. Don't fuck it up, Dave. It'd be a catastrophe.'

'All right. I'll talk to her. Tomorrow.'

'Tonight if she's still awake. What time is it now? Twenty past eleven. Maybe tomorrow'd be best. And let me know, Dave. Let me know what happens. Give us a ring. Any time over the weekend. All right?'

Dave said that he would and Tom got out of the car.

'Well goodnight, mate,' he said. 'And good luck. It might not be as bad as you think. Keep in touch.'

Dave said goodnight, switched on the car's headlamps and Tom watched as the Capri did a three-point turn and moved away towards the main road. Then he let himself into the flat where he found Peggy in the sitting-room watching *Newsnight* on television. He took off his coat and threw it on the sofa.

She rose and switched off the set. 'What you been doing?' she said. 'I heard the car stop ages ago, didn't I?'

They both sat down in the armchairs in front of the gas fire.

'Yeah. I've been talking to Dave.'

'Why didn't you bring him in?'

'He didn't want to come. Wanted to talk about something personal.'

'Big man talk? Something the little woman wouldn't understand.'

'No. Something he didn't want the little woman shouting her mouth off about.'

Peggy's chin jerked up and her eyes widened with surprise and some indignation. 'What d'you mean? Since when have I been shouting my mouth off about Dave's business. As if I'd be interested enough.'

'You'd be interested in this bit of business. Since you started it in the first place . . . well, in a way.'

'What bit of business? What the hell are you talking about?'

'Nothing. Forget it.'

'Oh come on, Tom. What's up? What's the matter with you? You look as if you've been given a death sentence. What are you talking about?'

'Dave's got himself a woman. I don't suppose I should tell you really but as long as you promise to keep it to yourself. And I mean that. Don't tell anybody. At work or anywhere.'

'Of course I won't.' She waited. 'Well, go on. Who is she?'

'That singer you told me about. Judy Styles. The one he met at the studio.'

Peggy looked surprised, then a slow smile spread and little sparks of excitement in her eyes. 'So there was something between them! I sensed there was. What's happening? What did Dave want to talk about?'

'What's happening is a bloody disaster.'

'Why. In what way a disaster?'

'He's daft about her. Besotted. Can't think of anything else, he says.'

'And what about her? Did he tell you?'

'I don't know. I've never seen the bloody woman. She may be stringing him along. After his money. God knows. They're certainly screwing. No doubt about that.'

'But what's so terrible? I mean I don't want to sound bitchy but that wife of Dave's isn't the kind of lady you'd go out and fight dragons for, is she? She's probably a dab-hand at making Yorkshire pudding but I bet she's a bit of cold pudding herself in the sack. And you've not seen Judy, as you say. If you had, you'd probably see why Dave's so wild about her. She's quite something. She'll be good for him. I hope they're having a ball.'

'You hope they're having a ball! And what about Aileen? Okay, you say she's a lump of cold pudding. But she's married to him. She's a woman and she's going to be hurt. Dave knows that and he's worried sick about it. And if Judy's the dreamboat you say she is, I find no cause for rejoicing in that. He's a fighter. He's got two fights coming up in the next five months and even if he survives the first one Hayes'll tear him apart. He'll murder him. You can't train for this game in the bloody bedroom. He's got to give every inch and ounce of himself to getting ready for Hayes. I tell you. It's a disaster.'

Peggy's eyes narrowed and she nodded to herself. 'You're not worried about Aileen,' she said. 'You're not really worried about Dave. All that matters to you is this damned boxing thing, isn't it? You don't really care whether he's happy or miserable, only as far as it affects his fighting. I think you're bloody mad, Tom. I really do.'

'Of course I care about Dave! He's a fighter. He's the World Champion. Take that away from him and he's nothing.'

'You tell that to Judy Styles. He's supposed to be your great friend. Ever since you were kids. Are you telling me the only thing you care about's his boxing? It's not the man you like? If that's the case—and it seems as if it is—then I'm disgusted.'

Tom shook, not just his head but hands and shoulders too, in a galvanic movement of denial and protest. 'No. No, you don't understand. 'Course he's my friend. It's him I like. It's him I'm worried about. But it's true what I say. He's a fighter. You can't understand what that means. It's not just his job. Not just what he does for a living. It's a lot more than that. More than a vocation even. It's his reason for being. It really is. I know this sounds daft to you but boxing's his art, religion, his faith. Everything. It's his language and grammar. It's the only way he can really say what he believes, what he is. And if he gets distracted now. If he loses one tiny scrap of concentration, he's had it. And if he's beaten he'll be finished. He'll hate himself and sooner or later he'll hate the woman. Do you see what I mean? If Hayes was to beat him anyway. I mean supposing Dave'd never met Judy Styles. Supposing he went into the ring a hundred percent fit and ready. No worries. And he still got licked. That'd be all right. He wouldn't be destroyed. He'd know that he'd done everything he could. There's nothing disgraceful in being beaten by a fighter like Hayes. Dave'd still be the man he was. But if he got beaten because of her—or not necessarily *because*, but if he *thought* she was the reason—he'd be finished . . . I wish—oh, I don't know. What's she like, this Judy woman? I wonder if I ought to go and talk to her.'

Peggy shook her head. 'I don't think that'd do anyone much good.'

'It might. If she really cares about him. She might—'

'Oh Tom! You're so bloody naive at times. She might what? Say she'll give him up for the sake of his career? Sacrifice her love to the greater glory of the World Championship? Never! I don't know what she's like really. She seemed okay. Smart, sexy. Not stupid but not overbright either. I don't know. I heard a bit of gossip at the club. Nothing much. Some stuff about her and a bloke called Colin Hunter.'

'Yeah. I've heard of him. He's a local tycoon. Owns a lot of property in West Yorkshire. Got one or two clubs, gambling places. Used to run the odd dinner show at the Lonsdale Club. I think Dave boxed there a couple of times. What about him?'

'Only vague stuff about her being his chick. Apparently he's married with kids and all that but he takes Judy around quite a lot. Or used to. Maybe she's ditched him now Dave's on the scene.'

'Maybe.'

'Hey! You're not thinking of stirring things up with that bit of information are you? Telling Dave she's two-timing him? Because I'd forget it if I were you. For a start you might be quite wrong. And another thing. Even if she was still seeing this chap, Hunter. If she was running the pair of them at the same time. You wouldn't be doing Dave any favours if you told him—you're looking doubtful. Well, you needn't be. You can take it from me. Even if you had definite evidence of Judy having another bloke. If you could prove she was cheating on Dave, you don't think he'd say, "Oh dear. I've made a big mistake. Back to the old gymnasium and the Yorkshire pudding. Forget sex. Forget love. Forget Judy." Of course he wouldn't! He'd be torn to pieces. He'd be a lot less likely to be able to concentrate on his practising or whatever you call it. He'd be demented. Maybe from the boxing point of view it wasn't a good thing, him and Judy. But the best thing to be done now is make it as smooth as possible. It's happened and nothing can make it unhappen. And to tell you the truth, I'm quite glad. I think it's romantic.'

'You won't think it's so romantic when Hayes cuts him to ribbons.'

'Then he can retire. From what I've heard he'll have heaps of money. She can kiss him better. And they can live happy ever after.'

Tom grunted. 'What you heard was probably a load of rubbish.'

'What d'you mean? I heard he was getting over a quarter of a million for the fight with the black man.'

'Yeah. It sounds a lot. But when the manager—or managers in Dave's case—and all the training expenses have taken their slice and then the Inland Revenue has a grab it doesn't look such a huge fortune. You'd be surprised.'

'But still quite a lot.'

'I suppose so. But it's a short working life. Anyway, to hell with the economics of it. You think the best thing for Dave'll be to sort out everything with Aileen and somehow get

158

himself settled with Judy. That right?'

'If she's serious. Yes.'

Tom thought for a moment. Then he said, 'That's what I thought really. I suppose he could have a kind of honeymoon with the—with Judy—before he goes to London. That's in about four weeks time. I only hope he doesn't get any daft ideas about taking her down with him. Though come to think of it Phil Richardson'd soon squash that one.'

'Why shouldn't she go with him?'

'Because sex and boxing don't mix. I believe in the old-fashioned view. It softens you. Sex is for multiplying. Even if the last thing you want's a kid. That's what it's for. Making. A figher's got to be mean, vicious, destructive. Fighting's murderous.'

'But you've often said it's aesthetic! You've said—'

'I don't give a fuck what I've said. You've got to have the killer-instinct. The tiger. If you haven't got it you're finished. That's the truth. Whether you like it or not. Whether I like it or not. It's the truth.'

'Then I think it's horrible.'

'Yeah. But my God, it's magnificent too.'

Peggy shook her head slowly. 'You're a funny bugger, Tom Darwin,' she said. 'Sometimes I don't think I know you at all.'

CHAPTER TWELVE

O N SUNDAY MORNING Dave awoke and so
immediate were his thoughts of Judy and
the previous eveing that they seemed like an uninterrupted
continuation of the play of images that had dissolved with the
coming of sleep. Aileen lay with her back to him, curled into
the foetal position, either fast asleep or pretending to be.
Weak daylight filtered through the bedroom window
curtains. He lay for a couple of minutes, luxuriating in his
recollections; then he moved out of bed with great care,
slipped into his underclothes and let himself out of the room
closing the door gently behind him. Downstairs, in the hall
cloakroom he put on his track-suit, socks and heavy boots and
pulled his knitted woollen hat on to his head. Then he let
himself out of the house and set off at a trot towards Roundhay
Park.

The fabric of mist was wearing thin and pale sunlight
promised a day of brightness. The streets were deserted and he
encountered no one as he jogged along Prince's Avenue, into
Mansion Lane, past the hotel and down the grassy hill to
Waterloo Lake which lay, spread like grey hammered metal in
the cold morning air. Dave increased his pace a little as he
began his first circuit of the lake and, while he pounded along
the uneven path, he thought of Aileen with anxiety and guilt
and exasperation.

When he had got home on Friday night after his talk with
Tom she had already gone to bed and though she was still
awake he had judged it an inopportune moment to speak of his
love for Judy. Saturday, too, had not provided what seemed a

suitable moment and, in the evening, he had gone to see Judy, offering Aileen only the most perfunctory explanation of 'going out to see a bloke'. As had recently become usual Aileen had shown neither curiosity nor positive resentment, but she had smiled and nodded with that kind of patient, indulgent acceptance which a mother will sometimes show in the face of a child's obstinate naughtiness. But he would talk to her soon, he promised himself. Today if possible. Tell her the truth. Everything. Get things sorted out. Tom had been right when they'd talked on Friday. Things couldn't go on much longer the way they were.

Judy had been lovely the night before. Every time he saw her it was like the first time. He sometimes thought, in those hours of waiting, when they were apart, that he was building her up in his mind into something more wonderful than she really was. But never. She was always even more beautiful. It was always a shock. And she was always so right, so exactly what he wanted. Never sulky or miserable or unfriendly. And passionate and sexy. Jesus, he didn't know girls could be like that. Not unless they were whores or something.

Last night he had got back home at about one-fifteen. So he'd had about six hours sleep. But he felt terrific. All that talk the old-timers gave you about sex being bad, weakening. It was all cobblers. He felt great. As strong as a lion. He'd show Wayne Harvey whether he was strong or not. And Hayes. Like Phil said: Hayes was going to get a shock. They thought British fighters was pushovers, did they? Well they'd find out a bit different.

He had reached Carriage Drive and looked back, over his shoulder to the Wetherby Road entrance and thought of Judy, in her flat just beyond there; probably—almost certainly—still asleep. He had to push down the rising flood of tenderness and desire and force his thoughts towards the harsher imagery of ring and gymnasium, the unerotic machines of the fight-game, ropes, gumshields, protectors, jock-straps, bandages; sweat, snot, blood. He ran on, driving himself harder, faster. A light sweat was beginning to shimmer beneath the woollen garments. Muscles were supple, obedient; his breathing heavier but quite regular and easy. He ran on, keeping his rhythm, opening lungs to the cold sweet air. Four circuits, he decided, and then back for a bath. Think of the London gym. Working out with the lads. Slamming the heavy bag. Your fists bunched hard to iron weapons. Crashing them in. Hard. Hard. Hard.

He ran and ran and ran. He could feel the sweat in his hair, prickling on forehead, slippery on his torso. He had always enjoyed training. That was one of the reasons why he was a champion. Some of the lads—good fighters, bags of guts, clever movers—but they didn't like the graft. They had to do it but they didn't like it. They'd go through the motions, hating it, the pain, the sweat, the going on and on when your body was screaming out 'No more! Pack it in! That's enough!' But he liked it, always had. He was a glutton for it. That's what dad used to say. Right from the start when Dave was a kid in the Schoolboys and the Juniors. 'By,' he used to say, 'you're a glutton for it. If I'd been like you, son, I'd a been a world-beater.'

But, behind the bleak images of his trade, the presence of Judy persisted like the pale sun behind the mist and cloud of the morning, so that when, towards the end of his fourth lap round the lake, he again reached Carriage Drive, he hesitated and then turned towards the Wetherby Road, trotting more slowly towards the park gates where he stopped for a few irresolute moments. She was there, so close; all he had to do was cross the road and run a mere hundred yards or so and he would be at her door. He could not deny himself.

A couple of minutes later he was at the now familiar back door, pressing the bell and hearing the urgent blurt of noise inside the flat. He waited. There was no sound from within. He pressed the bell again, keeping his forefinger on the button for a longer time. A glance at his watch told him that it was ten minutes past eight. Surely she could not have risen and gone out at such an early hour. And then doubt was suddenly hatched, small but alive in his consciousness. Perhaps she would not want to be awakened. She might even now be warm in bed, awake, and cursing whoever was ringing her doorbell, disturbing her Sunday morning lie-in. And here he was, scruffy in his old track suit and silly hat, hot and sweaty from his run. She'd probably be bloody mad at him, tell him to piss off.

He was about to turn away when he heard the sound of the bolt being slid back and the door, still on its safety chain, was opened a few inches and he glimpsed Judy's perhaps alarmed eyes peering from the shadows before the door was briefly shut to be reopened wide.

'Dave!' She exclaimed and seized one of his hands in both of hers and pulled him inside the hall where she promptly flung both her arms around him and pressed her mouth to his.

'Oh love,' she said when she had withdrawn her lips, 'How lovely. What a wonderful surprise. That hat! It's beautiful. Come on. In here. I'm bloody freezing.'

He pulled off the woollen hat and followed her into the bedroom where she threw off the dressing-gown that she had obviously slipped into when she heard the doorbell and beneath which she was naked, just as she had been when he had left her a few hours before. She wriggled into bed, pulling the coverings up to her chin.

'Come over here,' she said.

He sat on the bed and stared at her. 'You look terrific,' he said. 'Your hair all over the place like that. Terrific.'

She held up her face, lips pouted in invitation, and he kissed her again.

She said, 'Come on. Into bed. Hurry up.'

He laughed. 'I can't love. I'm all sweaty. Horrible. I've been running.'

'I don't care. Into bed. That's an order. Quick-sharp!'

'Honest. I stink. You can't—'

'Shut up. Don't argue and get those things off, Dave Ruddock. You've got to warm me up. You dragged me out of bed at dawn and made me get cold so you've got to get me warm again. Pronto!'

'But...'

'Come on!'

He heard the real impatience behind the bantering tone and it excited him. When he had removed his boots and his clothes Judy pulled back the sheet and blankets for him to join her. As he climbed in she said, 'Oh you're beautiful Dave!' and then

163

they were clinging together, moving and caressing and kissing and moaning before he spread her thighs and entered her, crying his triumph and joy and despair as they struggled both to postpone and arrive at the sweetly savage, soft explosive goal of consummation.

'Some minutes later Judy said in a smaller, different voice, 'Yes. You do pong a bit.'

'I told you,' he said. 'It was you said it didn't matter.' He sounded offended.

'I love it. It's a lovely pong.'

'No. I'll go and have a bath.'

'I mean it, love. I like it. It's you. Come here and kiss me.'

More time passed. Then she said. 'It must be getting late.'

'Nearly half-past nine.'

'Would you really like a bath?'

'I'll wait. I can have one when I get back. I've only got those mucky things to put on anyway.'

'Can't you stay all day?'

'Wish I could. But she'll have dinner got ready. Anyway, like I said, I haven't got clothes.'

'You don't need clothes.'

'Aye . . . well . . . I'd best be up.'

'All right love.'

But neither moved except to touch and caress each other and kiss.

Quite a long time later he said, 'Right. This won't do,' and he disentangled himself from her and got out of bed.

She watched him dress.

'You're a beautiful man, Mr Ruddock,' she said.

He grinned, self-conscious, embarrassed but pleased. Then he said, suddenly very serious, 'No. You're the beautiful one. Most beautiful in the world. That's a fact.'

Now dressed he stood looking down at her. Without any make-up, her fair hair in disarray, lips looking swollen from his kisses and her green eyes hazed with secret, pleasing thoughts, she looked younger yet more wanton than when she was dressed and made up for public scrutiny.

She said, 'Do you want some coffee? Breakfast?'

He shook his head. 'I'll have something when I get back.'

Then he sat on the side of the bed and took one of her hands in his. 'Listen,' he said. 'I were thinking. I reckon I ought to tell Aileen. You know. About us.'

She did not answer but looked up at him from the pillows, her eyes serious, perhaps a little wary.

'What d'you think? D'you reckon it's a good idea? I mean—well, me and you. Is it serious like? I mean we never talk a lot about it. Neither of us. What we going to do, Judy?'

She squeezed his hand. 'I know. I know what you mean. This's lovely seeing each other like we've been doing. But it can't stay the same forever. We both know that. We've both got to make up our minds what we want, what we really want. And don't think I haven't been worrying about it because I have. Ever since we started. And I'm still not sure. I don't mean not sure about what I feel. That's simple enough. I mean about the future. I don't want to make promises I can't keep. I care about you too much for that Dave. You see?'

He nodded but did not really understand all that she said. She was not sure about the future but she was sure about her feelings for him. Yet she had not said what those feelings were.

He said, 'Then you don't think I ought to say nothing to her—to Aileen.'

'I don't know. I think that's your decision, Dave. I'm not the one to give advice there, am I? I mean I'm not exactly a disinterested party. The only thing is—from everything you've told me—your marriage is a wash-out anyway. Even if you'd never met me. If I didn't even exist. So it's for you to decide what you tell Aileen. I'm not saying don't tell her about me. About us. I'm not saying tell her. It's your own choice.'

He released her hand and stood up. 'Aye. You're right. It's up to me.'

He turned and took a few paces towards the door and then hesitated, looking back at Judy. A frown wrinkled his forehead and his eyes looked thoughtful, morose.

She said, 'What's wrong, love?'

'Nothing.'

'Come on. What is it? You're worried about something. Is it because I'm not going to say get rid of your wife. Tell her to pack her bags. And then we'll get married and live happy ever

165

after. You disappointed in me, Dave? Is that it?'

He shook his head. 'No. It's . . . nothing really. I was just thinking . . . '

'What? What were you just thinking?'

'Well. I know I asked a while ago. Soon after we met like. I asked you about other blokes an' you gave me a right roasting. None of my business. I was married and all that. Okay. Fair enough. But if I'm going to tell Aileen about us and that's what I want to do—I reckon I ought to know.'

'Ought to know what exactly?'

'Well . . . ' Dave's head jerked to one side as if he were slipping a left lead. 'You know. Is there anybody else. Am I the champ or just one o' the contenders.' Neither his attempt at a jocular tone nor his grin was very successful.

Judy watched his embarrassment for a few cool seconds. Then she said. 'Come here. Come on.' She patted the side of the bed.

He did as he was told and when he was sitting there she took his hand and said, 'One thing you don't have to worry about is what I feel about you. You understand? You're the only one. You're not the first. You don't need to be told that. Maybe you won't be the last. But the way I feel now I wish I could say just that. You're the only man I want and, as far as I can tell, you're the only man I'll ever want. I've never believed in this till death us do part stuff before. But for the first time in my life I'm beginning to see why people feel like that. So you don't have to worry about that. You go home and tell your little wife whatever you feel you've got to tell her. But it's your decision. Whatever happens I'll be here. Okay? Oh, before you go. What about tonight? Are you coming round or have I got to make do with this morning?'

'No. Yes. I mean yes I'll be seeing you tonight.'

'Good. I think I'll have another little sleep. You're an exhausting man, Mr Ruddock, as well as beautiful.'

They kissed a few more times and then Dave left and began to run back, returning through the park where the lake was now silvery in the strengthening sunlight.

On the kitchen table vegetables had been prepared for cooking but the oven had not been lit. Dave looked into the empty lounge and then called 'Aileen!' from the foot of the stairs. There was no answer. He ran up to their bedroom but it, too, was empty. He called again, and still there was no reply. Obviously she was not in the house. He returned to the kitchen and drank some orange juice. Then he went up to the bathroom and turned on the tap. He stripped and threw his track-suit and underclothes into the laundry basket. Back in the bedroom he performed a few press-ups before returning to the bathroom, where he added cold water until the temperature was acceptable and climbed into the bath.

Half an hour later, dressed in polo-neck sweater and jeans, he was sitting in the lounge with a mug of instant coffee on the table at the side of his armchair reading in the *Sunday Express* an article about the English cricketers who had accepted a lucrative invitation to tour South Africa. He did not understand what the fuss was about. Politics was something that other people, educated people like Tom Darwin, got excited about. Tom had told him that the government of South Africa was evil. Dave could understand the injustices of discriminating against the blacks. It was their country. They were as good as whites as far as he was concerned. Look at all the great black fighters. But he couldn't see what harm the cricketers were doing playing cricket in South Africa. Unless the black people weren't allowed to play against them or even watch the matches. The article didn't say whether this would be the case.

He dropped the newspaper, finished his coffee and took the mug into the kitchen, rinsed it under the hot tap, dried it and returned it to its place in the china cupboard. The long, colourless Sunday lay before him, eight hours at least before he would see Judy again. Perhaps he would go and see Tom in the afternoon. Or he and Aileen could go for tea with his mam and dad. But where was Aileen? It wasn't like her just to go out for a walk and he'd never known her go and visit any of her friends on a Sunday. Not that she had many friends. Just that copper's wife and the other one, Madge somebody-or-other.

Suddenly he was troubled by a small but sharp stab of

anxiety. Aileen had seemed odd lately. That funny little smile, as if she was miles away with her own little secret thoughts. Sometimes he'd spoken to her and she hadn't heard. He'd had to say it again, whatever it was, and she'd sort of come awake with a jump and even then she'd not really listened. It was worrying. It was bad enough when she got nasty tempered and complaining. But he could handle that. If somebody went for you, you could hit back. Like that time she said she'd smelt the scent. If she went for him like that again it would be easy. He'd tell her straight. Tell her about Judy. But it wasn't so easy when she was all dreamy, living in another world, not really listening to anything he said.

He looked at his watch. It was almost noon. He went into the hall and put on his coat. He'd drive around. See if he could see her. Maybe call in at mam and dad's, though he doubted whether she would go there on her own. But you never knew. It was worth a try.

Outside, he unlocked the garage and got into the car, started it and reversed into the open. He was moving down the drive when she appeared, walking towards him, and he stamped on the brake pedal and clutch, slipped the gears into neutral and put on the hand-brake. He watched her as she approached. She was dressed in her new wide-skirted woollen coat with short cape, small-brimmed felt hat and court shoes. The effect was one of neatness, respectability, rather than charm. She did not change her pace or show any sign of having seen him. He lowered the car window and waited for her to draw level.

He said, 'I were just coming to look for you. Where you been?'

She stopped and looked down at him. 'You'd gone out when I got up. I waited till after ten.'

'You should've left a message.'

'I never thought you'd be bothered. Never thought of it.'

'Where've you been then?' he said again.

'Out.'

'I know you've been out. Where to? Where'd you go?'

She said, 'I've to get the roast on,' and walked towards the house.

Dave reversed and returned the car to the garage. Then he

went into the kitchen where Aileen, divested of hat, coat and formal shoes and wearing over her dress a plastic apron, was busy at the stove. She did not turn to look at him as he entered, but shifted pans and turned away from the cooker, wiped her hands on the kitchen towel and then removed her apron, hanging it up on the back of the door.

'I asked you where you'd been?'

'Nowhere special,' she said, and walked out of the kitchen and into the lounge where she picked up the newspaper which Dave had been reading and sat down in one of the armchairs.

He followed and said, 'What's the mystery, Aileen? What's up with telling me where you been?'

She looked up from the newspaper. 'It's not your business where I've been. If you think it is, then it's got to work both ways. If you've got the right to ask me where I've been, same goes for me, don't it? So where did you go last night? And last Thursday? And the night before that?' She spoke quite reasonably, without rancour and, though she was not smiling, her eyes held that curious look of secret knowledge which had recently been perplexing him.

He walked to the french windows and looked out at the garden for a few seconds before turning away and taking the chair opposite hers.

He cleared his throat and said, 'I know, Aileen. I know I've been acting rotten. I've been wanting to talk to you. About that. About me being out late an' everything.'

She waited, looking at him with patient, only mild interest. She looked nice, he thought, in her navy blue suit and white lace blouse. Not glamorous and breath-stopping like Judy, but very neat and clean and shiny. Like a secretary.

A shaft of thin golden sunlight leaned from the french windows into the room. Dave felt the faint, muffled pang of regret that the uncomplicated, calm, domestic comfort and certainty were threatened, a small nostalgia for the lost days when his professional ambition and obsession dwarfed every other consideration, when life outside the gym and the arena was simply a peaceful haven from the bruising hardships, the grinding procedures of training and the tensions, excitements and euphoria of battle; a nostalgia for the pre-Judy days. This

169

sensation, tiny and evanescent though it was, left behind a feeling of guilt and betrayal, almost an outrage that he should be capable of such ingratitude. And an image of Judy, as he had last seen her, beautiful, unruly, vulnerable, naked and achingly desirable made his heart melt with protective longing.

He said, 'It's hard to tell you, love. I don't really know how to say it.'

Still she said nothing.

Dave flicked his nose quickly and lightly with his right thumb, an old-fashioned boxer's habit, first acquired in imitation of his father, but now an involuntary gesture of embarrassment and confusion.

Then he said, 'I've been going out with somebody else. A girl.'

Her expression did not change. She put down the newspaper, nodded and said, 'I know.'

Dave stared. 'You mean . . . ? How did you know? Who told you?'

A very faint smile, sad, almost pitying, touched Aileen's mouth then went away. 'I didn't need telling. It were obvious.'

He released a long exhalation of breath that he had been unaware of holding. 'Aye . . . Aye, it must've been obvious.'

She nodded.

'Well,' he said. 'I thought I ought to tell you. Get it in open like. So's we can talk about it. See what we're going to do.'

'Who is she?'

When Aileen had said that she knew that there was someone else Dave had taken it that she also knew the identity of the woman. Now he realised that her apparent acceptance of the situation would probably have been much less cool had she known that the girl was Judy.

He said, 'I don't see as that matters.'

'No? Well, I'll have to know sooner of later, won't I? If you're going on seeing her. Or are you telling me about it 'cause you've finished with her?'

'No.'

'You're not finished?'

'No.'

'So you'd best tell me who she is, hadn't you?'

'You don't know her.'

'No. Well I didn't think I would.'

'So I don't see sense in telling you her name.'

She shrugged. 'All right. What d'you want me to do about it?'

.'I don't know. I mean I thought we could sort of talk about it. See best thing to do like. For both of us.'

'What d'you want then? Me to go away? Get a divorce? Marry this other one or what?'

Dave moved uncomfortably in his chair. 'I don't know. What's best for you really. I mean you don't have to worry. About money. Things like that. You can have the house if you want. I know it's too big but you could sell it. Get a smaller place.'

'I don't want your money.' For the first time since they had been talking, she showed a flicker of anger.

He said. 'No. No, love. But it's only right, i'n't it? It's all been my fault. We shouldn't've got married in first place. I should've known better.'

She nodded. 'It looks that way now. It didn't at time though, did it? You was keen enough then.'

'Aye...well...' Dave knew that he had to move carefully if he was to avoid hurting her more than necessary. 'I thought it were going to be all right.'

'It was till you went off and found this other woman. Whoever she is.'

'No. No it weren't, love. Not really.'

'Why not? What were wrong with it? It were all right. Good as most marriages.'

'No.'

'Why not? Why d'you keep saying that? What were wrong with it then?'

'Aileen...you never was...well, you know. What's the word? You was never very loving. You know. Romantic like. In bed and that.'

Now she was unequivocally angry. 'Romantic! Romantic! what d'you mean romantic? I'll tell you what you mean. You mean dirty. Mucky. Sex. That's what you mean. You talk about loving. I was loving all right. I loved you Dave. I used to come up to London every weekend. That horrible flat. An' all you wanted was to get into bed. I never said no. Not after the first time. I knew it were wrong. I knew it were a sin. There weren't nothing I wouldn't've done for you, Dave. Even that. Even sin.'

'For Christ's sake, don't—'

'And don't use the Lord's name in vain!' Her voice was high. The ripples of sound and passion slowly settled.

Dave said, 'It looks like we can't really talk without we get upset.'

'I'm sorry. I shouldn't have shouted at you. But you know I hate that. Blasphemy.'

'No. It's me should be sorry. It were my fault.'

Another short silence.

Then Aileen said, 'Listen Dave. I want you to understand. I'm not asking you to change your mind about anything. But I want you to understand. About love. About the way I felt . . . No, listen . . . When I were—what?—twelve, thirteen, about that kind of age—I used to see you in school. See you with other lads at playtime. Never spoke to you. You know that. You was older. Anyway you wasn't interested in girls. So they all said. But I thought you was fantastic. I used to dream about you all the time. Asleep and awake. And after you left school I used to hang about near your house. Hoping just for a look at you. You never knew that, did you? I never told you that. But it's true. And that day, in park. That day Carole and me was there and you an' that lad Brian May got talking to us. It were like a dream come true. I couldn't believe it. Dave Ruddock. Taking me to pictures. It were like magic. Romantic! There weren't anybody more romantic than what I were, Dave. It were lovely. I can't tell you. Magic.'

Dave had been listening with growing incredulity and a kind of horrified pity. Aileen had felt about him just as he had felt about Judy years ago when he was a kid.

He said, 'I never knew.'

'No.' Her slow smile was gentle, and again almost pitying. 'No I never told you. I didn't think you'd understand.'

He shook his head. 'But . . .'

172

She waited. Then, when he did not continue, she said, 'But what?'

'Well. I mean if you felt like that. If—well, wouldn't it . . . I mean shouldn't it've been great? When we made love like?'

'That's not love, Dave. That's lust.'

'Ah now. No. No. Wait a minute. I won't have that. Not for most people it isn't. You're wrong there, Aileen. I mean if you do it with somebody you don't like. Just for your own pleasure. Aye. That'd be wrong. That'd be what you call lust. But if the two of you—like you said—loved each other, well it's natural then i'n't it? It's what it's all about. It's what people get married for. Make love and have kids an' everything.'

'We wasn't doing it to have kids. That's what it's for. Procreation of children. If it's not for that, it's physical,' she said. 'Like animals.'

'We *are* animals! Tom told me about it. It's commonsense anyway.'

'Tom! You think he knows everything. Just because he's been to college and that. He doesn't know nothing. He's wicked. He's an atheist, that's what he is.'

'Hey. Wait a minute. He's all right is Tom. He's a good mate. I've known him best part o' my life. He knows what he's on about does Tom.'

Aileen shook her head. Her face had gone pink, her lips were pressed tightly together and her eyes had narrowed.

Dave said, 'Look. Forget Tom. we're not getting anywhere like this. We've got to make up our minds what we're going to do.'

'It's up to you.'

'No. We're married, aren't we? It's not just me. We've got to decide things. I'm not just going to walk out on you. We've got to fix money an' all that. Where you're going to live. Here or somewhere else. Things like that.'

Much of Aileen's composure had now returned.

She said, 'You never told me when I asked you. You want to marry whatever-her-name is? This woman that's not got a name?

'I don't know. Me an' her's never talked about it. Not marrying, we haven't.'

'No. I expect you're too busy with other things.'

Dave decided to take this jab without countering. 'She's got her own work an' that. She knows I'm married. So we never said nothing about getting married.'

'She knows you're married, does she? But she's no objection to stealing somebody else's husband then. That doesn't worry her. And what about her? Is she married? Or does she just use other women's men?'

'It's not like that, Aileen.'

Her small show of bitterness and resentment faded quickly and she seemed again almost uninterested. 'No. All right then. You'd better decide what you want to do. If it's divorce. Or what. And you might as well tell me the woman's name 'cause I've got to know sooner or later, haven't I?'

'I'd better talk to her first.'

Aileen stood up. 'Do as you like. I've got other things to do.' She began to walk to the door.

'Aileen.'

She paused with a hand on the door handle.

He said, 'Where was you this morning? When I was out running.'

A tiny smile moved on her lips but her eyes were vague and perhaps sad. 'I've got secrets too,' she said, and opened the door, went out and closed it softly behind her.

CHAPTER THIRTEEN

INDECISION AND PROCRASTINATION, the spell of erotic enchantment, collaborated to perform that cunning sleight of time which flicked the days past so rapidly that, when they were suddenly displayed as complete weeks, Dave was shaken by a panic of disbelief. After his Sunday morning talk with Aileen she had moved into one of the spare bedrooms, a manoeuvre on which neither of them had commented. At first he had watched her carefully and uneasily for signs of unhappiness or anger, but it seemed that she had simply resumed the strange, placid, drifting life which she had adopted during the two or three weeks before the unresolved discussion of their future. Dave continued his light training, running each morning in the park, though he always now resisted the temptation to interrupt or conclude his exercise with a visit to Judy and the perhaps no less strenuous but agreeably different exercise that she would provide. He worked out in the gymnasium two or three times each week and, when Judy was fulfilling singing engagements at Pontefract and Huddersfield, he went round to chat with Tom and Peggy.

Judy had dissuaded him from going with her when she sang. At first he had protested that he wanted to hear her but she had been firmly dismissive, pointing out that he would not like the kind of people he would be obliged to meet and in any case, until he had made up his mind what to do about his marriage, it would be prudent for them not to be seen together in public. Then, at the beginning of April, the Argentinians invaded the Falklands and the British taskforce set sail for the South Atlantic and even Dave, who had never before felt the slightest interest in political events, became concerned, though his anxiety was almost entirely for the fate of his brother, Martin.

Tom Darwin angrily condemned the way in which the Government were mishandling the situation, telling Dave that he must not be taken in by the propaganda spewed out by the Tory press. Margaret Thatcher had grabbed the opportunity to whip up a mindless patriotic frenzy so that public attention would be deflected from her disastrous economic policies, rising unemployment and her determination to dismantle the Welfare State. She had no intention of negotiating a peaceful solution to the invasion, Tom said, and she was quite ready to sacrifice any amount of lives, British as well as Argentinian, over a worthless fag-end of empire which the Foreign Office had been trying to get rid of for ages.

On the Sunday after Martin had embarked with his battalion Aileen and Dave visited his parents' home for the ritual midday meal and Dave was troubled by the change in his mother's appearance. She seemed to have grown older: her face had become pale and gaunt; there were shadows in the hollows of her cheeks and her eyes were large with fear and worry. She did not respond to her son's attempts to distract her and, when she spoke, it was of nothing but her anxieties for Martin's safety.

'Martin'll be all right,' Dave said. 'He's a tough lad. A lucky 'un too. He'll be all right, Mam, don't you worry.'

But Dot was inconsolable. She spoke, not so much to Dave or Aileen as to the unheeding fates: 'What they do it for? Where's the sense? Men. Fighting. Killing. Women too is as bad, some of 'em. That Mrs Thatcher. Her son's not going to get killed.'

When Jimmy came back from the pub and they were sitting at the dinner table he began to talk, with unconcealed excitement, even relish, about the likelihood of what he called a 'real punch-up with Argies' until his wife told him to shut up and eat his dinner. He winked at Dave but obeyed and, when the meal was finished, he suggested a walk round Potternewton Park.

Dave said, 'I don't know. Maybe not today, Dad. I thought Aileen and me'd do washing-up. Give Mam a rest. You put your feet up, Mam, you look tired.'

Dot spoke sharply: 'I can wash pots. Aileen can give us a hand if she wants. I'm not bothered.' Then, evidently hearing and repenting of her brusqueness, she added, 'It's nice of you to offer though. Go and have a walk with your father, there's a good lad.'

So Dave and Jimmy walked to the park through the quiet streets, the pavements and gutters of which were littered with empty beer cans and the discarded wrappings of take-away food.

'Cherry blossom's coming out,' Jimmy said. 'Look at buds. Aye, another spring. They come round quicker and quicker when you get older.'

'You'll see a lot more yet.'

'Oh aye. I'm not planning to kick bucket yet a while.' Then after a pause: 'Your mam's worried sick about Martin. I tell her them Argies'll pack it in without a fight but she don't listen to me.'

Dave said, 'She's bound to be worried.'

'Aye. Martin's still a baby to Dot. To me an' all in a way. But lad'll be all right. He can look after himself. I'm not too bothered.'

'Maybe it won't come to fighting, like you said.'

'Aye, maybe. But if it do, them Argies won't stand a chance. Our lads is trained see? An' they're all volunteers, regulars. The Argies is conscripts, it's like the fight-game. Like putting a raw novice in with a class fighter. It'll be a walk-over.'

Dave could see weaknesses in the analogy but he decided not to point them out. Instead he said, 'I'll be off to London a week tomorrow. Training for Harvey.'

'Soon as that, is it? You must have been back home three month or more. It don't seem anything like that.'

'Nearly four month.'

'Things going better with you and Aileen? She don't look so down in mouth.'

'Not too bad. But listen, Dad. When I'm away I want you to talk to Mam. I want you and her to get out of Harehills. A bungalow maybe. A nicer part. Shadwell or somewhere. A bit of garden. The old place was all right but it's getting rough these days. When the Hayes fight's over I'll have more brass 'n I can handle. So don't you let Mam go on about me throwing money about an' that. You two look around for something you really fancy and I'll tell Harold. Him and that lawyer and the accountant bloke'll fix it for you. I'll be seeing him on Tuesday and I'll tell him what you going to do. All right?'

'Ah. I don't know, son. I'll tell your mother what you said but I can't guarantee she'll say yes. You know what she's like. Nothing'll budge her once she's makes up her mind. Any case we're all right where we are. Be it ever so humble, like the song says. It's where we've lived all our married life. Brought up kids an' everything. We're happy enough where we are son.'

'But you'll tell her? You wouldn't mind moving, would you?'

'I'm not all that bothered. We're used to it. And you give us that money and got us the colour telly and the new washing-machine. It's all right. We're luckier than lots of folk. But I'll tell Dot what you said, son. Don't worry.'

They continued their walk in silence for a while. Then Jimmy said, 'How d'you feel about this training plan that Phil's got for you? Changing your style and that. Reckon you can do it?'

'If Phil says so. He's never been wrong so far.'

'Aye, he's smart one is Phil, I give you that. He did wonders with that featherweight from Belfast. What were his name? Turner?'

'Freddie Turnbull.'

'That's the one. Phil switched him round, didn't he? From southpaw. Lad that'd been in the game for five years. You wouldn't think he'd be able to switch. But he did it. And he took the European title. Marvellous was that.'

Jimmy went on to reminisce about fights and fighters, relating anecdotes, many of which his son already knew by heart, until he suddenly exclaimed, 'Eh! It's time we was getting back. Ten past four. They'll have a cuppa tea for us if we're lucky.'

They left the park and made their way back through the desolate streets, past waste areas which looked like small battlefields, towards the road in which Dave's parents had lived for almost thirty years and which, for Dave himself, possessed the bleak but still comforting aspect of long familiarity.

That evening Dave had left his own house and, as had now become customary, he offered Aileen no explanation or excuse. His departure had been made easier because she had gone to her room soon after their return from his parents' home and it was with a sense of relief as well as the usual excited anticipation that he had arrived at Judy's flat. They were in her living room where they had eaten a light meal of cheese soufflé and fruit. Judy had drunk a couple of glasses of white wine with her meal and they both now sat with cups of coffee.

In the earliest days of their relationship Dave had worried a great deal during the periods when they were apart that, once the attraction of the strange, the totally different, which he felt he must represent to her had dimmed, Judy would find him a boring companion, that they would have so little in common that communication would be scarcely possible. But he had been delighted to find that this was not so. She seemed fascinated by anything that he had to say about his life and profession. She had asked him for photographs and had borrowed his album of press-cuttings which, from the questions she subsequently asked, he could tell she had read thoroughly. And, responding to her interest, he had felt himself becoming more articulate. His gratitude was vast. Not only were they lovers, they were also truly friends. They enjoyed each other. Or so it seemed.

She said, 'What's it like before you go into the ring? I mean the few hours before. And then, as it gets closer and closer, the last minutes. Do you get scared?'

'Aye... well, no. Not scared exactly. It's not like being scared of being hurt and that. It's not the pain. But you do get like nerves. You get so's you need to—well, you know—have a leak every ten minutes.'

'That's what they call the adrenalin causes that.'

'That's right. I've heard of that. My dad told me about when he was in army, PT Instructor. He was training a boxing-team, lads that'd just been called up. Some of 'em never'd had gloves on in their lives. Real novices. Well, dad got this team together and they had to go and box at some RAF station against some o' the Brylcreem Boys as dad calls 'em. One of dad's team—a big fella, light-heavy I think—he'd been fine in gym. Quick learner. Natural mover. Very promising. But when he'd got to go in ring he was in a terrible state. Teeth chattering like a machine-gun. Couldn't hardly climb up to get in his corner. And when the poor bugger finally got up there and they was waiting for the bell for first round dad says he suddenly saw a pool of wet spreading round lad's feet. Aye. Poor bloke'd pissed himself!'

Judy was moved more by sympathy than amusement. 'Oh no! Oh dear. What happened to him? They didn't make him box, did they?'

'Far as I remember dad says he just chucked the lad's greatcoat over him an' bundled him out the ring back to dressing-room. 'Course he might've made the whole thing up. You never know with dad's stories.'

Judy said, 'It must be terrible when you're waiting in your corners. And those huge crowds shouting and yelling. I get nerves just going on stage to sing a couple of numbers. But I expect you're used to it, going in the ring I mean.'

'No, you never get really so's you don't feel nerves. I mean I've been fighting about twelve years now, if you include the amateurs, an' I still get jitters. Mind you. A little bit of the old tingle's good for you. I've known one or two lads, no nerves at all. One kid I knew used to sit in dressing-room and read a comic. Never bothered him in slightest. But fellers like that—well, they're a bit same in ring. No zip. No sizzle. Sparkle. They're a bit sluggish like.'

'Yes, I think I can see that. But the other kind—the stodgy ones who can read comics—I'm surprised they go in for boxing. I mean isn't the tingle, as you call it, a big part of what makes you want to be a boxer?'

'Aye. That's good. Hadn't thought a lot about that but you're right. That feeling, that sort of buzz. It's funny—it's sort of horrible but lovely. No, not horrible. That's not the word. Kind of scary. It's a bit like what I feel when I'm on my way to see you. Excited like. A bit scared you won't be there or maybe everything'll've changed. Sounds daft, don't it?'

'No it doesn't. I know just what you mean.'

' 'Course you can only talk for yourself. I mean other lads take up game for different reasons. Makes you wonder sometimes. We had a lad in St Joseph's Club used to get a hiding every time he fought. Seemed to love it. Trained like a Trojan. Keen as mustard. But he hadn't got no idea. Couldn't even punch. He used to go in there and jig around the ring waving and pumping his arms and other fella'd knock the stuffing out of him. Human punch-bag, he was. And he wasn't like some of 'em. He didn't do it 'cause he wanted to act the part like. D'you know what I mean? He didn't wear flashy gear and all that. Like some do. Like another fella at St Joseph's. This one were a posh lad, university student or something. He used to come to training-nights an' he had everything, the whole bloody lot. Better stuff than a 'pro. Satin trunks, boxing-boots, best kind of protector, headguard, flashy dressing-gown, the lot. An' he'd put this stuff on and work away at the heavy bag, pulling horrible faces and snorting and snarling every time he threw a punch. Tony his name was. Tony Davenport. But as soon as the trainer said what about getting gloves on, do a bit of sparring, old Tony always had something wrong with him. He'd sprained his thumb. Or he'd got a spit lip or a cold sore inside his nose or something. In all the time he were coming to club I never saw him in ring. An' you know why? He didn't like it. Not the real thing. Not going in there and throwing punches and having 'em back. Oh no. Old Tony was a play actor. Like little kids with cowboy or soldier suits. Aye, it's a funny old game.'

181

'It's fascinating.'

'Hey,' he said. 'I've been going on like an old washer-woman. Never talked so much in my life. You should've shut me up.'

'Don't be silly. I've told you. I'm interested. You'd soon know if I was bored. The more you tell me the more interested I get. I'm longing to see you in the ring. In a way, that is. As long as you don't get hurt.'

Dave grinned. 'You'd better not come to the big'un then,' he said. 'But you'll come down for the Harvey fight next month, won't you? That one should be all right. Unless Phil's made a horrible mistake an' picked a tartar.'

'When do you go? To start the training. Very soon isn't it?'

'Aye. A week tomorrow.'

'As soon as that!'

Dave nodded and they looked at each other suddenly shocked by the knowledge they they were so soon to be separated.

Then he said, 'Time'll pass quick. I'll phone you every day. I'm not much of a letter writer.'

'I'd rather hear your voice anyway.'

'And when you come down for fight may be we can fix something in London. I mean stay somewhere after the fight. Hotel for a couple of nights if you're not working. Another thing. We'd best fix how you're going to get there, to Wembley. I mean you can't go on your own.'

'Oh, I'd find my way.'

'No I don't mean that. I mean—well, you've never been to a big show, have you? It's a bit rough like. Big crowd, nearly all men. Some of 'em a bit dodgy. You'll be all right as long as you're with somebody. My dad and Harold and Micky'll be going, but—Ah! I've got it! You could go with Tom Darwin. If you was driving you could give him a lift. Or better go by train so's I can drive you back.'

'Hadn't I better meet your friend, Tom, before you go? It'd be a good idea, wouldn't it? If he's going to be stuck with me for a few hours when we're going to the boxing.'

'Aye. I'll fix it next week. I'll give him a ring and we'll meet somewhere.'

'All right. The only evening I'm busy's Friday. Any other day or evening. You can ask him here if you like. Or we could go out to Ilkley or somewhere. Whatever you think's best.'

Dave was surprised to find how pleased he felt at the prospect of Judy and Tom's meeting. This pleasure proceeded partly from his simple desire to impress Tom with Judy's beauty and, less creditably, to flaunt his own possession of a woman of such beauty, but also from an impulse to bring together the two people who, apart from his family, he cared for most. He was deeply anxious that they should like each other.

He said, 'I'll ring him tomorrow. He's a funny one is old Tom. Not everybody likes him.'

'No. You told me.'

'Clever though.'

'Yes. You told me that too.' Judy was smiling.

'Aileen don't like him. Never did really.'

'That's a good reason for me to think he's great. How is Aileen by the way? Still sweet and dreamy?'

'Aye. I don't understand it. She does all the things, round the house an' all that. Cooks me dinner. Does washing. Everything like that. Then you never see her. She's either up in her room or out somewhere. And she's got this look. Just like you say. Sort of sweet and dreamy. If I didn't know her better I'd say she'd got a bloke. She was in love or something.'

'Why you so sure she hasn't?'

'Aye. That's what Tom said. But you wouldn't ask if you knew Aileen. No. I don't believe it.'

'But it looks like it, doesn't it?' All the signs. Dreamy, absent-minded. Doesn't care what you're up to. Sneaks off out. Won't tell you where she's been.'

'Sure. That's what I said. You'd think she'd got a bloke. All signs is right. But I don't believe it. Unless...'

'Unless what?'

'I don't know. Unless he's—well, not normal. Not natural. I mean I can't see Aileen having a-what-you-call-it—love affair—like us fr'instance. She reckons sex and that's dirty. Wicked she calls it. Evil. It was that mam of hers. Dragging poor kid off to church nearly every day. Mass, she used to call it. All them statues and pictures and things they had in house. I only ever went there a couple of times. Enough to give you the willies.'

'Maybe she's got herself a nice Sunday school teacher or something.'

'I wish she would.'

'Wouldn't you feel just a little bit upset? Just a teeny bit jealous?'

Dave shook his head. 'No. I'd be happy as anything. It'd be great.'

Judy put down her cup and saucer and walked to the piano, sat down on the stool and raised the lid. She looked back over her shoulder at him.

'What's it to be, love?'

'What was that thing you played other night? You laughed at me 'cause I said his name wrong, the fella that wrote it.'

'Chopin? Yes, I know the one. Nocturne in F sharp minor. Okay.'

She began to play, and Dave watched the shaded lamplight on her hair and the agile, knowledgeable fingers delicate but authoritative on the keys, and he felt the music in the room and inside himself, as if it were being echoed in his skull and then in his heart, the seeking, questioning notes, the consoling reassurances and final serene affirmation. He thought that the sound was more beautiful than anything he had heard before and Judy's own beauty of face and form was in some way contained in that music just as her physical features seemed a corporification of those haunting patternings in time and silence.

When she finished the piece he said, 'Eh. That were lovely. I'd sooner be able to play like that than anything. Well almost anything.'

She looked at him and smiled. 'Rather than knock out Earl Hayes?'

He grinned. 'Ah well. Maybe not quite. As long as I've got you, it's all right. You can play the music. I'll do the fighting.'

Her smile did not disappear but it was modified to

184

something still affectionate but more serious. 'You'll always have me,' she said. 'As long as you want.' Then suddenly more business-like and cheerful. 'What now? How about a song? Or more Chopin?'

She played a couple of Waltzes and then accompanied herself as she sang a Gershwin song. Then she closed the piano lid and returned to her chair.

'You want more coffee?' she said.

Dave who was still dazed with admiration and enjoyment of the music shook his head. 'By, that were a treat, Judy. Honest. You're terrific. I can't think why you're not a big star.'

She laughed. 'Oh no, love. I'm nothing much. I don't fool myself about that. You'd find dozens of sopranos like me. Not bad. Better than any amateur, but still a long way down from the top. Quite a way down from the middle, come to think of it. I bet you get the same thing in boxing, don't you? Boxers who're okay in their own class. Put up a good show. Please the audience—crowd I mean. But an expert could spot them right away as second or third rate. No hopers. Isn't that right?'

He gazed at her, slowly shaking his head in wonderment. 'You're dead right about the fighters. Dead right. You get hundreds of 'em. What they call preliminary boys. Never get beyond boxing eight twos—that's eight two-minute rounds. Mostly six-rounders. They're all right. They can fight. Take a bit o' stick. One or two of 'em can punch a bit. In their own class. But step outside and they wouldn't last a couple of rounds with any of the rated boys. You're right. But I still can't believe you couldn't be a star. I've heard a lot worse than you on telly and on records an' that.'

'You're the star,' Judy said. 'No arguing about that. Champion of the World. You can't get any higher.' She looked at her watch. 'We'll just get the ten o'clock news on radio. See what's happening with the Falklands thing. Then we'll get to bed. If I'm permitted to make such an unladylike suggestion.'

She switched on the radio for a few minutes but there was no information about the Falklands crisis except that the

British Government was still hoping for an Argentine with-drawal and it was proposed to establish an exclusion zone of two hundred miles radius around the islands.

'What did you say your brother was in?'

'Parachute Regiment. Second Battalion.'

'Does he look like you?'

'No. He's dark. More like me mam, they say. The lasses seem to fancy him. I think I'll keep you out of his road.'

'You don't have to worry. I can't see what any man looks like when you're around. Come on. Let's go to bed, love. We've been hanging about long enough.'

She took his hand and drew him from his chair and together they went into the bedroom, switching off the living-room lights as they closed the door.

Dark silence was startlingly drilled through by the repeated double rasp of noise and Dave was instantly awake, muscles tensed and eyes wide open. At his side Judy moved and muttered and he was aware of her turning and leaning away from him to the bedside table.

He heard the click of the telephone being lifted and then her voice, slow and drowsy: 'Hullo...who is it?...Oh... yes...just a minute...' More fumbling movement and then the table lamp was switched on. She said. 'It's after one...all right. Never mind...yes...Yes, I see...'

Between her brief interjections Dave could hear from the instrument a flow of rapid speech, incomprehensible but unquestionably spoken by a masculine voice. He turned his back on Judy, pretending indifference or sleepiness, but straining to catch even a word or two of what the man was saying, but the noise was a meaningless mockery of the rhythms, the rise and fall, spurts and hesitancies of spoken language.

'No,' Judy was saying, 'I'm a bit tired. You woke me up...Yes okay...it doesn't matter...that's good...Yes. All right. I'll try...Goodnight then ...yes...goodbye.'

She put the receiver down and lay back again, pulling the bed-coverings up to her chin but leaving the bedside lamp on.

Dave turned on to his back so that they were side by side, both staring up at the ceiling. As he waited for her to speak a feeling of misery and fear grew within him, increasing with each second of her silence. Although he could feel her shoulder and hip lightly touching him he was aware of the estranging distance between them and it seemed unbelievable that an hour earlier they had been gasping, sobbing and murmuring together, heaving, writhing and thrusting in a passionate, reciprocal hunger for each other. He waited. But still she said nothing. Then an impulse of anger moved below the weight of desolation, not a bright glitter but a sluggish undertow of resentful protest. Why didn't she speak? Who was the man who'd called her up at one in the morning? Dave had a right to know. She'd said she wasn't interested in any other men yet here she was being rung up by some bloke after midnight. And it couldn't have been just a friend or relation or someone like that because she'd have said so, straight away. Her silence was a confession. She had been taking him for a ride. Two-timing him. He might have known it couldn't be genuine, it couldn't last.

He said, 'Who was that then?' and when she did not immediately reply, he added, 'Eh? On phone.'

'Nobody you know.' Her voice was dull, toneless.

'I never thought it would be. I don't know any of your friends do I? You make sure o' that.'

'Dave,' she said, drawing out the vowel sound in a long reproachful "Eh", 'don't go on love. There's a good lad.'

The patronising, weary note, as if addressed to a refractory child, stung him. 'All right then! Keep it to yourself,' he said, and swung out of bed and began to scramble into his clothes. His back was turned to her so he did not know whether she was looking at him but he guessed that she was still staring up at the ceiling.

When he was dressed he said, still without looking at her, 'Well I'm off.'

He heard her move and he looked towards the bed and saw that she had lifted herself on to one elbow and had turned to look at him.

She said, 'Don't go, Dave. Don't leave me. Stay for a bit. Come and sit here.'

He had never before seen her look so unkempt, her hair not so much in disarray as dishevellment, her facial contours oddly blurred, almost pudgy, and eyes blank and colourless. She looked almost ugly, yet he had never before been so moved by a protective tenderness which rose against, almost vanquishing, jealous antagonism and curiosity.

He sat by her side but did not touch her.

She said. 'All right, Dave. What's worrying you?'

'What's worrying you's more like it. That bloke on phone. Who was he?'

'I told you it was no one you know. If I gave you his name it wouldn't mean anything to you. He's just a man I've known quite a long time.'

'What's he doing ringing up at that time?'

'He didn't realise it was that late. He was ringing from America. He'd forgotten the time difference.'

'America...? Oh...aye...I see. That explains a lot.'

'What d'you mean?'

'How long's he been in America?'

'About six months. A bit longer perhaps. Why?'

'Obvious isn't it?' Anger was returning, dominant again. 'He's out the way. You get a bit lonely like. Feel like a bit o' fun. I'd do as good as the next fella. Till he comes back. That's it, i'n't it? When *is* he coming back, anyway?'

She said, 'It wasn't like that at all.'

'When's he coming back I said.'

'I don't know.'

'Well, you'll let me know, won't you? So's I can be well out the way. I mean we wouldn't want him to know what we've been up to, would we? I don't think he'd see funny side on it.'

'Dave...please...please listen. It isn't like what you—'

But the rage was swelling and drumming in skull and throat, and it was engendering a cruelty that he had never experienced before. It was frightening, dangerous, exciting. 'I know! I know! It i'n't what I think it is. You just good friends? That it? You and him don't do things we do. That right? You don't get on top of him and bounce up and down like a bloody Derby winner. Eh? You don't take his—'

'Stop it!'

Her eyes were alive now with an anger that seemed to equal his. She said, 'Before you go any farther. Just listen will you? I've told you more than once. You've got no rights that I'm not ready to grant you. D'you understand that? You're married. You're no different from any other man who's having a bit on the side. That's the truth, whether you like it or not. Whether *I* like it or not. We've known each other—what?—less than four months. We've both had our lives before that. You went and got married. I picked up a—whatever you want to call him. A man. A lover, except that's not a very good word for this one. His name's Colin Hunter if you must know. But I'm not getting at you and trying to hurt you because you talk to your wife. For all I know you'll be going back from here into her bed— hold on! I know what you've told me. But it doesn't have to be the truth, does it? You've never told her you want a divorce, have you? You've never said, "I want a divorce because I want to marry Judy Styles," have you? Oh shit! You bloody men're all the same. You're all selfish bastards. Go on. You can go now. Go if you want to. And don't come back. I don't care... I can do without you... I don't...' She was sniffling and the words were lost in rising sobs: '... damn you... Oh Christ... I wish... Oh God...' Then as he reached out to pull her close and hold her to his chest, stroking and kissing the top of her head and murmuring consolatory sounds and promises, she began to cry in earnest.

'It's all right, love,' he said, 'Don't worry. Everything's going to be all right. Don't worry. Everything's going to be fine. You see. It'll all work out all right...come on love...come on, darling...don't my sweetheart... everything's going to be fine... you see... I'll never be like that again... sorry, love... I should never've said things like that...come on darling...don't cry... sorry my love... it's all going to be all right... you see if it's not... it's going to be all right...'

Then like a sudden sunlight after a downpour of rain, she

was laughing, tears still on her lashes like rain-drops wet on her cheeks as she was saying, 'Oh Dave! Oh love! I couldn't manage without you! Honest. There's no one else. There really isn't. He's nothing. Never was. It's the truth, Dave. I don't mean we never—you know—went to bed. But it wasn't often and it was nothing. I swear that, darling. It was nothing to me. Nothing. You don't have to worry. You're the only one. Ever. I'll tell him it's all over. I was going to finish with him anyway. It wasn't much in any case, even to start with. I'll tell him, love. I'd have told him then, on the phone. I wanted to. But it was awkward, with you there. I mean we'd never talked about it. I should've done, I know. I can see I should've done. I'm sorry. I never wanted to hurt you darling. Never. Oh Jesus. Dave darling, I love you. I love you. I love you. Oh God I've said it now. I didn't mean to. I didn't mean to say it but it's true. I love you. You beautiful, horrible, jealous lovely monster!'

Then they were both gabbling endearments and nonsense and both of their faces were damp and salt with tears as they muttered and murmured and kissed and murmured again and, finally, Dave began to take off his clothes until he was naked again and back between the sheets.

'Dave,' she gasped, 'I love you so much. You're marvellous...oh!...oh God...yes...oh my darling...oh my love...oh...yes that's it...yes...yes...yes...'

Part Two

Part Two

CHAPTER FOURTEEN

PHIL RICHARDSON'S EALING gymnasium was no bigger but was far more comfortable and better equipped than Harold's place in Leeds. It was contained in a rectangular stone outbuilding in the spacious yard of the Bricklayer's Arms. You went in through a door on the right and in front of you, in a row across the room, had been suspended four heavy punch-bags. On your immediate left shelves had been put up holding mitts, skipping-ropes, medicine-balls and weights and further to your left, running the entire length of the gym, was a plaster-board wall which concealed three showers, a toilet and dressing accommodation with two massage tables and a set of weighing-in scales, two long seats and pegs for a dozen boxers' clothes. On your right, two speed balls were attached at intervals of twenty feet to their platforms in the wall and the main space of the gym was occupied by two ground-level, single-roped, boxing-rings. At the farthest end more shelves had been erected against the facing wall and on these lay training-gloves and head-guards. On the walls above the shelves had been stuck posters advertising past and future boxing shows. The smell of sweat and rubbing oils was strong and although it was familiar to Dave the first whiff as he entered the gym always stirred feelings of excitement. It was the scent of his earliest ambitions, of promise and threat, danger and glory. He knew that he would always be thrilled by it.

It was a Friday afternoon approaching the end of his second week in London and Dave was working on the heavy bag. Phil

193

and Paddy Whelan were standing watching him, the trainer holding a stop watch. Paddy barked out hoarse instructions: 'Left! Jab! jab! jab! Hook off the jab! Go on. Again! Off the jab! Hook! To the body! To the body again! Smash it in! Combinations Dave! Combinations now! Left-right to head, left to body, right to head! Okay Dave, let 'em go! Smash 'em in! Head, body, head! Last ten seconds! Both hands now! Every one a killer! Go! Go! Go! Smash 'em in! Bang! Bang! Bang! . . . Time! . . . All right, keep moving Dave. Keep moving around. Nice going, son. Bit of work on the ground now. Down you get. On your back like the Bishop said. First, your legs straight. Fifty like that. Then we'll do fifty with the knees up. Okay. That's right. Hands behind your head. Get them elbows right back. That's it. Okay. Begin! Up, press, sl-ow-ly down!'

Dave forced himself through the routine of exercises. After the ground-work he skipped for twenty minutes, scarcely aware of the other fighters in the gym who were labouring at their own work-outs or sparring in the ring. His rope whirled, whistled and slapped out a steady tempo and his feet performed their mechanically adroit movements without need of conscious thought. The unchanging rhythm and the purely physical demands of the exercise made any kind of sequential thinking impossible. When he was our of doors, running over the common in Gunnersbury Park, he could indulge in thoughts of Leeds and of Judy, but here in the muscle-factory it seemed that he became as near to being a machine as it was possible for a human to become. The rope swished and slapped, hands and feet moved in perfect synchronization, sweat trickled from hair-line towards his eyebrows and he could feel it, sliding like a snail's spoor down his flanks.

After the skipping session Paddy said, 'That'll do for now, Dave. You're coming on nice. Go and get a shower, I'll see you tonight for sparring. Okay?'

Dave put the skipping-rope back where it belonged and disappeared into the changing-room.

Phil, said, 'What d'you think, Paddy?'

'He's fine. Had him on the scales yesterday and his weight's okay. Only a few ounces over eleven-six. Just what we want.'

'Yeah. He's fit enough. I'm not worried about that.'

'Worried? What you worried about?' Paddy Whelan, stocky, balding, ex-welterweight, despite his Irish name spoke with an unmistakable East End London accent.

'How d'you think the sparring's been going?'

'All right. Pretty good. He's punching hard. Harder than ever maybe. That left hook he caught Jake with last night was a bleedin' crippler. If he hadn't been wearing pillows he'd've put him out for ten minutes, never mind about seconds.'

'Yeah. He's punching hard enough.'

'What's up then?'

'You haven't noticed anything? He don't seem a bit—well, like his heart's not in it? No. Maybe that's putting it too strong. Just a bit sluggish? No, that's too strong as well. What I mean is he don't seem quite the boy he was. A little bit of the edge's gone. I dunno. Maybe I'm imagining things. I dunno.'

Paddy rubbed his bristly chin. 'I don't think you need worry. It wasn't only Jake he nearly murdered. Ron says he's punching harder than any light-heavy he's fought. He reckons Dave'll murder any middleweight in the world, including Hayes. And that's with the pillows. He was saying the other night. They ought to get danger pay sparring with Dave.'

Phil nodded. 'Okay. I'll be seeing you later.'

He went into the changing room where Dave was pulling on his shirt.

'Nice work-out,' he said.

Dave tucked in the shirt and fastened his belt. 'Aye.'

'No problems?'

'No.'

'Good. You going to have a rest till this evening?'

Dave nodded. 'I might go for a little walk first. Do a bit of shopping.'

'If there's anything you want you've only got to ask. Me or Rose'll get it for you. You don't need to go out if it's just to get razor-blades or something.'

'I like to get out now and then.'

'Yeah. Well, I just thought. You know. Anything you want.

If you want to phone Aileen or anything. You don't have to ask. Phone's there.'

Dave pulled on his coat and grunted what might have been thanks.

'How is she anyway? Aileen.'

'She's all right.'

'And your parents?'

'They're okay. Mam's a bit worried about our Martin.'

'Oh Christ. Yeah. I'd forgotten. He's in the Paras isn't he? That must be a worry.' Then he added: 'Are *you* worried about him, Dave?'

Dave was bending over the long wooden seat to zip up his bag. He looked up surprised and, before he could answer, Phil said quickly, 'Yeah. Of course you're worried. Silly question. But what I meant was, is it on your mind a lot? Is it getting you down a bit. I've got a younger brother. Little bugger used to ride a motorbike. A thousand cc Honda. Used to worry me sick. I was glad when he got a girlfriend who wouldn't go on the bloody thing. They're married now. Two kids and an Austin Maxi. You'd never think he used to be a tearaway.'

Dave picked up his bag and together they went back into the main gymnasium. One of the rings was occupied by two little men, bantam or featherweights, and Paddy Whelan was watching them with his stopwatch in hand. Phil waved to him and moved towards the exit with Dave close behind.

Outside in the pub car park Dave said, 'What was you trying to say, Phil? About me being worried. You think I'm not looking sharp or something?'

They walked towards the road. 'No. No, you're doing fine. I just wondered if everything was okay. You've been a bit quiet at home. Rose noticed it, too. And maybe I thought you was just a teeny bit sluggish when you was sparring with Nemko. Nothing much and I'm probably wrong.'

'He's very fast, is Jake. And he's a welter. He'd make any middleweight look a bit slow. And I nailed him a couple of times. Once with a left hook and once with a right. With proper gloves he'd a been gone. Both times.'

'Yeah. Sure. I'm getting over-fussy. Imagining things. Don't take no notice. You're doing fine.'

They walked back to Phil's large Victorian house overlooking the common where his wife, Rose, had tea waiting for them. She was a handsome woman of about forty-two, her hair still glossily black and her wide, full lips made up with bright red lipstick in a style that seemed to belong to earlier notions of feminine glamour than those prevailing in the eighties. When Dave had first met her almost three years earlier he had been overwhelmed by her expansive, warm femininity; she was given to wearing low-cut dresses and using heavy perfume and there had been a brief, uneasy period when he had wondered if her generous friendliness was not something else, something more sexual, even predatory. But he had soon learnt that her amiability was maternal rather than erotic and he had grown very fond of her. It had been she who, a couple of years ago, had taught him to drive the old Cortina that Phil had given him after the second Mark Price fight when poor old Pricey had been flattened in three rounds. Dave had been strongly tempted to tell her about Judy but the knowledge that she would almost certainly convey whatever information he gave her on to Phil prevented him from soliciting for the sympathy he was sure she would have given.

Each night after an intensive sparring session in the gym, he went to bed at half-past-nine so that he would be sure of sufficient rest before rising at six-thirty to run the statutory eight miles after which he returned to the house for a large breakfast. He then rested or went for a walk in the shopping area of Ealing Broadway until lunch and another rest period to help the digestive processes. Then to the gym for another work-out of bag-punching, skipping, floor exercises, weights and shadow-boxing. And all the time, even when working in the ring with Jake Nemko or Ron Vallance or Paul Benson, it seemed that a part of his consciousness was kept for images of Judy to inhabit. During the busy parts of the day these images were discreet icons, kept like photographs in a wallet, but, when he was alone in his room, at night or in the daytime, they grew in size and vitality until he ached with longing for the reality of which these phantasmal shapes were taunting reminders.

He telephoned her every day, always from a public call box,

though he had given her Phil's home number in the unlikely event of her needing to get in touch with him urgently. He also telephoned Tom, more from the need to speak to someone about Judy, if it were only to say her name aloud, than because he wished to discuss his preparations for the fight. Quite often he thought about Tom's meeting with Judy which had been arranged a couple of days before he left Leeds for London.

Dave had picked up Tom from his work at the Old People's Home at seven-thirty in the evening and driven him to Judy's flat where they were to collect her and go on for a drink at a country pub on the Pateley Bridge Road, a few miles north of Otley. Dave had been puzzled by their first reaction to each other when they were introduced. Each had shown a similar watchfulness, a cautious, polite but slightly mistrustful affability and later, even when they had both swallowed a few drinks, though their friendliness seemed far more relaxed, Dave still sensed on both sides a reserve of wariness and even suspicion. When he had spoken of this to Judy that night, after they had dropped Tom at his flat, she had dismissed his doubts and said that she and Tom had both felt a little shy on first meeting and that she had liked him, although finding him 'a bit of an oddball'. Tom, too, on the telephone the next day had said that he thought Judy was a lovely girl and, as far as he could tell on brief acquaintance, was nice with it. Then he added, with an exaggerated meaningfulness, like an audible leer, that he was looking forward to taking her to the Harvey fight. Dave had felt largely reassured and when he recalled those moments of indefinable tension and the expressions on both Tom's and Judy's faces which bizarrely reminded him of two well-matched fighters circling for an opening in the first few seconds of a contest, he dismissed these recollections as symptoms of his anxiety that they should like each other without reserve.

He had telephoned Aileen a few times and on a couple of occasions had been puzzled, though not worried, at receiving no reply. After the news of the sinking of the *Sheffield*, he asked her to go round and see if she could offer any comfort and reassurance to his mother to whom, he suspected, his father would be of little help. Aileen had agreed at once and he had been surprised by the little spark of affection that was struck from his gratitude. The next time he had spoken to Aileen she told him that she had done her best to allay his mother's fears for her soldier-son but it had been difficult, and when Aileen had said that she would pray for his safety Mrs Ruddock had been, to put it mildly, distinctly sceptical of the value of this offer.

On May 10th Wayne Harvey arrived in Britain from the United States and at noon on the fifteenth, a press conference was held at the offices in Old Compton Street of Bernie Slater, the promoter, at which Dave and Phil met the American fighter and his manager for the first time. Dave did not enjoy these occasions when he was supposed to act a part dictated by the promoter's idea of what would attract public interest. He found it as difficult to smile to order in his role as blue-eyed, upstanding British athlete as he did to scowl ferociously when he was cast as the 'blond destroyer', the tag which had, since he had won the World Title, been attached to him by the sporting press.

Harvey was an inch or so shorter than Dave. He looked tough with a square, dark head of tight, oiled curls set on a short and very thick neck and wide shoulders, a small flattened nose and scarred eyebrows. His rather closely set eyes met Dave's only once, as they were shaking hands for the photographers, and they registered no identifiable feeling at all. They were so lacking in expression that they might almost have been the inanimate, button eyes of a soft toy.

'Hold it!' the photographers were shouting as the flashes startled the gloom in the office. 'Give us a smile, Dave!'

'Over here! Look confident!'

'Show us your left hook! Shape up, Wayne. Both of you!'

'Big grin, now Dave!'

Bernie Slater said, 'All right gentlemen. Any questions?'

Phil put an avuncular hand on Dave's shoulder, pressing him down to sit behind Slater's huge desk. They all took their seats, promoter, the two managers and fighters. Harvey's manager did not resemble the popular stereotype of the American boxer's representative except for the cigar which he worked from one corner of his mouth to the centre and back again as he watched the pressmen with the bleak and sceptical gaze of a man who had witnessed similar scenes too often for this one to be of the least interest. He was dressed in a neat dark suit, white shirt and plain blue tie and might easily have been mistaken for a small town doctor.

One of the journalists said, 'A question for Wayne. You fought Earl Hayes a year ago. Wayne. I think I'm right in saying he stopped you in the sixth round. No disgrace there. What chance do you give Dave Ruddock against Hayes?'

Before Harvey could answer—if he had any intention of answering—Phil said, 'Wayne hasn't fought Dave yet. Hasn't even seen him in action as far as I know. How can he give an opinion? So let's stick to the fight we've got here, shall we?'

Another reporter called from the back of the office, 'What d'you know about Dave, Wayne? Seen him on film or anything?'

Harvey looked at his manager whose head moved in the slightest nods before the fighter spoke: 'Sure. I seen him on film. I seen him fight that Frenchman, Fournier. He fought okay. But Fournier ain't nothing. I figure he wouldn't last a couple of rounds with Hayes. Your man Dave Ruddock's a fair fighter but he ain't been around in the kinda company I'm accustomed to keeping. I guess you're gonna see a big upset on the twenty-fifth.'

'Any prediction? Knock-out? Points? What round?' someone asked.

Harvey shook his head. 'I'm a fighter, not a prophet. If I was a prophet I wouldn't be in this business. I'd play the horses I guess.'

His manager removed his cigar from his mouth and permitted himself a faint smile and another nod, a small show of something like paternal pride.

One of the tabloid men said, 'What about you Dave? You any predictions how it's going to go?'

Dave shook his head. 'No. I'm not a prophet neither.'

'Supposing you blow this one,' said the same reporter. 'Supposing Wayne beats you like he says he will. What happens then? With the Hayes fight? It'd take the shine off that one a bit wouldn't it?'

Dave shrugged and glanced at Phil who said, 'For a start I don't think we'll lose this one. I'm not saying it's impossible. Anything can happen in this game. Harvey's got a good record but he's been licked six times, four inside the distance. We've never been beaten, not once. And look at Dave's inside-the-distance wins. Eighteen out of thirty-one bouts! And Wayne talks about the company he keeps. Okay. Look at Dave's last five opponents—Barny Corrigan, Joe Kimbu, Roberto Ramirez, Jose Vallejo and the Champion, Fournier—all world class fighters, all licked inside the distance. And may I remind you that Vallejo stopped Wayne inside eight rounds.'

'Cuts,' said Harvey's manager.

'He'd a been stopped anyway. Vallejo had dropped him three times in the sixth and seventh.'

Harvey's manager examined the top of his cigar with an expression that suggested that he was in possession of some satisfying private knowledge unavailable to Phil.

Bernie Slater said, 'The main thing is, gentlemen, whatever the outcome we're going to get a chance to see our new World Champion in action here in England. And one thing you can be sure of. It'll be a real fight. You can't accuse Phil Richardson here of picking an easy touch for his boy's warm-up. Wayne Harvey's been in with the very best and he's only lost six out of nearly forty. And he's won the last three. So don't let's hear any talk of him being over the hill. Like Wayne says, there could be an upset. I expect you all know Wayne's finishing his training at the Thomas à Beckett at the Elephant and Dave's at the Bricklayer's in Ealing. You can watch 'em work out and form your own conclusions. And when you've seen Wayne in action in the gym I think you'll agree with me. We've got a good match here.'

When, at last, the press conference was over Phil and Dave immediately left the promoter's office, where the reporters were being supplied with drinks, and took a taxi back to Ealing where they had a late lunch after which Dave went to his room to rest until the evening training session. He took off his shoes and lay on top of the bed with a copy of *Boxing News*, but he soon let the paper fall and closed his eyes and thought, with a hollow ache of longing, about Judy and Leeds. Yet his erotic and nostalgic reverie was disconcertingly adulterated by the intermittent appearance of other, opposing presences; the hard, ungiving, watchful little eyes of Wayne Harvey, set deep beneath the black eye-brows which showed, gleaming pale through the wiry hair, the marks of old scars; the faces of the newspaper men, blotched and thick with booze and second-hand experience, grinning or bored in the haze of cigar and cigarette smoke; the faces of his sparring-partners, dehumanized below the leather head-guards, jaws clamped on gum-shields, eyes like gun muzzles, fixed dark, menacing, as they ducked, rolled and weaved.

Another ten days to go before the fight: it seemed a long time. Judy would be there at the ringside. The prospect thrilled. She would be looking up at him in the ring. She would see him, for the first time, doing what he was so very good at. She would see the way he moved, the perfect balance, the way his feet stayed exactly the same distance apart whether he was moving back or forwards or to one side, the way the jab moved in, fast as a cobra's tongue, looking like a mere flick but smashing in with all of his weight, the power like an uncoiled spring, starting from the rear foot, the way he switched from head to body and back again, the way he could glide and fade on the ropes, looking as if he was moving to the right when he was going the other way; the way he could throw the finisher, the big bomb, either hand. Bang! Out! Flat! Finished. The referee, arms flung wide, crucified in the air above the fallen victim, and the hero, dancing and leaping to the crowd's hoarse and brainless music.

He suddenly expelled a long-held breath and unclenched the hands that he had been unaware of gripping into fists of concrete. He grinned slightly and thought that Old Phil's magic always worked. Just thinking about fighting tensed him up now, ready to throw the killer punches. As Phil had said, you gripped hard, you clenched like a vice, your fists, your teeth and your mind. That was the tricky part and the most important. Clenching hard with your mind. Almost every punch he threw now had all of that behind it. He wasn't worried by Harvey. Or by Hayes if it came to that. He'd only got to catch them with one punch and they'd go. He was a big puncher, like Dempsey, Louis, Sugar Ray, Marciano, and he could box a bit as well.

He swung his feet down to the floor and bent and put on his shoes. At the open bedroom door he paused and, hearing no sound below, ran lightly down the stairs, grabbed his coat from the hanger in the hall and left the house to walk quickly to the telephone box at Ealing Common Station. He would tell Judy to look out in the sports pages the next day for pictures of him and Harvey. And he wanted to tell her that he had booked a double room with bath at the Cumberland for the night of the fight and the following five nights so that they could have almost a week in London before returning to Leeds. He would also tell her how much he missed her and that he loved her.

On Sunday, May 23rd, two nights before the fight, at nine-twenty in the evening as Dave was playing a final hand of rummy with Phil and Rose before going to bed, the telephone rang and Phil threw down his cards and rose to answer it.

He spoke the number into the mouthpiece then said, '...Yeah...he's here...Sure...Is that—? Who's speaking please?...Okay I'll get him.' He turned to Dave, holding out the instrument with one hand over the mouthpiece: 'It's for you. Somebody called Judy.'

Dave felt the thump of surprise and delight and apprehension in his gut as embarrassment warmed his face. He rose and took the telephone from Phil. 'Yes?...This is Dave.'

Her voice sounded surprisingly close. She spoke rapidly, a little breathlessly as if she had been hurrying. 'Dave darling. I had to ring you. I hope it's all right. I mean I hope you don't mind. He sounded—your manager—he sounded a bit dis-approving. I hope he's not. Is it all right? Can you speak?'

'Yes. Yes, it's okay. What's up? Anything wrong?'

'Well yes. But don't worry, love. It's going to be all right. I just hope you're not too disappointed . I can't make it on Tuesday. It's terrible, I know, but it's going to be impossible. I've tried every way I can think of but it can't be done.'

The disappointment was sickening, draining. Then it was followed by suspicion, unfocused but painfully jagged and probing. He said, 'What you on about? Why? Why can't you come?'

'It's work darling. Mike—Mike Carpenter, you remember I mentioned him, my agent?—well he's just phoned and offered me a stand-in engagement in Manchester. I can't get out of it Dave. He'd said yes before he'd spoken to me. It's a big concert, love. He thought I'd jump at it, whatever plans I had. Veronica Crossley's got a bad throat—she's the one whose place I'm taking. She's very well-known. I mean this is a big chance. Good fee too. But I wouldn't've done it Dave. I wouldn't've let you down. Not if it'd been up to me. But Mike's booked me. There's nothing I can do. I've got to do it, love.'

Dave felt a tightness in the throat. He tried to cough it away but when he spoke his voice sounded strangely pitched. 'That's all right.' Again he tried to clear his throat. 'I expect I'll see you when I get back.' Then with an attempt at enthusiasm he said, 'Good luck anyway. I'm glad you've got the job. I mean you must be pleased.'

'No Dave. Honestly. I wouldn't do it except I'm committed. Mike gave them a firm yes. But listen. It's not so bad. You've booked the hotel room, haven't you?'

'Aye. Till next Sunday. I'd best let them know we don't want—'

'No! No love. Listen. Don't cancel. When your fight's over you go to the hotel. Just as we planned. Tell them your wife's joining you the next day. See? I'd come on Tuesday night, after the concert if it was possible but it isn't. I won't get back to Leeds till well after midnight. But I'll get an early call and I'll catch the ten to nine on Wednesday morning. You can meet me at King's Cross or I'll come straight to the Cumberland. Perhaps the Cumberland's best. I'll be there before twelve. You have a lie-in. You'll be tired after your fight. You stay in bed and I can come and join you. In bed darling. How's that sound?'

Dave glanced at Phil and Rose, irrationally embarrassed, though commonsense assured him that they could not possibly hear what Judy was saying.

She was speaking, quickly, anxiously: 'Is that all right Dave? Dave . . . are you listening? You will keep the room booked, won't you? It'll be lovely having a few days together in London. Going out together. Not having to worry about gossip or anything . . . Dave . . .'

'Yes,' he said. 'Yes, it'll be great.'

'Is it difficult for you to speak now?'

'Aye. A little bit.'

'All right. Will you ring me tomorrow from a call box? Can you ring before twelve? I'm rehearsing in the afternoon. Can you do that?'

'Yes.'

'Are you all right love? Not too disappointed?'

'I'm all right.'

'Still love me?'

Again a nervous look towards where Phil and Rose were elaborately not listening.

'Aye. Yes. Yes, I do. A lot.'

'Oh . . .' It was a long sigh. 'That's all right then. Ring me tomorrow morning. Okay? Goodnight my darling. Love you, love you, love you.'

Two kissing sounds and the line was disconnected.

Dave returned to the table and picked up his cards. 'Who's go?' he said.

Phil was looking at him with a steadily enquiring gaze. Then he said, 'Yours.'

They played out the rest of the game without much sense of involvement and Dave announced that he was off to bed.

He was about to rise from the table when Phil said, 'Everything all right? The phone call. Nothing wrong at home?'

Dave shook his head.

'Judy. That's not your sister's name, is it? She's called Joan or Jane or something like—'

'Jean.'

'Jean. That's it. I remember you told me. So Judy's not family then?'

Rose said, 'Leave the boy alone, Phil. You're not his father and he's old enough to choose his own friends even if you were.'

'No. I'm not his father. I'm his manager. Sure he can choose his own friends. But when he's got an important fight—any fight at all for that matter—in a couple of days I'm entitled to get a bit concerned when strange women ring him up with what sounded to me like bad news.'

'It wasn't bad news,' Dave said.

'I'm glad to hear it.'

Rose said, 'Don't let him bully you Dave. You don't have to tell us anything you don't want to. I won't say we're not interested. Of course we're interested. We've always thought a lot of you and it's not just because you're a great boxer. We want you to know you can come to us about anything. I mean any little worries or troubles or anything on your mind. Anything. We might neither of us be able to help but we'll always be ready to listen. And that can be half the cure for a troubled mind. Just a sympathetic ear to pour your worries into. Get rid of 'em like that.'

Dave said, 'It was just a friend.'

Phil left the talking to his wife. 'That's nice. Nothing wrong then? Just ringing you for a little chat was she?'

'Aye. Well, she was coming down for fight. I'd got her a ticket. She was coming with that mate of mine—you've met him—Tom Darwin.'

'Oh, I see. She's *his* girl-friend.'

'No.'

Rose smiled. 'Listen dear,' she said. 'Don't say anything you don't want to. But if there's anything you'd like to talk about. Like Aileen or being homesick or this girl, Judy. You know we'd never take the other side. You understand? You're like family to us, Dave. What you want for yourself is what we want for you. I mean that. I wouldn't hold anything against you. Unless you'd committed a murder or something and even then I'd want to know every circumstance.'

'I haven't murdered nobody.'

Rose waited.

'Aye. Well, it's a bit disappointing. That's all. This girl Judy was coming down to watch me and Harvey. Expect I wanted to show off a bit like. Anyway she can't make it. She's singing in Manchester on Tuesday.' He added: 'She's been on telly. She's a great singer.'

'And you're very fond of her.'

Dave nodded. 'I am that.'

'And Aileen?'

'I don't know. She don't seem to worry all that much. I can't really understand it. At first I thought she were upset like. But she don't seem bothered now.'

Rose said, 'Well, don't you worry. I'm sure things'll work out all right. Perhaps we can meet Judy one day soon?'

'Aye. I'd like that.'

'Anyway. Off you go to bed now. And promise us you won't lose any sleep about Aileen or anything. I think everything'll turn out for the best. You see. Love'll find a way as the old song says.'

After Dave had gone to bed Phil went to the sideboard and brought out the whisky, a syphon of soda and two glasses. He poured drinks for both of them and sat down again.

'What d'you think, Rose?' he said.

'I think he's fallen for Judy, whoever she might be. I'm not surprised. That Aileen always seemed a cold little fish to me. We'll just have to see how things go. This Judy might be good for him. Thing is, you mustn't lose his confidence. He trusts us, Phil. We've got to make sure we keep it that way. Not just because he's worth a bloody gold-mine either. There's something about young Dave you don't come across these days. Innocence I suppose it is. Not stupidity, though he's not all that bright. But I've met plenty thicker than Dave and they've been anything but innocent. I don't know. I'm very fond of the boy.' She raised her glass and said over its brim before she drank. 'And so are you.'

'Yes,' Phil said. 'So am I.'

CHAPTER FIFTEEN

JUDY POURED TEA and handed the cup and saucer to her friend, Sue Davitt, who had arrived at Judy's flat a few minutes earlier. They sat in armchairs with the small table between them.

Sue took a sip of tea, then said, 'Looks as if you've landed yourself right in it, love. You'd better tell me all about it.'

Judy said, 'It's nice of you to come straight away like this. What've you done about Emma?'

'It's all right. Don't worry about Emma. Mrs Troop's looking after her till four-thirty. So we've got—what?—a couple of hours nearly. Tell me exactly what's happened so far. You said on the 'phone that Colin's back already?'

'Yes. Last Tuesday.'

'And your—what's-he-called?—Dave. You haven't told him anything? And Colin, of course, doesn't know anything about Dave. Is that right?'

'Yes. Well, no, not quite. I told Dave a bit but not much. Not enough.'

'What did you tell him?'

'I told him—this was a few weeks ago, just before Dave went to London. Colin 'phoned from Florida when Dave was here. About half past one in the morning. Dave knew it was a man. And of course he was curious, jealous I suppose—anyway, I told him. I mean I didn't go into details but I said there'd been somebody, another man, lover, whatever you want to call him.'

'You told him there had been?'

'Yes.'

'But that means it was over, past. And it isn't really?'

'Yes. Well, I want it to be. It's going to be. I'm going to tell Colin it's all over.'

'And what about the flat? Did you tell Dave who owns it?'

'No. It wasn't the right time. It's too complicated. I meant to tell him before he went away but somehow it never seemed the right time. I mean it sounds so awful. It's so hard to explain.'

Sue drank more tea and held out her cup for a refill. Then she said, 'You were silly. You should've told Dave everything. I mean once you'd got started on the confessional bit you should've gone the whole way. I know it sounds like preaching but it really is the best thing to be honest.'

'But it'd look as if I was cheating on him, wouldn't it? Cheating on both of them. Dave'd be bound to think of this place as a kind of—you know—sordid love-nest. If he knew Colin owned it.'

'Perhaps so. But you could explain, surely. When you rented the place you didn't even know it was Colin's property.'

'Sounds a bit unlikely, doesn't it?'

'Judy! It's the truth! For God's sake stop complicating things. Colin was somebody you'd worked for a couple of times. He heard you wanted a flat and kindly put you on to an agent. You didn't find out till later why the flat was such a bargain. Tell Dave the truth. Colin not only owned the flat but he owned the agent as well. All right, maybe you needn't have let him into your bed, but, for whatever reason it happened, if Dave really cares about you, he'll accept it.'

'I know. I know you're right. I should've told him everything. But he's so easily upset. And he's got this fight in London tomorrow night. I thought it might worry him. Put him off training.'

'Well, what's going to happen now?'

'I'm seeing Colin tomorrow. He phoned me after he'd got back last week. I said I wanted to see him urgently, something important to talk about, but he didn't give a damn. Said he was busy till Tuesday—that's tomorrow—and even then it'd mean having dinner with some Keighley business men at the Box Tree. They're going to talk about setting up a new Casino or club or something. They'll have their women with them so Colin'll want me tarted up to put their poor old bags in the shade. I'll have to wait till I can get him on his own. Then I'll tell him we're finished. Absolutely.'

'What about the flat? Will you want to say on?'

'That's one of the problems. I'll have to stay till I—or we, Dave and me—find somewhere else. That's if Dave's going to leave his wife. I've got my piano here and quite a lot of stuff. I thought I'd see if I could give Colin a month's notice. Something like that. That's why I wanted to see you, love. You're so good at thinking things out. What would you do? I rang Dave last night and he phoned me this morning. He's all tensed up, poor darling. This fight tomorrow at Wembley. I should've been going to watch but I've got to get this Colin business settled first. Do you think I ought to tell Colin about Dave?'

'Yes. Of course. Maybe you don't need to say exactly who it is but you must tell him everything else. How d'you think he'll react? Is he likely to get nasty?'

'I don't know. I've never really seen him when he's not got his own way. I don't care much. I mean I don't feel I owe him anything. He's used me as much as I've used him. More, really. I'll just tell him the truth. I don't suppose he'll care a lot. He'll find somebody else easy enough.'

'You said you were going to watch the fight but you're seeing Colin instead. What did Dave think about that? You seeing Colin instead of going to London.'

'Oh, I didn't tell him I was seeing Colin.'

Sue gave her friend an oblique look of exasperated reproof and shook her dark, sleek head: 'Oh Judy! Really!'

Judy protested, 'Yes, really! What the hell d'you think I was going to say? A couple of days before the boy's going into the boxing-ring to fight some Yankee thug who looks as if he'd murder you for ten cents. You think I should've said I was sorry I couldn't go and watch him but I'd got other things to do? Like having dinner with my ex—or hopefully ex—lover? You go on about telling the truth. I think you're right. I wish I'd told Dave about Colin right at the beginning. But I didn't and that's meant I've got tied up in a tangle of lies. I couldn't tell Dave that I was seeing Colin instead of going to the fight. He was so thrilled at the idea of me being there. Surely you can see that. It'd 've broken him up. I know it would.'

'So what *did* you tell him?'

Judy looked defiant. 'I told him I'm singing in Manchester on Tuesday night.'

They stared at each other. Sue was the first to laugh; then Judy's challenging expression disintegrated and she joined in.

'Oh Judy!' Sue gasped. 'Singing! Singing in Manchester! Couldn't you think of anything better than that?'

'No, I couldn't,' Judy controlled her voice and features. 'No. All I wanted to do was stop him worrying. I told him Mike's booked me as last minute substitute at a concert in Manchester and I just couldn't turn it down. I said the soprano had been taken ill suddenly with a sore throat.'

'D'you think he believed it?'

'Of course he did. Why shouldn't he?'

Sue did not look entirely convinced. 'I don't know. It wouldn't be hard to check up on.'

'He'd never think of doing that. Wouldn't know how to set about it anyway.'

'So you're going to tell Colin you've finished with him, hope he'll take a month's notice on the flat and not be awkward. And what then? Wait for your Dave to come back north and—well, what then? You think he's going to leave his wife?'

'It's not quite like that. Dave's booked us into a hotel in London, the Cumberland. We were going to go there straight after the fight. So I've told him to stay there by himself tomorrow night and I'll join him as soon as I can on Wednesday. At least I'll have settled things with Colin then. I hope.'

'And how long are you staying in London?'

'Till the following Sunday. That's next Sunday.'

'And you'll come back here? To the flat?'

'I don't know. I s'pose I'll have to see what happens. About giving notice and about what Dave decides. I think he'll leave his wife. They don't seem to have anything going for them at all. I know I've only got his version of her but she does seem just about the dreariest kind of girl you could imagine.'

'Well, I suppose he would paint her in the worst possible light, wouldn't he?'

'No. I told you before. He doesn't, believe it or not. I mean he doesn't deliberately. In fact he's quite defensive about her at times. Blames himself. But, even when he thinks he's singing her praises, the impression you get of the girl is pretty depressing. Very depressing in fact.'

'And would you want to marry him? If things go the way you want them to. Can you really see yourself married to a prizefighter? Looking ahead a few years I mean. When all the glamour, or what ever it is, has gone. He'll probably have his face battered a lot worse than it is now. Maybe a bit funny in the head. Don't they get punch-drunk or something? I've seen pictures of him. Saw one the other day in the *Post*. Nice-looking in a way. But a bit battered already isn't he? I mean it's fine when he's a fighting-fit youngster in his twenties but what's he going to be like in his forties? Fifties?'

'Oh I don't know, love. About marriage, I mean. Everything you say makes sense. In a way. I can see it as clear as day. With my mind. But not my heart, not my feelings. I don't know. I've never felt like this before about anybody and that's the truth. I think if he said he was going to divorce Aileen—that's his wife—and wanted to marry me. If he said that, I'd most likely say yes. I think I would. I'm sure I would. And all that stuff about him getting his face bashed in or his brains addled. Well, I don't know. What about most men? Ordinary men in ordinary jobs I mean. They don't usually look so bloody marvellous when they're in their forties or fifties, do they? And come to that, I don't suppose I'd look so sensational myself.'

Sue smiled. 'All you want from me is approval, isn't it? You just want me to say go ahead. Get your man. Love makes its own laws. You don't want advice. You want my blessing. Isn't that it, Judy?'

'No—well—yes. In a way. I don't mean I don't want your advice. 'Course I do. But yes, I suppose I do want your approval. I've a feeling it's not going to be a very popular move. Dave and me getting together. Ending his marriage. I don't know what my parents are going to say. And I expect his won't be too pleased. I think we're going to need all the friends we can find.'

'You know quite well I'll always—we'll always be your friends. Whatever you do.'

'We?'

'Me and Andy.'

'Oh . . . Yes . . . Don't you think he might disapprove?'

'He'd better not. No. He wouldn't. You'd be surprised. Andy's a lot less conventional and conservative than you'd think. In any case he'd make an awful lot of allowances if it meant he could meet a famous boxer.'

'Would *you* like to meet him?'

'Your boxer? Yes. Yes I would. If it's only to see what kind of man's turned you in to a dewy-eyed romantic.'

Sue looked at her watch.

'Oh don't go yet,' Judy said. 'We've plenty of time. I'll make a fresh pot.'

'All right. Another half hour.'

Judy took the tray into the kitchen and filled and switched on the electric kettle.

Sue called from the living room, 'If old Colin gets nasty tomorrow night and you want somewhere to run to. Well, you know where you'll be welcome. We can always put you up.'

'Thanks,' Judy answered. 'But I don't think it'll come to that. It's nice to know though.'

She made a fresh pot of tea and carried the tray back into the living room.

'Now,' Sue said, 'let's talk about me for a change.'

CHAPTER SIXTEEN

Y OU COULD HEAR the crowd faintly now, in the distance, like the noises of an enormous farmyard or zoo, the roars and yelps and squawks; excitement, hunger, frustration, vicarious triumph. Dave sat on the massage-table after the fight while Paddy Whelan removed the bandages from his hands. Paddy was chuckling and muttering to himself as he worked. 'Jesus Christ!' he kept saying, over and over again, 'Jesus Christ! What a beauty! What a wallop! Jesus Christ! What a punch! Oh boy, oh boy, oh boy! What a lovely punch!'

Phil was ushering the reporters out of the dressing-room: 'Thanks a lot lads. You've seen the boy's not got a mark on him. So Hayes'd better watch out in September.'

When the pressmen had gone Micky Rice began dancing around, hooking and jabbing into the air and chortling and grunting to the rhythm of his efforts. Then the dressing-room was again invaded and the noise from the arena swirled in and was abruptly reduced as Harold King, Jimmy Ruddock and Tom Darwin came in and shut the door behind them. Harold and Jimmy were beaming and Tom's eyes were brilliant with excitement and pleasure.

Jimmy flung his arms round Dave and kissed him somewhere on the side of the neck. 'By! What a punch! Oh, Dave lad! What a cracker! He never knew what hit him. Must have thought the bloody roof'd fell in! Poor bugger were out for three minutes.'

Harold stood back, grinning and nodding. Tom stayed near the door looking at the scene with a small, intent smile, his eyes still gleaming with a kind of joyful satisfaction.

Dave said, 'I'm going to get cleaned up', and he heaved himself from the table and disappeared into the shower cubicle.

Jimmy was saying to Phil. 'What d'you think then, eh? What about that left hook, eh?' And the right to the body? That's the one that brought Harvey's hands down. That's how Dave got to his chin. But what a punch. Third round! And it took Hayes six! Dave did it in half the time. What d'you make of that then?'

Phil said, 'I'd sooner he'd waited another four or five rounds.'

'What! Why? Quicker the better. Get the job done, that's what I always say. Why hang about? You might walk into one yourself. That Harvey weren't no mug. He were always dangerous. No. Dave did the right thing. Bang! All over. That's the way to do it.'

Phil smiled. 'Yeah. It was a nice punch. Very nice. The boy did a very neat job. It's just I'd've liked to seem him go a few more rounds. A bit more working behind the jab. Upright. What the Yanks think's the British style. Remember what I said in Leeds? Fool the Hayes camp. Make 'em think he'll be an easy touch. The way he handled Harvey's going to make 'em think different.'

'You can't fool around in a fight. It's all right in the gym. But in a fight. You see your chance you've got to grab it. Happen you'll not get another.'

'Yeah. Perhaps you're right. Maybe it's not such a bad thing, this quick win. Come to think of it we might be able to make very good use of it. Hayes'll be watching out for that left hook. That's the one that's finished Dave's last three knock-outs. We know—and the Hayes camp very likely doesn't—that Dave packs as much dynamite in his right as he does in his left. Yeah. We might be able to work on that.'

Dave emerged from the shower and began to dry himself and get dressed. He looked pale in the harsh strip-lighting, the flesh drawn tautly over the facial bone but, except for a slight bruising high on the left cheek, he was quite unmarked. His eyes, like Tom's, glittered with excitement. As he bent to tie his shoes a small, secretive smile touched his mouth but when he straightened up again it was gone.

He said, 'What you doing, Dad? Harold? You going back tonight?'

'No,' Jimmy said. 'Harold booked us in Regent's Palace. We thought we'd all go back an' have a bit of a celebration like. Except young Tom. He's got to be at work tomorrow morning, poor lad. Getting last train, aren't you son?'

Tom nodded.

Dave said, 'I'll take you to station. I've got the car here.'

'No,' Tom said. 'You go with your dad. I'll be able to get there all right on the underground.'

There was a knock on the door and Bernie Slater, the promoter, came in. His perspiring red face was jubilant.

'Great stuff, Dave!' he said. 'Terrific! My God this is going to make the Hayes fight a dazzler. Talk about the fight of the century! Phil, I'd like a few words. When you're free. Okay?'

Dave, now fully dressed, moved over to Tom's side. 'Listen,' he said. 'I want to talk to you. I'm not going with dad and them. They'll only be boozing. I'll just tell Phil and we'll bugger off. All right?'

Tom nodded. 'Whatever you say.'

Dave spoke to his father, 'I'm going to take Tom to station, dad. Then I'll be off to bed. I'm a bit tired like. You know. Need to wind down on me own. You have a good time. An' I tell you what. We'll have a real celebration after the Hayes fight. That's the real big 'un. We'll have a right slap-up do then. That's a promise, dad. All right?'

Jimmy looked a little disappointed but he accepted his son's decision. 'Aye. That's all right, lad. You young 'uns'll likely have things you want to talk about.'

Phil was watching Dave attentively. He said, 'Will we be seeing you later? At home?'

Dave hesitated. 'Aye . . . well, maybe not. I'll give you a ring.'

'Just a minute.' Phil turned to the others. 'Excuse us a minute.' He took Dave's arm and led him to the farthest end of the room near the shower cubicle and spoke in lowered tones,

216

almost a whisper: 'What's the trouble, Dave? Something's going on. You can tell me, son. What ever it is. Like Rose said the other night. We're with you. Hundred percent. Is it that girl? Judy? I just want to know where you are, what you're doing. That's all. It's only fair, son. Rose'd be worried sick if we didn't know where you was.'

Dave's head was lowered and he was slightly flushed. When he spoke his voice sounded uneasy yet defiant, very young, like that of a guilty schoolboy. 'I'm going to Leeds.'

'Tonight! Can't you wait till tomorrow?'

Dave shook his head. 'I've got to. I'm all right. I'm not tired. I can be there by one. Easy. I've got to go, Phil. Whatever you say.'

'Okay, son. That's all right. I just wanted to know. That's all. Paddy'll take your gear back. Will you give us a buzz? Tomorrow?'

'Yes.'

'Take it easy then. Keep in touch. Okay?'

Phil put one arm about Dave's shoulders and they went back to the others who had been discussing the spectacular knock-out of Wayne Harvey and the possibilities of a similar dramatic ending to the coming defence of the World Title against Earl Hayes.

'Dave's off now,' Phil said. 'Look after him, Tom.'

Outside the dressing-room Dave said, 'Come on. We can get out to car park this way.'

They set off down the long corridor.

'What was all that about?' Tom said. 'You and Phil in a huddle there?'

'I was telling him I'm going back to Leeds.'

'What d'you mean? *Now*?'

'That's right.'

'You mean you're going to drive back?'

'Aye. Both on us.'

They mounted a small flight of stairs and went along another corridor towards a door at the end marked 'Emergency Exit'.

'I thought you were staying at the Cumberland. Judy phoned me the other day and said—'

'Aye. I know. But I've changed me mind. I'm going back now.'

They did not speak again until they were out in the night air, moving past the phalanxes of parked cars.

'It's over there,' Dave said. 'We'll get out easy. It's bloody murder if you wait till end of show . . . Here we are.'

He unlocked the driver's door, slipped into the seat and leaned across to release the catch and allow Tom to climb in.

'I'm going to get an XJS Jag after the Hayes fight,' he said as he started the engine and switched on the lights. 'It's a great car is that.'

The Capri moved forward, nosing towards the exit.

Tom said, 'Why've you suddenly decided to go back tonight?'

Dave drove out into the road without answering. Then he said, 'I've got to see her. Tonight.'

'Judy.' It was not really a question.

'Aye.'

Tom nodded and made a small noise of what was both understanding and confirmation of something already known.

They drove towards Neasden and the North Circular and they had almost reached the M1 before Dave spoke again.

He said, 'I s'pose you think I'm daft.' Then when Tom did not reply: 'I couldn't wait. Not till tomorrow. It's like—I don't know how to say it. Like I won the fight and Judy's part of the win. It's not a proper win without her and me sort of sharing it. Sounds daft, don't it?'

'No.'

'Aye. But I bet you think it is really.'

'No. I can understand it.'

'I've been working all this time for the Harvey fight. Five weeks. Seemed like bloody years. I rung her up every day, but that's not the same. I was working for tonight, for the fight. You know the way, when you're training, you've got target there in front of you like. The big night. That's what you're working for. Every day you're getting closer. Then you're there. Up there in ring. The fight. An' when it's over, you've won. Like tonight, you've flattened the other bloke. It's great. Marvellous. You're on top o' world. Everything you've been

218

working for. Everything you want's in that fight. You win it and you've got it all. Everything you've ever wanted. But tonight was different. A great win. I knew I'd find him. Right from first bell. You can tell sometimes. Only a matter of time. I brought his guard down and cracked him on the chin. Simple as that. Lovely. But after—when I got back to dressing-room and media boys come in an' all that—it weren't same. Something missing. I'd been working all them weeks for something else. As well. See what I mean, Tom? It weren't just the win, it were winning an' getting back to Judy. Judy's the prize. She's what I want as much as winning. An' I'm going to get her. I can't wait Tom. And that's a fact.'

They had reached the motorway now and the car was humming along at a steady eighty-five miles an hour.

'Yeah. Well, take it steady. Another half hour won't make much odds.'

'I tell you. I can't wait.'

'Isn't she in Manchester tonight? She said something about a concert. Standing in for someone that was ill.'

'Aye. But she's getting back to Leeds about midnight. Soon after. That's what she said. What time d'you make it now?'

Tom held his wrist close to the dashboard light. 'About twenty past ten.'

'Not bad. We'll be back before one, rate we're going.'

'Does she know you're coming?'

'No. I'm supposed to be at Cumberland. That's what we fixed. I've got me case in boot. All me stuff. I'm s'posed to spend night there. She was coming by train tomorrow morning. But—you know, like I said—I can't wait to see her.'

'Did you cancel the room?'

'Bugger the room.'

'I'll ring 'em up when I get back if you like. Give some excuse.'

'Don't worry Tom. I'm not bothered.'

'Perhaps you'd better phone Judy. We could stop at one of the service stations.'

'No. I told you. She won't be back till past twelve. That's what she said. Any case I want to give her a surprise.'

There was not much traffic on the motorway and Dave

kept to the outside lane. Their progress was punctuated by his headlights illuminating signs which rushed towards them and were flung by speed into the darkness behind. Tom began to feel drowsy but his mind was tennanted by images of Dave's triumph in the ring. Again and again, like film being replayed, he saw Dave moving forward against the shorter, powerfully muscled American who tried at intervals to arrest the Champion's advance by holding his ground and launching sudden barrages of hooks and swings to the head and body. These counter-attacks were nullified every time by Dave's stabbing left jabs and thumping right uppercuts to the solar plexus or straight to the head. Then the end: two very fast left jabs into the mouth, and the right smashing upwards into the body. Harvey wincing, bending a little and involuntarily lowering his gloves for that part of a second which left the jaw unprotected to receive the scything left hook that lifted him clear of the canvas and dumped him in a sprawling, motionless lump close to the ring-apron. Then Dave walking, almost casually, to his own corner, raising both gloves above his head in what was, compared with the antics of most fighters, a modest acknowledgement of the crowd's shrieks and yells.

'What did you think of her then Tom? Aye. I know what you said on phone. Very nice girl. You wouldn't say nothing different though, would you? But what you really think? Honest to God. Did you really like her?'

Tom had to snap himself away from the remembered spectacle of the arena and for a second he could not think what Dave was talking about. 'Oh yes,' he said. 'Judy. Yes I did. I mean I really did think she was nice. Very. Lovely looking girl. I don't blame you at all for falling for that one'

'But did you *like* her? I know she's beautiful an' all that. Anybody can see that. But never mind what she looks like. Did you like her anyway, as a person like?'

'Yes I did.'

'You're not just saying that?'

'No, I'm not. I did like her. 'Course it's not easy to separate what people look like from what they are. If you see what I mean. You can't really do it. It's no good saying would you like Judy just as much if she looked like Margaret Thatcher. Fact is Judy *couldn't* look like Margaret Thatcher any more than Mrs T could look like Judy. In other words Judy looks nice at least partly because she *is* nice. It's not just shape of features, colour of eyes and hair, size of tits and that kind of thing. These are a help of course. Judy's lucky like that. The scaffolding's very nicely made. But what makes people—women, maybe men, too—what makes 'em attractive is a lot to do with what they're like, what they are. Good nature, kindness, generosity, humour, intelligence. All these things show. Put it another way. You could probably find a woman not all that much different from Judy in the way of eyes and nose and hair and figure. But if she was a nasty mean unsympathetic, greedy, cruel cow I don't think you'd find her good-looking or attractive.'

'So you like her.'

Tom laughed. 'Yeah. I liked her. Very much.' But he was troubled by a tiny itch of uncertainty as he asked himself if he was telling Dave the truth. Certainly, he thought, he had not disliked Judy. Certainly he had found her sexually attractive, even a little uncomfortably so, though he hoped that he had concealed this fact from both her and Dave. But unambiguous liking was something he could not honestly claim to have felt.

Another sign zoomed towards them and fled away, behind.

'We'll soon be coming up to Leicester turn-off,' Dave said. 'What time is it now?'

'Nearly half-eleven.'

Tom felt the car's speed increase and he saw the speedometer needle move to ninety.

He said, 'What about Aileen?'

'Eh?'

'Aileen. You said you'd tell her about Judy. What's happening there?'

'Oh. Aye. Well. I'm not sure about that. It's hard to tell. She's such a funny one is Aileen. I wish I knew how she really felt.'

'She's still the same as you said then? Fairly happy? Not too worried? As far as you can tell.'

'Seems like it.'

They drove on in silence for a while. Then Tom said, 'How do you feel about tonight? The fight. Easier than you expected?'

'I felt good. Right from start, like I said. Never felt better. I reckon I'm punching harder than ever. I know what papers'll say tomorrow. They'll say Harvey's over the hill. Past it. A push-over. But they don't know. Bloody reporters. Never had gloves on in their lives. They don't understand. You're as good as other bloke lets you be. I never give poor lad a chance. I was boss and he bloody knew it, right from first bell.'

'Hayes'll be a different proposition.'

'Aye. He will that. But he'll go. He's a clever bugger, no doubt about it. And he can dig a bit. But I'll get to him, sooner or later I'll find him an' he'll have to go. That sounds big-headed I know. But it's not really. I'm at my peak. I'm so bloody strong I could knock a wall down. I can't see anybody staying there for fifteen threes. Not even Earl Hayes.'

A few minutes later Dave said, 'What's time, Tom?'

'Quarter to twelve.'

'Won't be long now. Should be there inside an hour.' A pause: then he said, 'By! It'll be great to see her.' He chuckled. 'And won't she get a surprise!'

Judy watched the one called Dennis light another cigar and gaze sideways at her from beneath heavy greying eye-brows, his dark, slightly bloodshot eyes holding a knowing yet querying look, speculative and obscurely insulting.

He then turned and raised his right index finger to summon a waiter.

'Same again my friend,' he said. 'Remy Martin for the gents and whatever the ladies are on.'

Colin Hunter sat at the head and Judy at the foot of the table with Dennis on Judy's left and the other man, Arthur, on her right. Next to Dennis sat Arthur's wife, Vi, who was opposite Shirley, married—poor bitch, thought Judy—to Dennis. Colin wore a dark lounge suit and his sun-tan looked theatrically implausible in the shaded lights of the restaurant and in contrast to the grey pallor of Arthur and Dennis's jowly pinkness. Both women were in their mid forties and striving, with the aid of cosmetics and the beautician's arts, but without much success, to appear younger. Vi was a good deal the plumper of the two and she had managed, perhaps assisted by a generous amount of alcohol, to remain cheerful, occasionally embarassingly so. Unlike Shirley she made no attempt to conceal her Pudsey origins and she spoke, more loudly than necessary, with an unaffected West Yorkshire accent. Shirley, on the other hand, was resolved to sustain a demeanour of fastidious ennui and when she spoke it was with an unhappily judged attempt at standard Southern speech in which her vowels emerged in astonishing forms, as when she asked her husband to 'pess the shugger' when she wished to sweeten her coffee.

The men had talked business over drinks before the meal and during the earlier part of it, but they had now shifted on to more general conversation. Dennis had expressed his admiration for the Prime Minister's resolute handling of the Falklands crisis and his loathing of all bleeding-heart pacifists, left-wingers and do-gooders. Colin did not say much, nodding with indulgent good-humour as Dennis extended the virulence and range of his attack to include the molly-coddling Welfare State, football hooligans and criminals who needed to be taught a lesson in the only language they understood—the lash and the rope.

Judy sipped some black coffee and glanced surreptitiously at her wristwatch. Ten to twelve. Surely they would be finishing soon. Then she was suddenly alert as she heard Arthur say, 'I wonder how Ruddock got on with what's-his-name, the Yank. It'll put the cat among the pigeons if he gets beat tonight, won't it?'

'Gets beat?' Dennis said. 'He won't get beat old son. It's a fix. Stands to reason. They're not going to take any chances with the title fight coming up in September or whenever it is. Those boys know what they're up to. This guy he's fighting's

223

a has-been. He'll go in there and mess Ruddock about for a few rounds. Then the Yank'll take a dive when he's told to and pocket a few thou' and get the next plane home. Old Bernie Slater's on to a winner. The Hayes fight I mean. Closed-circuit TV all over the world. Packed out stadium. The lot.'

Arthur said, 'It'll be a great fight.'

'A great what!' Dennis's eyes bulged with incredulity. 'You must be joking Arthur. Hayes'll kill him.'

Colin said, 'What odds would you give, Dennis?'

'On Ruddock? Oh, I don't know. Six to one. Something like that.'

'Hey, he's a good lad, is Ruddock,' Arthur protested. 'never been beaten. I saw him knock that Mexican out last year. He's got a helluva wallop.'

'He fought for me a couple of times at the Lonsdale Club when he was on his way up.' Colin said. 'Arthur's right. He could punch hard. Even then.'

Dennis said, 'You say he's never been beaten, Arthur. But who's he fought? Nobody in Hayes's class. Sure Ruddock's a useful lad and he can punch. In his own class. But this nigger's something special. They're not like us. They're animals. Primitive. He'll murder Ruddock.'

Judy said, 'Excuse me', and rose from the table and made her way to the women's cloakroom.

Dennis watched her cross the restaurant floor. He drew on his cigar and exhaled smoke. Then he nodded in the direction that she had gone. 'Little lady's not got much to say, Colin. Hope we're not boring her.'

'*We're* not,' Vi said, but her expression was amiable.

Shirley said, 'It's time we were going, Dennis.'

Briefly he looked as if he might become angry but the moment passed and he grinned, 'All right, love, I'll just finish this.'

Colin signalled to the waiter and asked for the bill.

Vi said, 'It's been lovely, Colin. Hasn't it, Arthur? Been smashing.'

When Judy returned she saw, to her great relief, that they were preparing to leave. Colin took her coat from one of the attendant waiters and held it for her to slip into.

Vi said, 'It's been really nice meeting you love. I'll watch out for you on telly.'

Judy smiled and murmured thanks. Her eyes were smarting from the tobacco-smoke and a slight headache had began its delicate drilling at her right temple.

Dennis was watching her with a smile that was ingratiating yet not without a hint of a sneer. Then Shirley tugged at his elbow and he allowed himself to be led towards the door. The others followed to a murmuration of thanks and farewells from the staff and, outside, Judy held up her face with gratitude to the cool night air.

Colin did not speak to her until they were in his Mercedes and heading back to the city. He lit a cigarette as he drove and then he said, 'You tired?'

'Yes, a bit.'

'Feeling off colour? You didn't seem very lively tonight. To put it mildly.'

'No. I'm sorry.'

'That's all right. They're not the best of company. Still you could have made a bit of an effort. Dennis's a slob but he's a good man to do business with. Straight. Says what he means. Sticks to his word.'

'I thought he was repulsive.'

'Yes. You made your feelings pretty obvious.'

'Not as obvious as I'd like to have done.'

'Oh come on now, Judy. No harm in being civil. Even if it's only for my sake. After all, you weren't exactly suffering, were you? I mean a lot of girls'd be only too happy to swap places. Best food you can get around these parts. Good wine. Service. A bit of an effort wouldn't have been too much to ask.'

Judy said, 'I told you I wanted to talk to you, Colin. Earlier, when you picked me up at the flat. You said later . . . Okay . . . It's later.'

A brief pause and then he said, 'Go on then.'

'You just said there'd be a lot of girls who'd like to swap places with me. Maybe you're right. Perhaps you ought to find one of them.'

'Oh . . . I see . . . Ah, mm.' A brief monotonous low humming, then: 'Yes. I might've expected it. A good six months I've been away. Too long to expect anything else . . . mmm . . . still, not a very nice welcome back is it?'

'You'll get over it.'

'Yes, I expect I will.' Again the low, ruminative humming. 'Well go on then . . . or is that it?' He stubbed out his cigarette in the ashtray.

Judy closed her eyes and tried to will the increasing discomfort of her headache to recede.

She said, 'I've met someone. It's serious. I've got to—I mean you and me—we've got to finish. I'm sorry.'

Colin did not speak for what seemed quite a long time. Then he said, 'You'd better tell me more.'

'There isn't any more. It's quite simple. I told you. I've met somebody I like. Very much. It's obvious we can't go on, you and me. I'd have told you before. I'd have written if I could but that wasn't my fault, was it? I mean I hadn't got any address to write to. You made sure of that.'

'No need to get aggressive, dear. Let's both try and be reasonable.'

'But it's true, Colin. If I could have written to you in the States I could've told you. You didn't want to risk your wife getting hold of—'

'Let's leave my wife out of this!' Then he softened his voice again: 'She's not a strong woman, Judy. I've told you that before. I've got to take care she doesn't get any kind of unnecessary worry, anxiety. It's her nerves. The other thing's psychosomatic. That's what the doctor's say. She's got to avoid stress, any kind of stress, as much as possible. So let's just stick to the point. What concerns you and me. And this other person of course.'

'I was only saying—'

'I know what you were saying. You could have told me by letter. That would've been easier wouldn't it? Dear Colin, Sorry to tell you I've met someone else. So just disappear, will you? It was nice knowing you, Love from Judy. That kind of thing?'

'No. But at least you'd've had time to think about it. Think what's the best thing to do.'

'The best thing to do? What is there to do? You tell me.'

They were now on the Otley Road and on their left Judy could see scattered light shimmering far away in the great bowl of the valley. Soon they would be on the city's outskirts and then only a matter of minutes before arriving at her flat. Her headache was intensifying and she felt slightly sick. Dave would be at the Cumberland now. He had said that he would telephone at twelve-thirty. He would be in the hotel bedroom, maybe bruised and tired from his fight, wanting to hear her voice.

'Well?' Colin said.

She said, 'I don't know. I've got a headache.'

'Perhaps it would be a good idea to tell me something about your—this—whoever it is. You say it's serious. How serious is serious? I mean can we expect wedding bells? Who is he? What's he do? How old is he? A lot younger than me I imagine. And what have you told him about me? Let's start with his name, shall we?'

'You don't need to know his name.'

'I don't? Isn't that for me to decide? After all I've got some rights haven't I? I mean we've known each other for—what? Three years? It must be a bit more than friends. At least I'd have thought so. I think you owe it it me to give me a few details. I mean you can't really expect me to say okay. You've found true love. God bless you and goodbye. Can you?... well, can you?'

'All I want is to run my own life. I've told you. I've met somebody who means a lot to me. I want to—I want a clean start. You and I've never been—well, you know, we never pretended we were in love or anything. It was just something that happened. I happened to be free. I hadn't got any ties. You wanted— I don't know—somebody young and presentable. Somebody to take out. Meet your friends. Like that lot tonight. Go to bed with once in a while. I suppose I shouldn't've got myself mixed up in the first place. I'm sorry if I've hurt your feelings. But don't let's kid ourselves it's anything more than pride. I'm no more to you than anything else you own—or think you own. Your dog or your car or your boat. That's true and you know it.'

'That's how you think of yourself is it? A thing, an object a possession? You really think of yourself like that Judy?'

'No. But you do.'

His left had released the steering-wheel and settled on her right thigh and squeezed gently. Quite involuntarily she pulled away from his touch.

'Oh,' he said softly, 'we're untouchable, are we? Keeping ourselves pure and unsullied for Mr Right.'

Anger sparked and flared. She said, 'Don't be funny! And stop dodging the issue. All I want to do is tell you it's all over. You and me. We're finished. And I want to know what you expect me to do about things. About the flat really. I know I'll have to get out. I want to know if it's all right to give you a month's notice. Just so's I can have time to find somewhere else. Move my stuff. I just want you to accept things the way they are.'

'The way they are. Accept things.' Again the low musing noises. 'Look Judy. I'm a reasonable man. You know that. But I'm not a patsy. I'm not the kind of person that gets pushed around. You ought to know that, too. I think you do know it, don't you? Now let's get things into perspective. You've been living in a very nice little flat for the last three years. I've—'

'I paid rent,' she interrupted. 'You talk as if it was a gift.'

He laughed quietly but the sound was not pleasant. 'Rent! Have you any idea what that place would bring in on the open market? Yes, of course you have. Central heating. Double-glazing. Self-contained in Roundhay. And what've you been paying? Forty quid a month, isn't it? Judy, my dear, let's be realistic. You know damn well the only reason you paid anything at all was your own self-respect. I let you have it for peanuts to save your face. You must've known that my dear. You're not a fool. You must know I could've been collecting at least four times as much. Think about it. A bit of simple arithmetic'll tell you in three years I've lost over four and a half thousand on that place. Not that I'm complaining. At least I wasn't complaining. Not till now. But what do you expect? You want me to say no hard feelings? Leave the flat when ever you feel like it? Or maybe you'd like to keep it on with your new boy friend. Mr Anonymous. Is that what you'd like to do?'

They were now approaching the Oakwood traffic lights. In a couple of minutes they would be at the flat. Judy felt a kind of muffled panic clogging her mind, heavy on her spirits, a sense of tired despair and frustration. She struggled to hold back the suddenly importunate tears.

She thought, without much hope, that she must do something to change the mood of antagonism that had been established, attempt to engage his sympathy, use her femininity.

'Colin,' she said, 'I'm sorry I've sprung this on you. It must be a nasty shock. I can see that. But honestly it's not my fault. I would have written and explained everything if I could have done. I wanted to. And it's not as if I've deceived you or anything. I couldn't help it. I couldn't help falling in love. I suppose it was bound to happen some time. I mean we both knew what we had—you and me—we knew it wasn't forever, didn't we? I remember you said, ages ago, right at the beginning, that I mustn't expect more than you could offer. You'd no intention of leaving your wife and children, ever. Don't you remember? I mean it was never permanent, was it Colin? We both knew that.'

He turned off the Wetherby Road and brought the car to a halt near the entrance to the drive that led to the flat.

He said, 'Are you going to ask me in?'

'It's late. Nearly half past twelve. I've got to get up early tomorrow. I've got to catch an early train. I'm going to London.'

'And you expect me to drive away now and disappear completely? You've decided it's all over. Time to give me my marching-orders, eh? The old sugar daddy's served his purpose. He can go and get stuffed. Is that it?'

'No. No, love. You know I've never thought of you like that. Be fair, Colin. Try and see it from my side. I've got my whole life ahead of me. You never expected me to give up any hope of a life of my own. Maybe marriage. You must have known it couldn't go on forever. One of us was bound to end it sooner or later. You must have known that.'

He took out another cigarette and lit it. Then he said, 'I'm not going to sit here all night. Either I come in and we talk a bit more—find out just what you've been up to, who this fellow is—or I'll drive off now and find out in my own way. That won't be difficult, you know. And don't think I'll be a fairy godfather to you both. I'm not feeling too happy about the way things are going. Maybe if I knew a bit more, knew who I was being ditched for, if the man's worth it. Maybe I'd be a bit more sympathetic. It's possible. But I'm not going to be told it's none of my business. Because it is. It's very much my business. You understand?'

She hesitated, the said, 'All right. But you can't stay the night, Colin. I'm sorry but you can't.'

He opened the car door but paused to say before he began to climb out, 'Don't worry. The last thing I want to do is curl up with your tender little body. About which, incidentally, I could compare notes with your new friend some time perhaps.'

They both got out of the car and walked to the rear of the house where Judy unlocked the door for them to enter the flat. She switched on lights and in the livingroom she said wearily and from habit, 'Would you like some coffee?'

He took off his coat and threw it on to the sofa. 'That would be very nice,' he said sitting down. 'And get me an ashtray will you?'

'Will Nescafé do?' Judy called from the kitchen as she looked in a cupboard and found an ashtray.

She went back to the living-room and placed the ashtray on the arm of his chair. Then she returned to the kitchen to prepare the coffee.

Had Dave telephoned? she wondered. How had he got on in his fight? She must get rid of Colin quickly yet somehow manage to placate him. But was that possible? She knew now with a miserable clarity that she should have told Dave the truth about her relationship with Hunter right from the beginning. She had been a fool to deceive him. On one thing she was firmly resolved: tomorrow—no, it was already today—she would tell him everything about the whole wretched business and hope that he would be forgiving. She would explain that she had been ashamed and afraid of losing him. He would understand. Surely he would understand and forgive her.

The kettle began to boil and she made the coffee and took the tray back to where Colin was finishing his cigarette.

He said, 'It *is* a nice little flat, isn't it love?'

She said, 'Look Colin. I'm feeling rotten. Got an awful headache and I told you I've got to be up early. Please let's get this over with. There's really no point at all in quarrelling. All I'm asking is for you to tell me how and when I leave the flat. And I'm asking—I'm begging you—not to make things difficult with me and—the person I'm going with.'

'Oh yes. The person you're going with. Now that's what interests me. Would I know him? What kind of a chap is he? One of those down-at-heel fiddle players or something? A singer maybe? I'd like to know. Can't you see that, Judy? I'm interested. Of course I am. Anyone would be interested. I'd like to know what kind of man you think's better than me. Do I know him, I wonder.'

'No you don't. And it's not a question of being better than you. It's not a competition.'

'No? I happen to believe everythings's a competition. Life's a competition. But don't lets get philosophical. All I want to know is who the fellow is. What's his name? What's he do?'

She thought, 'If Dave phones now Colin will interfere. He'll either grab the phone or shout so that Dave can hear him. And it'll be obvious there's a man here. I've got to get him out. Quick.' And, with the renewed feeling of urgency, anger was fuelled. Aloud she said, 'I've had enough! You've got to go. You're obsessed. You're jealous of—'

'Jealous! Of you! I think you're—'

'Shut up! Listen. You're jealous because I find somebody—as you put it—better than you. And, my God he's a million times better. No mistake about that. All right. You've been laying down the law. You've been trying to blackmail me. You'll tell him what a tramp I am. All about me being your bit on the side. Okay. Two can play that game. If you don't get out of here, now, in two minutes, I'll ring your wife up and tell her a few interesting things about her loving husband. And if she blows a fuse or bursts a blood vessel or whatever's supposed to be wrong with her it'll be your fault. So get out!'

He leaned forward, a hand on each arm of the chair as if he were preparing to launch himself at her. His eyes widened and seemed to swell with disbelieving rage. She saw veins suddenly appear, prominent on his forehead.

He spoke very softly, almost in a whisper: 'You little bitch! You wicked little cow! You think you can get away with this! By Christ you're going to find out different. You're going to pay! Believe me you're going to pay! I'm going to make you suffer.'

He rose to his feet, his bulging glare unwinkingly fixed upon her as they both stood facing each other across the little table. Then the bell rang.

For a fraction of a second Judy was utterly disconcerted. 'Dave!' she thought. 'The telephone!' But almost before the idea had taken shape she realized that the noise was not that of the telephone but of the doorbell.

'Who the hell can that be?' Colin muttered to himself, moving towards the kitchen and the rear of the house. 'Maybe the police. I must've left my lights on.'

Judy followed him through the kitchen into the hall and, as he was reaching for the outer door handle, the bell rang again.

'All right, all right,' Colin grunted and swung the door open. He peered out at the man on the threshold. 'Who're you?' he said. 'What do you want?'

Dave came quickly forward and pushed him forcibly enough to make him stagger and collide with Judy who was at his elbow.

'What the hell . . . !' Colin exclaimed.

Dave was in the hall now, staring from Judy to Colin and back again, first with an expression of total bewilderment that, in other circumstances, would have been comical, mouth open and eyes very wide. Then his face was suddenly contorted, lips tightly compressed, eyes narrowing and forehead creased. He shook his head, opened and shut his mouth, and then his face was no longer simply twisted with shock and perplexity but it seemed to break into jagged angles and planes and he was almost unrecognisable as the Dave that Judy knew.

She tried to speak his name but no sound came out. She heard a voice that must have been Colin's, but was weirdly unlike it, breathless and high-pitched , a tremulous squeak.

'Jesus Christ!' he was retreating, backwards, into the kitchen.

Dave threw back his head; his face was raised to the ceiling. She could see the tendons and muscles of his neck stretched taut. She thought he was going to scream. It was almost as if he was screaming without making any sound. Then, very slowly, he lowered his head and stared at her with terrible intensity, pain and hatred.

She tried again to say his name but still the sound died in her throat.

Then his eyes closed very tightly and his head fell to one side, and began a slow, rolling, circular movement. Twice this happened and then his head came to rest, chin lowered upon his throat, before it came up and his eyes reopened and stared at her again.

At last he spoke. 'Him! You was with him all the time!' he said in a thick growl. 'You never went to Manchester.'

At last her voice was audible: 'I can explain. He's nothing. Dave. He's nobody. I can explain.'

Dave said, 'Was you in Manchester? Singing?'

She heard the sitting-room door close and knew that Colin had retreated to what must have seemed a safer place.

She said, 'No. I wasn't. But I can explain. Let me explain. Don't go Dave . . . Please . . .' She began to move towards him.

'Get away from me!' It was a snarl. She saw his fists, bunched, rock-hard.

She thought, 'He's going to hit me. He's going to kill me.'

Then 'Please . . . please Dave . . .' She was whispering, hopelessly, but already he had turned away and, moving with a curious stiffness, like someone much older or suffering from a painful muscular disease, he stepped out through the open door and disappeared into the darkness.

CHAPTER SEVENTEEN

S UNLIGHT WAS DAZZLING at the uncurtained
window, rinsing the bedroom furniture, as
he awoke and quickly turned his head away from the painful
brilliance and closed his eyes again. At first, for no longer than
two seconds, he was aware only of an appalling sense of sick
desolation, of blank, engulfing misery, before the full memory
came razoring into the darkness with images and the
explanation of his condition.

He was lying, fully clothed, on top of his bed. He had not
even removed his shoes. He brought his wrist watch close to
his face and, without moving his head, looked at his watch. It
showed the time to be a quarter to ten. He closed his eyes again
and tried to escape back into forgetful sleep but he knew at
once that there was no hope of such an easy sanctuary from the
knowledge that was insisting on being recognised.

He recalled walking from Judy's house and getting into his
car where he had sat for some time trying to control his nausea
and the destructive rage which urged him to return and smash
the pair of them. And then he had driven the car away, at first
forgetting to switch on his headlights, so that he had scraped
the side of the Mercedes that had been parked in front of him.
He had driven at great speed, quite without conscious
direction, and he now had indistinct recollections of passing
through deserted Harrogate and leaving the main road to
hurtle along narrow, winding country lanes, hearing the
tingling lash of branch and briar on the bodywork of the car
until he had reached a road that took him high over the moors
and here he had stopped the car and remained hunched in his
seat, gripping the steering-wheel, struggling to impose some
kind of order on the thrashing confusion of thoughts and
feelings that tormented him.

234

Colin Hunter, the oily bastard who used to run shows at the Lonsdale Club and treated fighters like cattle. Dave remembered him coming into the communal dressing-room and looking at the lads with a kind of contemptuous smirk and telling them he didn't want any free-wheeling or play-acting in his ring. He'd said that his customers expected real action and if they didn't get it none of the lads need expect any more work at the Lonsdale. This shit-house was the man Judy preferred. She had told Dave that she would finish with Hunter, that she wouldn't see him again. Dave had believed her. He had believed that she loved him and that she was truly his girl. And what had happened? She had chosen to be with the bastard on the very night when she should have been at the ringside watching Dave's victory. She had lied and lied and lied. Everything was lies. She was a cruel, lying, dirty bitch. She looked like an angel but she was evil. There was no punishment bad enough for her. He ought to have smashed her face in. And Hunter's. He ought to have murdered the pair of them. The bitch. How could she have told such lies? How could she have been so loving and passionate and tender and all the time known that she was going to deceive him, get back with Hunter as soon as he returned from America? Even then, at that moment, the two of them were probably laughing at him. In bed. Together. They had probably made love, just as she had made love to Dave, all her open, clinging, moist welcoming for that creepy old man Hunter. Judy. Her sweetness and tenderness, her cries of need and rapturous fulfilment. For Hunter!

Dave remembered.

He had sat in the car as rage filled him, its dark fermentation generating images of murderous violence, until he was trembling and sick with the black taste of it and then, quite unexpectedly, it drained away, leaving briefly a vast cold emptiness which was then flooded by such sorrow as he had never known or dreamed possible. The harsh grief rose and clawed in his throat, pressed and burned his eyes, expanded to bursting-point in his chest, and then it was released and he wept, great choking sobs rending him as the tears flowed, blinding and soaking and salting, going on and on as if his pain would flood the world and drown all sweetness there. It seemed that he must have cried for a long time before the storm of grieving passed and he was left shamed and weakened and now filled by a dull sense of loss, of something infinitely precious that had been taken from him forever.

He could not recall how long he had stayed there after his bout of weeping but it must have been for a considerable time because he remembered at last driving on and being quite lost until he had reached a cross-roads with a sign-post, one arm of which pointed to Otley, and noticing that the sky was beginning to blanch and, by the time he was driving into Leeds, the street lights were pallid against a grey and misty sky. Now, as he lay on his bed, he felt the weight of his misery pressing down on him and a hollowness in his stomach that might have been hunger, though the thought of eating made him feel so sick he almost retched.

Presently he heard a sound on the stairs and then his bedroom door opened and Aileen looked into the room.

She said, 'Didn't you hear the phone? It's Phil Richardson. He'd like to talk to you.' Then, when he neither moved nor answered: 'Dave! What's up with you? What you been playing at?'

Still no reply.

'Dave! What am I going to tell him?'

He muttered half into the pillow, 'Tell him I'm asleep. I'll ring him later.'

She went away but in a couple of minutes she was back at his side. 'What's the matter, Dave? What happened? I thought you wasn't coming back till next week. When you came in s'morning—it were about five— I were right scared. I wondered who it could be. What's wrong love? What's happened?'

Her voice showed concern and it must have been this that touched the vulnerable centre of hurt and self-pity from which the shocking tempest of tears had been engendered a few hours earlier and Dave was appalled to feel again grief struggling for release in his breast and throat. He pressed his face into the pillow but he could not prevent the muffled sound of a sob from escaping.

236

He bit hard on the pillowcase and clenched his fists so tightly that the fingernails were cutting into the palms of his hands.

Aileen said, 'Oh lovey! What is it? What's wrong. Tell me. You're not hurt, are you? I heard you won your fight. Heard it on news this morning. You never got hurt, did you? What's up Dave? . . . Is it her? Is that it, love? It's her, isn't it? What's she done to you? What is it, love?'

He turned his head slightly so that, with one eye, he could see her face on which he expected to find at least a hint of satisfaction, if not malicious triumph, but there was no sign of any other emotion except tender, almost motherly concern for his distress and it was this look of compassion that he found unbearable. Again the irresistible, shaming, almost orgasmic rush of tears was released as he turned his face to the pillow and felt his shoulders shaking and heaving. He could hear Aileen's voice, but only faintly, unable to distinguish the words, though the consoling rhythm communicated sympathy, and, as the paroxysms became more controllable, he felt her hand lightly stroking his head. Then she sat on the edge of the bed and put both arms about him and drew him close so that his face was now against her breast and she began to rock slightly and gently to and fro, murmuring timeless maternal sounds of comfort until the depredations of misery and hopelessness had subsided.

The modified and temporary relief from pain and his feeling of gratitude to Aileen prompted him to raise his head and reach out to draw her down beside him on to the bed. At once she stiffened against him and firmly disengaged herself from his embrace.

'No,' she said. 'Nothing like that, love. Why don't you get up and have a bath and put some clean clothes on. You'll feel better for it. P'raps you'd like to tell us about it then if you want to.'

She went to the door and paused there for a moment. She looked very fresh and healthy and he was puzzled by, and even a little resentful of, the serenity of her faint smile.

'I'll make you some breakfast,' she said and went out of the room.

Dave did not eat that breakfast, nor did he eat anything for two days.

After his bath, in a desperate attempt to find later oblivion in a sleep of exhaustion he set out on a long walk, avoiding the city centre, where he would certainly be recognised and stopped for his autograph, and striding out towards the villages of Shadwell and Wike, returning in a great circle through Eccup, over the Headingley golf-course to Alwoodley and Moortown, but, although he was physically tired at the end of the journey, he could not sleep. At first he thought incessantly of Judy and Hunter but later, perhaps from an unconscious wish to escape the anguish of these cruel images and the murderous impulses they generated, his thoughts dwelt more and more on the earlier and idyllic moments of love and, while these recollections were in a sense palliative, the undeniable knowledge of the subsequent betrayal now filled him with a great, dragging pain of emptiness.

Two days later, a Friday, he got up and again left the house before Aileen had risen and again set out on another long walk, this time going east through Sandhills and Thorner to Scarcroft Hill. Still utterly obsessed with thought of Judy he seemed now no longer troubled by vengeful fantasies, only weighted down by the sense of loss, and gradually he began to seek for some small glow of hope in the embers of his desolation. Now that he could reconstruct the events of Tuesday night—or, rather, the early hours of Wednesday morning—he remembered that Judy had said that she could explain Hunter's presence. He, Dave, had not given her the chance. And, he thought with a flicker of something close to optimism—she had not been scared—surely, if she and Hunter were together for what he had thought they were, she would have been afraid of Dave's anger. She wouldn't have called him back as he left. She would have been only too glad to see him go. Perhaps—if only he dared to believe it—perhaps there was some explanation.

It was almost eleven o'clock when he reached Wellington Hill and joined the Wetherby Road. By now he was walking very fast for he had made up his mind. As he approached the road where she lived he began to trot and he only slowed to a walk again as he turned into the drive and approached the back of the house. He pressed the bell and listened to the sound of its summons inside the flat. No hint of movement from within. He pressed the bell again, keeping his finger hard on the button for ten seconds or longer but still there was no response. Perhaps she was out shopping, he thought. Yes, of course she was. Her Mini had not been parked in the drive. He ought to have noticed that it wasn't there. The best thing to do was leave now and phone her or return to the flat later. He had to see her, talk to her. Maybe there was an explanation other than the impossible, agonizing, obvious one. Maybe. He knew one thing was certain: he could not bear the thought of never seeing her again.

But Dave did not see her that day. He dialled her number two or three times each hour and returned to ring hopelessly the door-bell of her flat, in the afternoon and early evening and, finally, at about eleven o' clock at night. Then he walked slowly home to find that Aileen had gone to bed and that another night of virtually sleepless torment lay before him. It proved to be a long darkness.

While he was awake he re-enacted in his mind the brief scene of his discovery of Judy and Hunter, but the more often he tried to visualize its every detail the more blurred the images became until it seemed possible that they existed only inside his imagination, that his jealousy and suspicion had re-shaped events which could be explained in quite different and more innocent terms. Perhaps she had, after all, been singing in Manchester and Hunter had just happened to be there and—But no! She had admitted that she had not been to Manchester. He could remember asking her. She admitted it. But she had said that she could explain and he had not permitted her to offer that explanation. Yet how could she satisfactorily justify being with the man who had been her lover, the man she had promised to finish with, on the night when she was supposed to be at the ringside watching Dave's triumph, and what possible excuse could there be for telling the lie about the job in Manchester?

It all came back to that. She had lied to him She had deceived him. And yet, and yet, how beautiful she was, how wonderful they had been together. And it seemed that, if the dear creature of his memories had indeed proved so cruelly treacherous, then she must have been a monster of wickedness, and Dave simply could not believe this to be true. Sometimes she had shocked him with her surprising toughness of mind and occasional profanity of speech and, in the earlier days, by the candid hunger of her sensuality but, even in the few moments of conflict and doubt when they had come close to quarrelling, she had always shown, beneath the rebarbative surface a gentleness and tenderness and, above all, an emotional honesty which he was convinced could not be assumed.

As his weariness increased, sleep was still held back by an uncontrollable feverishness of mind which transmitted a tension and restlesness to his body so that, as he lay in bed, he was unable to remain still for more than a very few seconds. And the thoughts of Judy led to visions of her in postures of sexual need and excitement so that his own senses and flesh were roused until his yearning became unbearably intense and, in such shame and anguish that any possible pleasure was extinguished, he was compelled to ease the importunacy of his longing for her. He lay naked, sweating a little, feeling contempt for himself and a guilty sense of having insulted and defiled the image of Judy, but some physical relief must have resulted for he soon drifted into a shallow sleep, though one which was populous with disturbing presences of another kind, distorted yet recognisable faces of his mother and father, of Tom Darwin and Phil Richardson, all of them feasting on chunks of meat cut from an enormous red, steaming boxing-glove. This strange banquet faded and he found himself in the ring at Wembley, wearing his dressing-gown before the start of a contest. The Master of Ceremonies was making the announcements and he knew that, in a few moments, his gown would be discarded and its absence would show that, apart from his boxing gloves, he was quite naked. In the opposite corner his opponent was an immensely fat, bald old man who was at least decently covered though oddly clad in yellow silk pantaloons and he carried a curved, scimitar-like sword.

When he woke Dave found that he had slept for only twenty minutes or so and the time was a little after two o'clock. He sat up and swung his feet out from beneath the sheets to the floor and perched for a while on the edge of the bed. His eyes were sore and inside his skull was a faint but insistent buzzing and his mouth was dry and sour. He stood up and took his dressing-gown from the peg on the door, slipped it on and, bare-footed, left the room and went down to the lounge where he switched on the lights. Then he picked up the telephone receiver and dialled the number of Judy's flat. In his right ear the faint double rasp went on and on and he could visualize the dark and now empty bedroom where he and Judy had lain that night or early morning when Hunter telephoned from the States.

He let the ringing continue a few more times before he replaced the receiver. The prospect of returning to his bedroom was so uninviting that he wandered about the room, picking up ornaments from mantelpiece and sideboard, examining them sightlessly, almost wholly unaware of what he was doing until he came to the glass-fronted cabinet which contained a selection of his more important amateur trophies, the two National Schoolboy's Championship gold medals, the ABA Junior and Senior cups and international prizes, and the sight of these familiar objects was suddenly focused and unexpectedly poignant. He remembered those very early days when winning a fresh trophy was deeply thrilling and the way he would hurry home from school to look at and touch his latest prize; how he preserved any report that mentioned his name from *Yorkshire Evening Post* or *Boxing News* and stuck it carefully into his scrapbook. Even after he had turned professional something of the glamour and excitement had remained although that first innocent delight of the early days had become dulled and tarnished like a neglected medal. He mourned the lost simplicity of the world of his boyhood and felt a vague but quite deep need for some kind of comfort and reassurance that had once existed but was no longer available.

He moved away from the cabinet and picked up the newspapers and magazines, which Aileen had piled neatly on the shelf beneath the coffee table, and sat down with them. His current *Boxing News* was among them but none of its pages could hold his attention for more than a few seconds so he threw it aside and flicked through a fashion magazine until he came to a coloured photograph of a smiling model who so piercingly reminded him of Judy that he could scarcely endure either looking at the picture or putting it out of sight. Again he walked round the room a few times before returning to his chair to pick up the *Daily Telegraph* which Aileen arranged to have delivered though Dave could recall having seen her read only the *Sun* over her morning toast and tea.

The front page of the *Telegraph* carried stories of the enthusiastic reception given to the Pope in England and reports from the Falklands War including some casualty statistics from the sinking of the Royal Naval Frigate, *Ardent*. Mrs Thatcher's popularity was increasing, it seemed, in direct proportion to the number of people being killed and maimed in the South Atlantic. Dave thought of his brother, Martin, and tried to imagine what it must be like to be under constant threat of violent death or mutilation but he could see only a kind of snapshot of a young soldier, confident, tough, grinning beneath the jaunty angle of beret and, less clearly, moving pictures of military combat, all derived from the cinema, brightly coloured, pyrotechnic but essentially unthreatening, cosmetic, fictional.

Dave dropped the newspaper and went into the kitchen where he drank a glass of water. Then he switched off the downstairs lights and returned to his bedroom and lay in the darkness, waiting and hoping for an oblivion which refused him its mercy until another couple of hours had crept past and, even then, was of brief duration for, as the darkness thinned to a penitential grey and the first low growls of the waking day sounded in the city's throat, he awoke again and knew that he could remain in bed no longer. He got up and took a shower, dressed and left the house. Outside the garage he paused for a few seconds but, deciding not to take the car, he set off on the walk to Tom's flat in Headingley. If he walked slowly, he thought, he would be there by about seven. Tom and Peggy would almost certainly still be in bed but perhaps they would not mind too much being disturbed so early. Tom would be able to help. He was clever, and he was Dave's friend. He would be able to think of some way to find Judy. And, as Dave walked steadily onward, pale sunshine filtered through the mist and he noticed that birds in the suburban gardens were singing.

CHAPTER EIGHTEEN

Tom said, 'Don't worry, Dave. It'll all work out. You see if it doesn't. We'll find her all right. And from everything you've told me there'll be a perfectly good explanation for what happened the other night. There's a dozen reasons why Hunter could've been there. You see that now, don't you? So stop worrying, mate.' He got up from the kitchen table and took both of their mugs to the stove. 'I'll make us another coffee and take one in to Peggy. You don't mind if I tell her a bit about all this, do you? 'Cause she could be helpful. Finding Judy I mean.'

He made the coffee and took one of the mugs to the bedroom. Peggy was awake but still drowsy.

He said, 'Here you are, love. Aren't you the lucky one. Waited on hand and foot.'

She uncurled and sat up and yawned. 'What's going on? Who was it? You've been gone ages.'

'Dave. He's still here.'

'At seven-thirty in the morning! What's wrong? What's he want?'

'I'll tell you about it later on. He's had a rough time the last couple of days. He looks bloody awful.' Tom had taken off his dressing-gown and was climbing into jeans and pulling his sweater on. 'His girl-friend—you know, Judy—she's disappeared. I said we'd try and find her.'

'Disappeared? What d'you mean disappeared? Kidnapped? Murdered? What?'

'I'll tell you all about it tonight when you get back from work. She's left her flat. Maybe she's scared of Dave. He found her with that bloke, Colin Hunter, when he got back on Tuesday night. She'd told him she was working, a concert in Manchester or something. That's why she couldn't be at Dave's fight. Dave thought he'd come back and give her a surprise. I told you didn't I? Looks as if he surprised her all right. Both of 'em.'

'But I thought you said Judy was all right. Really fond of Dave.'

'That's what I thought. That's what we've got to find out.' He moved to the door. 'Must go. I don't want to leave him on his own. Time you got up anyway. You've got to be at the studio at nine, haven't you? See you in a minute.'

He went back to the kitchen. Dave had not touched his coffee and was sitting at the table with lowered head and vague, dull stare. The dark-golden stubble of beard, the thumbprint smudges beneath the eyes and the shadows in the hollows of his cheeks, with the unusual pallor of his skin, gave him a curiously ambiguous appearance, desperate, tough, yet spiritually tormented, the look of a fanatical political or religious prisoner.

Tom said, 'It's ten to eight. A bit later when people are up and about we'll start making a few phone calls. We'll find her for you. Bet you anything you like.'

Dave attempted a smile and nodded without much conviction.

'When did you last eat anything?' Tom asked.

'I dunno. I had some—I don't know.'

'Okay. I'm going to have a bacon butty. I'll make you one as well.'

Dave watched his friend go to the refrigerator and bring out a packet of bacon. He said, 'Don't bother for me, Tom. I'm not hungry.'

Tom began to slice a loaf. 'We'll see.'

A few minutes later Peggy came in. 'Hello Dave,' she said. 'You're an early bird. God, that bacon smells good!'

'Want some?' Tom spoke over his shoulder.

'Can't. Haven't got time. And anyway it'd make me fatter than the pig it came off. It's all right for you skinny guys.'

'Listen,' Tom said. 'When you get to work will you look up

any number or address that we might trace Judy Styles through? Places she's worked. An agent. Didn't she have an agent?'

'I think so. Yes. I'm sure she did.'

'Could you get his name and number?'

'Yeah. They'll have it next door if we haven't.'

'And ring us here as soon as you get anything. Okay?'

'I won't be able to do anything till after ten-thirty. I'll be on the air till then.'

'As soon as you can then. It's important. Don't forget.'

'I won't.'

She kissed Tom on the ear and said goodbye to Dave and left.

Tom finished preparing the bacon sandwiches, brought them to the table and sat down. He pushed one of the two plates over to Dave and said, 'Dig in.' He began to eat.

Dave watched him for a time then picked up his own sandwich and took a small bite. He chewed, at first slowly then more rapidly. Then he helped himself to a much larger bite and, as he munched, he said, 'By, this is great!'

Tom grinned. 'You can have my other half if you like. I've had enough . . . Go on take it. I'd only chuck it away if you don't.'

Then, as Dave ate hungerily, Tom went away to return with a telephone directory. 'What about her parents?' he said. 'Maybe she's run home to mummy. Any idea where they live?'

'Not in Leeds. Robin Hood's Bay Judy said.'

'What's their name?'

'Styles.'

'Right. Of course. We'll try directory enquiries. Come into the living room. Bring that with you.' Tom nodded towards the remains of the bacon sandwich. 'The phone's in there.'

In the living room Dave sat in one of two armchairs and watched Tom dialling. He ate the last of his food and felt, for the first time in four days, a relaxed drowsiness and with this comfortable feeling came a flowering of gratitude. It seemed that he could simply hand over the burden of his fear, uncertainty and pain and that Tom would dispose of it. Dave thought how lucky he was to have a friend like Tom, who was now speaking to the operator: 'No, sorry, I don't know the initials. Or the address... No... Just Styles... I see... In Robin Hood's Bay itself... Okay, give me them all...' He was jotting with a ball-point and reciting numbers. 'Fine. Thank you very much. Bye.'

He broke off the connection with the pressure of his forefinger, removed it and began to make calls. Each time he began with the same words: 'This is BBC Radio Leeds. I'm sorry to bother you but I'm trying to contact Judy Styles, the singer. Have I got the right number?'

On the third attempt Dave heard him continue '... I see. But she's not there... yes, I've got the Leeds number but I don't seem to be able to get her there... No, nothing very important. Just wanted to talk about her plans... Yeah, I'm sure I'll find her... Sorry to have bothered you... 'Bye.'

He put the telephone down. 'Well, she's not with her parents.' He lifted the receiver again. 'What's her number at the flat? We'll try it just once on the off-chance she's come back.'

Dave gave him the figures and he dialled again. He waited a few moments then gave up.

'Don't worry,' he said. 'Peggy'll find out. We'll just have to wait till she rings.'

He took the armchair opposite Dave. 'You like more coffee?'

Dave shook his head. His eyes were glazed with tiredness.

'Heard anything of Martin?'

'No.'

'You know you're on the telly today? One-fifty on Grandstand.'

Dave's eyes closed and his head fell forward, then lolled to one side. His mouth was slightly open and he was breathing deeply and slowly.

Tom watched him for a few seconds, then took a book from the table at his side and began to read. Dave slept.

It was a couple of hours later, shortly after eleven o'clock, that Peggy telephoned. Tom pounced on the instrument to prevent its ringing a second time and he saw, as he answered, that Dave had not been awakened by the noise.

Peggy said, 'I've found her! I had a helluva job getting hold of her agent—a bloke called Mike Carpenter—and even then he wasn't—'

'Where is she?'

'Bramhope. Staying with a friend. Woman called Sue Davitt. I'll give you the address in a minute. This bloke Carpenter said he'd sworn not to tell anyone where she's living but I told him I was the Beeb and we'd got big plans for—'

'Yeah. That's marvellous, love. You've done well. But what's the address?...Just a sec, I'll write it down...good ...fine...No. I won't phone. She might be so scared she'll scarper again...I'll just go round there straight away...he's asleep. Out to the world...I don't think he's slept for days...yes...Okay. I'll see you later. Tell you all about it.'

He said goodbye and replaced the receiver. Dave had not stirred. Tom tore the top sheet from the scribbling-pad and put it into his jeans hip pocket. Then he picked up the ball-point and wrote on the fresh sheet of paper a message telling Dave that he had gone out to see Judy and that he would soon return either with her or with news of her. He placed the note on Dave's lap and then let himself out of the flat and walked to the main road where he did not have to wait very long before the Bramhope bus arrived. Twenty minutes later he was ringing the doorbell of the smart little detached house with double garage and well-kept lawn and flower-beds.

A man in his early thirties with a large, amiable face and reddish curly hair opened the door. He was dressed in a shirt with red and black horizontal stripes and an open white collar, like those worn by rugby players, corduroy slacks and canvas shoes. From inside the house came the sound of a young child's voice raised in imperious demand.

'Yes?' the man said. 'Can I help you?'

Tom had not prepared himself to be confronted by a man and for a moment he was uncertain how to explain his presence. Then he said, 'I'm sorry to bother you. I've come to see Judy Styles. I've got some important news for her. Very important. I wouldn't have troubled you otherwise.'

The man looked unsure. 'How did you—I mean no-one's supposed to know she's . . . I don't know. I'd better talk to my wife . . . ' He turned his head, facing back into the house, and called, 'Sue! Can you come here a minute?' Then he looked back at Tom and said with an awkward grin, 'I'm sorry not asking you in. Seems daft. I don't know what the hell it's all about. Ours not to reason—ah, here she is. This is my wife, Sue.'

Tom said, 'My name's Tom Darwin. I'm a sort of friend of Judy's. I've got a message for her. It's very important. I think she'll want to see me. I'm sure she will.'

Sue was looking at him suspiciously. 'How did you—I mean what makes you think she's here?'

'I know she's here. All I want's a few minutes to talk to her, that's all. I'm certain she'd want to hear what I've got to tell her. I'm positive. In any case what's the harm? Just ask her if she'll talk to me. Tell her I've got a message for her. I think it's the one she'll be glad to hear. What's the harm?'

Mr Davitt said, 'Sounds fair enough to me.'

Sue hesitated, then said. 'Wait here,' and she disappeared into the house.

Her husband shrugged. 'I wish I knew what it's all about,' he said. 'They love their little dramas, don't they? All they've told me is Judy's being threatened or she might be in danger or something. All incredibly vague. Ask for details and they talk in riddles. Do *you* know what it's about?'

'I've a good idea. It's a bit complicated. But they're wrong about Judy being in danger. She's not. I'm sure about that.'

'Well I hope—oh here's Sue again.'

Sue said, 'You can come in.'

Tom followed them both into the hall.

Sue nodded to her right. 'In there.'

Tom thanked them both and went into the room she had indicated. Judy was standing looking out of the window. As he closed the door behind him she turned and came towards him, smiling faintly, with an expression that was both rueful and quizzical, even, perhaps, apprehensive. They faced each other questioningly for a moment; then Judy said, 'Have you seen him? Dave. Is he all right?' Then she added, 'Sit down.'

He ignored this. 'Yes. I've seen him. I've just left him at my place. He's asleep.'

'Does he know I'm here?'

'No.'

'How did you find me?'

'Peggy got on to your agent. Told him some nonsense about a big deal with the BBC. Said she had to get in touch with you. I suppose he thought he might lose his ten per cent if he didn't tell her where you were.'

She sat on the arm of one of the chairs. 'How is Dave? I expect he'd like to strangle me.'

'No. That's not what he wants to do at all. He just wants to see you. He's been going crazy trying to find you. I don't think he's slept more than a couple of hours since Wednesday. He looks terrible. Hasn't been eating. Worrying himself sick. You've got to see him, Judy. If you care anything at all about him. You've got to see him and put his mind at rest. Tell him that night—you know, when he came back from London—well, tell him anything. Tell him what he wants to hear. He'll believe it. I'm sure you can think of something.'

Judy stood up. 'Here. Just a minute. What are you talking about? What's he told you? Dave. What does he think?

'He didn't tell me a lot. I haven't seen him till this morning. He came round about half past seven, out of his mind with worry. He just wants to see you. That's all.'

'But what did he say? About that night.'

'Well...' Tom shrugged. 'He just said what happened. He got to your place and found you and this bloke—what's his name—Hunter. Together. That's all.'

'But we weren't! I mean we weren't doing anything. The only reason I saw Colin that night was to get rid of him. Finish with him. I wanted to be able to tell Dave I was—Oh Christ, this sounds like soap opera. What I mean is I didn't want trouble, mess. I wanted to be able to say to Dave, I'm here if you want me. No complications. We can forget about what's happened in the past. See what I mean? I wanted to start clean. D'you understand?'

Tom said, 'Yes. Yes, I can understand. But it seems a funny time to choose. Why the hell couldn't you have got rid of the bloke ages ago? I mean you and Dave've been seeing each other, as they say, for quite a while now. Four or five months, isn't it? Why pick the night Dave's fighting in London. Wanting you to be there more than anything. Why wait till then?'

Judy sat down again on the chair arm. 'It was the first chance I had. Colin—Hunter—he'd been away in the States since last November. He only got back a couple of days before the fight and he couldn't see me till that Tuesday. Maybe I was wrong. I don't know. But I felt I had to get things cleared up before I saw Dave again.'

Tom moved to the window, looked out, then turned back and he, too, perched on the arm of the chair so that he and Judy were face to face, like fighters in opposite corners.

He said, 'Why didn't you tell Dave about Hunter before all this? Dave must've known a girl like you—don't get me wrong—I mean a girl as attractive as you, he must've known you'd have lots of men keen enough to make it with you. Wouldn't it've been easier to tell him? Say okay. There's been this guy, Colin Hunter, but now I've met you I'm going to send him packing. Couldn't you have said that?'

Judy's head moved first in a denying shake which then became a nod of assent. She said 'I know. I know. I should've told him everything. I did tell him. Some of it. I told him about Colin. Told him how things had been. But I was afraid. If I told him everything I thought I'd lose him. So I didn't tell him Colin owns the flat. I pay a rent but it's not much. I thought if Dave knew Colin owned the place he'd think—oh, you know—he'd think he owned me too. He'd think I was his property, his private tart. I didn't think he'd be able to take that.'

'Dave'd take anything rather than lose you. That's how it seems to me. He's just falling to pieces. What do you feel? I mean how do you—' Tom paused, then went on: 'This is bloody difficult to say. You can tell me it's no business of mine. Go and get stuffed. Okay. All the same I'm going to say it. What do you feel? About Dave. I mean how serious? Do you—you know—really care a lot about him. Not just a . . .'

'You mean do I love him.'

Tom looked both relieved and abashed. 'Well . . . yes. Yes. That's what I mean. Whatever that means. If you see what I mean.' His grin was fatuous, but Judy's unsmiling seriousness quickly erased it.

She said, 'Yes. I love him.'

Tom was surprised by the way the simplicity of this moved him and he was conscious, too, of another less easily defined emotion, a shadowy feeling of something close to envy, even to jealousy.

He said, 'Then you'll come and see him?'

She nodded.

He saw a sudden brightness of excitement in her eyes and a small smile on her mouth.

She said, 'I'll tell Andy and Sue I'm going out. Wait there.'

When she came back five minutes later he saw that she had been re-arranging her hair and attending to her make-up.

He grinned. 'You look fine.'

She smiled and there was a moment of curious complicity between them. Then she said. 'I've got the car outside. Come on,' and they went out of the house.

Dave was awakened by the sound of the outside door being slammed and he was at first bewildered by his surroundings though, by the time the living room door was opening he had remembered and was rising to his feet.

Judy came in.

She moved a couple of paces inside the room and they stood staring at each other. Tom was behind her, his dark face intent, smiling slightly, watchful.

Dave opened his mouth as if to speak, but no sound came out. Then Judy moved forward again, swiftly, lightly, as if in flight, and Dave spread his arms and she came into them and he held her close and could smell the fragrance of her hair and could feel the remembered softness and suppleness and strength of her pressing closer and closer to him, and then his heart or some great sweetness began to expand inside his chest

252

and swell and flood his whole being with ineffable relief and joy and longing.

Tom said, 'I've got things to do,' and he went out and closed the door.

Neither Dave not Judy heard him go.

When Judy raised her face to Dave's it was wet with tears but she was smiling.

He said, 'You're not crying, love. There's nowt to cry about. It's all right. Everything's all right.'

'Yes,' Judy said. 'Yes, yes, yes. Everything's all right. I'll tell you everything. I want to. I'll tell you—'

'Shush . . . there, there, love. Don't you fret. Everything's going to be fine. Don't worry. We're back together. That's all that matters.'

'I want you to know. I want you to know everything, Dave. Oh God, I love you. I do, I do.'

'That's all I want to know.'

They kissed.

She said, 'You're bristly.'

'Sorry.'

'I like it.'

They kissed again. Then Dave said, 'Come on then, love. We've got to make some plans.'

CHAPTER NINETEEN

Dave thought afterwards that, without Tom's help, he would never have been able to find his way out of the cave of misery in which events had seemed to imprison him and, even when the miracle of restoring Judy to him had been effected, Tom continued to be of assistance by suggesting what steps next to take. First he had said that the wisest—and probably the pleasantest—thing for them to do was get out of town, at least for the weekend, and talk matters over, decide on what they were going to do about Judy's possessions, which were still in her flat (he recommended that she should have them put into storage for the time being), and, most important, what action Dave was going to take over Aileen. He telephoned an Inn which he knew of near Ingleton in the Dales and booked a room for Mr and Mrs Ruddock. There was no point, he explained, in Dave's adopting a false name. Someone would be sure to recognise him. On the other hand no one would be likely to know that Judy was not in fact the real Mrs Ruddock which—and at this Dave and Judy grinned and nodded happily—she would indeed become before very long.

Dave went to his home to pick up his car, collect some clothes and to tell Aileen that he would be going away for the weekend. He was relieved to find that she was not in so, after he had shaved and packed a case, he wrote a brief note saying only that he was going away but would be back to see her some time Monday. Judy left her Mini in the road outside Tom's flat and Dave first drove her back to Bramhope where she, too, collected a weekend case and assured Sue that all was well before they continued their journey into the Dales.

Their stay in the country was entirely successful. On Saturday night they had dinner at the inn and went early to bed to make love, at first with a kind of cautious tenderness as they re-explored remembered and idyllic territory but, later, with the wild improvisatory passion of mutual certainty. The weather was fine and warm on Sunday so they spent most of the daylight hours out of doors and in the evening they avoided the bar where Dave would most probably have been recognised. It transpired that the proprietor of the inn had indeed recognised Dave though it was not until they were leaving on Monday morning that he approached them, with engaging diffidence, and asked for autographs. Dave and Judy drove back to Leeds in a state of intense but nervous happiness.

They had telephoned from the inn to the Queen's Hotel in Leeds to book a double room for a couple of nights. Dave was to return to his house and tell Aileen exactly what had happened: he and Judy were in love and intended living together until it was possible for them to get married. He hoped that Aileen would agree to a divorce. He and Judy would then find a furnished flat or house to rent for the next four months, the last five or six weeks of which he would be spending in London with Phil and Rose Richardson, preparing for his title defence against Earl Hayes. Neither he nor Judy wished, at least for the time being, to leave Yorkshire. Perhaps later, after the fight, they might decide to buy a house somewhere else in the country but for the time being they would look for a temporary home in or near Leeds.

Dave had suggested that Judy might come with him to the show-down with Aileen but she had instantly and emphatically rejected the suggestion and only a few moment's reflection was needed to assure him that she was right to do so. But she would have to see his mother and father, he said. Perhaps they could visit his old home that evening or the next day. He ought to have gone earlier particularly since his mam would be worried silly about

Martin and the fighting at Goose Green, news of which they had heard on the car radio. Judy had said that of course she would love to see Mrs Ruddock again after all these years and Dave would have to meet her own parents, but first of all the Aileen situation had to be settled. Once that was done, everything else would be comparatively simple.

It was a little before noon when they deposited their luggage in their room at the Queen's Hotel and went out into City Square to walk along Boar Lane towards Briggate. The sun was shining and the pavements were busy with people hurrying or strolling with that secret self-absorption of city pedestrians. Many of the young women were wearing flimsy summer dresses and the bright colours moved like floating petals along the grey sun-splashed streets and arcades. Three times, Dave was stopped by strangers who congratulated him on his victory over Wayne Harvey and assured him that their money was on him to give Earl Hayes a hiding, and Judy noticed how the men glanced with furtive appreciation and curiosity at her as they gave Dave their good wishes.

At half-past twelve they had lunch in an Italian restaurant on the Headrow and then walked back to the hotel. There they went to bed and made love, after which they dozed for an hour or so before Dave got up, bathed and dressed. Then, after kissing Judy and promising to be back soon, he left the hotel and drove to his house, but, as he approached it by the familiar ways, his sparkling happiness was suddenly dimmed and, as he drew up before the front door, a sense of foreboding and of guilt settled upon his spirits. He thought of his euphoria of a short time ago, the feeling he had experienced while walking with Judy throught the city, an intoxicating sensation of joy that was strangely magnanimous, generous, embracing, a wish to share his delight with or extend sympathy to those who would never be blessed by such good fortune as his own, and suddenly it seemed that all of this had been false, that he was entirely selfish and his love, or need, for Judy was ruthless, greedy and dishonourable. There was no one he would not be ready to sacrifice if the alternative would be to lose her.

He got out of the car and went into the house. At once he

could feel its emptiness, its lack of human occupancy and, though he called Aileen's name and went from room to room, he knew that she was not there. On the kitchen table he found the note that he had left for her on Saturday but no clue at all as to her possible whereabouts. Perhaps she had been tempted out by the fine weather for a walk in the park but it was not very likely, for Aileen had always shown a disinclination for what she regarded as unnecessary physical effort. She would work strenuously enough at domestic tasks but the notion of walking simply for pleasure had always seemed inexplicable to her. She might be out shopping at Oakwood, but this did not seem probable either. The vegetable-rack was well stocked; there was fruit in the bowl. He looked in the refrigerator: no shortage of supplies there. His vague uneasiness increased.

She had changed so much. Ever since that Sunday, way back in March when she had refused to tell him where she had been, she had become almost a different person from the girl he had so stupidly, so wrongly, married. She was up to something and he could not guess what it was. She had been out when he came to pick up the car on Saturday and now she was out again. On a Monday afternoon. It was a mystery and he was obscurely troubled by it.

He went to the telephone, dialled the number of the Queen's Hotel and asked to speak to Mrs Ruddock, giving the number of their room.

Judy came on the line: 'Hullo darling. What's going on? Where are you?'

He said, 'I'm at home. My place. She's out. Aileen's not here.'

'Oh. Well, I expect she'll be back soon. Had she locked up?'

'No. She never bothered. I used to tell her about it but she never seemed to remember. Or she left the place open on purpose.'

'On purpose? You mean she wanted to be robbed?'

'No. She reckoned you ought to trust people. It were the ones with burglar-alarms and double locks an' all that what got robbed. Maybe she were right. Anyway she's not here.

What's the best thing to do?'

'Wait till she gets back, I suppose. We want to get everything settled, don't we, love?'

'Aye.'

'You don't sound so sure. What's up darling? You having a change of heart?'

'No. No, 'course I'm not. It's just—I don't know. Seems funny her being out. I can't think what she's up to.'

'You make yourself a cup of tea or something and sit down and wait. I expect she'll be back soon. And Dave . . .'

'What?'

'Remember I love you.'

'Aye. Me too.'

'Be nice to her. Try to keep calm. Don't let things get out of hand, start a shouting-match, anything like that. Okay? I'll see you back here whenever.'

'Right.'

They exchanged endearments and farewells and Dave went back to the kitchen and, because Judy had suggested it and in order to pass the time, he made a pot of tea. When he had drunk two cups he washed up and then wandered into the garden. The flower beds looked well cared for and the lawn had been recently mown so he guessed that his father had probably been round, unless Aileen had found someone locally to help out while he had been in London training for the Harvey fight. Certainly there would be no difficulty obtaining a part-time gardener with the number of unemployed increasing all the time. No wonder more and more lads were turning pro these days, though not many of them would make a proper living. He, Dave, was one of the very few lucky ones. He had never ceased to be thankful for his good fortune and he knew what an important part luck had played in his success. He was lucky to have the natural talent, the physical strength and stamina, the right temperament and the ability to graft. Without that luck he would still be working in the butcher's shop. Or not at all. And, without it, he would never have met Judy again and, even if, by some freakish chance, they had encountered each other she would not have been likely to show the least interest in him.

He looked at his watch: nearly ten past five. Perhaps he should leave another note asking Aileen to telephone him at the Queen's. But no, this was not such a good idea. There was something evasive, something cowardly about it. He would wait for another hour but if she had not returned by then he would have to postpone the meeting. He went back into the house and switched on the television, but switched it off again before any picture had appeared on the screen. Then he went upstairs and into Aileen's room.

On the dressing-table stood a few small bottles and pots of creams and lotions, a hairbrush and large comb. Aileen did not use much make up. He walked across the room and looked down at the cosmetics and then saw a small porcelain bowl which had perhaps once contained pot-pourri or some kind of unguent but had been thriftily preserved by Aileen as a useful ornament. In the bowl were a few hairgrips, a crumpled hair-net, four or five fancy buttons of different shapes and sizes and the gleaming, pale yellow of her wedding-ring. Dave picked it up and looked at it thoughtfully. When had she discarded it, he wondered. It was not the kind of thing he noticed. Aileen had often teased him, though with an underlying sadness and, perhaps, some bitterness, that he never really looked at her, and it was true. Once he recalled, she had been in town one afternoon and had returned to get his tea ready. She had been back almost an hour before she had asked him if he had noticed any change in her. It was only then that he saw that she had been to the hairdressers and was wearing a new skirt and blouse. No, he would be unlikely to notice whether or not she was wearing her wedding-ring. He would notice any change in Judy, he was sure.

He put the ring back in the bowl. Then, feeling oddly guilty he opened the top drawer of the dressing table. A faint lavender scent sweetened the air. He looked down at the neatly folded garments, nightdresses, slips and plain, unprovocative knickers, a packet of tampax. There was something chaste and vulnerable about these things which moved and shamed him. They belonged to a stranger. He shut the drawer and went out of the room and into his own. The bed was neatly made and the clothes which he had left lying about had been tidied away. He thought he might as well pass the time by collecting a few more of his things and stowing them in the car but, as he reached for a suitcase which rested on top of the wardrobe, he heard a sound below and then Aileen's voice calling his name.

He hurried down the stairs. She was standing in the hall and she was wearing a pale blue suit with a small matching hat, white gloves and shoes. She looked very neat, wholesome, unmagical but pleasant. Outside, in the drive, he heard a car's engine cough into life and the rasping of its tyres on the gravel as it moved away.

Dave said, 'Who's that?'

'Nobody you know.' It was not said with any note of sharpness or coquettishness: a calm, factual statement.

He followed her into the kitchen. 'Where've you been? I've been waiting over an hour.'

Aileen smiled slightly. 'Oh dear. I'm sorry.'

He waited for a further answer but when none came he spoke again: 'Well? Where've you been then?'

She put her handbag down on the table. There was no smile now. 'I don't see it's any of your business really. You've been away all weekend. You was in a terrible state last time I saw you. Like somebody drunk or sick or something. Now you come back looking all bright and cheerful. I expect you've made it up with your woman. Or got another one. I don't want to know. I'm not interested. I've got my own life thank you very much. I expect I'll be leaving here very soon.'

Dave stared at her as she removed her hat and gloves and filled the kettle. She did not seem to be aware of having said anything unexpected.

He said, 'What do you mean, leaving?'

She was setting out the cups and saucers and teapot on a tray. 'What do I mean? It's easy enough to understand, i'n't it? I said I'll be leaving. Going away. Getting out. That suits you don't it?'

'But where? What you going to do? Where will you go?'

She scooped tea into the pot. 'I told you. That's my business.'

'Aye. Sure. I'm not saying it i'n't your business. That don't mean I'm not interested though. 'Course I'm interested. An' I want to know what's happening so's I can make arrangements. I'll want to know where you're living. Send you money an' that. An' I'm interested anyway. I feel I've let you down. I want you to be all right. Happy like. I want to know you're being looked after.'

Again the small, private smile. 'Don't worry. I'll be looked after all right. I've got me mam's solicitor. He'll tell you.'

He wanted to see if she would say any more and when she went on with brewing the tea he said, 'Then you've got somebody. A bloke. You've got somebody to go to like.'

Her smile deepened and he saw the dimple in her right cheek which, he now recalled, had once charmed him. 'Yes. I've got somebody to go to,' she said, again without any coyness or complacency.

Dave was very surprised, almost shocked, and far less relieved than he would have expected. It seemed that his near-disbelief had thrown his expected responses into disorder.

He said, attempting but dismally failing to strike a jocular note, 'Well, this is a turn-up for books! You've been going on at me about playing around an' all that an' look at you! It's amazing.' Then he added quickly: 'I'm not getting at you, love. I mean it's all right. Best thing could've happened really. We was never right for each other, was we? Not really. I mean you wasn't interested in the fight game. We wasn't up to much in bed like. You didn't really want kids or anything. It's great you've found somebody more suited. I'm very glad, love. I really am. I hope the two of you's going to be happy.'

She finished pouring the second cup of tea, put the pot down and looked at Dave steadily and with an expression in her eyes of tired, wondering disbelief, with a suggestion, too, of pity: it was the look that often accompanies a slow, hopeless shaking of the head, though in fact her head remained still.

She said, 'I sometimes think you're not quite all there, Dave.' Then she picked up the tray and carried it into the lounge.

Dave followed and she handed him a cup of tea. They both sat down.

He said, 'What's that supposed to mean? Not all there. You never tell me anything straight. How the hell d'you expect me to know what you're getting at? I said I hope you'll be happy with—well, whoever the bloke is. I don't see anything daft about that. It's true. It's what I feel. If you don't want to tell me who it is, then that's all right by me. I just hope you don't think I'd do him any harm. Or maybe you're ashamed of me. Happen that's why you didn't bring him in when you saw my car. Or doesn't he know you're married? Is that it? I saw you've stopped wearing your ring. You've not been daft enough to kid him you're single, have you?'

Now Aileen did shake her head. 'Oh Dave . . .'

'Well I don't know. I don't know why you don't tell me who the bloke is anyway. Was that him that just drove away?'

'That was Father McGraw.'

'Oh. Aye. Well he's not . . . I mean they can't marry can they? They don't . . . anything. Not RCs. That's right, i'n't it?'

'That's right, Dave. Priests don't marry. They're celibate. That's what they call it.'

'But what . . . ?' He was silent, frowning, utterly confused.

Aileen took a sip of tea. Then she said, 'I've been to York. Knavesmire Race Course.'

'Race course! What you been doing there?'

'Not riding a horse. The Pope was there. Didn't you know? It's been on radio, telly, in all the papers. We went to see him.'

'You and this vicar bloke?'

'Me and a party from St Peter's. We had a coach. Father

McGraw come with us. He gave me a lift home after we got back. He had to come this way in any case, visiting. It were wonderful at York. Fantastic.'

Dave grappled with this further disconcerting change in the expected pattern of events. He said, 'You've gone back to all that then, have you? Going to church an' all that.'

'Yes. I've gone back. Thank God.'

'An' you haven't got anybody else. A bloke, I mean.'

She smiled. 'No bloke. Not what you mean. Not on earth.'

He frowned. 'You mean . . .'

'I mean Jesus.'

Dave took a gulp of tea and, in his embarrassment, looked wildly round the room. Then he said, 'I thought you'd finished with that lot. I mean when we got married. I thought they kicked you out.'

'No. I'm not finished with that lot. I've gone back where I belong. It's like you've been lost, like a lost child, scared and lonely and miserable. And then your mam or dad finds you and cuddles you close and takes you home and you're safe and warm and nothing can hurt you any more.'

'I dunno,' he muttered. 'I don't really understand. It seems like—I dunno.'

'I know you don't. That's why I never said nothing all these weeks. But don't worry about me, Dave. I'm all right now. You'll be able to get your divorce an' everything. I don't mind. Fact is it's just what I want, what I've always wanted really. Father McGraw's giving me a reference. He thinks they'll take me as a postulant. The Carmelites in Wales. That's what I've always wanted, Dave. I just got sort of led off the track for a bit. But I'm back now.'

'What's a postulant?'

'It's the first stage you've got to go through if you want to be a nun.'

'A nun! By, that's terrible!'

Aileen laughed aloud. 'But it's not terrible, Dave! I knew you wouldn't understand. It's great. It's the most wonderful thing any woman can be. It's not for everybody. I know that. There's lots of women, very good women, that'd never suit. It doesn't mean they're any smaller in God's eyes. They've got a different calling different ways to serve. You said you hoped I'd be happy. Well, I'd be happier this way than ever I could be with a man, any man. Make no mistake.'

Dave nodded, but looked less than convinced. Then he said, 'Well, it looks like things are working out all right for both on us. Judy and me want to get married as soon as—'

Aileen interrupted. 'I don't want to hear anything about that, Dave.' For a brief moment her old look of tight-lipped, hard-eyed disapproval came and went. 'I'm not interested in your love life, if that's what you'd call it. It's nowt to do with me. I'll get solicitor to write to you. You're lucky, Dave, you and your woman. I'll not get in your way. I'll make things as easy as I can. And I won't want your money. No more'n what I'll need for a few weeks while I'm living at St Mary's Hostel.'

'You don't need to go to a hostel! You can have as much—'

'Dave! Why can't you understand? It's what I want. The sooner I get out of here the better. I'll be out by next weekend. You can bring her here if you like. It wouldn't bother me.'

'I wouldn't do that.'

'Well that's up to you.' She stood up. 'You finished with your cup?'

He drank the cool dregs of his tea and handed Aileen the cup and saucer.

As she was carrying the tray into the kitchen she said, 'Oh I forgot to tell you. I went to see your mam while you were away. I told her what I was going to do.'

Dave followed her. 'What did she say?'

'She didn't understand neither. I never expected her to. But she was very nice, considering. She meant to be. Poor woman's got enough troubles. Martin out there in that war an' her husband boozing. You ought to go and see her, Dave. Try and give her a bit of comfort.'

'Dad don't drink much. He just likes his pint. No harm in that.'

'No. Well, I expect you're right. But he does leave poor woman on her own a lot and as far as I can make out he's always at pub.'

'Dad's all right.'

'Oh, I'm not saying he's not a nice friendly man. I'm saying he could spend a bit more time at home. Anyway I hope you'll go and see your mam soon.' She began to wash up the tea things.

Dave said, 'You say you're going the end of the week. Does that mean I won't see you again after that?'

She turned from the sink and looked straight at him. 'Yes, that's what it means, Dave. So don't let's be soppy about it. I'm doing what I want to do. And we're lucky because it's what you want as well. I expect I'll miss you quite a lot. But there's plenty of things I'll miss. And it'll be worth it. I mean what I'll be given—the happiness—that's worth paying anything for. It'll be my kind of happiness. Not everybody's. Certainly not your kind. But you take my word for it. I'll be happier than anybody you've ever known. So you don't have to fret or feel guilty or anything. If you want to go away now and stay with your woman that's all right. I'd sooner you did, to tell the truth. I'd rather be on my own till I leave here. If that's all right with you.

Dave was shocked, not so much by Aileen's surprising and apparently new-found steeliness of purpose as by his own feeling of resentment which was strong enough to give a slightly sour flavour to his relief that things were working so smoothly in his favour.

He said, 'You'll be all right on your own then?'

The small explosion of her laughter was mocking. 'I was on my own about five or six weeks when you was in London. What's the difference?'

'You ought to lock up when you go out.'

'Aye. Well, we've not been robbed so far.'

He turned away. 'I'll go and pack a few things then.'

She made no reply to this so he went upstairs and threw some clothes into the suitcase and returned with it to the kitchen.

He said, 'When you go. How you going to manage? I mean all your stuff and that.'

'I'll manage.'

He turned as if to leave, but paused. 'You all right for

money? I'll keep the joint-account the way it is till I hear what you want to do. About money and that. From your solicitor. You can get what you want from bank.'

She nodded. 'I'm not bothered.'

He moved towards her with the intention of offering a token embrace or farewell peck but she raised one denying hand. 'No. Dave. I don't want owt like that.'

He shrugged, turned away and picked up his case.

'I'll be going then.'

She nodded. Then she said, 'Oh that Phil Richardson keeps phoning. You'd better get in touch with him.'

He nodded. A pause, then: 'You sure everything's all right?'

Aileen simply smiled and said nothing.

'Cheers then.' Dave said.

'Tarrah,' she answered and watched him leave and then moved over to the kitchen window to see him heave the case on to the back seat of his car, climb into the driving seat and drive away.

Aileen went into the lounge and sat down with the *Evening Post*. But she did not read it. She sat gazing before her, her eyes unfocused and a faint smile on her lips. Tomorrow she would go to early mass for her daily refreshment of spirit and restoration of strength. After today's excitement at York, the almost hysterical adulation of the multitude for that tiny figure in the white skull cap and robes, inspiring and thrilling as it was, she would be happy to return to the familiar and reassuring welcome of the church she had known since very early childhood. She could visualize it clearly now: the small, scattered congregation hollowing and shadowing the vaulted cavern and the flickering petals of yellow and blue brilliance from the chaste candles, the gleam of gold and the sanctuary light at the altar; she could hear the voice of the priest and then the high, starry sound of the sacring bell as the Host was elevated, the holy, fragrant silences.

On Wednesday she would see Mother Mary Joseph again and her admission to the hostel would be confirmed. Then the pre-entrance programme could properly begin. She would read and she would study and she would pray. Dave did not understand. His mother had not understood. They were sorry for her, she could tell. And this was funny and sad because, if anyone was in need of pity, it was them. She was lucky. She had, by the mercy of God, escaped from the snares of the world before it was too late. She was very happy.

It was nearly seven o'clock when Dave got back to the hotel. Judy was dressed and made-up, ready to go out.

She said, 'You've been a long time. Was it hard going?'

They both sat on the bed, side by side.

'No. It were unbelievable. You'll never believe it.'

'Well? Tell me.'

'Well. I went there to tell her it were all over. I wanted a divorce. Give her her cards. Right? And what happens? You won't believe it, Judy, but it were the other way round. She give me my cards. It's her that wants a divorce. No kidding. She's moving out at weekend.'

'Has she got somebody else?'

Dave released a snort of unamused laughter. 'That's what I asked her. Aye. She's got somebody else all right. You'll never guess who it is. Jesus. That's who she's got. That's who she wants a divorce for.'

'You mean . . . ?'

'She wants to be a nun.'

'Good God!'

'Aye. That's the fella.'

Judy laughed. 'But . . . had you any idea?'

'No. I thought she'd been acting a bit funny past three or four month. I told you. Acting kind of mysterious. Coming and going odd times. Funny kind of look on her face. Secret like. But I thought. I don't know. Well, I began to think maybe she had got a bloke. I never thought of religion. I thought she'd gave all that up when she got married. I don't understand it but I remember she said something about being in sin or something. She couldn't take the what-y'm'-call it, the blessed something.'

'Sacrament. Communion, I expect.'

'Something like that. It must've been worrying her a lot all that time we was married. I never knew.'

Judy took his hand. 'Don't worry love. It's all worked out for the best. You're bound to feel a bit—I don't know. A bit guilty maybe. A bit sad. You knew her a long time. You did marry her, after all. You did live with her. But as long as you're sure about us.'

'Aye.' His head was lowered, chin down, eyes on the carpet.

'You *are* sure, aren't you?'

He looked up at her and saw the slight doubt, the faint stirring of panic in her eyes and suddenly the uneasy gloom that had oppressed him during the drive back dissipated and he felt a flood of tenderness and gratitude and need and he took her other hand and said, 'Of course I'm sure. 'Course I am lovey. Never been surer of anything in my life. Sorry I were a bit down in dumps just then. It were seeing her like that. She were all right were Aileen. In her funny way. I just want her to be happy, that's all.'

'Seems as if she is.'

'Aye. It does that. I just don't understand it. Religion an' all that. It's a mystery.'

'We all need love. We need to love and be loved. That seems to be the kind Aileen needs. Not me though. You're what I need. You and nobody and nothing else.'

They kissed and then looked at each other solemnly, awed by what seemed to be the grandeur and singularity of their passion. Then Judy grinned and rose quickly to her feet. 'I'm hungry,' she said. 'Being in love gives me an appetite. I expect I'll get as big as a house.'

'I'd sooner that than you stopped.'

'Stopped loving you? Never. I couldn't. You're stuck with me for good.'

They kissed again and they were about to leave when Dave said, 'Sorry love. I've just remembered. I've got to make a phone call. I won't be a minute. Phil, my manager in London's been ringing every other minute. I'd best put him out of his misery.' He picked up the telephone, asked for the number, and replaced the receiver. A few seconds later it rang and he said into the mouth-piece, 'Hullo . . . Phil. It's me Dave.'

Judy watched him as he grinned at the immediate flow of speech that followed and of which she could hear only an incomprehensible gabble.

At last Dave said, 'Okay, Phil . . . Aye. I'm fine . . . Sure . . . Don't you worry. I'll be all right . . . When d'you want me there? . . . Okay . . . Listen we'll come down and see you and Rose . . . I don't know. Pretty soon. We'll come for a weekend or something. Okay? I want you both to meet her . . . Sure . . . I'll let you know. I told you not to worry. I'm in fine shape . . . Aye . . . Okay then. See you. Love to Rose . . . Cheers . . . 'bye.'

He replaced the receiver. 'We're eating downstairs are we? You don't want to go out, do you?'

Judy said the hotel restaurant would be as good as anywhere and they went out into the corridor and rode the lift down to the ground floor.

When they were at their table and had given their order Dave said, 'I told Phil we'd go down to London and see him and his missus, Rose. You heard me I expect. We'll fix that later on. First thing though is book our room here for rest of week. Till next Monday'd be best. Give us time to find somewhere. A furnished flat or a house or something. And tomorrow we'll arrange about storing your stuff. Eh, we've got a lot of things to sort out, haven't we?'

A waiter brought prawn avocado for Judy and minestrone soup for Dave.

She said, 'We ought to get in touch with Tom. He'll be wondering what we're doing.'

'We'll do that. I'll give him a ring later on. Take him and Peggy out for a meal. Tomorrow p'rhaps or whenever they can make it. That all right?'

'Lovely. What else did what's his name say? Your manager.'

'Oh, the Hayes fight's been put off a week. It's on the twenty-first. September. And they've switched it to the Albert Hall. Don't ask me why. I leave all that stuff to Phil. He wants me to be in London in early August. The ninth.

That's to start strict training. I'll be starting the light stuff end of June, beginning of July. That's here, in Leeds. So we've got about a month we can do whatever we like in. Go away on holiday if you like. Anything. Oh—of course . . . maybe . . .'

Judy looked at him questioningly, smiling. 'What?'

'I've been forgetting. Your work. Your singing. What you going to do about that?'

'Ah, my career.' The phrase seemed to amuse her.

'Well, yes. That's what I were thinking about.'

'I don't know, Dave. How do you feel about it? I mean for a start we don't need the money do we? What little there is of it.'

'No. Money's not going to be any problem. Harold King's accountant looks after it for me, investments, building societies and that. Income tax and stuff. We're going to be rolling in it after the defence. Phil reckons I'll be able to retire a millionaire after three or four more fights, maybe less. Another couple, if I go to States.'

'Well . . .' She drew out the word slowly, judicially. 'I've got as far as ever I'm likely to get. Not very far. It's pretty boring stuff I do as a rule. Same old thing. It wouldn't worry me if I never sang in public again. I might change my mind, but that's the way I feel now.'

Dave could not hide his pleasure and relief at this information. He said, 'You're sure, love? I mean you're a great singer. Lovely. It seems a terrible waste.'

Judy laughed softly and shook her head. 'No, darling. I'm not. I'm very ordinary. Not a great singer at all. If I was I'd feel different I expect. No. I think I'll be very happy just being Mrs Dave Ruddock.'

The waiter took away their first course and came back with a steak for Dave and Chicken Kiev for Judy.

He said, 'What will you do while I'm away in London? It's going to be well over a month.'

'Can't I come with you?'

'When I'm in full training! No. Never. Phil'd have kittens if he heard you even mention it.'

'Oh.'

270

'It's nothing against you, love. Not against women. As such. See what I mean? It's not the old fashioned idea neither. You know, they used to reckon it—' He glanced round to make sure no one was within hearing '—weakened you. Making love like. It's not that. It's your mental state. You've got to be mean. And you've got to be single-minded. I've got to win this one, Judy. And I will. You wait and see.'

'I know you will.'

'Aye. Well . . . yes. Still, we haven't said what you'll do with yourself while I'm away. August and September.'

'Oh, I'll find plenty to do. I'll go and stay with mum and dad for a week or so. They'd like that. And I'll see a bit of Sue and Andy. You know, the couple I was staying with at Bramhope. And Tom and Peggy. I hope I'll be able to see a lot of them. They're your friends. We'll be able to talk about you. It'll bring you nearer—well, make you not quite so far away. And your parents. We're going to go and see them tomorrow, aren't we. That'd be lovely if I could visit them now and then. Oh, don't worry darling. I'll be all right. I don't get bored easy, you know. I'm a lazy cow really. Love doing nothing. Listen to a bit of music, read a bit, watch the box. Go and see my friends. Dream about you.'

'Aye. Best make sure those friends are my friends too.' His voice and smile were meant to be flippant but both contained a steeliness, a hint of threat.

'Dave,' she said softly, and reached across the table for his hand. 'You don't have to worry. Believe me. I'm yours. All of me. I'm not interested in anybody else. You've got to believe that. A month. Two months. Whatever it is. It's nothing. I could wait for years as long as I knew you wanted me. That's not Barbara Cartland stuff. It might sound like it but it's not. It's true Dave. I love you and I'll never let you down.'

His smile softened and he returned the pressure of her hand. Then he said, 'I'm a lucky bugger.'

She smiled back. 'No. It's me. I'm the lucky one—well, perhaps we both are.'

271

CHAPTER TWENTY

The next day Judy and Dave were up quite early and, over breakfast in their room, they made their plans for the day. Judy was going to pick up her car from outside Tom's place and drive to her flat where she would take away what clothing and other necessities she would be needing during the next few days. Her main concern was for her piano which, they now decided, could be moved to Dave's house the following week when Aileen, they assumed, would have left. Judy's few boxes, sheet music, records and record-player could also be removed and stored with the piano so, when Dave's fight was over, they would find storage for both his and her possessions while they put the house on the market and found a permanent home for themselves. While Judy was tidying up at her flat Dave would visit his parents and give them the news about his intention to re-marry and suggest that he brought his future wife around to meet them. Then he and Judy would return to the hotel for lunch.

After breakfast Dave telephoned the principal estate agents in the town to find out what furnished accommodation was immediately available and made a note of each possibility. Then he drove Judy to where her Mini was parked and, after making sure that its engine started without any trouble, he kissed her goodbye and drove back into town. He parked his car on a meter space in Merrion Stret and walked to Briggate where he entered one of the large jeweller's shops. He was smiling, a small private smile which brought to his eyes a glint of suppressed excitement and pleasure.

A girl in a black dress said, 'Can I help you?' She was blonde, quite pretty but her mouth and eyes were petulant and, at the same time, a little calculating and suspicious. Judy, he thought, made all other women, even good-lookers, seem ordinary.

He said, 'Looking for a ring. Engagement ring. Diamond.'

She turned away and returned to the counter with two trays of rings. 'Do you want a solitaire? A row? Cluster? What sort of ring?'

He said, 'Let's have a look . . . Eh, that's a nice one.'

'That's sapphire and diamond. Victorian style. Half hoop.'

'And that one. What's that? I like that one.'

'That's a bit more expensive. Single stone diamond. Eighteen carat gold. Very nice ring.'

Dave nodded. 'What d'you think yourself like? I mean if you was to have your pick. Which one'd you go for?'

She frowned and pouted thoughtfully and made a little purring noise. Then she said. 'That one I think. The one you just said. It's a lovely stone. See how it sparkles? And not too heavy. Delicate like.'

'Aye.'

'What size did you want?'

'I don't know. About . . . can I look at your hand?'

She extended well manicured fingers, flexing them daintily.

'That's about it, I reckon. About same.'

'Well, if there's any problem you can bring it back and have it altered.'

'Aye. Okay. I reckon I'll take that one. How much is it?'

'Four hundred and ten pounds.'

'Fine. I'll take it.' He got out his cheque book. 'I've got a card. But p'raps you'd like to phone bank as well. It's Oakwood branch.'

She said, 'Just a moment sir.'

She carefully removed the trays of rings from within reach and then tapped on a door behind the counter and disappeared into the room behind it. Within a few seconds she reappeared with a man in his late thirties or early forties who wore gold-rimmed glasses and a pale moustache.

He began, 'You'd like to pay by—'Then he broke off for a moment before exclaiming. 'It's Dave Rud—Mr Ruddock, isn't it? I'm right, aren't I?'

Dave nodded. 'That's right.'

'This has made my day! *Your* cheque's all right sir. We don't need to bother about formalities as far as that's concerned. I'm proud to be of service.' He turned to the girl. 'You know who this is, don't you Laura?'

She looked doubtful. 'I thought he looked ...'

'It's Dave Ruddock! The boxer. Middleweight Champion of the World! That was a great performance last week. Terrific. I wish I'd been there to see it.'

Dave felt himself blushing. 'Aye ... thanks,' he muttered. 'Four hundred and ten, you said, wasn't it?' He spread his cheque book on the counter and bent over it with his ballpoint. 'June the first. That right? Who do I make it out to ...?'

The man placed a printed invoice on the counter. 'There you are sir.'

Dave wrote out the cheque and was given a receipt for his purchase.

'One little thing sir.'

'Yes?'

'Could you give me your autograph? My little lad'll be very thrilled to get it. Here we are sir. If you could write it on this. Maybe a little message—you know: Good wishes. Something like that.'

'What's his name?'

'Jason.'

Dave wrote on the piece of paper. 'To Jason. All the best from Dave Ruddock, World Middleweight Champ.'

'How's that?'

'That's marvellous. Very good of you sir. If there's any trouble about the ring, wrong size or the lady wants to change it, you've only got to bring it back with the receipt.'

Dave left the shop and walked back to his car. After three days of fine sunny weather the sky was bruised to a dark purple and the air was warm and still. He drove along North Street towards Roundhay Road, turned right into the street where his parents lived and came to a halt outside the house.

He knocked loudly on the door, opened it and went in calling, 'Anyone at home! It's me, Dave!'

At once his father came out of the living room. He was wearing baggy trousers and a woollen vest. On his feet was the pair of ancient boxing-boots that he habitually used as slippers.

'Eh, by! It's great to see you, Dave. Come in lad. Yer mam's got kettle on . . . Hey Dot! Look who's here!'

Dave followed his father into the living room where his mother was sitting at the table filling in some kind of form printed in multicoloured inks. It was, he guessed, one of the many competitions for cars, washing machines, holidays in Tenerife or cash prizes for which she was continuously and unsuccessfully submitting entries.

He said, 'Hullo, Mam. How are you, love?'

He bent over her and kissed her cheek. She did not look at him or say anything. Jimmy wrinkled his forehead and drew down each corner of his mouth in a grimace which might have been warning of simple helplessness in the face of female unpredictability.

'What's up?' Dave said to her. 'You don't seem all that glad to see your eldest lad.'

She did then look at him. He felt a quick stab of anxiety at his heart when he saw how pale and tired she looked. Her eyes were miserable and, he thought, accusing.

She said. 'You don't seem very interested in my youngest lad neither, do you?'

Dave looked quickly at his father, then back to Dot. 'Martin? What about him? What d'you mean?'

Jimmy said, 'He's wounded. But he's all right, Dave. It's not serious. He's going to be all right.'

'He's going to be all right!' Dot repeated. 'That's what they say. He's only been shot in both legs. That's all. He's going to be all right. What does that mean? He's going to keep his legs? They're not going to cut 'em off? Just one maybe. They don't care!'

'No, no Dot! They told us,' Jimmy protested. 'They told us. Gun-shot wounds in both legs. Left leg superficial flesh wound. Right leg, fractured something-or-other. One of them foreign words. Latin. That's not bad, Dot. They'll never amputate. Never. Gun-shot wounds. They go straight through, see. It's a blighty one. He'll be back home right as rain in a few weeks.'

'When did you hear?' Dave said.

Jimmy answered: 'Yesterday. They give that number to ring on telly. After they'd said about Goose Green and Two Para being there. Your mam's been down road about fifty times ringing 'em up.'

Dave said. 'I've told you often enough you should've got phone fixed up here. You wouldn't listen. It don't cost much. I told you to send bills to me, didn't I? Then you wouldn't have to go down to stinking phone box and get change an' all that. An' another thing I could've rang you. I could've rang you to see about Martin an' everything.'

His mother reached out and he held her right hand in both of his for a moment. She smiled very faintly, apologetically. 'I'm sorry love. You're quite right. I'm out of my mind with it all. It's terrible is this Falklands thing. You can't hardly believe it. Lads being burned to cinders. Drowned. Smashed. Killed. And their parents! My God, you wouldn't believe it. One of the mothers the other day on telly. Her young lad killed on one them ships. The *Ardent*. And what's she say? She says she's proud! Proud! When your little lad—the baby you—eh, I don't know. It's madness. It's wicked!'

'Dad's right,' Dave said. 'Martin'll be okay.'

'Aye,' Jimmy confirmed. 'He'll be back here in a few weeks. Maybe sooner. Leg in plaster for a bit then he'll be skipping around like a two-year-old. He'll be a hero.'

'Hero!' Dot echoed with deepest scorn.

'Aye . . . well . . . lad did his bit. You can't let them Argies get away with it tha know'st. It's British soil, see.'

'Oh shut up you old fool,' Dot said, but there was a small note of indulgence behind the exasperation. 'I'll go and make tea.'

While she was in the kitchen Dave said, 'Listen dad. I'm telling you. Get that bloody phone fixed up here. All you've got to do is get form from Post Office. Get mam to fill it in. Or I'll do it if you like. Aye. Leave it to me. I'll do it. All right?'

Jimmy nodded but his son could sense the uncertainty.

When Dot came in with the tea, Dave said. 'I was just

telling dad. I'll get form from Post Office. You've got to be on phone. I'll see to it. So don't let's have no arguments. It's for me as much as you. I'm going to be in London six weeks in August and September before the fight. I'd want to keep in touch. You're so obstinate. Old-fashioned.'

She handed him his tea. 'All right.'

'Good lass.'

They sat round the table. Dave was aware of his mother's mildly sardonic gaze fixed speculatively upon him.

He said, 'You heard about—Aileen told me she come to see you. While I was in London. Training. She told you then?'

'Aye. She told me.'

'About—you know—being a nun an' that?'

'That's right. And a few other things as well.'

'About . . . ?'

Dot waited.

'About a divorce and me . . . well . . . getting married again?'

'Getting married!' Jimmy exclaimed. 'You must be barmy, lad. You get out of this one, you want to stay free for a bit. Enjoy yourself.'

Neither Dave nor his mother took much notice of this.

Dot said, 'No. She didn't say you was getting married again. She wanted a divorce so's she could be a nun. She said you was running around with other women though.'

'A nun!' Jimmy echoed with amazement and perhaps distaste.

Dave said, 'Aye. Well, that's it. I want to get married again. Aileen's wrong about other women. There's just one, that's all. We're going to get married when divorce's through.'

'Oh yes?'

Dave felt the flush of embarrassment spreading on his face and neck. 'You know her,' he said. 'Well, you used to. A long time back.'

'Oh? She's an old friend of mine? She must be getting on a bit for you, love.'

He grinned awkwardly. 'You used to do a bit of work for her mam. Look after the kid, Judy Styles. Remember?'

His mother nodded slowly and thoughtfully. 'Judy? Oh yes.

I remember all right. Yes. A right little minx. Pretty little thing. Didn't she take up singing?'

'Aye. That's right. She's a great singer. Or she was. She's going to give it up.'

'And you're going to get married.'

Dave nodded. 'Yes.'

'How long you known her?'

'About six months.'

'An' where is she now?'

'What? This minute?'

'Don't be daft. Where's she live? Where are you two going to live when you get married? What are you going to do with house?'

'Sell it. We're going to get a furnished place for time being. Then we'll look for a regular place after the Hayes fight.'

'What you want to sell the house for?' Jimmy said. 'What's up with living there?'

Dave said, 'I don't think Judy'd fancy that. I know I wouldn't.'

Jimmy shook his head in perplexity.

'Where are you staying now?' Dot asked. 'D'you want to come here for a bit or what?'

Again Dave felt the warmth on his face. 'We're staying in a hotel just for a few days. Till we get a flat or something.'

'Oh...you're not waiting till you get married.'

'No.'

'No. Well, things is different nowadays.'

He said, 'I'd like to bring her round. You haven't seen her since she's grown up. She remembers you well. Is that all right?'

'I don't see why not. I expect we'll have to meet our next daughter-in-law sometime, won't we father?'

'She's nice,' Dave said. 'You'll like her.'

Dot smiled suddenly and the irony lingering about the mouth and eyes disappeared. 'Of course we will. Bring her to tea on Sunday. I expect she's used to something a bit posher than this but we'll do what we can.'

They sat for another half an hour or so and talked, among

other things, of Aileen's vocation.

'It's beyond me,' Dot said, 'but I never did understand that one. She seemed happy enough about it when she come and see me. I can't think what she got married for in the first place if that's what she's wanted. I can see why you—you know—how things—never mind.'

'As long as she's happy,' Dave said.

'Not much happiness in that life,' Jimmy observed. 'They shave their heads and they've got to wear scratchy vests and that. Terrible grub like in solitary—bread and water—saying prayers all day. Can't think how anybody'd want that lot.'

'No. You wouldn't,' his wife said. 'But you're not exactly a religious kind of man, are you love.'

'I know right from wrong. I wouldn't do nobody a bad turn. Not if I could help it.'

She looked at him for a moment indulgently and with some affection. 'I know you wouldn't,' she said gently.

A little later Dave got up to go.

He said, 'We'll see you Sunday then. About half past four. An' I'll do something about a phone.' He kissed his mother. 'Look after yourself. Don't worry about Martin. Dad's right about bullets. It's the big stuff and the flames and all that that's the killers. He'll be all right.'

His father went out on to the pavement with him.

'Listen dad. I'm staying at Queen's for a few days—' Jimmy's eyes widened and his mouth formed a whistling shape signifying awe '—so give us a ring there if you hear any more about Martin or anything. Just ask for me. All right?'

'Queen's, eh? That must cost a bob or two.'

'Aye. Well, I can afford it.'

'Right son. See you Sunday tea-time.'

Dave could see Jimmy in his rear mirror as he moved away, the stocky, untidy figure with one hand raised in farewell, and he pressed the car horn a couple of times in answering valediction before he turned into the main road and drove back to the city centre.

Judy was surprisingly nervous as they approached Dave's parents' home on the following Sunday afternoon.

She said, 'I hope they don't hate me.'

He grinned. 'Aye. They'll likely spit at you. Lock you in coal shed.'

She had spent a long time in the hotel room deciding what to wear for, as she explained, she didn't want to look like the scarlet woman who had enticed their little lad from the path of righteousness but, on the other hand, she didn't want to look like something the cat brought in. The weather had been fine and warm since the thunderstorm which had exploded on the afternoon of his last visit to Dot and Jimmy, but again the atmosphere was weighted with threats of thunder and great turgid clouds were massing above the office blocks of the city. Judy finally decided to put on a simple sleeveless cotton dress and dainty, low-heeled sandals.

Dave said, 'You look bloody marvellous. So stop worrying.'

The storm broke as they reached the house, a few vast raindrops splattered out like great shattered pale asterisks on the windscreen and then the chilling flash of lightning which was followed almost instantly by an alarmingly close shell-burst of thunder. Then the rain was slashing and sizzling and spitting and dancing all about them.

Dave slipped out of his jacket and draped it about Judy's shoulders. He said. 'I'll get out and open door. Then you make a dash. This is going to go on for hours.'

She nodded and he opened the car, slid out and was standing in the open doorway within a couple of seconds. He beckoned to her and she left the car and sped for the shelter of the house. Then they were both inside, grinning and wet, as Jimmy appeared from the living-room. 'Eh, I thought I heard something. By, you've brought some funny weather with you. Come on in. Are you wet?'

Jimmy was wearing his best trousers and had been persuaded to put on a tie which had already slipped to one side so that the knot was partly concealed beneath one wing of his shirt collar. Dot was carefully dressed in black skirt and shoes and a white blouse and Dave thought she looked much better than when he had seen her five days earlier, though she was still very pale.

The fuss over their being wet helped Judy to get over the potentially difficult preliminaries of meeting Mrs Ruddock again after so long and, when Judy returned from the bathroom, where she had gone to dry and tidy her hair, Dot was busy laying the table with salad, cold meats, bread and butter and cake.

Dave noticed with amusement his father's covert and entirely appreciative glances at Judy.

Jimmy said, 'Dot tells me you used to come here as a little lass. Can't say I remember. But you must've changed a bit since then. Aye, for the better too, I reckon.' He grinned and winked at Dave.

Dot said, 'Judy only come here two or three times. 'Course you wouldn't remember.'

'I remember coming.' Judy said. 'I used to look forward to it. It was always cosier. Nicer than at home. And you always had lovely ginger cake.'

'Parkin!' Jimmy exclaimed. 'Aye it's champion is Dot's parkin. Fancy remembering. Got us some for tea, love?'

Dot's smile was meant to be self-deprecatory but she could not exclude from it a hint of complacency. 'If you behave yourselves I might find some.'

The storm rumbled, cracked and flashed as they sat down at the table. Rain rattled and sprayed against the windows. The lights had been switched on against the darkness.

Dot poured tea and served food and they began their meal.

'Any more news about Martin?' Dave asked.

Jimmy turned to Judy on his left. 'That's my other lad, Martin. He's been wounded in Falklands. Two Para.'

'She knows. I told her,' Dave said.

'Aye. He'll be back before long. Not right away like. They're flying the very bad ones back but he's not all that serious like. Gun-shot wounds.'

'Sounds serious enough to me.' Judy said.

'That's a lovely ring.' Dot was looking at Judy's left hand.

'Yes . . . yes, it's nice isn't it?' She glanced up at Dave who was sitting opposite and he saw that she was blushing faintly.

He said, 'I got it in a lucky dip.'

Dot smiled and nodded. 'Very nice.' Then she said, 'You was talking about a house or flat. Somewhere to live for time being. You found anything yet?'

Dave and Judy began to answer in unison that they had been lucky but Dave was quick to stop speaking and allow Judy to give the details.

She said, 'It's a flat. Shire Oak Road. That's up in Headingley. Very nice. We went to see it on Thursday. The couple that's in it now—he's a lecturer at the Poly, I think—they're going to America for about nine months. Something to do with his work. We've got it till the end of March next year. Gives us lots of time to look around after Dave's got back from London.'

Jimmy said, 'I still can't see what's wrong with the house in Lidgett Park—'

'And no one's asked you,' his wife interrupted briskly. 'More tea, Judy?'

'The flat's very nice,' Dave said, 'Handy too. Only down road from Tom Darwin's place and not all that far away from Bramhope. Judy's got an old friend there. She'll have somewhere to go when I'm away. Won't be without company.'

'You'll be very welcome here, love,' Dot said. 'Any time.'

Dave saw the women exchange small, delicately significant smiles of an understanding that need never be stated and he knew that each had made a kind of declaration.

'When d'you start training, son?' Jimmy asked. 'I mean light stuff with Micky and Harold.'

'I reckon I'll start the end of month. About four, five weeks, harden up a bit for Phil. Then the torture sessions. I'll go an' have a word with Harold about it before we go away.'

'Go away?' Dot said.

'Aye. For a few days later on in month. Down to London. Phil and Rose wants us to stay with them but we reckon we'll find a hotel. I'll be seeing enough of old Phil later on.'

Dot asked Judy about her parents and said that she would like to be remembered to them. Then she added, 'I don't know how your mother's going to feel about you and my lad,' and there was a dryness in her voice and a minute glitter in her eyes which suggested that speculation yielded some satisfaction.

Again the smiles they exchanged contained hints of conspiracy.

They began to talk about the past, the way in which Leeds, like the rest of the world, was changing for the worse and Judy began to question the older woman about her own youth and then about Dave's earliest days. Jimmy talked to Dave, at first about the forthcoming defence against Earl Hayes and very soon about his own experiences in the professional ring.

At about seven-thirty Dave and Judy prepared to leave.

'Don't forget,' Dot said to Judy. 'You're welcome here any time. When he's away in London I mean. Don't be lonely. I don't suppose we're much company for a young woman like you but we'll always be glad to see you.'

They came together and brushed cheeks.

Judy said, 'It's been lovely. Smashing. And you're both lovely company. And that ginger parkin's wicked and gorgeous. You'll have to give me the recipe.'

Jimmy was grinning, bashful and with a kind of elephantine mischievousness. He went with them to the street where the rain had stopped and beneath a smeared and slatey sky the gutters ran with swollen rivulets and debris.

Judy said. ' 'Bye Mr Ruddock,' and pecked him quickly on the forehead.

His grin spread to an almost alarming size. When Judy had been settled in the passenger-seat and Dave was about to climb into the car, he said, 'Eh, she's a right corker Dave! You lucky young bugger.'

Dave nodded. 'Aye I know that,' he said. 'You don't have to tell me.'

As they drove away Judy said, 'You were right Dave. If we'd had any lunch I'd have been finished. What a banquet! I won't want to eat for a week.'

Dave nodded, smiling. 'Mam's ideas about grub's what you might call a bit basic. Stoke up with as much you can as often as you can.'

'It doesn't seem to have done you any harm.'
'I reckon not.'
'They're lovely,' she said. 'They really are.'
He nodded. 'They liked you too,' he said. 'I could tell.'

CHAPTER TWENTY-ONE

THE FLAT WAS on the first floor of a large, early Victorian house. It comprised a living-room and a bedroom, a spacious kitchen which also served as a dining-room, a small study, which, it had been agreed, Dave and Judy should not use, and a bathroom of heroic size with an old-fashioned, large tub. Judy found the décor and furniture acceptable, if rather drab, and she liked the high ceilings of the rooms and the huge windows which overlooked a well-kept garden at the back of the house. To Dave the place was romantically different from anywhere that he had lived or aspired to live before. He felt that there was a kind of splendour about its very shabbiness and he was delighted by the shelves of books which lined completely two of the living-room walls. Not that he read or intended trying to read any of them but he was flattered by their presence and he was pleased when, as quite often happened, Judy would browse among them and sometimes pick one out to settle down with. Occasionally she would read aloud some passages which had taken her fancy and Dave enjoyed these moments deeply, even when he had little idea about their meaning.

Gradually Dave had lost what might best be called the sense of social awe which Judy had originally inspired in him. This did not mean that she was any less mysterious, enchanting and exciting, but simply that she had drawn closer to him on plain human ground. He was no longer intimidated by what he had formerly regarded as her general superiority of class, education, breeding, style. Her good nature, liveliness and generosity of spirit were qualities which brought them together in a way which insisted on equality and reciprocity. But the power of the erotic spell which she cast over him was undiminished; her femininity, the contrapuntal ferality and submissiveness, the at times shocking directness of her sexuality became more, rather than less, thrilling. And this interflow of sensual awareness, the consciousness of each other's bodies as both objects of delight and temples of the treasured selves, was continuous. Her simple domestic acts, her merely reaching for a dish or adjusting a curtain, were gestures of not only extraordinary grace and eloquence but commentaries on and reminders of physical joys, of outrageous excitement. To watch her dressing or undressing was a privilege he could not imagine ever failing to delight in and the sight of her possessions alone, a shoe, a lipstick, hairbrush, flimsy under-garments could stir him to a desperation of longing.

Since that first night of their reconciliation at the pub in Ingleton when Judy had given Dave a full account of her relationship with Colin Hunter neither had referred to that area of her past at all. Dave's mind refused to admit the man's presence and to imagine him and Judy together in the act of love was something that, mercifully, proved impossible. Aileen was not mentioned either, though Dave thought about her quite often with feelings of residual guilt and fervent hope that she had found the happiness she seemed confident was waiting for her in the religious life.

At the end of June, when they had settled in the flat, they packed their bags and went to London where they stayed in a Kensington hotel and twice saw Phil and Rose Richardson, the first time for a visit to the Prince of Wales Theatre to see *Underneath the Arches* followed by a meal in a Soho restaurant, and the second at the boxing manager's home. Rose and Judy found each other immediately compatible and Phil, though a little apprehensive of the possible threat presented by Judy's potentially distracting and softening charms, was fairly quickly disarmed by her vivacity and by what seemed a genuine and intelligent interest in the fight game. The other theatrical experience that Dave, with some private misgivings, agreed to submit himself to was to attend a performance of *Tosca* by the English National Opera at the Coliseum and this, to his astonishment, he enjoyed. Afterwards he was almost inarticulate with wonder: 'By!' he exclaimed in the taxi, 'it were bloody wonderful. Imagine me. Opera! Going to bloody opera. An' it were terrific! I really enjoyed it!'

When they returned to Leeds Dave began light training. He got up at six-thirty and put on boots and track suit and, rather than discover another route for his road-work, he drove to his old training-ground of Roundhay Park and pounded out his daily six miles of steady running before driving back to the flat. Judy had his breakfast ready for him after he had bathed and dressed and at ten-thirty he drove to the gym in Roseville Road and worked with weights, heavy punch-bag, skipping rope and at his exercises on the floor for an hour and a half. Three evenings each week he returned for a second short work-out which included sparring four rounds with a variety of partners. He worked conscientiously but without that gritty, self-punishing fierceness that he would bring to his work once the strict training in Ealing began. Then, he told himself with a kind of bitter satisfaction, the real, the cruel preparation would start, monastic, merciless, lonely and uncompromising. Both physically and mentally he would be transformed to a man of steel.

While he was at the gymnasium in the mornings Judy would sometimes visit or be visited by Sue, and Dave was finally persuaded to dine with the Davitts, an occasion to which he did not look forward but, in the event, found quite enjoyable. Andy, Sue's husband, was, Dave realised with amusement and mild incredulity, in awe of him and listened to the fighter's pronouncements as if they were oracular. The Davitts were, in their turn, entertained by Judy and Dave, and, with a couple of visits for Sunday dinner to Dave's parental home and a number of meetings with Tom and Peggy life was, socially, quite sufficiently occupied and, indeed, there were times when, in restaurant, pub or someone's home, they looked at each other covertly and they would both see or sense an answering need to be together, alone.

On the Sunday evening preceding the day at the beginning of the second week in August on which Dave was to leave for London he and Judy joined Tom and Peggy at their flat for a farewell meal. After they had eaten they remained in the kitchen, sitting round the table, Dave with a mug of instant coffee and the others finishing the second of the bottles of red wine which Tom had provided.

They had been talking about the aftermath of the Falklands campaign and the recent IRA bombings in Hyde Park and Regent's Park when Tom, who had drunk more than his share of the wine said suddenly, 'You heard any news of Aileen, Dave? Is she out of the swing of the sea yet?'

Dave frowned, puzzled by the last words.

Peggy said, 'He's being clever, Dave. It's a poem about a nun taking the veil.'

'Oh . . . no. Nothing about that. Just something from solicitors. About divorce. I give it to Harold's bloke to deal with. Seems she's started divorce going. Doesn't want to claim nowt except costs and that. Judy and me ought to be able to get married next year.'

'And what about Martin? What news?'

'He's back, in hospital. Aldershot. I'll get over an' see him next week or week after. He reckons he's going to be all right. Still got one leg in plaster but he's on his feet. Wants a couple of tickets for the Hayes fight. Him and his mate. Looks like there'll be right bunch of you lot at ringside.'

Peggy said, 'Can you get as many tickets as you like?'

'No. No, they're a bit funny about ringside tickets. Some of 'em's booked every show for VIPs. There's not all that many seats at Albert Hall. But I'm getting half-a-dozen. That's you—Tom—and Judy. Dad and Harold'll be there. And Martin and his mate. Micky'll be in corner with Phil and Paddy.' He looked at Peggy. 'You don't want to go do you love? Great party after fight. We're all staying at same place. The Rembrandt.'

'I do not!'

Judy said, 'I don't know whether I want to go or not. I've

never seen a boxing match. Except a few times on telly and I never took all that much notice. But I don't know . . . seeing Dave. I don't think I could stand seeing him hurt. I'm not sure. I'd probably scream or faint or something.'

Dave said, 'You don't need to worry. Nobody gets hurt. Well, not the way it looks. You see lads bleeding like pigs, but they're all right really. They're not feeling nothing. You don't when you're in there. Not unless you crack a rib or a hand or something and even then you don't notice it much till after.'

Peggy said, 'Till after. That's the trouble isn't it? All those blows on your head and face. Every one's doing some sort of damage. As you say, Dave, you don't notice it at the time. But the harm's done and it's irreversible.'

'You don't know what you're talking about,' Tom said. 'Not that that's ever stopped you laying down the law about anything.'

'I know that a bang on the head can cause serious brain damage. Everybody knows—'

'For Christ's sake, Peggy! Dave's fighting for the World Title in a few weeks' time. He doesn't need you to tell him what the risks are.'

Dave said, 'You don't need to worry about me, Peggy. Anybody banging away at my head's more likely to hurt his hands than anything else.'

Peggy looked prepared to argue but Tom's warning expression made her pause. Then she said, 'Well, whatever you say, I think boxing's barbaric. It'd be banned in any civilised country. In fact it is banned in Sweden, isn't it? And Cuba.'

'No,' Tom told her, 'it isn't.'

'I think you'll find I'm right.'

'Professional boxing. That's illegal. Not amateur though. Sweden and Cuba are no different from the Eastern Bloc countries. Well, Cuba, anyway. There's no pro boxing behind the curtain either. Plenty of boxing though. What they call amateurs spend as much time at it as our pros. Same in Cuba. One of their national heroes is a boxer. It's not barbarism they object to, Peggy. It's capitalism.'

'All right. How do you justify it on those grounds then? You're always sounding off about the evils of capitalism. I mean even if it's accepted that boxing's what you claim it is—splendid exhibition of skill and courage and all that stuff—you've got to admit it's wrong for big business to exploit it. I've heard you say it yourself. The days of the hungry fighters are coming back. Unemployment, poverty, a heartless government. Lads who wouldn't become professional fighters in better times are going into the game because the alternative is miserable poverty. How do you justify that?'

'I don't.'

Dave said, 'All I can say is I'm glad they haven't banned game in this country. I wouldn't be nobody if it wasn't for boxing. And I've heard them going on about exploiting young lads an' all that. But nobody makes you go in ring. It's up to you. Nobody puts gloves on if they don't want to. And these people that say we're being exploited. What do they think we are? Daft kids or something? We understand risks all right. Better than what they do. We're not as ignorant as they think. We know there's been three hundred and forty boxers died from injuries they got in ring. That's since Second World War. Nearly fifty years. Sounds a lot. There's been millions, billions of fights. Three hundred and forty out of that lot's a drop in ocean. See what I mean? Boxing's no more dangerous than a ride on a push-bike. Maybe less.'

Peggy said, 'What would you do, Judy, if you had children? Sons? Would you like to see them box?'

'I don't know. I haven't thought about it. I think I'd leave it to Dave. I know he wouldn't make them want to do anything they didn't want to do.'

'Aye. It'd be up to them,' Dave said. 'I wouldn't push 'em one way or t'other.'

Peggy looked scornfully at Judy. 'You really mean that? This is man's stuff, nothing to do with the little woman. I mean that's a bit close to the attitude of those women who sent sons off to be killed in the Falklands isn't it?'

Tom and Dave responded to this simultaneously.

'Balls!' Tom exclaimed. 'It's not the same thing at all.'

'That's not what Judy meant,' Dave protested.

Judy answered, 'No. I don't think it's a fair comparison, Peggy. All I'm saying is that Dave knows more about boxing than I do. You wouldn't argue with that, would you? And if we had kids—boys—and they wanted to box I'd be inclined to leave it to Dave to encourage or discourage or whatever he thought was right.'

'But he's not an impartial judge of—'

'Of course he's not impartial,' Judy interrupted with spirit. 'He'd be the boys' father. He'd be on their side. He'd want what's best for them.'

'Anyway. No more argument,' Tom said. 'Let's finish the plonk.' He topped up the girls' glasses and filled his own empty one. 'We won't be seeing you till after the fight, Dave. That's a solemn thought.'

'Aye. That's right.'

'Oh darling!' Judy's eyes widened with the sudden realisation. 'I hadn't thought of that! Won't I even see you at the hotel before you go to the hall?'

Dave shook his head. 'No. It's best that way. I think Phil's right. He reckons I'm in the right state. If it all works out I'm physically at the peak and I'm mentally ready to go. I'll be feeling mean. I'll be blaming Hayes for everything. Not seeing you all those weeks. I'll be wanting to take it out on him. It's him stopping me from seeing you, love. If I was to see you, even if it was just for a few minutes before the fight, I'd be feeling different. Sort of gentle. That bit of edge'd be gone. Can't afford no sweet loving thoughts. Just hard, concentration on job. That's the ticket.'

Peggy said, 'Well, much as I disapprove of the whole business I still hope you win. And if one of you's got to get hurt I hope it's him and not you.'

'And don't worry about Judy,' Tom said. 'We'll look after her for you. Don't worry about anything this end. Just concentrate on giving Hayes a hammering. Okay?'

Dave nodded. 'I'll lick him all right. I've got to. For everybody's sake. It's going to be a tough 'un. But I'll win it. You wait and see, I'll win it all right.'

Part Three

CHAPTER TWENTY-TWO

TRAINING HAD NEVER been so hard. Little of the old bitter, almost masochistic, pleasure was left. Dave worked his way through each day's routine with a bleak, self-punishing determination to force himself beyond the limits of what the human body could endure. His morning run was gradually extended from six to ten miles and the pace he set himself became more and more exigent. If, as happened quite often during that August and early September, rain was falling when he rose at six o'clock in the morning, he did not consider waiting to see if the weather would improve. Running in the grey drizzle, being splattered with mud, feeling the malicious cold trickle of water from drenched hair, down between the collar of his track-suit and the warm skin, satisfied this new, steely compulsion to be merciless to himself. On those mornings when the park was fresh and glittering beneath bright sunshine and a blue sky he felt mocked by the weather's geniality.

In the gymnasium Phil watched him with an approval which was modified by an underlying puzzlement and anxiety. The grimness of Dave's approach to his work, the uncompromising pitilessness of his aggression in the sparring sessions, were encouraging portents for the defence against Hayes, but his continued and uncharacteristic darkness of mood after the work-outs gave cause for concern. The danger was that Dave could over-train and, as Paddy Whelan put it, 'leave the fight in the gym'.

At the beginning of his fifth week of intensive training, after a private evening sparring session during which Dave practised the tactical manoeuvres which Phil believed would prove successful against Earl Hayes, the fighter was getting dressed after his shower when his manager came into the dressing-room and sat on the bench. Leroy Coombes and Tommy McGuire, the boxers who had been working with Dave, were also getting dressed.

'How was he tonight, Leroy?' Phil said to the tall, lean black fighter. 'You find him easy to hit?'

Coombes's grin was broad and his teeth gleamed white as the flesh of a newly split coconut as he looked up from tying a shoelace. 'I was kinda busy stopping Dave hitting me,' he said. 'Some o' them body-shots just about bust you wide open, man. Yeah. He kept coming on pretty strong there. He ain't easy to hit. Slips the jab pretty good.'

'What about you, Tommy?'

McGuire, shorter, with heavily muscled arms and shoulders and a head of close-cropped ginger hair, said, 'I think I caught him a couple times with a right hand underneath. Not to worry him though. Like Leroy says, his body punching's wicked. I wouldn't fancy taking many of them shots with eight ounce gloves.'

Paddy Whelan came in and started to change his boxing-boots for outdoor shoes.

'What d'you think, Paddy? How'd the boy go tonight?'

'Pretty good, considering.'

'Considering what?'

'Well, he was fighting one-handed really wasn't he? I mean you says to nurse his right. He never threw it, not proper. Not once. All left hand work. Jabs, hooking off the jab. He only used the right a coupla times inside, to the body, when he went two-handed.'

'You think he'll keep up with Hayes? For speed?'

Paddy finished tying his shoes. He stood upright. 'You know he's not as fast as Hayes. There isn't another middle in the world as fast as that boy. But you know what old Joe Louis said about Billy Conn? He can run but he can't hide. I've never seen Dave more aggressive. The way he's been going the last two or three weeks he'll catch Hayes sooner or later. If Hayes don't catch him first. 'Cause that's one thing we mustn't forget. Hayes can bang a bit too. The way I see it, Dave's got to work bloody hard and maybe take a bit of stick in the first six or seven rounds. After that Hayes ought to lose a bit of speed and Dave'll begin to get to him. That's the way it'll go. We hope.'

'You hear that, Dave?' Phil said. 'You got to be ready to take a lot of stick. And don't forget Hayes can dig. There's always the chance of a big bomb. So if you did walk into one don't let it shatter you. See what I mean? You've got to keep your head. Keep it together. Follow your plan. Work away inside. Keep close. Don't throw your own bombs till you know they're going to land. And hold your right. Throw plenty of lefts. Jabs and hooks. Then show him the left and throw the right. That's the plan. You can do it, son. Never doubt it. You can beat the bastard.'

Dave put on his jacket and picked up his bag. 'I could've let the right hand go a coupla times tonight but I held it back. I'm saving it for Mr Hayes.'

'That suits me,' Coombes said. 'Let's keep it that way, man.'

Phil said, 'We'll be going now lads. Make sure all the lights are off when you lock up, Paddy. See you all tomorrow.'

He and Dave left the gymnasium and started to walk quickly back towards the manager's home. The light was fading into a blue mistiness and the street-lamps gleamed and spilled their yellow light in pools on the surface of the road. Already there was the slight chill and pungency of autumn in the air. Two young men and their girls approached and passed them on the pavement and Dave could detect the faint sweetness of the scent the girls trailed behind them like invisible veils. The click and tap of high heels faded and he felt a small dark emptiness in his stomach. It was like a hunger-pang, though he had no wish to eat.

Phil said, 'We've got the television boys in the gym tomorrow morning. I expect they'll want you to punch the bag and skip. Maybe spar a bit with Ron or Paul. Then a bit of chat. They're putting out a Big Fight preview on Saturday's Grandstand. They wanted to get you and Hayes together but

I told them no way. You and him don't meet till the weigh-in.' When Dave did not answer Phil went on: 'You all right, son? You seem a bit quiet. You feeling okay?'

'Yeah. I'm fine.'

'You missing Judy. That it?'

'Aye. I am that.'

'Won't be long now. Remember it's his fault. Hayes. It won't be long now. Week on Tuesday. Stay mean till then Dave. You're doing great. You're punching hard. I could see those hooks to the body going in tonight. That's what you've got to do. Get close and stay close. Bang away downstairs. Hurt him. Worry him. Keep working at his belly and ribs. Don't go throwing big right hands. Not at first. Not till you're sure they're going to get there. Sooner or later you'll catch him. And if you stop one yourself. Well, you don't need me to tell you. Be ready. He's a puncher. Don't let's kid ourselves about that. He can dig all right. Probably harder than anyone you've met so far. So you've got to be ready, Dave. No surprises. Be ready for the worst. The big bang on the chin. You know what it's like. You've been tagged before. And you know as well as I do that half the kids that get counted out aren't real knockouts. They're bloody shock-cases. They come in not prepared. Mentally. You've got to be ready. There's not more'n one punch in every dozen knockouts is what you'd call a real KO. The others are good punches. Hard enough to put you on the floor, scramble your brains for two, three seconds. That's all. But these kids that haven't got their minds right, haven't prepared their selves, it takes 'em another two, three seconds to get over the shock after they've come round. Then they think Christ, I'm on the floor. The ref's counting. I'm knocked out! And they don't get up. Now you're going to be ready. Maybe the big one won't come over but you've got to be ready in case it does. You've got to be in that state of mind where you're expecting to be hit. Hard. Where your mind's made up he can't knock you out. However big the bombs. You're the guy that knocks 'em out. You're not going to be knocked out. No way. Like Marciano. He was like that. Hit him with a fucking axe and he'd come back at you And that's the way you're going to be, Dave. You're going to give this bastard a bad time.'

When they reached Phil's house Dave said that he would go straight to bed but Rose persuaded him to stay downstairs and drink a cup of hot chocolate. They all watched television for a while and at ten o'clock Dave said goodnight and went up to his room. He laid out his track-suit, heavy boots and socks for the morning's run and undressed and climbed into bed. He lay in the darkness but did not sleep. Nearly a fortnight to go before the fight; nearly a fortnight before he would see Judy again. He wondered what she was doing at that moment. Was she thinking of him? Could it be possible that she missed him as much as he missed her? Certainly she claimed to, when they spoke daily on the telephone, and she sounded as if she meant it. After the fight, whatever the result, he would go with her to the hotel and stay around with the others who would be boozing, either in celebration of his victory or in mourning for his dethronement, and he and Judy would each know what the other was thinking, wanting, longing for. Then, when the party was under way, they would give each other the nod and they'd escape, up to their room and then, and then. And then. Oh Christ, it was too shattering, too crazily exciting, too agonizing and dizzying and sweetly heart-wrenching to think about.

He turned on to his side and struggled to dismiss the seductive, debilitating images by invoking the harsh and unlovely pressures of the gymnasium and ring. He saw Leroy Coombes's black, intent face, the wary, unblinking eyes beneath the leather headguard, heavy lips blubbered by the gumshield; he could hear the sounds of combat, the slither and hiss of feet on canvas, the grunt and snort of expelled air from flattened nose, the smack and thud of glove on bone and flesh. He smelled the bitter reek of sweat. He heard Paddy's voice: 'Keep 'em up! Hands high! Keep 'em up . . . underneath! Bring it up from under! . . . Both hands now . . . work! Move! Worry him! Rough him up! . . . Last ten seconds! Slam away inside . . . Both hands! . . . Time!' But there was something lacking in his response, something of the old grim excitement, and he knew that he had changed; he was no longer enjoying the game as he once had done.

He was training as hard and as conscientiously as ever. He was boxing as well and punching with at least as much power as at any other time, but he was not experiencing that fierce, ruthless glee that used to fill him every time he put on the gloves. Perhaps it would come back on the night, but certainly it was absent in his sparring sessions. He knew that he was moving with all the old smoothness and economy, that he was slipping punches with split-second timing and throwing his counters with accuracy and explosive venom, but the old joy of battle was missing. He had become a fighting machine.

In the old days, by which he meant the shadowy time before he had known Judy, it seemed that he had been a different person. When he had first joined Phil's stable in Ealing he had been home-sick for Leeds but this had not interfered with his enjoyment of the game. He had revelled in every moment of training, indoors or out, running, skipping, exercising and sparring. And, always, the prospect of the fight itself had been almost unbearably thrilling. He would not have believed then that, in a few months' time, he would be looking forward to a World Title defence against a great fighter, possibly one of the greatest ever, with an impatience caused not by the eagerness to test himself against Hayes but by the consuming longing to be with his woman. And, faintly but recognisably present, was a small undertow of regret for those days which had possessed a kind of innocence. Aileen had been there, to comfort him with a whiff of home when he needed it, but her absence had never troubled him with clamorous needs and his enjoyment of and commitment to boxing had remained absolute.

The thought of Aileen brought instantly a conflict of feelings: he felt disloyal to Judy and indignantly reproving of his own ingratitude, but he was also stabbed by uneasiness and guilt for his abandonment of Aileen. He tried to imagine her in a nun's habit but found it difficult to visualize her in any other guise than the familiar one of his not very exciting girlfriend and, later, his wife, and despite her evident happiness in the rediscovery of her faith he found it impossible to believe that the religious life could be a permanently fulfilling one for a woman. It seemed that Aileen was being made to pay for his happiness with Judy and the unfairness of this left a sour taste. He was, he thought, a bit of a bastard. He had once thought of himself as an easy-going, kindly sort of bloke, good-hearted. But events had proved otherwise. He was as selfish and cruel as anyone when it came to the crunch. And he was lucky, lucky beyond all likelihood. One thing was for sure, he told himself. There wasn't much justice in life. So there wasn't much sense in expecting things to be fair. Grab what's on offer and enjoy it for as long as you can. You're a long time dead so make the most of it while you're still on your feet. But, before he slept, there was, close to his own face, yet slightly out of focus, the features of Judy, smiling, gentle and infinitely understanding, and he was moved, not by sexual passion but a deep hunger of the spirit and flesh, a yearning to be close to her, to protect and be cherished by her for the rest of his life, and he was perplexed though strangely unashamed to feel the delicate, warm progress of a single teardrop move from the corner of his left eye, down his face to the side of his mouth. He was turning, he told himself, into a right cissy and he grinned in the darkness so that, a little later, when he was fast asleep, his mouth still showed a touch of that self-mockery.

The next day Dave skipped rope, sparred a couple of rounds with Coombes and punched the heavy bag, while the television cameras recorded his actions. Then, still sweating from his exertions, he and Phil recorded an interview with the presenter of the programme, Barry Parsons.

'This'll be going out on Saturday,' Parsons said before they began to film, 'so I'll be talking about the big fight like it was in a couple of days' time. Okay?'

Dave sat on a straight-backed chair with Phil on one side and Parsons on the other. He had slipped into his jeans and a T-shirt after his work-out. The producer signalled to Parsons that the cameras were rolling and the interviewer turned to Dave and said, 'Well, you certainly seem in good shape,

Dave, for your first defence of the title you won back in January when you knocked out Marcel Fournier in the eleventh. Since then you've had one non-title fight with Wayne Harvey. You took him out in the third so you'll be feeling pretty confident for Tuesday's defence against Earl Hayes. All the same I think you'll be the first to agree that Hayes is going to be a very different proposition from Harvey. Or from Fournier come to that.'

Dave nodded. 'They're all different. No two fighters is the same.'

Parson's smile was knowing. 'Yeah. But some are more different than others. Hayes is reckoned to be just about the best middleweight since Sugar Ray Robinson—maybe *including* Sugar Ray. And everything we've seen of him on film and in the gym confirms all the claims they make. He really seems something out of this world.'

Phil said, 'Why isn't he the champion then? Dave Ruddock's the undisputed Middleweight Champion of the World. There's no argument about that. He's never lost a fight since he turned pro and he's won over half inside the distance. In fact his last six fights—all against World class opponents—everyone was a knock-out or a stoppage. You can't ask for more than that.'

'Sure. No one's knocking Dave. We're all very proud of him. But I'd like to hear what *he* thinks of Earl Hayes.'

Dave said, 'He's a good fighter. Anybody can see that. But I don't think he's been tested the way I'll be testing him.'

'Not been tested? Over twenty contests and only one lasted the distance!'

Dave shrugged. 'He's fought a lot of has-beens. Like I said. He's a good fighter. So am I. They say he's a hungry fighter. Me too. He can punch a bit. So can I. If you think publicity worries me you're wrong. I don't take no notice of what the experts say.' He managed to put the 'experts' into ironical inverted commas.

'All right,' Parsons said briskly, with the air of a man who has cut the cackle, 'how is it going to go then? You going to outbox him? That'll take a bit of doing. Or you going to take him out with one punch? Or do you hope to wear him down?

That's the one thing we don't know about, isn't it? Hayes's stamina. How he's going to travel fifteen rounds. If it goes that far, of course.'

Dave said nothing.

Parson's smile faded. 'Well,' he said, almost tetchily, 'what's it going to be?'

Phil intervened: 'We don't play that game, predictions. But I'll say this. Anybody thinks Dave's going to be a push-over's got it all wrong. He can match Hayes in every department except, maybe, Hayes is a bit faster. But Dave's at least as big a puncher. And when it comes to stamina I think my boy's going to have the edge. I know there's a lot of people saying Hayes is phenomenal. But there's an old saying in the fight game. You're as good as the other fella let's you be. And Dave's not going in there on Tuesday night to make Earl Hayes look good.'

'Well, I'd like to wish you the best of British luck. Unfortunately we won't be seeing the fight live though it's being shown on closed circuit in cinemas all over the world. Except here in Britain. But we'll be showing the complete fight on Wednesday's Sportsnight. So, until then, good-bye.'

Dave went off to finish dressing and when he returned Parsons and the team of technicians were leaving the gym.

Phil said, 'You did well there, son. He was a bit sick at having to come out here for the interview. They wanted us to go into the studio on Saturday like I said. Bugger them. We've got the title. We call the shots. Let's go back and have some grub.'

At home Rose had prepared a lunch of steak and salad, fresh fruit and cheese. After the meal Dave rested for an hour in his bed. He thought of the television programme being transmitted on Saturday and reminded himself that he must tell Judy to watch it. He would ring Martin at Aldershot who would, no doubt, like to see his famous brother on the small screen, if only to impress his army friends. His parents, too, who had at last had a telephone installed, would like to be told, though Jimmy would almost certainly be in the pub when the fight preview was transmitted. If there was a television-set in the bar he would be a very proud and happy man.

Thoughts of his brother and parents seemed to nudge his speculations back into the shadowy archives of his childhood and he grinned with half-mocking self-congratulation as he reflected that the small boy who pored over the action photographs in his father's *Ring Magazine* and *Boxing News* and indulged in prolonged solitary fantasies of heroic triumph in the boxing-ring would scarcely have dared to hope for the reality that in fact had been achieved. He remembered his first pair of proper boxing-boots, a present on his twelfth birthday, and the following Christmas when he had unwrapped the dressing-gown of orange towelling with black piping and the inscription in black letters on the back: St Joseph's ABC. And the ring itself, the podium, altar, scaffold, stage, an artefact capable of stirring depths of feeling, superstitious awe, reverence, fear, tremulous excitement, that only initiates could share or understand; that roped square under the bleaching power of the arc-lamps, even seen in an empty hall, could set the engines of hope, terror, ambition and the sheer exhilarating zest for action pounding into vibrant life and when he had first seen a boxing-ring used, on television, for that travesty of physical combat, commercial wrestling, he had been sick with disgust and rage to see what seemed to him, quite seriously, a desecration of a sacred object. His almost tearful anger had seemed comical to Jimmy, who had witnessed it, and the old fighter's incomprehension marked the beginning of Dave's withdrawal of respect, though not of love, for his father.

He remembered boys at school getting together in little groups in the bogs and sniggering over some photograph torn out from a girlie magazine, or maybe something more blatantly pornographic, and when he had rejected their invitations to join their furtive covens he had felt both superior yet uneasily aware of his priggishness which, had he not been a boxer, would have invited rough treatment from the hard-cases. Tom Darwin's contempt for what he called the 'Shithouse Mafia' or the 'Witless Wankers' was one of the causes of Dave's admiration for and sympathy with his clever and unlikely friend and it was Tom who understood most completely his feelings about boxing and his reverence for the ring. The only thing he had never confided in Tom about was his romantic schoolboy obsession with Judy. That had always been his secret until he had told Judy herself and now, not only had his dreams of becoming a great fighter, a World Champion, come true but he had been granted the real presence of his ideal fairy princess who, miraculously, had proved to be human, warm, passionate and loving. He was, surely, the luckiest man alive.

The weekend before the fight seemed interminable. Dave had finished his training and he was at that stage of mental and physical readiness when only the most violent activity could provide release for the compressed coil of tension inside him. After breakfast on Sunday he and Phil walked for most of the morning, and, after lunch, they read the newspapers. Of the ten sports writers who were previewing Tuesday's fight only two suggested that Dave was in with a likely chance of retaining his title. The rest were unanimous in picking Hayes as the almost certain winner though there was some diversity of opinion as to the likely manner of his victory. Three of the journalists believed that Hayes would win by a knock-out or stoppage early or, at the latest, in the middle of the contest while the others were less sure of the duration of the bout or the precise manner of its conclusion, though fairly certain that Hayes would be the winner. One 'expert' who had been watching Hayes in training was of the opinion that Dave's only chance of survival was to enlist the aid of the marines and to make sure that they had plenty of ammunition. This writer went on:

> 'I yield to no man either in my patriotism or admiration for Dave Ruddock as a good, honest fighter whose courage and skill have never been in doubt. But more than bravery and ordinary know-how is needed to combat Hayes's lethal brilliance. In more than twenty years spent at the ringsides and in gyms all over the

world I can honestly say I have never seen such lightning reactions, such cunning ring-generalship or such murderous punching power as this black panther from Atlantic City has displayed. With the best will in the world I cannot see Ruddock lasting more than five rounds with the challenger. I hope I am wrong but commonsense and Hayes's record and performance tell me I'm right.'

'You read this bloke in *Herald*?' Dave said to Phil.

'Yeah. He's like a lot of 'em. I've seen him at a few of the shows. Always half-pissed. Face like a bloody great strawberry. Don't take no notice of him, Dave.'

'I'm not. It don't worry me what he says.'

'It shouldn't neither. This fella in *The Observer*'s got a bit more sense. He's the only one that's pointed out what everybody's suddenly forgotten. Your record's just as good if not better than Hayes's. And he puts his finger on it when he says we've never seen Hayes hurt. We don't know how he takes a punch. And that's what we're going to find out on Tuesday. That right, son?'

Dave nodded. 'Right.'

Rose said, 'It's a nice afternoon. What about a ride out into the country? Have tea somewhere.'

Dave said, 'I've got to stay in. Judy's ringing some time.'

'Why don't you phone her? Then we can go out. You don't want to sit around all day. You give her a ring now. Come on Phil. I've got something to show you in the other room . . . and give her our love Dave.'

Phil and Rose left the room and Dave dialled the number of the Leeds flat.

Judy answered. 'Dave! I was just going to phone you. How are you darling?'

'I'm fine. I thought I'd ring so's we can go out for a bit. Rose wants to go for a drive in the country.'

'I can hardly wait till Tuesday. Tuesday night. When it's over. Oh my god, Dave. I never knew it was going to be like this. Waiting. It's terrible. I think I've lost about a stone. I don't think I could face it again.'

'It'll soon be over. Day after tomorrow.'

'I saw Tom and Peggy last night after I phoned you. They came round. Tom brought a bottle of vodka. He was blowing his top about the sports writers. Says they don't know what they're talking about.'

'Aye. Well, I hope he's right. Most of 'em say I'm in for a hiding.'

'Oh my love. I can't bear it. I won't be able to watch. I won't be able not to either. I'm so scared. Every time I think about Tuesday night I have to go and have a pee.'

Dave chuckled. 'I know the feeling.'

'Dave...'

'What love?'

'I miss you. I love. I want you. Now. This minute.'

He said, 'It won't be long now.' His voice was hoarse and he cleared his throat.

'It seems years away.'

'Yes.'

'Darling...'

'Yes.'

'Tell me.'

'I love you,' he said. 'You know I do, don't you?'

'Yes darling. But I like to hear you say it.'

'I'd better go. Phil and Rose are waiting to go out. They send their love by the way.'

'Give them mine. And tell them they've got to look after you. Because you're very precious.'

He said, 'Ring me tomorrow. Any time. I've finished training so I'll be in most of the time. If I'm not, leave a message. All right?'

'Yes...Love you, Dave. Very much.'

'Me too.'

They exchanged a few more endearments before Dave finally said goodbye and replaced the receiver. He stood for a few moments, still hearing echoes of Judy's voice, tempted to dial her number again. Then he turned slowly away and moved towards the door.

'Tuesday night,' he thought. 'Roll on bloody Tuesday.'

CHAPTER TWENTY-THREE

T HE CROWD WAS pumping out great waves of noise that came thundering and shrilling from the smoky darkness, bursting over the ring so that Dave could scarcely hear the referee's brief homily. But the words were familiar enough. 'All right, boys. Let's have a nice clean fight. When I say break you break clean. Keep your punches on target. If you score a knock-down you go to a neutral corner. Wait for the order and signal to box on. Deliberate fouls, low punches, use of the head, gouging, biting, you'll be warned first. Persistent fouling and you'll be disqualified. You know the rules as well as I do. So back to your corners now, come out fighting and good luck to you both.'

Hayes, his skull completely shaven and brown eyes expressionless, almost bored, had been rhythmically moving from one foot to the other, quite slowly bending each knee as if he were treading water. He was perhaps an inch taller than Dave and when he turned to his corner the ripple of back and shoulder muscles moved fluently under his chocolate-coloured skin as he flexed his arms and began to dance lightly on his toes, waiting for the bell.

Dave stood for a moment and looked out over Phil's shoulder down to the ringside where he could see Judy staring up at him, her eyes unsmiling, big with concern. He gave a quick, ducking nod and grin in her direction and then came the time-keeper's call: 'Seconds out of the ring!...First round . . .' and the single clang of the bell.

Tom could feel Judy trembling as the two boxers moved to the ring centre and began to circle each other. He took one of her hands and placed it on his right sleeve and felt it grip hard. Martin, sitting on his left, immediately bellowed, 'Come on Dave! The old one-two! Show him who's champion! Show him who's boss!'

Dave had adopted a slight, uncharacteristic crouch. His gloves were held high, elbows close to the body and, as he moved forward, his head was moving from side to side, up and down, bobbing and weaving in the pattern favoured by aggressive, hooking fighters. Hayes, by contrast, looked more relaxed and his hands were quite low, the right carried at about chest height, around the left nipple, and his extended left lower still, both gloves moving continuously in an almost lazy motion as if conducting his own private music, and it was from this fluid, graceful rather old-fashioned stance that the first blow was struck, a long, stabbing left, aimed at his opponent's head, which Dave deflected with his right without countering. Again the left shot out and this time Dave slipped it, moving inside the lead so that Hayes's glove slid past his right ear and, with the sway to his left Dave released a right to the solar plexus which Hayes took on his elbow and the two fighters clinched. But only for a couple of seconds. They broke, without the referee's intervention, and immediately Hayes leaped back into action with a left hook to the body and right to the head. Dave took the body punch but ducked under the following right and countered with his own left and right to the body.

The noise of the crowd had changed from the raucous, dithyrambic chant, which had started with the bell for the opening of the bout, to a deeper growl and muttering that could explode at any moment into a tempestuous roar. Tom's teeth were grinding together and his abdominal muscles were already beginning to ache with the strain. In the white gush of brilliance from the lamps above the ring Dave's skin looked marmoreally pale and the heavy satin of his crimson trunks glittered with an opalescent, contradictory prettiness. Hayes wore black trunks with white waistband and stripes and his dark-brown muscular body seemed less vulnerable than the pale Britisher's, though the experienced eye would immediately detect the power and durability of Dave's physique.

There was a sudden, excited, almost hysterical note to the crowd's din as its voice swelled and shrilled and rumbled in support of a quick, determined attack by Dave who took one left jab on his forehead, slipped a second, and let fly with a combination of short body punches with both hands followed by a fast left hook to the head which Hayes succeeded in evading by moving forward so that the force of the blow was spent as Dave's glove landed harmlessly behind the shaven head. The fighters clinched again and, this time, the referee pulled them apart. Immediately Hayes took up the offensive, shooting out two rapid straight lefts followed by a hard right to the head and left hook to the solar plexus, driving Dave back towards his own corner where he executed a skilful side-step, fading away from another threatened attack then coming back with his own barrage of short arm body-blows and a right uppercut which jolted Hayes's head back and brought an eruption of noise from the crowd. Then the bell ended the first round.

Martin said to his army friend, 'He walked it! He bloody walked it!'

Jimmy Ruddock sitting next to Harold King shook his head. 'I don't like this new style Phil's got him using. Dave's a left-hand merchant. A stand-up, straight puncher with a left hook for afters. He's no in-fighter.'

'He's doing all right though, i'n't he? Got in a few good digs to the body there.'

'Aye. We'll see.'

Judy gazed up at the corner where Dave was sitting, nodding as Phil talked urgently, close to his ear.

Tom said, 'He's doing very well, Judy. They were just feeling each other out in that round. I think we'll see more action in the next.'

The timekeeper called, the bell sounded and Hayes came from his corner very fast and leaped into the attack straight away with a left jab to the mouth, a right to the body and a left hook to the jaw, the punches delivered with such speed that the three blows seemed to form a single flowing movement. Dave managed to drop his head instinctively so that the hook landed too high to be dangerous but it stung his right ear and set steel wires twanging inside his skull. He stabbed back with two straight lefts but Hayes moved away easily and threw a right cross over the second lead. The punch landed squarely on Dave's jaw and he felt the stony weight of his opponent's knuckles numbing and setting off warning lights in his head as he feinted with his own right and threw a left hook at Hayes's chin with all the power at his command. The punch did not connect. He felt or heard a mighty clash of black cymbals, darkness flooded into his skull and, in this sudden midnight, glittering burs of brilliance floated. The echoes from that first apocalyptic explosion quickly faded and, with them, the darkness as he found that he was still on his feet and holding on to Hayes's arms with his gloved hands, his head burrowing into his adversary's shoulder, the smell of sweat strong in his nostrils. The referee was heaving at his right arm and snarling, 'Break! Ruddock! Leggo for Christ's sake! Break it up!' At last he managed to pull them apart. The engines of the crowd's excitement were now thunderous.

Dave bit hard on his gumshield and began to move forward behind his high guard. There was no sense in retreating. This man could hit you from any distance. He had three arms. At least. He was faster than light. Phil had been right. The only thing to do was get in close and rough him up. And hope he slowed as the fight went on. Dave slipped a left but was caught by a jolting short right. Then he drove his own left to the body and tried a right hook over Hayes's lead. It landed too high on the head but it carried enough weight to force Hayes back a couple of paces and Dave drove forward, digging in short-armed blows to the midriff. Hayes grabbed him and the referee separated them and ordered them to box on. Three left jabs flashed and thudded into Dave's face before he slipped under a right hook and dug another left into the body. He could feel a swelling coming up above his right eye, a little sore lump, weighting the brow and threatening to grow big until it blocked his vision. He feinted with a left to Hayes's head, slipped under a right counter and again got through with a cluster of stiff shots to the body before Hayes trapped his arms and the referee parted them as the bell ended the round.

Dave went to his corner where Paddy Whelan took his

gumshield and at once applied an ice-pack to the swelling above his eye as Phil said urgently, 'You're doing fine Dave. You took that big bomb and you showed him you could take it. Now keep going forward. Worry him. Keep your hands high as you go in. Try to get him against the ropes. And try that right hand again over the top. And keep banging away at the body. He can only take so much of that. You'll slow him down sooner or later.'

Judy, at the ringside, said to Tom, 'It's horrible! Look at his poor eye. It's all swollen.'

Tom patted her hand which was still clutching his sleeve. 'Don't worry. Dave's all right. He's doing very well.'

As the bell sounded for the third round Martin and his friend added their shouts to the yells of the crowd and Dave left his stool, biting on his gumshield as he went straight into the attack, taking a jab and moving inside the next one and hooking his right glove to the pit of Hayes's stomach. He heard a small grunt and, encouraged by this, he slammed with both hands at the belly and ribs, taking a hard right upper cut to the chin but still punching away and forcing his man back to the ropes.

The din was thunderous, shouts, screams and stamping of feet. Hayes slid along the ropes and got back to the ring centre. Then he sprang in to take the offensive, hooking off the left jab to the head and slinging in a thunderbolt of a right to the body. It was Dave's turn to grunt and gasp for breath, but he fought back from his crouch, hooking to the body with left and right and then throwing a quick scything left to the head which Hayes partially blocked with his right glove but took enough of its force on his upper jaw to cause him to move away fast and raise his guard. Dave followed, taking two more left jabs but getting through with a hard right to the heart. Then Hayes, perhaps feeling that the initiative was being taken away from him, began to dance on his toes, using the whole space of the ring, darting in and out with stabbing left leads, and then throwing a combination of lefts and rights to body and head, some of which Dave took on gloves and elbows, though he was staggered for a moment by the weight of a cruel right uppercut that snapped his head back. Hayes, confident again, began to stalk him, flicking out measuring left jabs, varying them from head to body and back again.

Dave was retreating for virtually for the first time. He moved back towards a neutral corner, gloves high, perhaps a little apprehensive. The crowd were screaming at him to attack. Hayes shuffled to his right to cut off Dave's attempt to avoid being trapped; then he sprang forward with another dazzling combination of punches, a one-two to the head, a right to the body and a left uppercut to the chin. Dave was on the ropes. He was frowning behind his guard. The swelling over his right eye was coming up again. Tom, on the edge of his seat, was swearing monotonously, sick with anxiety. Judy now had both hands over her eyes and her head lowered. Hayes stabbed out a range-finding left and, as he delivered it, Dave flashed over his right-cross. It looped over the probing left and crashed against Hayes's unprotected jaw. Hayes was bowled over on to his back. The din of the crowd was skull-drilling, deafening, crazy.

Martin and his friend were on their feet, jumping up and down like enormous puppets on wires, roaring their triumph and delight. Tom grabbed Judy's arm and yelled, 'He's done it! By Christ he's done it! Oh, you beauty! Oh my God, he's done it!'

Jimmy Ruddock and Harold King were clutched in a mad, hilarious embrace.

Hayes rolled on to his side and scrambled up into a kneeling position. Then he was resting on one knee as the referee, taking his count from the time-keeper, tolled the seconds while the right arm rose and fell: '. . . six, seven, eight . . .' Hayes started to rise. He was upright, on his feet, as the ninth second was called. The referee looked into his eyes, examined his gloves for dust or resin, then signalled to both fighters to continue the fight.

Dave moved forward. He was not fighting from a crouch now. He was upright, prodding out an orthodox straight left, looking for an opening. Hayes was retreating, guard high, replying with similar left jabs. Then Dave jumped forward with a left to the stomach and another powerful, smashing right to the head. But Hayes moved back with the second punch, riding it, robbing it of its full force and with tigerish speed and ferocity he fought back with his own left and right to the head. Dave's knees seemed momentarily to wobble and sag, but he was still able to counter with a couple of solid shots to the body and Hayes, apparently recovered from the knock-down, resumed his earlier exhibition of fast, elusive boxing, dancing on his toes, darting in and out with rapier left leads, threatening with the right but content to score points with the jab until the round ended.

On his stool Dave was distantly aware of the surging, crackling flood of noise from the hall as he closed his eyes while Paddy took his gumshield out of his mouth and again applied the ice-bag to the swelling on his right brow. He breathed deeply and a small grin, so faint as to be undetectable by an onlooker, moved the corners of his mouth. He was feeling good. He could take anything Hayes had to offer. The man was a good fighter, but he was human. Those punches were harder than anything Dave had been forced to take in the past but they were not the killers he had been told to expect. He could soak them up all night if he had to, until Hayes got tired and a bit discouraged. Then he, Dave, would move in and take over. Because he was the harder puncher.

Phil, leaning through the middle and top rope, standing on the ring-apron, was hissing in Dave's ear: 'That's the one, son. You've done it once. You can do it again. But don't be in too much of a hurry. Keep banging away at his guts. Guard up. Bob and weave. Get inside. Hurt the bastard in the belly. Then over the top. If you get the opening throw your left hook. Try and nail him with it. Get him scared of the left. Okay? Then you can throw the right. But be patient . . .' The time-keeper shouted, 'Seconds out of the ring!'

'Good lad!'

Dave opened his eyes. The ice-bag was removed and gum-shield slipped back into place. He felt Phil's hand massaging the back of his neck.

'. . . fourth round!'

Then the clang of the bell.

Dave rose from the stool, tapped his gloves together, shrugged into his slightly crouching stance as he moved towards the tall dark figure of his adversary. The swelling above his right eye had not wholly subsided. He was aware of the tiny pressure on his eyelid. He could see almost perfectly but he knew that the eye was beginning to close.

Dot Ruddock was sitting with her daughter, Jean, in the living-room of Dot's house where they had lit the gas-fire because the evenings were beginning to bring, with the misty twilight, an autumnal chill which could become quite sharp as the night wore on.

Jean said, 'It's nearly ten o'clock. I'll have to be getting back, Jeff'll start to get worried if I'm much after ten.'

'That's all right, love. It was nice of you to come and keep me company.'

'You going to be all right, mam? All on your own. I told you. You're welcome to come back and stay with us.'

'Eh, no. I'm not bothered. They'll be back tomorrow some time. Martin's coming with a pal of his from Paras. They've got leave now he's had plaster off. I've got lots to do, love.'

'The fight's on radio, Jeff says. Radio Two. If you want to listen. It'll have started by now. Half past nine I think he said.'

'No. I never could stand listening. I watched Dave a few times on telly. But that's after I know what's going to happen. Not live. I couldn't stand that.'

'He'll be all right. Jeff reckons he's going to give 'em all a surprise and win on a knock-out.'

'Aye. Well, if Jeff says so . . .'

'Now don't be sarcastic, mam. I know Jeff's a bit hard going at times but he's a good lad really.'

'Of course he is, love. I just thought—well, I wouldn't have said boxing was something he knew a lot about. Some things, yes. But not boxing.'

'Everything,' Jean said. 'He knows a lot about everything.'

They exchanged smiles, Dot's sceptical and her daughter's tolerant and affectionate.

Then Jean said, 'Anyway. You're on phone now. You can give us a ring if you—well, I dunno . . . want anything . . . Get lonely . . . Anything.'

'I'll be all right. I'll go to bed soon. So don't you worry about me.'

Jean collected her handbag and coat, kissed her mother's cheek and let herself out of the house. Dot heard the car engine start and the sound of its dying away. Then she took the cups and saucers, from which they had been drinking tea, into the kitchen and washed them up. A portable radio stood with her cookery books on one of the shelves above the gas-cooker. She finished drying the last saucer and put it away. Then she hesitated for a moment before reaching up for the radio and carrying it into the living-room where she placed it on the table. She stood, looking down at it with an ambiguous expression of dislike, suspicion and, perhaps, fear. Then she switched it on.

A man was speaking about the massacre of refugees by the 'Christian Militia' in a camp in the Lebanon, an act of sickening brutality condoned if not encouraged, it seemed, by Israel's Minister of Defence, Mr Sharon. Dot turned the control knob and the pounding tempo of a rock band blared out of the speaker. Then she tuned in to the urgent voice, cockney with transatlantic overtones, of the boxing commentator who was raising the pace and volume of his account of the fight as he tried to combat the swelling din from the crowd and to keep up with the rapidity and violence of the events in the ring.

'. . . Hayes jabs again with the left. And again! Ruddock takes them both and still comes forward. He throws a left to the body. And a right! But Hayes takes the right on his elbow and cracks over his own right to the head. And Ruddock staggers! Here in the sixth round of this contest for the Middleweight Championship of the World at the Albert Hall, London, Dave Ruddock the British holder of the title is fighting desperately to hang on to the crown. And so far it's anybody's fight. Ruddock comes back yet again and yet again he walks into that snaking left jab and he takes a right uppercut to the heart for good measure. But still he goes forward. And still Hayes picks him off with that lightning left jab! There it goes. Again and again! You could probably hear the smack of it hitting the target . . . But Ruddock's slipped under that one and in goes his own left to the body. And a right. And—oh

316

boy!' The commentator's voice was almost a shriek yet it was frail against the jungle howl and thunderous stamping of the crowd. 'He's caught him! Ruddock's caught the challenger with a smashing left hook to the chin and Hayes is on his bike. He's back-pedalling for all he's worth and Ruddock's after him, trying to trap him in a corner. Can he catch him again! That left hook really shook the challenger. You could see his knees turn to jelly. But he's back on his toes and using the ring to get away from the champion. Ruddock drives in again with a left and right to the body but Hayes ties him up. And there goes the bell for the end of round six. Come in Freddy and tell us what you make of that round.'

A hoarse unmistakably East End London voice replied, 'Well that was another good round. I give it to Hayes. Dave was forcing the fight, going forward all the time but he wasn't landing that many punches. Hayes was taking most of them on his gloves or elbows or getting out the way. And he was scoring all the time with his left hand as well getting in a few digs with the right. But near the end there Dave clobbered him with a real beauty. A left hook. He's been working for that all along. That's the punch he put Wayne Harvey away with last time he fought. A real cracker. Dave's been hammering downstairs and taking quite a bit of punishiment himself. Trying to get Hayes's guard down so's he can throw the big one to the chin. And that's what he did. And it nearly come off. Hayes looked very shaky for a bit but he's a tough, strong fighter as well as a brilliant boxer and he's going to take an awful lot of stopping.'

'Thank you Freddy. We're just coming up for round seven of this fifteen round contest for the Middleweight Championship of the World . . . There's the bell . . . that right eye of Ruddock's is almost completely closed now . . . and Hayes's very first punch of the round lands smack on it! That sizzling left jab. Right on target. And again! And Hayes moves away as Ruddock tries his own left jab. Can Ruddock connect with that left hook again? That's the question. Like Freddy said. He's been working away at the body for six rounds now and he's absorbed quite a lot of leather. But he's got in quite a few solid thumps to the body and

Hayes's ribs must be feeling a bit sore. Dave wants him to leave his chin—wow! Hayes jumps in with a combination there—two, three, four punches—head, body, head—and Ruddock seems to be floundering. Maybe that swollen eye's affecting his vision. He didn't seem to have any answer—'

Dot switched the radio off. The room seemed very quiet. Out in the night the desolate wailing of an ambulance siren grew louder, then faded away. She sat down and extended her hands to the warmth of the gas-fire. What fools these men were, she thought. What unbelievably childish, violent, stupid creatures they all seemed to be. They went off to foreign countries. No, not really countries at all. Little barren rock islands where nothing grew and the sheep outnumbered the humans by thousands. They went off there with their guns and bombs and battleships and killed and burnt and maimed hundreds of young people and then they came back—the lucky ones—and everybody said what heroes they were. Medals. Bands. Parades. Vicars and bishops and priests who ought to know better joining the old generals and politicians and talking about freedom and bravery and patriotism. It was all childish rubbish. The flags and the cheers and the hymns and prayers. All they wanted was the thrill of playing soldiers, playing with their big, noisy, murderous toys. And now. Tonight. There in London at the Albert Hall. Grown-ups, fully grown adults, yelling their stupid heads off, bawling and shouting for blood. That's what they wanted. They wanted to see blood. Pain. They didn't really care whose blood it was or who suffered as long as somebody did. They paid good money to watch it. To watch her boy, her son, Dave, being smashed in the face, cut, swollen, bleeding. And he was another hero. A hero because he could hit somebody else's lad quicker and harder than they could hit him. It was a mad world. And it would never change.

She crouched down and turned off the fire. Then she stood, looking at the radio, tempted to switch it on but afraid of what she might hear. Suddenly she gave her head a quick, impatient shake, walked to the door, flicked off the light and climbed the stairs to the bedroom. There she lit the bedside lamp, undressed, put on her nightdress and got into the double bed.

She lay on her back for a while, her eyes open, staring up at the ceiling. Then she turned off the lamp and closed her eyes, waiting for sleep, which would be a long time coming.

Colin Hunter was driving on the M62 from Liverpool where he had been attending an agreeable and, he hoped, profitable Masonic dinner. He had made his excuses and left just after ten o'clock and was now speeding smoothly past the M57 exit when he switched on the radio. Immediately his full attention was captured by the voice that issued from it.

'Hayes is beginning to dominate. He must have won the last three rounds and now, in the tenth, Ruddock's looking the worse for wear . . .' A slow smile of satisfaction spread on Hunter's face. '. . . His right eye's completely closed. It looks very nasty indeed and he must be finding it difficult to see those punches coming. Specially the left. And again Hayes pierces his guard with the jab and moves away, using the ring, as Rudddock tries to counter. I don't know how long the referee's going to let this go on for. Oh and there's another jab from Hayes. And another, and—ouch!—a cracking right-cross. But Ruddock takes it well and comes fighting back. Still going for the body. And he gets in there with a left to the stomach, misses with the right and Hayes ties him up. The referee pulls them apart and Hayes immediately moves in with a left and right to the head, a left to the body and another left smack on that injured eye. Ruddock is backing away now. The challenger's really taking charge here. He lands another left to the head, and another! Ruddock comes back to the attack. You've got to give him full marks for courage. He's soaked up a lot of punishment but he's never stopped trying. He gets through with two, three jolting punches to the ribs. Then a left hook to the head! But Hayes moves inside it and—oh yes! What a punch! A short right counter, inside the hook, and Ruddock almost went down. His knees buckled and he staggered. And now Hayes is after him. A left jab and then a hook. Then that right again! I think Ruddock's in trouble . . .'

'Kill him!' Hunter muttered aloud. 'Kill the bastard!'

'. . . Hayes backs him up against the ropes. Throws a right

to the head and left to the body. And Ruddock's fighting back! He's fighting back two-fisted! He's come off the ropes and he's throwing lefts and rights. They're swapping punches. Toe to toe! This is fantastic! Unbelievable! Ruddock's caught Hayes there with a straight right to the chin. And Hayes backs away. He's the first to break off. And he's on his bike again. Using the ring as the bell goes for the end of the tenth round . . . Come in Freddy and tell us what you think of that!'

Tom said, 'It's all right, Judy. He's all right. He's still strong. He's still punching hard. That right hand shook Hayes. Dave's not licked yet. Not by a long chalk.'

She was trembling and tears had stained her face and smudged her mascara. He held her hand. 'Don't worry, love. He's as strong as a bull.'

'His eye!' she said in a thin, quavering wail. 'His poor eye!'

'It's only swelling. It's not serious. He's going to be all right. I promise you.'

Jimmy Ruddock was peering up at his son who was rinsing his mouth and spitting out the water as Phil, his right hand automatically kneading the muscles at the back of Dave's neck, offered a continuous flow of advice. Martin, who had been opening a packet of cigarettes and lighting up for his companion and himself, shouted, 'Come on Dave! This round! The old one-two!'

Tom thought, 'Jesus Christ, how can they do it? How can he go back for more? Ten rounds. Half an hour's non-stop fighting. Forty minutes if you count the rests. And he's got to go in and face more of it. Muscles aching, lungs bursting, driving yourself on. Pain and more pain. They're both mad. Or brave beyond belief.'

The time-keeper shouted, 'Seconds out of the ring . . . round eleven . . .' and the bell sounded. The swelling noise from the crowd was like a tidal wave. A falling mountain. Dave left his corner and it was obvious to the initiated that, either on his manager's instructions or from his own decision, he was going to alter his style and tactics. He was no longer crouching and trying to duck and weave his way through

Hayes's armoury to get to close-quarters. He was more upright, his stance fairly orthodox, feet not now so far apart. his left glove already prodding forward in a conventional, exploratory jab. Immediately Hayes's right flashed over the top of the lead and exploded on Dave's cheek bone. It was a hard, perfectly timed and executed punch and it staggered the champion who took a couple of paces back. Hayes followed, stabbing out his own left twice to the face, then dropping it and whipping in a hook to the solar plexus. Dave tried to find the sanctuary of a clinch but Hayes was unaccommodating, using his feet to frustrate the attempt and again snapping out his left jab. Dave retreated to the ropes. Hayes followed, stalking, feinting with his left, then right, and finally throwing the left hook to the head which connected heavily, directly on the bruised and grotesquely swollen right eye.

'Get off the fucking ropes!' Martin was yelling from the ringside. 'Move Dave! Move!'

Jimmy's head was miming defensive tactics, ducking and slipping imaginary punches.

Judy, eyes covered again, was moaning softly. 'Oh God. I wish they'd stop! Oh God it's horrible! I hate it . . . I wish they'd stop!'

Dave's back was against the ropes. Hayes took his time, feinting, measuring, coaxing his man to leave an opening for the blow that would fuse all the lights. He prodded out a reconnoitring left, waiting for Dave's defensive move. Dave slipped it with a flick of his head to the right and, at the same time, he unleashed his own left hook, moving forward, fast from the ropes. The blow landed high on Hayes's cheekbone. Had it connected a litte lower down it might have put him on the canvas. As it was he was shaken and he at once began to make use of the whole ring area, moving fast, clockwise, guard high.

Tom shook Judy's arm. 'Look Judy! For Christ's sake look! Dave's caught him! Dave's going after him. Look!'

She peered, sideways, fearfully from behind her fingers and saw that Dave was moving after his man, not punching, threatening, looking for his chance.

'Hayes's slowing a bit.' Tom said. 'He's lost a bit of speed.

Dave's going to get him. He's slowing down.'

As he spoke Dave went into action: a left jab that fell short, another left that also missed, then a right, travelling upwards into the pit of the stomach. This one connected solidly and Hayes grunted and for the first time in the contest his face registered dismay; his mouth opened, showing his gumshield and his eyes seemed to swivel in his skull as he grabbed Dave close and hung on.

The referee pulled them apart and Dave immediately returned to the attack, taking two left jabs to the face, walking through them to hurl his left hook again. This time Hayes picked it off with his right glove, circling to his left, jabbing and dancing again on his toes. Dave stalked him, accepting two, three, four jabs, not bothering to deflect or slip them, simply tucking his chin down and taking the blows on his forehead. Hayes was boxing well, moving with grace, shooting out the straight lefts with speed and accuracy, but there seemed to be a hint of, not apprehension, certainly not desperation, but a temporary resignation to a negative role. Not since his knock-down in the third round had he looked to be on the defensive. Until now. Dave was the aggressor, the menacing one. Again Hayes's left flickered out and again Dave took it on the forehead. The crowd had sensed the change of pattern and they were bellowing and stamping their encouragement. Tom was gripping the edge of his seat, saying, almost whispering, 'Come on Dave . . . You can do it . . . come on lad . . . you're going to get him . . . now . . . now . . .'

Hayes suddenly braked on the left foot, swayed to the right, then leaped forward with a combination of left to the body followed by a right and left to the head. Every punch was on target. The first blow brought down Dave's guard so that his jaw was exposed to the two head punches. His knees buckled and he seemed to be going down but, astonishingly, he converted the slight stagger into the launching of his counter-attack, a hard straight left to the mouth and again the upward curving right to the solar-plexus which crashed into Hayes's body with bone-crushing impact. Hayes's head came forward and he grabbed frantically for the respite of a clinch but Dave

322

tore himself free, jabbed again then showed the left in a menacing feint but smashed over his right to the jaw. Hayes must have sensed the coming blow and at the last moment he dropped his chin and rolled with the full force of the punch which connected with the ridge of bone above his left eye. He staggered back, three paces, recovered and began to dance and feint and swerve and jab as Dave went after him.

Then from the vast cave of the hall came the growl and rumble, rising to a howl, a pulsing, feral ululation of a terrible excitement and lust. Hayes was cut. The crowd could see the blood spurting from the wound above his left eye, glittering on his dark skin. He pawed at it with his left glove. Then he sprang forward to meet Dave's attack, abandoning his defensive manoeuvres and releasing a barrage of hooks, jabs, uppercuts and swings, delivered at dazzling speed, switching from head to body and back again. And Dave fought back. His punches were slower, perhaps being thrown at a rate of one to three to those of his opponent, but they were heavier. The two fighters slammed away at each other in the middle of the ring. Blows smashed into face, ribs, stomach. Blood was smeared on gloves, both faces, bodies; it flew like crimson rain as the jolting, crushing punches hammered home. The noise of the crowd was an avalanche of thunder, a dark, rolling, engulfing tonnage of noise that drowned the sound of the bell so that the referee, at great risk to his own safety, was compelled to drag the fighters apart and send them to their corners.

Martin and his friend were yelling and laughing and weeping and punching each other. Tom sat quite still but his eyes were crazy with a staring brilliance of wonder and triumph. He kept saying very quietly. 'He's done it. He's done it. He's got him. I knew he would. He's unbeatable. He's done it. He's got him.' Jimmy was babbling incoherent joy, and tears were bright on his scarred cheeks. Judy, ignored by all the others, was pale, shocked, and looked as if she might easily be sick.

The referee was in Hayes's corner looking at the cut. He signalled over the ropes and the Board of Control doctor climbed up on to the ring apron and joined him in his scrutiny of the challenger's injury. The noise of the crowd subsided.

The doctor was seen to say something to the referee before he returned to the ringside. Then the referee crossed to a neutral corner. The fight was to continue.

Phil was hissing in Dave's ear. 'That cut's a bad 'un. Don't take no chances. Dave. Go for the cut. Don't mix it for Christ's sake. He's still strong and he'll be going for the finish. He's got to get you this round. Work on the cut and you've got him. He's yours. He can't last more than this round. Open it up Dave. Box him. Use your jab. Don't take no chances.'

'I'm going to knock him out,' Dave said.

'For fuck's sake, no! Listen to me. You do as you're told. Get out there and box him. You mix it you'll come unstuck. He's yours for the taking Dave. So don't be a silly bastard. Go for the cut.'

The time-keeper called for the seconds to leave the ring. The bell sounded for the twelfth round.

'I'm going to knock him out,' Dave said as he left his stool.

Hayes's corner men had done a good job on the injury which was no longer bleeding and had been smeared with a thick film of grease. Dave, upright, gloves high, went forward, spearing out the long left lead, once, twice, and Hayes moved back just far enough for the punches to fall short of their target. And then, before Dave could release the heavy, following right, the challenger sprang into the attack with a barrage of jabs and hooks to the body and head, the punches travelling with such speed that spectators in the cheaper seats a long way from the ring could have seen little but a blur of red leather, though they must have witnessed the straight, pile-driving right that landed flush on Dave's jaw as he tried to throw his countering left hook. The force of the last blow sent the champion staggering back to the ropes and Hayes followed, moving with smooth, unhurried deliberation, feinting to the body with his left before unleashing a thunderbolt of a right which again crashed on to Dave's jaw, violently twisting his head so that his chin almost touched his right shoulder.

The screams and roars from the crowd contained dismay, alarm, sheer atavistic excitement and exultation. And then, impossibly, the noise swelled even louder as Dave came off the ropes to hurl his own right in an overarm, clubbing blow which smacked on to the wound over Hayes's left eye and brought the blood again spurting from it. Hayes took a couple of paces back, wiping at the injury with his left glove. He seemed to move further back and sway to his right. But this was a feint of the body and feet, a *trompe-l'oeil* of movement, to lure his adversary forward to meet the savage attack he then launched, another combination of vicious, snapping punches, hurtling from different angles as Dave tried to fight back with his own two-handed counters. For a thrilling, blood-spattered minute, the fighters swapped blows and it was Hayes who was the faster puncher and it now seemed that he was hitting with greater power than Dave. The blood was again splashed on both fighters, masking Hayes's face, gleaming on his chest as if he had been wounded there, smeared over Dave's features and torso. The referee was crouching, legs apart, peering at Hayes's injury.

'He's going to stop it!' Jimmy Ruddock said to Harold. 'That's cut's a bad 'un. The ref's going to stop it!'

As he spoke Hayes broke off the toe-to-toe slugging match, moved back, then, as Dave came forward to throw his left and right Hayes sprang in and drove an upward left to the body followed instantly by a straight, crushing right to the head. The second punch landed on Dave's lower jaw on the left side of his chin. His head snapped sideways and his hands dropped leaving him, for a second, defenceless. A second was quite long enough for Hayes to whip over a flashing left hook, a blow that was thrown with every ounce of his weight behind it, the elbow lifting and the knuckles driving downwards, crunching against the right jaw-bone. The force of the punch almost lifted Dave into the air. He went over backwards, his feet kicking upwards and, when his back hit the floor, he rolled over on to his left side and began at once to paw at the canvas and bend his knees in the effort to regain his feet.

The vast, bulging noise of the crowd contained anger, frustration, outrage, as well as pure excitement.

'Get up Dave! For fuck's sake get up!' yelled Martin. 'You've only got to see the round through! It's in the bag!'

Phil was hammering with both fists on the ring-apron. Jimmy's mouth sagged open and his eyes were wild with disbelief and misery. Judy's face was buried in Tom's shoulder and he could sense rather than hear her sobbing protests. Tom stared at the ring, hands clenched into fists, his fingernails biting into his palms, stomach muscles knotted, teeth clenched, as he prayed silently: 'Get up . . . for God's sake . . . please! please! get up!'

Dave heaved himself on to all fours. Then, as the referee's count reached six he managed to get on to one knee. He knelt there looking up at the tolling arm, rising and falling. His face was unrecognisable. The right eye was completely hidden by the enormous swelling, and the other eye was beginning to close. The swellings were discoloured and there were raw abrasions on his jaws and on the bridge of his nose. The whole face had been not so much dehumanized as caricatured by punishment. It was misshapen, hammered, distorted until it had become a mask of human suffering, primitive and, raised beneath the harsh white brilliance of the arc-lamps, sacrificial. Hayes, standing in a neutral corner, gloves not in the position of attack or defence but held close together in front of his chest, ready to become shields and weapons again should his fallen adversary rise, was, despite the deep cut like a small mouth above his left eye, still quite recognisable as the fighter who had entered the ring almost an hour earlier. The wound and the blood on his face were extraneous, incongruent.

The count reached nine as Dave rose and stood. The referee came close, held the fighter's gloves, wiping them on his own shirt. He peered into the ruined face and said something. The crowd bellowed their relief and approval when they saw Dave nod and raise his gloves in readiness to continue fighting. The referee gave the signal to box on and Hayes moved from the corner, purposeful, predatory, his gloves weaving patterns of menace. He feinted with his right and unleashed a left hook similar to the one which had floored his opponent. It was obvious that, with his right eye totally covered, Dave could not see the approaching blow which crashed against his jaw and sent him staggering against the ropes. Except for their support he would have gone down again. He stayed there, gloves held high, waiting for Hayes to attack again.

The challenger did not hesitate. He moved in, smoothly, calculatingly stabbing the straight left out, measuring his man for the savage, thunderbolt of the right hook that followed. The punch was deflected from Dave's left glove to high on his temple. His head snapped backwards and to the right and it seemed that only the ropes at his back prevented him from falling. The referee seemed about to move in and stop the bout. And then the unbelievable, magnificent, preposterous thing occurred. Dave came back off the ropes with a desperate, looping right hand counter, a punch which would not have connected had Hayes not been certain that his opponent was a beaten fighter, ready for the taking. But it did connect, crashing into Hayes's mouth, knocking the gumshield loose which flew through the air and skittered across the canvas. The challenger staggered back three paces, recovered his balance as Dave moved forward swinging both hands. But the blows were wild and Hayes moved away from them until he saw the opening for his own right. He did not probe first with the left but threw the blow from the back foot, a brutally crunching cannonball of a punch that carried the weight of his entire body behind it and into which Dave was moving forward. It caught him flush on the point of the chin and knocked him flat on his back where he lay quite still except for his left leg which beat up and down at tremendous speed, the heel of his boot rapping out a mechanical tattoo on the ring floor. Then after only a few seconds it, too, was perfectly still.

The referee had begun to count but he got no further than the fourth downward beat of his arm before he bent over the fallen fighter, pulled the gumshield out of his mouth and began signalling frantically to the ringside. The uproar of the crowd faded and the darkness beyond the ring was filled with a susurrus of unease, fear, perhaps even some shame. Phil, Paddy Whelan and Micky Rice were in the ring and they were joined by Hayes and his handlers. The doctor pushed his way through them and bent over the prostrate figure of the ex-champion. The crowd noise grew louder, a buzz of speculation, still fearful, but excited too.

The referee had been sent by the doctor to the ropes and he was shouting instructions down to someone at the ringside.

Martin had limped to Dave's corner and was trying to climb into the ring but was being held back by two stewards. Jimmy was pale and sweating. He stayed in his seat, swearing monotonously, repetitively. Tom sat with both arms holding Judy who was sobbing and trembling.

When the St John's Ambulance men came with the stretcher the crowd was almost silent. The ropes were slackened to facilitate the removal of the stretcher and its burden. It was carried down the ring-steps into the aisle leading to the dressing-rooms, followed by the train of seconds, the promoters, managers, Jimmy and Martin. They walked after the stretcher like mourners.

'Come on love,' Tom said to Judy. 'Let's go and see what's happened,' and he helped her from her seat as if she were an invalid or an old lady and, still holding her arm, he led her in the direction that the doom-laden procession had taken.

CHAPTER TWENTY-FOUR

THEY SAT UNDER the icy fluorescent lights of the hospital on a long bench against the wall. The reporters had at last been driven away by a small but very determined Sister to wait in the reception area on the ground floor or to file their stories for early editions. Martin and his friend, Hughie, a short, thick-set Glaswegian with close-cropped colourless hair and a tough, pock-marked face, were smoking beneath a notice which forbade the practice. The Sister had not failed to observe their disobedience but she had not protested. Phil Richardson and Paddy Whelan were sitting a little apart from Jimmy, Harold and Micky Rice; and Tom and Judy were next to, but not with, the two soldiers.

Martin got up and limped down the corridor to the men's toilet.

Hughie said to Tom, 'It's a right carry-on, this. They never tell you nothing. They're all the same, the medics. Bloody secret service.' Like Martin he was wearing uniform and he had not removed his red beret which was worn in the usual Para fashion, angled, pulled down low over the forehead, foreshortening the temple and increasing the natural or conditioned look of belligerence, brutality and arrogance.

Tom said, 'I don't suppose they know anything yet. They'll be doing tests.'

'Fucking medics,' Hughie said, 'you can't tell me nothing about they bastards.'

Martin came back and spoke to his father. 'Didn't we ought to ring mam?'

Jimmy looked up. His eyes were wretched with fear and

anxiety and he was scowling with bewilderment, shock and frustrated anger. At last he shook his head. 'She'll know soon enough, lad. Anyway, there's nowt to tell her. We don't know nowt, do we.'

'If she's heard it on radio, she'll be worried silly.'

'She never listens. Not to fights. Never has done.'

Martin looked unconvinced but he shrugged and went back to where he had been sitting with Hughie.

He spoke across Tom to Judy who was hunched in blank and silent misery. 'You want a fag, love? Some coffee? There's a machine up corridor. I'll get you one, eh?'

She took no notice of him at all.

He waited for a moment, still wearing the smile of solicitude and solicitation, but then it faded. 'Suit yourself.' Then he turned to his friend. 'You want a coffee, Hughie? Expect it'll be piss but it's better'n nowt.'

Hughie nodded. 'Okay. I'd sooner have a wee dram but.'

Martin grinned with that look of self-conscious, reckless wickedness that the mention of strong drink so often seems to elicit from those accustomed to the rougher kinds of masculine society and he set off again along the corridor, moving with what Tom uncharitably suspected was an exaggerated limp.

The door opposite which they were all sitting opened and the Sister came out. She was plump and she wore metal-rimmed spectacles. Even beneath the unfriendly strip.lighting she looked pink and healthy.

She said, 'Who's the closest relative?'

Jimmy stood up. 'Me. I'm his dad.'

'Mr . . .'

'Ruddock.'

'Yes, of course. Mr Ruddock.' She drew him a little apart from the others but not so far that Tom could not hear her words: 'Now, Mr Ruddock. The doctor's carried out some tests on your son. I must tell you at once. The news isn't good at all. We've tested reflexes—you know the kind of thing, knee-tapping and so on—to find the type of lesion in the brain that we might be dealing with. And we've put him on an encephalogram—this is a sort of machine that gives us the site of the haemorrhage. What he's got is what we call a diffuse haemorrhage and it's in the upper part of the brain which I'm afraid is the most serious. If it was a clot we could operate. But it isn't. So there's not a lot we can do at this stage except wait and hope. I'm so sorry I can't give you better news.'

'You mean . . . ?'

'We've made him as comfortable as we can. And we'll just have to wait and see. He's completely unconscious of course.'

'Can I see him?'

'Yes no reason why not. You do understand he won't be able to see you or hear anything, don't you?'

Martin had returned with two small, plastic containers of coffee.

He said, 'You're going in to see our Dave, dad?'

Jimmy looked round and then nodded. 'Aye . . . Then he spoke to Judy: 'You want to come, love? Come and see Dave?'

She looked up and her eyes were preternaturally large in her white, drawn face. She shook her head without speaking and then lowered it again.

Martin said, 'Can I come in? I'm his brother.'

The Sister nodded. 'I've just told you father. He's not conscious. He won't hear you or see you.'

Martin handed the cup of coffee to Hughie, and Tom watched the old fighter and his son follow the Sister into the room.

Hughie said, 'Medics. I've shit 'em.' He put one coffee down on the seat at his side and drank from the other.

Tom looked at his watch. The time was a little after midnight. They had been at the hospital for less than an hour but already it seemed that time had stopped in that unchanging frozen light in the bare windowless corridor. Phil Richardson had said almost nothing since the newspapermen had left and to them he had been almost entirely uncommunicative. Paddy Whelan and Micky Rice both looked, despite their ageing and battered faces, like frightened, even guilty children. Harold was breathing heavily and staring at the opposite wall with stricken eyes which saw no trace of consolation there.

When Jimmy and Martin came back into the corridor the older man's face changed. Where anger, puzzlement and fear had been there were now only pain and grief. Tears threatened

331

to well from his eyes. He sat down between Harold and Micky. Harold began to offer some feeble words of comfort or hope but they crumbled quickly into silence.

Jimmy said, 'My lad . . . my little lad . . . it's not right . . . I can't . . . I . . . oh Dave . . . Dave . . .' and he gulped, swallowing the sob.

'They should've stopped it,' Harold said. 'That referee should've stopped it.'

Phil, sitting a little apart from Harold overheard this and shook his head. 'No. He couldn't stop it. Not then. Dave was still strong. He was still punching hard enough to finish it. And Hayes was cut. Hayes couldn't have gone another round, not with that cut. If the ref had stopped it the crowd would've lynched him. You can't blame the ref. You can't blame anybody.'

Judy stood up.

Tom rose after her and said, 'You all right?'

She nodded. 'Feel sick. Want the loo.'

'It's up there. Come on. I'll take you.'

'No . . . it's all right.' She pulled her arm free of his hand and set off, a little unsteady on her high heels, along the corridor.

Jimmy was blowing his nose and wiping his eyes on a white handkerchief.

Hughie said, 'What did the brother look like? Pretty bad, eh?'

Martin nodded. 'Fuckin' awful. Like a corpse.'

Then they all sat in silence. Judy was gone for quite a long time and Tom had become anxious by the time she re-appeared. She had obviously tried to repair the damage to her make-up but she still looked pale and ill and the harsh lights scooped blue hollows beneath the cheek-bones. She sat down again at Tom's side.

He said, 'How do you feel?'

She shrugged.

'Do you want to go? You could come back to the hotel. I'll take you. Then I'll get back here and let you know as soon as there's any news.'

'What kind of news? What's going to happen? Is he going to

die? He can't die, can he? That's not what she meant is it? That nurse.'

'I don't know. We'll just have to wait and see.'

'Wait and see! How long? What's happening? Why can't they do something? This is a hospital isn't it? They've got doctors. Surgeons. Operating theatres. Why don't they do something?'

'You heard the Sister. It's the kind of injury he's got. There's nothing you can do with that kind of haemorrhage.'

'You mean . . . ' she did not finish her question.

They all sat in silence. Martin and Hughie lit fresh cigarettes. Then the Sister and doctor came out of the ward into the corridor. The doctor was Asian, slightly built, with a small beard. A stethoscope protruded and dangled from the pocket of his white coat. He murmured something to the Sister who answered briefly, nodding towards Jimmy.

The doctor moved across to Dave's father. 'I'm very sorry about your son's condition. Sister has told you the position. There's nothing we can do at present. There is a nurse with him and if there is any change in his condition she will send for me at once. Now, I understand you are staying in London, Mr Ruddock. What I recommend is that you all go to your hotel or wherever you're staying and tomorrow morning you can telephone the hospital and you will be told about the patient's progress. That would be the sensible thing to do.'

Martin said, 'What's the chances, doc? How bad is it?'

'It is a very serious injury to the brain. It is impossible to predict the outcome. But I think you should be prepared for the worst.'

'Isn't there nothing you can do?'

'I have told you. Sister has told you. With a diffuse haemorrhage of this kind there is no question of surgery. I am sorry. I can assure you that everything that can be done to help the patient will be done. But you cannot expect miracles.'

The doctor and Sister moved away along the corridor and disappeared through some swing-doors at the end.

Jimmy said, 'He's right. You lot go an' get a kip. We're paying for—well Dave's paying—' He stopped, aghast at what he had said.

Harold stood up. 'Aye. I think you're right Jimmy. We might as well get a bit of shut-eye. Doing no good sitting here. Nothing we can do to help. You coming, Micky?'

Phil Richardson said, 'We'd better get back, Paddy. Rose'll be going spare. I'll ring the hospital first thing in the morning.'

Martin looked at his friend. 'You go with Harold and Micky. I'm staying on for a bit.'

Hughie shook his head. 'No. I'm not ready for ma bed yet. I'll stick around a while. If that's all right with you.'

'Okay.' Martin turned to his father. 'You go back, dad, and get the head down. I'll let you know if anything happens here.'

Jimmy remained seated on the bench. 'I'm not leaving till I know what's happening to Dave. I couldn't leave him . . .' He stopped and choked back another upsurge of misery.

Finally Martin and Hughie, Jimmy, Tom and Judy were left on the bench in the bleak corridor. They were all silent, a silence which became the more unbreakable the longer it lasted. At one point Jimmy, without a word, got up and made a journey to the toilet and back. Later, Hughie stabbed out with his heel the cigarette he had been smoking and disposed himself full length on the bench. It seemed a precarious perch but he put his hands behind his head, closed his eyes and soon appeared to be sleeping.

'Sleep on a tightrope, could that bugger,' Martin grunted.

After a while Jimmy's head began to nod and every now and then it would fall forward and then jerk upright and he would stare about him, bewildered and startled until memory came back and, with it, the realisation of the circumstances.

Tom thought with incredulity of the previous day, his setting out with Judy on the train from Leeds, her excitement and vivacity. He remembered their booking in at the reception.desk of the hotel, the momentary perplexity of the girl behind the counter when they said that Tom had booked a room for himself and Judy was to be given the key to the double-room reserved by Dave. Then their attempt to eat something in the Knightsbridge restaurant, both too excited to swallow more than a couple of mouthfuls. It seemed so long ago.

He glanced surreptitiously at her as she sat by his side, her head bowed and her hands clasped together, resting against her mouth. He could not see whether her eyes were closed or not. Of the fight itself only dislocated images flickered before his eyes. Dave flashing over that first tremendous right-cross that had floored Hayes; the two fighters slamming away at each other after Hayes had been cut; the blood smeared darkly on Dave's white skin and gleaming, rubescent on Hayes's face and torso; and persistent, inerasable, constantly returning, the image of Dave on one knee, his swollen, mutilated face raised in what looked like supplication as the signal arm of the referee recorded the falling seconds.

Martin stood up and lit another cigarette. He said, 'You want a coffee, Tom? . . . Dad?'

Jimmy started and peered up at his younger son. 'Eh? What's that?'

'You want a coffee?'

'No . . . Aye . . . might as well.'

Tom said, 'I'll get them . . . What about you, Judy?'

She did not move or answer.

Tom touched her shoulder gently. 'Would you like some coffee?'

At first there was no response, then she slowly shook her head.

Martin and Tom went to the dispenser and found between them the right coins for three plastic cups of coffee which they carried back to the seat. Hughie was snoring intermittently.

Martin said, 'This is the worst night I've ever spent. Worse than fucking Goose Green. No kidding.'

Jimmy sat, holding his coffee in both hands as if he were warming them, although the air in the corridor was anything but cold.

He said, 'What's happening? What's happening to my lad?' His voice sounded old, weak, querulous.

Martin dropped his cigarette and stepped on it. He finished his coffee and threw the cup into the litter bin.

'I'm going in there to see what's going on,' he said.

He pushed the door open and went into the room where his brother was lying. The others waited. Minutes passed and he did not reappear.

'What's going on?' Jimmy said. 'Why ha'n't our Martin come back?'

'He'll soon be back. He's just making sure Dave's all right,' Tom told him.

'That doctor, he ought to be doing something. They shouldn't leave him with just a nurse. Just a young lass. It's not right.'

'She'll be in touch with the doctor. If she needs him she'll be able to get through on the phone or inter-com or something.'

'It's not right. Leaving us like this. Not telling us nothing.' Then he said, speaking to himself rather than to Tom, 'Eh, I don't know what Dot's going to say about this.'

'Would you like me to phone her? You're on the phone now, aren't you?'

'What?... Oh... No. No thanks, son. Nowt she can do. Better let her sleep if that's what she's doing... What time is it anyway?

Tom looked at his watch. 'Nearly twenty to three.'

Jimmy nodded. He thought for a few moments before he said, 'That's over four hours. Dave's been out for over four hours... four bloody hours!' Then he added, 'I wonder what it's like? Does he feel anything? It's what they call a coma i'n't it?'

'He won't feel anything. It's like—well, being fast asleep.'

Jimmy did not say anything at once but a few seconds later he said, 'How d'you know? How'd's anybody know what he feels like. You can't tell, can you? Nobody can tell. He could be feeling pain, couldn't he? How'd you know? He can't say nothing. He can't move. He might be having bad dreams.'

Tom began: 'I don't think so. I believe they can tell by those—' but he broke off as the door opposite opened and Martin came out. He was smiling.

For a breathless, heart-thumping moment Tom thought that he was bringing good news of his brother's condition.

Then Martin said, as he sat down at Tom's side, 'She's all right is that bird in there. She comes on all snooty and posh at first but she soon got friendly like. Very nice too.'

Judy raised her head and looked at him with weary contempt

and dislike. 'How is you brother?' she said. 'Or didn't you notice?'

For a moment Martin's face showed only surprise but this was quickly replaced by a scowl of anger. 'Don't you get bloody funny with me. What the fuck's it got to do with you anyway?'

Jimmy said, 'Hey! Let's have less of it Martin! You don't use language like that in front of ladies. If that's what they teach you in Paras you'd best . . . any case, lass's right. What about your brother? What about Dave, eh? That's what you went in to see about wa'n't it? Not chatting up bloody nurses.'

'Dave's just the same. No change. Just lying there like—well, he's out to world. Same as he was from start.' Martin lit a cigarette and blew out smoke. 'Me mouth's like a fuckin' bird-cage,' he said to Tom.

After her small show of anger Judy had relapsed into silence and resumed her huddled position, head drooping, clasped hands at her chin and mouth. Jimmy began to nod again, snapping into wakefulness every now and then. Hughie continued snoring.

Martin said, 'Funny. I used to hate hospitals when I were a kid. Well, right up till I went to Falklands really. Till I were in dock myself. They used to scare me, tell you truth. I used to get bloody nightmares about them. Sometimes you'd hear of some lad at school having to go into hospital. Give me shivers it would. I'd think Christ! S'posing it were me! I didn't even like going past St James's. Bloody great building. All them sick and dying people. And the bloody smell. That were another thing. My grandpa were in there when I were a kid. About ten, eleven, I'd be. And they took me to see him. Dying he were. He never come out. Aye, I'll never forget it. The old fella. Thin as a skeleton he were. But it weren't that. It were all nurses and trolleys and stretchers and screens and things. Everything so quiet and shining and white and clean. And that fucking smell. Sweet, sickly. You could taste it. Made you feel sick. That's what illness smells like. Death. That's what I thought . . . Aye . . . But I were fucking wrong . . . Death don't smell like that . . . Aye . . .'

Tom knew that Martin was thinking aloud but he felt he

337

ought to make some sort of response. He said, 'I know what you mean.'

There was a brief pause before Martin said, 'About death? Aye . . . Maybe . . . but not the kind I'm thinking about.'

Hughie suddenly jerked his knees upward and a convulsive shudder moved his arms, shoulders and head as he snorted and gulped. Then he sat up and swung his feet on to the floor. He shook his head like a fighter shaking away the effects of a heavy punch. Then he got out a cigarette and lit it.

'How's the brother, Martin? Any change?' he said.

Martin shook his head. 'Just same.'

Judy got up and went again to the toilet where, as before she stayed for a long time. When she returned Tom asked her if she would now like to go to the hotel but she shook her head. Jimmy had fallen asleep, his head against the wall but likely to fall forward and at any moment wake him up. Hughie and Martin began a sporadic and esoteric conversation dealing with events and people in their enclosed military world, much of the language incomprehensible to a civilian. Tom felt tiredness pressing on his mind, prickling in his eyes, weighting his eyelids. His head began to nod and roll and intermittently jerk him back to full consciousness.

He must have been asleep when he was abruptly jolted back to wakefulness by a heavy nudge from Martin and the words; 'Hey up! Something's happening!'

The swing-doors had been pushed open and the doctor was hurrying along the corridor with the Sister close behind.

'What's up?' Martin called as they were going into the room.

The Sister said, over her shoulder, as she followed the doctor, 'We'll let you know.'

The door closed. Everyone was now awake.

Jimmy said, 'You reckon he's come round?'

No one answered at first. Then Tom said, 'Maybe.' But his voice did not carry much conviction.

Judy looked at him and her eyes showed doubt and fear and reproach, yet there seemed to flicker there the tiniest gleam of hope.

He said, 'We'll soon know.'

'Fuckin' medics,' Hughie muttered.

'You was glad of 'em when they dug that bit of shrapnel out.' Martin said, but his mind was fixed on what was happening behind the door.

They waited.

Jimmy kept making little shaking movements of his head and whispering under his breath what could have been prayers, or curses.

'Come *on*,' Martin said aloud.

And still they waited.

Tom could hear Judy's quick breathing and he knew that she was trembling. His eyes were gritty with tiredness, his mouth was dry and sour and his head throbbed with a dull, red ache.

Then the door opened and the doctor came into the corridor.

'Mr Ruddock,' he said.

Jimmy remained seated, staring at him, saying nothing.

The doctor glanced from him to the others and back again. 'You're all family, aren't you?'

Martin said, 'Yes. I'm his brother. What's up? How is he? What's happened?'

The doctor spoke to Martin. 'I'm very sorry to have to tell you. I have bad news. The worst... The patient—your brother—died a few moments ago. There was absolutely nothing anyone could do to save him. No one could have done anymore than was done here. I can assure you of that. And the only consolation I can offer you is to tell you that he suffered no pain. He never regained consciousness so he knew nothing about the end. That won't be much comfort to you now. But perhaps later... Sister will be out in a moment. She will bring you to my office, Mr Ruddock. There are some formalities... Ah, here she is... I will see you presently.' He walked towards the swing-doors and disappeared.

The Sister, still looking fresh and unruffled, said, 'The doctor's told you. We'll need you, Mr Ruddock, and perhaps ...' she looked at Martin, 'Your father might be too distressed...'

Martin glanced at Jimmy who appeared incapable of speech, 'I'll come and help sort things out,' he said.

'I'll come with you,' Hughie volunteered.

She looked enquiringly at Judy and Tom.

Judy stood up and began to walk away in the opposite direction from that which the doctor had taken. She was heading towards the lift that would take her down to the reception area and the main exit. Tom started after her.

The Sister called to him. 'There might be some of those newspaper vultures down there! I could show you another way!'

Tom paused but, seeing that Judy had ignored the Sister's words, he answered. 'We'll manage thanks . . . I'd better go with her.' Then to Martin: 'See you later. At the hotel perhaps.' He was hurrying after Judy as he spoke over his shoulder and he caught her up just as she was entering the lift. They rode down together, without speaking. If there were any newspapermen in the reception hall they did not approach Tom and Judy who went out of the building into the Fulham Road.

The grizzled light of early morning surprised Tom who, although he knew rationally that it was now approaching six o' clock, was emotionally and sensorily prepared for the darkness of night. The air was cold after the warmth of the hospital; it held the faint scent of urban autumn, a hint of decaying leaves and it was singed a little by garden bonfires. Judy set off, walking quickly, slightly ahead of him, moving he suspected without any sense of direction towards the Boltons. For a few moments he followed quite slowly, allowing her to draw further ahead, briefly tempted to let her go, let her take her solitary grief and confusion away for someone else to alleviate, but his own misery and bewilderment were suddenly pierced by a bright needle of pity. She looked painfully vulnerable and alone as she walked, her shoulders slightly hunched, both hands in the pockets of her camel-hair coat the collar of which was turned up against the chill breeze. He quickened his pace and drew level with her.

'Judy,' he said. 'Judy. You're going the wrong way.'

After a few more steps she stopped.

'The wrong way? Which is the right way? Where does that go to?' He was further moved by her look of desolation, the bleak misery in her eyes. And he was touched, too, by her beauty which, though changed, had suffered no diminution by sorrow.

He said, 'Come on love. Let's get back to the hotel. We've got to pick up our bags.'

She nodded. 'And then?'

'Well . . . get the train for Leeds I suppose.'

She stared at him. Then she said, 'You're mad. You're all mad. All of you. Crazy. You've killed him. He's dead. Dead . . . My . . . he's smashed up. Finished! Dead . . . And you want me to go back to Leeds! Back to that flat! Sleep in the bed where . . . Dave . . . Why did he do it? How could he? How could you all make him do it? He wasn't . . . he was . . . beautiful . . . Oh Christ! What have you done! She was now torn and shaken by sobs that clawed at her throat. Her mouth was misshapen, broken. Yet her eyes remained dry.

He put his arms about her and held her close to him. He felt and heard the cruel depredations of her grief. He held her tighter, more closely, willing the mauling claws of pain to go away. Over and over he said her name. He murmured and crooned to her like a parent with a hurt or unhappy child. 'Judy, it'll be all right, love . . . there, there . . . Judy . . . you'll be all right . . . don't love, don't . . . you're going to be all right . . . it'll get better. You see . . . oh Judy . . . don't . . . there, there . . . ' He found that he was kissing the top of her head, and though she might not be crying, he knew that he was very close to tears himself.

A van drove past and a hoarse voice shouted something derisive. A man in the uniform of a London Transport underground worker went by, turned, staring in surprise, and then walked on.

Tom said, 'We'll look after you . . . I'll do anything . . . Judy, love . . . Judy . . . it's going to be all right . . . it'll get better . . . it'll have to . . . '

Slowly she raised her head and looked at him. Her long steady gaze, still dry-eyed, was searching, perhaps accusing. Then her mouth moved in the very faintest of smiles, if the slightest movement at one corner of her lips could be called a smile. She shook her head slowly, just once, and he knew that he must release his embrace. Then, together, they turned and began to walk back along the grey, littered pavement as pale sunlight filtered through the clouds for a few seconds then withdrew, leaving the waking city as cheerless as before.